SOME LIKE IT HAWK

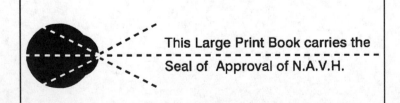

This Large Print Book carries the
Seal of Approval of N.A.V.H.

A MEG LANGSLOW MYSTERY

SOME LIKE IT HAWK

DONNA ANDREWS

THORNDIKE PRESS

A part of Gale, Cengage Learning

Detroit • New York • San Francisco • New Haven, Conn • Waterville, Maine • London

GALE
CENGAGE Learning®

Copyright © 2012 by Donna Andrews.
Thorndike Press, a part of Gale, Cengage Learning.

ALL RIGHTS RESERVED
This is a work of fiction. All of the characters, organizations, and events portrayed in this novel are either products of the author's imagination of are used fictitiously.
Thorndike Press® Large Print Mystery.
The text of this Large Print edition is unabridged.
Other aspects of the book may vary from the original edition.
Set in 16 pt. Plantin.

LIBRARY OF CONGRESS CATALOGING-IN-PUBLICATION DATA

Andrews, Donna.
   Some like it hawk : a Meg Langslow mystery / by Donna Andrews.
      pages ; cm. — (Thorndike Press large print mystery)
   ISBN-13: 978-1-4104-5093-7 (hardcover)
   ISBN-10: 1-4104-5093-7 (hardcover)
   1. Langslow, Meg (Fictitious character)—Fiction. 2.
Murder—Investigation—Fiction. 3. Large type books. I. Title.
PS3551.N4165S66 2012b
813'.54—dc23   2012032078

Published in 2012 by arrangement with St. Martin's Press, LLC.

Printed in the United States of America
1 2 3 4 5 6 7 16 15 14 13 12

ACKNOWLEDGMENTS

Thanks, as always, to the crew at St. Martin's/Minotaur, including (but not limited to) Matt Baldacci, Anne Bensson, Hector DeJean, Meryl Gross, Andrew Martin, Sarah Melnyk, David Rotstein, and my editor, Pete Wolverton. And thanks again to the Art Department for another wonderful cover.

More thanks to my agent, Ellen Geiger, and the staff at the Frances Goldin Literary Agency for handling the business side so I can focus on the writing, and to Dave Barbor at Curtis Brown for taking Meg abroad.

Many thanks to the friends — writers and readers alike — who brainstorm and critique with me, give me good ideas, or help keep me sane while I'm writing: Stuart, Elke, Aidan, and Liam Andrews, Renee Brown, Erin Bush, Carla Coupe, Meriah Crawford, Ellen Crosby, Kathy Deligianis, Laura Durham, Sally Fellows, Suzanne

Frisbee, John Gilstrap, Peggy Hansen, C. Ellett Logan, David Niemi, Alan Orloff, Valerie Patterson, Art Taylor, Robin Templeton, and Sandi Wilson. Thanks for all kinds of moral and practical help to my blog sisters at the Femmes Fatales: Dana Cameron, Charlaine Harris, Toni L.P. Kelner, Kris Neri, Hank Phillipi Ryan, Mary Saums, and Elaine Viets. And thanks to all the Buds, who do not quail when my subject lines contain the ominous words [long] or [rant].

Andy Straka gave me much useful advice on hawks, so if the falconry in the book is accurate, he gets the credit — and if it isn't, he can blame my memory and Dr. Blake's.

When I realized that my plot required placing Meg and the town of Caerphilly in legal peril, I turned to Barb Goffman and Dina Willner. Without their excellent advice, Meg's lawyer cousin, Festus Hollingsworth, would probably have been disbarred by now, and if you find any glaring legal errors in the book it's probably something I forgot to ask them about.

I was planning to write another book entirely before a brainstorming lunch with Chris Cowan, at which she asked, "Did everybody really leave the courthouse? What if there's still one guy holed up in the basement?"

And that's how Phineas Throckmorton was born.

CHAPTER 1

"Welcome to the town that mortgaged its own jail!"

The amplified voice blaring over the nearby tour bus loudspeaker startled me so much I almost smashed my own thumb. I'd been lifting my hammer to turn a nicely heated iron rod into a fireplace poker when the tour guide's spiel boomed across the town square, shattering my concentration.

"Mommy, did the blacksmith lady do that on purpose?" piped up a child's voice.

A few onlookers tittered. I closed my eyes, took a deep breath, then opened them again. I checked to make sure that all fifty or sixty of the spectators were safely behind the fence around my outdoor blacksmith's shop. Then I raised my hammer and began pounding.

Nothing like blacksmithing when you're feeling annoyed. The voice from the tour bus still squawked away, but I couldn't hear

9

what it was saying. And I felt the tension and frustration pouring out of me like water out of a twisted sponge.

Along with the sweat. Even though it was only a little past ten, the temperature was already in the high eighties and the air was thick with humidity. It would hit the mid-nineties this afternoon. A typical early July day in Caerphilly, Virginia.

But in spite of the heat and the interruptions, I managed to complete the current task — shaping one end of the iron rod into the business end of the poker. I flourished the hammer dramatically on the last few blows and lifted the tongs to display the transformed rod.

"Voila!" I said. "One fireplace poker."

"But it needs a handle," an onlooker said.

"A handle?" I turned the rod and cocked my head, as if to look at it more closely, and pretended to be surprised. "You're right. So let's heat the other end and make a handle."

I thrust the handle end of the poker into my forge and pulled the bellows lever a couple of times to heat up the fire. As I did, I glanced over at my cousin, Rose Noire. She was standing in the opening at the back of my booth, staring at her cell phone. She looked up and shook her head.

"What the hell is keeping Rob?" I mut-

10

tered. Not that my brother was ever famous for punctuality.

I wondered, just for a moment, if he was okay.

I'd have heard about it already if he wasn't, I told myself. I pushed my worry aside and kept my face pleasant for the tourists. After all, I'd been making a good living off the tourists all summer. However inconvenient it had been to move my entire blacksmithing shop from our barn to the Caerphilly town square, it had certainly been a financial bonanza. Maybe it wouldn't be a bad idea if the town held Caerphilly Days every summer.

I just hoped we didn't have to continue them into the fall. What if —

I focused on the tourists again and continued my demonstration.

"To work the iron, you need to heat it to approximately —"

"That tent on your right contains the office of the mayor," the tour bus boomed, even closer at hand. "Formerly housed in the now-empty City Hall building."

No use trying to out-shout a loudspeaker. I smiled, shrugged apologetically to the tourists, and steeled myself to listen without expression as the voice droned on, reciting the sad, embarrassing history of Caerphilly's

11

financial woes.

"Alas, when the recession hit," the loud-speaker informed us, "the town was unable to keep up with payments on its loan, so the lender was forced to repossess the courthouse, the jail, and all the other public buildings."

Convenient that they didn't mention the real reason Caerphilly couldn't make its payments — that George Pruitt, our ex-mayor, had stolen most of the borrowed funds for his own use. Actually, a few buses had, until he'd threatened to sue, so now they just mentioned the ongoing lawsuit against him. Not as dramatic, but less apt to backfire.

"And to your left, you can see the Caer-philly Days festival, organized by the citizens to help their troubled town out of its dire plight."

I always winced when I heard that line. It wasn't exactly false — but it did seem to imply that we craftspeople were donating our time and our profits out of the good-ness of our hearts, to benefit the town. We weren't — we were making good money for our own pockets. Our real value to the town lay elsewhere.

Not that we could let the tour buses know that — or worse, the Evil Lender, as we all called First Progressive Financial, LLC, the company that had foreclosed on so much of our town. Only our new mayor made an effort to call them FPF, and that was because he spent so much time negotiating with them and had to be polite.

I glanced into the forge and was relieved to see that my iron was hot enough to work. I glanced at Rose Noire and nodded, to indicate that I was about to start hammering again. She bent over her cell phone and began texting rapidly. To Rob, I assumed.

"Come on, Rob," I muttered. "Hurry up."

I pulled the rod out of my forge and began the much more complicated job of hammering the handle end into a sinuous vine-like coiled shape. Mercifully, by the time the iron needed reheating, the amplified tour bus had moved on, and I had only the tourists' questions to deal with.

"What happens if you break it?"

"Don't you ever burn yourself?"

"You shoe horses, don't you?"

"Wouldn't it be faster to do that with a machine?"

I spun out my answers in between bouts at my anvil. Finishing the poker required several return visits to the forge, followed by several vigorous rounds of hammering. I could see Rose Noire, cell phone in hand, keeping a close eye on my progress. I treated the rod — and the tourists — to one last crescendo, a great deal louder than it needed to be, dunked the rod into the water bucket, releasing a small but dramatic cloud of steam, and held up the finished poker for the tourists to admire.

And then I did it all over again. Several times. I answered what seemed like several hundred more questions — or more accurately, at least a hundred iterations of the same half dozen questions. Finally the clock in the courthouse building chimed eleven, signaling the end of my shift.

I finished up the andiron I'd been making and thanked the tourists. Then I changed my sign to the one saying that Meg Langslow's next blacksmithing exhibition would begin at 2 P.M. and slipped through the gate in the back of my enclosure. The cousin I'd recruited to mind the booth and sell my ironwork for me dashed in and began quickly shoving the tables of merchandise from the side of the enclosure to a much more prominent place front and center before the crowds dispersed.

Normally I'd have stayed to help her, but Rose Noire was waiting for me. She looked anxious. Not good.

"What's wrong?" I asked.

14

"Rob's been delayed," she said. "He's fine, and he'll try again later."

"Delayed?" I realized that I'd raised my voice. Several tourists were looking at us, so I choked back what I'd been about to say. "Back to the tent!" I said instead.

I strode rapidly across the small space separating my forge from the bandstand at the center of the town square. At the back of the bandstand was a tent. The town square was filled with tents of every size, shape, and description, but whenever anyone barked out "the tent!" as I just had, they nearly always meant this one.

Rose Noire scuttled along anxiously behind me.

As soon as I stepped inside the tent, I felt my fingers itching to tidy and organize. Even at its best, the tent was cramped and cluttered, since it served as the dressing room, green room, and lounge for all the craftspeople and performers participating in Caerphilly Days. Several coatracks held costumes for performers who would be appearing later or street clothes for anyone already in costume. And every corner held plastic bins, locked trunks, totes, knapsacks, boxes, grocery bags, suitcases, and just plain piles of stuff.

"Mom-my!" Josh and Jamie, my twin

eighteen-month-old sons, greeted me with enthusiasm. They both toddled to the nearest side of the huge play enclosure we'd set up, holding out their arms and leaning over the child fence toward me, jostling each other, and repeating "Mom-my! Mom-my!"

Eric, my teenaged nephew, was sitting at the back of the enclosure, holding a toy truck and looking slightly hurt.

"They were fine until you came in," he said.

"I know," I said. "They just want to guilt-trip me." Making a mental note to chivvy my fellow tent users into a cleaning spree later in the day, I stepped into the enclosure, sat down, and let the boys climb on top of me. Hugging them calmed me down.

"Thank you for watching them," I said. "And not that I'm complaining, but what are you doing here instead of Natalie?" Eric's sister had been our live-in babysitter for most of the summer.

"Grandpa says Natalie's ankle is broken and she needs to stay off her feet," Eric said. "So Mom drove up this morning to take her home and bring me as a replacement for the next few weeks. Assuming that's okay with you."

"It's fine with me." Having Eric babysit was fine, anyway. Should I feel guilty that

16

my niece had broken her ankle chasing my sons? I'd worry about that later.

"And thank goodness you're here to help out in time for the Fourth of July," I said aloud. "Everything will get a lot easier after the Fourth."

"I thought Caerphilly Days went on all summer," Eric said. "What's so special about the Fourth?"

"I haven't told him," Rose Noire said. "And evidently Natalie is very good at keeping a secret."

"But he's a resident now, at least for the time being," I said. "Eric, do you swear you won't tell a single soul what I am about to reveal?"

"Yes," he said. "I mean, I swear by . . . um . . ."

"Cross your heart and hope to die?" I asked.

He nodded.

"Okay. Then it's time we told you Caerphilly's sinister secret."

CHAPTER 2

"Sinister secret?" Eric repeated. I could tell I'd captured his attention.

"There's nothing sinister about it," Rose Noire said.

"It's a little sinister," I said. "And besides, I like the alliteration. So Eric, you heard about what happened with all the town buildings?"

"Yeah," he said. "Mayor Pruitt mortgaged them and stole the money."

"We don't know for sure about the stealing part," Rose Noire said. "It hasn't been proven in court."

"I know you're reluctant to think ill of any other sentient being, even a Pruitt," I said. "But if you want to make a bet on what the verdict will be if they finally manage to try the mayor for embezzlement . . ."

"Ex-mayor," she said. "And no. But I still think we should be careful to say 'alleged.' "

"If it makes you happy," I said. "I'm sure

our alleged horse thief of an ex-mayor will appreciate the consideration. Getting back to the secret — Eric, did you hear about Phineas K. Throckmorton?"

"You mean the crazy guy who refused to get out when the lender repossessed the town buildings? The one who barricaded himself in the courthouse basement?"

"Eric . . ." Rose Noire began.

"The allegedly crazy guy who allegedly barricaded himself," Eric said quickly.

"Not crazy, just eccentric," I said. "Reclusive. And there's nothing alleged about the barricading. He's been down there since April of last year."

"Wow," Eric said. "Over a year in the courthouse basement?"

I could see him turning the idea over in his mind. I wondered if he'd guess Mr. Throckmorton's secret — for that matter, the town's secret.

"He must reek by now," Eric said finally. "I stink if I go a day without a shower. And — does he even have a toilet?"

"There's a bathroom in the basement," Rose Noire said.

"You mean like an outhouse?"

"A real bathroom," I said. "Shower. Sink, Toilet. Running water. Installed in the forties, so it's old, but quite functional."

"And how fortunate that the town water system's idiosyncratic," Rose Noire said. "So that shutting down his water supply would mean shutting off the fire hydrants all around the town square."

"And that the phone and Internet cables come in through the basement," I said. "So they can't cut his communications off without cutting off their own — not to mention excavating the courthouse lawn."

"Still — he must be going stir-crazy there all by himself," Eric said. "And in a tiny, cramped basement?"

"It's not tiny," I said. "He's got the whole courthouse basement, except for the twenty-by-thirty-foot antechamber where the stairways come out. He barricaded the door from the antechamber into the main part of the basement where the archives are. I suppose you might call the archive area cramped — it's certainly a maze of paper-filled rooms and corridors. But it covers a whole city block."

"Okay, but what does he eat?" Eric went on. "He can't possibly have stashed away enough food to last all this time. What happens when he runs out?"

"He won't," I said. "Any more than he's going to go stir-crazy from being by himself. That's the town secret. Or rather, this is."

I hoisted Josh onto my shoulder and walked to the back of the tent. I stopped just before I stepped from the children's pen into the smaller pen containing Spike, our small and temperamental furball of a dog. Spike scrambled up as I approached, scampered to the front of the pen, and stood looking up expectantly.

"Bite me and you sleep in the barn for a week," I said. "Maybe a month. And no play time with the twins."

With Spike formally on notice, I stepped into his pen. Spike, wisely, stood aside. Eric, carrying Jamie, followed, clearly more anxious than me about the state of his ankles.

I strode to the back of the pen. It was flush with the side of the tent, just at the part where it backed up to the bandstand. I leaned down and, with a dramatic flourish, flipped up a low flap.

"Voila," I said.

Eric stooped down to peer through the opening, then jumped back and looked up at me anxiously.

"Holy cow," he exclaimed. "What is that horrible thing?"

Horrible thing? I bent down to peer through the flap. A pair of unblinking eyes peered out of a tangle of gray fur to meet mine. I was startled for a second, but then I relaxed.

"Good girl, Tinkerbell," I said. "It's only Rob's dog," I said to Eric. "She's an Irish Wolfhound. Not horrible at all — just big. Lie down, Tink."

I moved aside so Eric could look through the flap again. Tinkerbell, satisfied that Eric was with me, curled back up on the ground beside the flap. Josh began wriggling, so I set him down inside the pen. Eric followed suit with Jamie, then peered through the flap again.

"What am I supposed to be looking at?" Eric asked, after a few moments.

"That's the crawl space under the bandstand," I said. "And that trapdoor —"

"Trapdoor?"

I bent down to look again. The crawl space was lit only by streaks of sunlight that came through cracks in the weathered floor of the bandstand overhead. Junk littered the entire area, including a huge heap of old tires, faded wooden crates, battered sawhorses, and other debris in the exact center of the space. Tinkerbell had curled up at the foot of the heap.

I turned back to Rose Noire. She was sniffing Josh's diaper. In vain; I could tell just from his face that Jamie was the one who needed changing.

"Why is all the junk still on top of the trapdoor?" I asked. "Maybe it's not Rob's fault he's still stuck in the courthouse."

"Uncle Rob's in the courthouse, too?" Eric asked.

"Only temporarily. And what if he came all the way through the tunnel only to find he couldn't get it open?" I went on, turning back to Rose Noire.

"Tinkerbell would bark," Rose Noire said.

"Tunnel?" Eric said. "You mean there's a tunnel all the way into the courthouse?"

"I was waiting to uncover the trapdoor until I knew he was on his way," Rose Noire said.

"Awesome!" Eric exclaimed. "Can I go through it?"

"Not now," Rose Noire replied.

I'd have said not at all, but maybe she was right. An absolute prohibition would only make the tunnel more enticing. And I wasn't about to distract Rose Noire when she was in the middle of changing Jamie.

"The trapdoor screeches like a wounded banshee," she said over her shoulder. "We can't open it without some kind of noise to cover it."

"Like the calypso band that I thought was supposed to start playing at eleven," I said.

"Where's the schedule?"

"I have it right there." Rose Noire pointed a half-unfolded diaper at a well-worn clipboard lying on the ground nearby. "And that's probably them now."

Footsteps and a lot of dragging and thumping had begun happening up on the stage.

"They're late," I said.

"They're on island time." Rose Noire smiled indulgently.

"They're not actually from the Caribbean, you know," I said. "When they're not playing in the band, they're a bunch of CPAs from Richmond."

"Well, in any case, they should be starting soon." She glanced at her watch. "Eric, Rob was supposed to come out while your Aunt Meg was hammering so loudly on her iron."

"Call him and tell him to get ready to come over as soon as the calypso band starts up," I said.

"I'll try," she said. "But you know how spotty cell phone reception is over there."

Spotty? It was virtually nonexistent. Most of the time we had to resort to sending text messages to Mr. Throckmorton's computer.

"Awesome," Eric said. "Did Mr. Throckmorton dig the tunnel?"

"No, it's been there forever," Rose Noire

said. "No one knows how long."

"Actually, we do have some idea," I said. "The original courthouse was built during the 1780s and the trapdoor was mentioned in some documents from the 1840s, so presumably it was dug sometime between those two dates."

"I thought the courthouse burned during the Civil War," Eric said.

"Not by itself." I nodded with approval when I saw that Rose Noire was rapidly texting on her phone. "The Union Army burned it on their way south. But that was only the building. The basement and the tunnel survived."

"And it's almost certainly proof that Caerphilly was a stop on the Underground Railroad," Rose Noire said, looking up from her phone. "Why else would they dig such a tunnel?"

"So the early nineteenth-century mayors would have an escape route if the citizens showed up with tar and feathers," I said.

"You mean there were Pruitts here back then?" Eric asked. Strange how even a teen who only summered here automatically associated tar and feathers with the family that had misruled Caerphilly for so long.

"No, the Pruitt family didn't show up until Reconstruction," I answered. "They're not the only crooked politicians in the world. They don't know about the tunnel, and we all have to be very careful not to let them find out."

"They'd tell the Evil Lender, you know," Rose Noire said. "The Pruitts are the ones who brought the Evil Lender to Caerphilly in the first place."

"So don't brag about knowing where the tunnel is if any Pruitts are listening," Eric said. "Got it."

"Only a few people in town knew about the tunnel when the siege began," I said. "In fact, for most of the twentieth century, only the county clerks knew it had ever existed. After all, it was in the courthouse basement, and there's nothing worth stealing down there. Never has been anything down there except the clerk — currently Mr. Throckmorton — and over two centuries' worth of gently crumbling town and county records."

"For the first few weeks of the siege, we kept pretty busy hauling in supplies," Rose Noire said. "We all expected that sooner or later the Pruitts would remember about the tunnel and find a way to shut it down."

"We?" Eric repeated.

"A lot of townspeople are in on the secret," I said.

A cheer went up overhead. Eric had opened his mouth and was saying something, but he was drowned out by the thunder of half a dozen steel drums.

Eric drew closer.

"So this whole time everyone in town has been just strolling through the tunnel with supplies?" he asked. He had to shout to be heard.

"Heavens, no," Rose Noire said, with a shudder.

"It's no stroll," I said. "Here, I'll show you. Help me move this stuff."

Rose Noire went back to the front of the tent to keep watch. Eric and I crawled under the bandstand, where he helped me pull aside the tires and boxes to reveal an ancient-looking iron trapdoor with oversized hinges on one side and a huge, slightly rusty ring on the other. It was set into a wide slab of eighteenth-century stonework, heavily patched with early twentieth-century concrete. Overhead, the steel drums had subsided and we could hear the drama student who served as today's emcee formally introducing the band, his words punctuated by random notes from the drums or guitars.

"Grab the ring," I said. "Get ready to pull. But wait until the music starts."

The calypso players launched into their

27

first number. I nodded to Eric and we heaved on the ring. The trapdoor rose with a screech that would have alerted half the county if the musicians above hadn't been playing their hearts out, with occasional deliberate squawks of feedback.

We peered down into the tunnel, a three-by-three-foot shaft lined with stone for the first six feet and then with boards. A flimsy-looking ladder was nailed along one side. In the dim light, we couldn't see the bottom.

We gazed in silence for several long moments.

"Wow," Eric said finally. "How deep is that anyway?"

"I don't know for sure."

"Must be a hundred feet."

Actually, it was more like twenty-five or thirty, but if he thought it was a hundred, all the better. I was worried that he'd scamper down the ladder and disappear into the tunnel, but he stood looking down into the entrance with a slightly anxious expression on his face. Maybe Eric felt the same way about the tunnel as I did.

"Don't go down there," I said. "It's pretty narrow, and Rob's due out any minute, and you don't want to get in his way."

"Okay." He managed a fairly credible air of disappointment. "I guess they had to keep the entrance narrow so people couldn't find it as easily."

"The tunnel's even smaller," I said. "Not much over two feet high and wide. Remember, they didn't have power tools back then. It was all dug by hand."

"Amazing that it hasn't caved in after all these years."

"At least half of it was partly caved in when this whole thing started," I said. "But we dug it out and now we have it pretty well shored up. We've only actually had three substantial cave-ins, and one of those was last year during the big earthquake. We've always managed to get people dug out pretty quickly."

From the look on Eric's face, I had a feeling I'd eliminated the danger that he'd try to sneak into the tunnel.

If only I could eliminate my own constant anxiety that all the little cave-ins were warning signs that a great big one was coming. And my not entirely irrational dread that when — make that if — it happened, Rob would get caught in it.

"And the big deal about Fourth of July is that we're going to replace the trapdoor then," I said.

"You couldn't just try oiling it?" Eric asked.

"We do," I said. "Daily. Doesn't help much. So we're replacing it. Actually, the Shiffleys tried once before, but apparently back in the nineteen-twenties someone — possibly bootleggers — did some repair work. The trapdoor doesn't just sit on the slab — it's anchored by a whole lot of steel bars going down into the stone and concrete. They figured out they'll have to hack the whole thing apart with jackhammers and blowtorches. It'll make a hell of a racket. So they're going to do it under cover of the college orchestra concert, which will end with a bravura performance of *The 1812 Overture,* complete with cannons and fireworks."

"Cool." Eric perked up a bit at the thought. "There is one thing I don't understand, though."

"What's that?"

"My mom said you and Michael were worried that the Evil Lender might take your house," he said. "Does this have something to do with that? And how can they do that, anyway?"

My stomach tightened, as it always did when the subject came up.

"It's complicated," I said. And then I realized that if Eric was almost old enough to drive, he was also old enough to deal with a few complications. "The short version is that they can't. But the county might be able to seize our land if they needed it for some public purpose. And right now the county owes the Evil Lender a lot of money. What if the Evil Lender told the county board 'We won't sue you, and we won't make you pay back those millions of dollars — all you have to do is use your power to seize these people's land and sell it to us'?"

"But the county board won't do that — right?"

"I hope not. They don't want to, but what if the Evil Lender backs them into a corner where they can't refuse?"

"What does this have to do with Mr. Throckmorton?"

"Cousin Festus thinks having him there helps the county's case." Festus Hollingsworth, part of Mother's vast extended family, was representing the county in all of these legal matters. I found myself wishing, not for the first time, that Festus would explain why he thought Mr. Throckmorton's presence was so useful. Was it only for the PR value, or was there some obscure legal reason? But Festus hadn't become a respected litigator and one of the top property law experts in Virginia by sharing his strategies with the immediate world.

Or maybe Festus might have enlightened us if he'd had time. For the past six weeks, he and the team of attorneys and paralegals he'd installed on the third floor of our house had been putting in twenty-hour days sorting through the boxes and boxes of papers and diskettes the lender had delivered. "It's called document dump," Festus had explained. "In discovery, they're required to give me all relevant documents. But there's no rule to prevent them from hiding them in several tons of useless garbage." Festus was a veteran of many battles against slimy corporations. He knew how to deal with all this — didn't he?

"Festus is the expert," Eric said, echoing my thoughts.

"So until he tells us otherwise, we protect the secret of the tunnel," I said. "And help Mr. Throckmorton stay in place."

Eric tried to draw himself up to his full height, whacking not just his head, but even his shoulders on the low ceiling — when had he suddenly grown taller than me? He nodded with enthusiasm.

"You can trust me!" he said.

"Of course, protecting it doesn't mean we have to sit here staring at it," I replied. "Let's go out and keep watch. Always peek out before you reenter the tent; never leave the tent unguarded until the junk's on top of the trapdoor; and if someone catches you going in or out of the crawl space, there's your excuse."

I pointed to a mini-refrigerator tucked just inside the entry. I popped the door open to show its contents: sodas, water bottles, juice, fruit, and neatly stacked jars of the organic baby food Rose Noire still made for the boys.

"Our cover story is that I keep this back here because people were eating the boys' food," I said. "And drinking my sodas."

I peeked out and saw only Rose Noire in the tent, so I lifted the flap and we scrambled out.

"Just one more thing," Eric said. "What if — Oh my God!"

CHAPTER 3

My heart leapt as I looked to see where Eric was pointing. It seemed a harmless enough tableau. Apparently Eric had failed to notice that we were putting the boys down in Spike's pen. Spike was licking Jamie's face. Jamie was lying on his back, kicking his feet in the air, giggling happily. Then I realized what had alarmed Eric. Josh was waddling toward the two — in fact, as we watched, he reached down, grabbed a handful of Spike's fluffy black-and-white fur, and yanked. Hard. So hard he fell down, still holding a few tufts of fur.

Spike yelped and whirled toward Josh. Eric belatedly realized that as babysitter he should be doing something and scrambled to grab Josh. But Spike was faster. By the time Eric reached them, Spike was happily licking Josh's face. Jamie started crying.

"It's okay," I said, as I picked up the abandoned one.

" 'Pike!" Jamie said. "Want 'Pike!"

"Aren't they cute?" Rose Noire cooed.

"Wow, Spike really has mellowed," Eric said.

"Only where the boys are concerned," I said. "To the rest of the world he's as fierce as ever — maybe fiercer if he thinks you're a threat to the twins."

Eric nodded. I was relieved to see that he was still eyeing Spike warily, as if not sure how far to trust him.

I handed Jamie to Eric and turned to Rose Noire.

"So what's taking Rob so long?" I asked her.

"Apparently Mr. Throckmorton is helping him test a new game."

"New game?" Eric perked up. Not surprising — he was, after all, squarely in the age range targeted by Rob's phenomenally successful computer and role-playing games.

"I'm sure he'll be glad to show it to you — on this side of the tunnel, please. Josh and Jamie are too young to become tunnel rats. And can you keep an eye on them while I go get something to eat?"

"I have a better idea." Michael, my husband, had appeared in the doorway to the tent.

"Look," I said to Jamie. "Here's Daddy."

" 'Pike!" Jamie was unconsoled, and still struggling in Eric's arms.

"Let me have him." Michael gave me a kiss, then scooped Jamie out of Eric's arms and lifted him up as high as he could reach — which, since Michael was six feet four, meant Jamie was flying fairly close to the ceiling at this end of the tent. He squealed with delight.

"Eric, you bring Josh," Michael said, as he continued to wave the giggling Jamie overhead. "The hay ride's starting any second now."

"Cool," Eric said. He managed to snag Josh without getting bitten by Spike and the four of them were out of the tent before I had the chance to check the boys' diapers.

Though I did notice that Michael grabbed the diaper bag I routinely kept packed and ready, so I told myself not to worry.

Spike settled down to watch the door through which the boys had disappeared. I congratulated myself, not for the first time, at having found the perfect watchdog for the tunnel's mouth. If the boys were in the same enclosure as Spike, he would bark furiously when anyone approached and attempt to bite anyone foolhardy enough to disregard his warning and enter the pen — even, at times, Michael or me. If the boys weren't with him, he sulked, and usually snapped at intruders out of sheer crankiness without even the courtesy of a warning bark. I had no doubt that Spike had contributed more than any of us to ensuring that the existence of the tunnel remained a secret.

Tinkerbell just sighed and curled up to sleep.

"Now that the boys are in safe hands, I'm going for some lunch," I said to Rose Noire. "If I go now, maybe I can beat the rush. Call me when Rob's safely out."

"I have Tofu Surprise in the mini-fridge," Rose Noire said. "You're welcome to have some if you want to stay here."

"Thanks, but I was planning to get some chili at Muriel's Diner," I said. "Want me to bring you some? She makes a vegetarian version." Then a thought hit me. "Of course, if you already have Tofu Surprise, I suppose you won't want chili. Maybe you can give some to Rob when he gets out." I was eager to see the Tofu Surprise disappear before Rose Noire could browbeat me into consuming any more. The only surprising thing about it was how a pound or two of spices utterly failed to conceal the taste and texture of the tofu, which was probably my least favorite food.

"No, thanks," Rose Noire said. "But you go on. I'll stay here and wait for Rob."

I nodded my thanks and strolled out.

The calypso band was still playing — with more enthusiasm than skill, but the crowd seemed to be enjoying them. Or maybe they just enjoyed having a place to sit that was out of the sun — the Shiffley Construction Company had installed dozens of new, sturdy wooden benches in a semicircle around the front side of the bandstand, and hung giant tarpaulins over them, turning the whole place into a much more usable event space. Every bench was filled, and there were even a few people standing at the back or along the sides, braving the blistering sun to hear the concert. The Fourth of July decorations had turned out well. The bandstand's ornate Victorian wooden fretwork had been freshly painted so that it looked more than ever like a giant wedding cake, and it was so festooned with flags and red, white, and blue bunting that even the old-timers who hung out at the VFW hall allowed that the new mayor had done the town proud this year.

I glanced over at the courthouse. Normally it, too, would be decorated for the upcoming holiday with multiple flags and several square miles of bunting, but the new occupant didn't go in for holiday frills. A tour group was clustered on the sidewalk in front of the courthouse, listening to their leader, who was standing on the third or fourth step of the wide marble stairs leading up the front of the building. And predictably, on the veranda at the top of the stairs stood two uniformed guards — part of the force hired by the lender to patrol the vacant courthouse.

I sighed. I knew the guards would remain there, glaring down at the tour group until it moved on. Did they suspect the tourists of some evil intentions?

Or were they just hot and cranky about having to wear an outfit more suited to a Chicago winter than a Virginia summer, and taking it out by glaring at the tourists? The dark blue uniforms were long-sleeved, high-necked, and decorated on collar and cuff with a glitzy bright red lightning bolt. We'd thought they were ridiculous even before one of Michael's film students pointed out the strong resemblance between the guards' uniforms and those worn by the Flying Monkeys in the movie of *The Wizard of Oz.*

Of course, they might not know we'd started referring to them as "the Flying Monkeys." I wasn't about to ask.

The guards glared on. Maybe they were

afraid the locals would infiltrate the tour groups in the hope of sneaking inside the building to resupply Mr. Throckmorton. I had to smile at the image of a group of tourists, posing in front of the barricade for a group photo, while behind them a rebel sympathizer tried to slip bits of food through the barricade.

Which wouldn't be all that easy to do — the barricade was pretty formidable. In fact, it was actually two barricades.

Last year, after our creditor had seized the buildings, they hadn't noticed for two weeks that Mr. Throckmorton had locked himself in the basement. For that matter, it was at least a week before anyone else in town noticed either. But once the lender realized it had a stubborn squatter in residence, its staff took action.

They battered down the basement door, only to find that Mr. Throckmorton had erected an inner barricade of six-by-six-inch landscape timbers. When they took a chainsaw to one of the timbers they discovered that he'd drilled holes in the timbers and threaded inch-thick iron bars through them. At that point they gave up. They covered the outside of his barricade with chicken wire and erected their own external barricade, a flimsy affair of one by sixes nailed

40

in place.

Mr. Throckmorton's barricade was solid except for a few places where he'd put spacers to leave chinks an inch tall by a few inches wide — I assumed for ventilation. A well-intentioned visitor might be able to slip a few grapes or cherries through the chinks, or maybe a hot dog minus the bun. Anything larger would be impossible.

Not that they were letting tourists into the courthouse, much less down in the basement where the barricade was. The Evil Lender had originally tried to block off all access to the town square, to tourists and locals alike, but Judge Jane Shiffley had ruled that the streets and the town square were public property, and the appeals court in Richmond had upheld her ruling. So all the guards could do was frown menacingly at passersby, in the hope of scaring them away.

Far from scaring anybody away, the guards' presence had inspired the residents with a keen new interest in enjoying the town's public spaces. Weather permitting, the sidewalk in front of the courthouse normally teemed with people walking, power walking, dog walking, jogging, carrying on animated conversations with friends, playing musical instruments, singing (either with the instruments or a cappella), sunning themselves on the benches — and, of course, wishing the guards a good morning, afternoon, or evening, and offering them cookies and glasses of iced tea or lemonade.

The original guards had eventually mellowed, and become a little friendlier. And then a few weeks ago, just before Memorial Day, they were fired on suspicion of taking bribes to let townspeople sneak in supplies. It was a bum rap, of course, but we didn't dare tell the lender that. The Flying Monkeys had come in as replacements.

Maybe the Flying Monkeys would also mellow in time, but so far they tended to stay at the top of the steps, where they could sulk to their hearts' content without the danger that the locals' friendly overtures would spoil their fun.

I passed by the area where several dozen potters, quilters, woodworkers, and other craftspeople had booths, and in most cases, demonstration areas in multicolored tents. A little farther on was an area where the 4-H and the Future Farmers of Virginia had set up a series of agricultural displays along with an ongoing farmer's market.

My stomach rumbled, reminding me that it was time for lunch. I headed in the opposite direction from the courthouse, passing through the section where the food tents were arranged in a semicircle. St. Byblig's, the local Catholic church, sold Southern fried catfish with hush puppies and slaw. Next door, the New Life Baptist Church served up fried chicken, mashed potatoes, and greens. And beyond them was Trinity Episcopal's pit barbecue with fresh corn on the cob and hot German potato salad. Add in smaller stands offering cakes, pies, watermelons, funnel cakes, fresh-squeezed lemonade, and ice cream and you could see why the tourists sometimes spent half an hour staggering around in circles before finally deciding what they wanted to eat. And often trying to eat it all. Indigestion was second only to heatstroke at the first aid tent that was my dad's latest way of avoiding complete retirement from the medical profession.

But I'd had fried chicken on Wednesday, barbecue Thursday, catfish Friday, more fried chicken Saturday, and leftover fried chicken yesterday, when Rose Noire had tried to spring her Tofu Surprise on me. I wanted to start the new week out with something different.

Preferably something that didn't require waiting for an hour. As usual, the only food concession without a killer line was the newest one — a hamburger stand run by Hamish Pruitt, Caerphilly's disgraced former town attorney. Even the hungriest and most footsore tourist would take one look at the small size and inflated prices of Hamish's patties and go elsewhere. The stained, flyspecked, and generally seedy look of his stand didn't help either. Though perhaps the biggest barrier to sales was Hamish himself, who seemed unable to banish from his sagging, ruddy face the scowl he had so often used to intimidate opponents in court and over a bargaining table. I wasn't the only local who suspected Hamish had opened his stand not to make money but in the hope of finding out how Mr. Throckmorton was getting his supplies. Hamish's spot at the very edge of the food area was perfect for keeping an eye on comings and goings from the courthouse.

Then again, maybe the Hamishburger stand really was an attempt to make ends meet by flipping patties. It wasn't as if his law practice was going great guns. Most of the locals distrusted him because of his long history of favoring the Pruitts at the expense of Caerphilly, and now the rest of his own family was furious with him for failing to stop the recall vote that kicked his uncle George out of the mayor's office. I actually felt sorry for Hamish.

But nowhere near sorry enough to eat one of his burgers.

I noticed that the surly teenager minding Hamish's booth this morning was nibbling, under the counter, on what I recognized as a Baptist fried chicken leg.

"Oooh! Look!"

I glanced over and saw several tourists pointing up at the sky. I followed their glances and saw a red-tailed hawk soaring overhead.

"Isn't he beautiful!" someone said.

He was actually a she, and while she might be beautiful, she was also deadly if you happened to be a smaller bird. I turned and raced back to the tent.

Rose Noire was sitting in her rocking chair by Spike's pen, sewing. Probably making another batch of hand-sewed, organically grown aromatherapy sachets to sell at this week's farmer's market. She looked up as I came in and cringed slightly.

"No, he hasn't come out yet. You've only been gone five minutes. I don't know what you expect me to do if — Meg? What's wrong?"

I was ignoring her to race over to the left side of the tent where a large square birdcage sat on the ground. My abrupt arrival

45

startled the racing pigeons inside, who began fluttering around wildly.

"Help me count them," I said. "There are supposed to be eleven."

"I thought there were supposed to be twelve," she said.

"Yes, there were supposed to be twelve, until that damned hawk got one last week," I said. "Mr. Throckmorton is still inconsolable. That's why they're here instead of happily flying in and out of the courthouse basement. We're supposed to be keeping them safe, but if someone was careless or stupid enough to let one out and the hawk got it — damn! Why don't the silly things sit still long enough to be counted?"

"You're scaring them," she said. "Just sit over there and let me count them."

I put some distance between myself and the pigeons and fidgeted while Rose Noire cooed softly to them. After a minute or so, the pigeons had settled down and were seated on the rods that ran across the width of the cage, preening their feathers and cooing along with her.

"Eleven," she said softly. "All safe. I gather that nasty guard is flying his you-know-what?"

"His hawk, yes."

Rose Noire flinched, and the pigeons re-

46

acted as if startled, growing more restless and in a couple of cases, fluttering once or twice around the periphery of the cage before settling down again.

"See," she said. "Even the word upsets them."

"They wouldn't react if you didn't." I strolled over to the door of the tent and peered out. Out and up. The hawk was circling overhead, riding an updraft. Now that I knew all the pigeons were safe, I could appreciate how beautiful she was.

Just then she dived, almost too fast to see. I could hear exclamations on several sides and glanced around to see that other people had also been watching the hawk.

"I hear that's how the hermit is getting his meals," one tourist said. "By carrier pigeon. And the guards brought in a squadron of hawks to shut down his supply line."

"Poor man," the woman beside him said. "I guess he'll go hungry tonight, then."

No, actually Mr. Throckmorton would probably be dining well tonight. Rob was supposed to have taken in a care package full of Episcopal pulled pork and Baptist mashed potatoes. And the tunnel was so small that even Rob would have a hard time misplacing the package on the way.

They were wrong about the purpose of

the pigeons. They weren't carrying food, or even messages. After all, Mr. Throckmorton had a phone and a computer with Internet access. He just liked raising and flying pigeons, and for the first year of his self-enforced captivity, a tiny ventilation window near the ceiling at one end of the courthouse basement had let him continue doing so.

But slaying the pigeons was definitely the reason the guards had brought in the hawk. They'd probably call it psychological warfare — yet another tactic aimed at driving Mr. Throckmorton out of the basement. I called it pure meanness. I found myself hoping the hawk had caught a wild pigeon, or a starling — a bird that belonged to an invasive species, or at least one that wasn't endangered. And wasn't anyone's pet.

After all, it wasn't the hawk's fault that her handler worked for the bad guys.

I ducked back into my tent, pulled out my cell phone, and turned on the camera function. I moved it around until I had a good, clear shot of the cage from an angle that would let anyone who was so inclined count its occupants. Then I snapped a photo and e-mailed it to Mr. Throckmorton.

"Make sure they stay there," I said to Rose Noire, as I headed back out.

"I will," she said. "Trolls! Last week they

burgle Mr. Throckmorton's house, and now this."

"Vandalized, not burgled," I said. "Sammy and the other deputies couldn't find anything missing, remember? Lots of damage, but nothing actually missing."

"It's not as if Mr. Throckmorton has had a chance to inspect it himself," she said. "And anyway, vandalism is just as bad. Maybe worse."

I nodded my agreement as I left the tent.

Halfway across the town square, I heard the little ding that meant I had an e-mail. Mr. Throckmorton saying "Thanks."

The lines at the food concessions had grown longer. I could even see two people standing in front of the hamburger stand, trying to get the attention of Hamish's bored teenaged clerk. Maybe the teenager wasn't a slacker. Maybe he was trying to be a good Samaritan.

My stomach rumbled so loudly I was sure the nearby tourists could hear it, so I turned and headed for Muriel's.

CHAPTER 4

Even as hungry as I was, I knew better than to dash carelessly across Main Street. I had to wait until three tour buses and half a dozen cars full of gawking tourists had passed. Then I crossed to the other side, which contained a small block of businesses. In the center of the block was Muriel's Diner, a local institution since the fifties. In spite of Muriel's attempts to make it look like the sort of dive where you risked ptomaine poisoning just by touching the menus, word was getting out, and now on most days the tourists outnumbered the locals.

Locals still got a warmer welcome, though. Muriel beamed when she saw me walk in.

"Hi, Meg!" she called as she stepped out from behind the counter. "You all by yourself?"

"Michael's taking the munchkins on a hay

ride," I said. "I was craving some of your chili."

"Great!" she exclaimed. "You want a booth or a seat at the counter?"

I had actually planned to do carryout, since I'd assumed that Muriel's would be packed, as it usually was during the noon hour. But there was a line of three vacant stools near the far end of the counter, and the last two booths were empty.

"What's wrong?" I asked. And then I spotted the problem: the man sitting on the last stool, surrounded by a buffer zone of empty seats. He was middle-aged, balding, and utterly nondescript. Not someone who would normally draw a second glance. Except right now —

I lowered my voice. "Is that the private investigator the Evil Lender sent in?"

"My new regular," Muriel said, also in an undertone. "You'd think after two weeks he'd have figured out that no one in this town is going to tell him the first thing about Mr. Throckmorton." She glowered at the PI's back. Just then he turned around, holding his coffee cup up with the look, half hopeful, half apologetic, of someone seeking a refill. Normally Muriel would have refilled a customer's cup before he even

51

noticed it was getting low. Her scowl didn't change.

"Likes to linger over his dessert," she grumbled. "You think people would understand if I started charging for refills? Just for the time being, till he gets the message that he's not welcome?"

"You think he hasn't already gotten the message from those empty seats?" I asked. "And he's on an expense account — he doesn't care if his employer has to pay for his refills."

"Hmph. Chili and fries for you, then?" I nodded. Muriel sauntered over to the window and called my order back to Sam in the kitchen. Then she picked up the coffeepot and sashayed to the far end of the counter, where Seth Early, the farmer who lived across the road from Michael and me, was finishing off a burger and reading a copy of *The Banner Sheep Magazine.*

As she refilled his cup, I overheard her ask Seth about Lad, his border collie. Everyone in town knew that was good for half an hour. Clearly anyone who wanted a refill in a hurry was out of luck.

I strolled over to the counter and took the middle one of the three empty seats. The PI looked up and nodded at me. I nodded back. Then I reached into my purse to pull out my notebook-that-tells-me-when-to-breathe, as I called the small but fat binder that held my epic to-do list. Out of the corner of my eye, I noticed Sam, the cook, sliding a glass of water next to me.

"I'm just visiting Caerphilly," the PI said.

I glanced up. He was looking at me.

"We seem to be very popular these days," I said. "Hope you enjoy your stay."

I went back to my notebook. I had crossed off a few items and added one more when I heard the PI's voice again.

"So is there anyone in town who doesn't know who I am?" he asked.

I glanced up again. He had turned around sideways, the better to talk to me. Or maybe the better to study my fellow townspeople. I glanced over my shoulder and saw that everyone else in the diner was ostentatiously not looking our way. I pondered several possible answers and decided on the truth.

"You mean, is there anyone who doesn't know you're the private investigator hired by the Evil Lender?"

His face fell a little, but he nodded.

"Nobody really bought the story that you were a freelance reporter," I said. "We've seen quite a few of those over the last year, and we all know the kind of questions they ask, and yours just didn't ring true."

"So everybody had me pegged from day one?"

I shrugged.

"I don't expect the younger tots at the Wee Kinder Day Care have figured it out yet," I said. He winced slightly. "And there's an old guy over at the Caerphilly Nursing Home who's convinced that you're an advance scout for Ulysses S. Grant's army. But for the most part, yeah, everyone knows who you are and why you're here."

He nodded again and picked up his empty coffee cup. After a rueful glance inside, he put it down again, and reached for his water glass. It was nearly empty, too, but he finished off the last half inch of water and began crunching some ice cubes.

"Here," I said, shoving my water over to him. "I haven't touched this yet."

"Thanks," he said. "A pity it's bad business to say 'I told you so' to a client. Because I did warn them. Small town like this, situation like this, and someone nobody's ever seen before shows up and hangs around asking peculiar questions . . ."

He shrugged and sipped his new water.

"You're good," I said. "The whole rueful, self-deprecating manner. Bet most of the time it works pretty well."

He started to laugh and snorted out a bit

of the water.

"Sorry." He was patting his shirtfront and the counter dry with his napkin. He looked up and grinned at me. "Yeah, normally it does."

Nondescript looking but definitely charming. I was almost tempted to suggest that a PI who was the right age to be a student at Caerphilly College might have had a better chance of slipping under our radar.

Almost tempted.

"And you're right," he was saying. "The Evil Lender, as everyone around here likes to call my client, hired me to find out how Mr. Throckmorton is getting his supplies. At first they just thought he stocked up for a siege before they took possession of the building, but every week that's getting harder to buy. They're wondering what's going on."

"A lot of people are wondering the same thing," I said. Which wasn't a lie. A lot of people were wondering, just not a lot of people in town.

Except, of course, for the Pruitts, who had brought the Evil Lender down on us in the first place.

"I really thought my cover was pretty good," he said. "I mean, why wouldn't people want to talk to a freelance writer trying to do a sympathetic story on the Siege of Caerphilly?"

"Last I heard, they were talking to you," I said. "They just weren't telling you what you obviously want to know. Because if anyone's sneaking supplies into the courthouse basement, they're not going to admit it. And if they know that someone's doing it and how, they're not going to rat their neighbors out. Not to a reporter any more than a PI. Not to anyone who's not from around here. I mean, tell the press and you might as well just march up and tell the Flying Monkeys."

"The what?"

I winced.

"The Flying Monkeys," I repeated. "It's what we call the new security service. Someone started calling them stormtroopers, but then we all decided that was a little fraught and melodramatic, so we settled on Flying Monkeys. It's the uniforms."

"I see." His mouth was twitching.

Muriel appeared, coffeepot in hand, and refilled his cup.

"Thank you, ma'am," he said, tipping an imaginary hat to her.

Muriel was torn between responding to his courtesy and maintaining her righteous indignation. She settled for a curt nod.

"I have to admit, this has been a humbling experience," he said, as he added sugar to his new coffee.

"Normally by now you'd have cracked the case?"

"Not necessarily." He took a swallow of the coffee and sighed with contentment. "What I mean — you see, it's standard operating procedure for PIs to vet our clients before taking on a job. Make sure we're not going to be aiding and abetting something illegal or unethical. This one seemed like a no-brainer — potential client has a squatter on their property and wants to figure out how to cut off his supplies so he'll give up and come out. They showed me the legal documents. Seemed on the up and up. But the more I hang around this town . . ."

He let his voice trail off, clearly trying to draw me out.

My chili arrived.

"Things aren't always the way they seem at first glance." I picked up my spoon and dug into the chili.

"No, they're not," he said. "And I'm beginning to think maybe this time I'm not playing on the side of the angels."

"Good insight," I said over my shoulder as I applied myself to my chili.

A business card slid next to my bowl: Stanley Denton, private investigator; a P.O. box in Staunton, Virginia, and a phone number with a 540 area code.

"If you think of anything that might persuade me I should quit this assignment and go home, I'd be happy to listen," he said. "Have a good day."

I glanced up to see that he was tossing a few bills on the counter as he swallowed the last of his coffee.

"Thank you, ma'am," he called to Muriel.

I heard several sighs of relief as the door closed behind him.

"Overtipped me as usual," Muriel growled.

"Silly me," I said. "I thought it was undertipping that you wanted made a capital offense."

"Thinks he can buy me with a few lousy dollars," Muriel muttered as she cleaned off the place where Denton had been sitting. She shoved his dirty dishes through the hatch to the kitchen as if she'd rather toss them in the Dumpster, and scrubbed the entire vacant stretch of counter as if trying to eradicate all traces of some dire contagion.

"What did he want?" Sammy Wendell, one of our local deputies, sat down to my right.

"Just wants to cause trouble, that's what he wants," said a local farmer as he and his wife sat down to my left in the remaining empty seats at the counter.

In about two minutes, the entire population of the diner had convened an impromptu town meeting to discuss the PI. From the sound of it, he hadn't made too many friends during the several weeks he'd been in Caerphilly.

I ate my chili in silence, pondering our brief conversation. Was he just trying to gain my confidence? Or was he really starting to have reservations about working for the Evil Lender? And if so, what did he know that we needed to know? Because as much as I disliked the Evil Lender, I hadn't thought they were doing anything actually illegal. If they were —

He had said illegal or unethical. Unethical wouldn't help us. And for all I knew he could have just been trying to run some kind of scam on me.

I was still pondering that as I left the diner and headed back toward the town square.

I had plenty of time before my next blacksmithing demonstration. I called up Michael and learned that the boys were enjoying the hay ride. I reminded him to take some pictures for the grandparents. Then I decided to check out what was going on in the world before heading back to the tent. After all, chances were when I got back to the tent, I'd find that Rob had still not made his escape, and I wanted to postpone as long as possible the moment when I gave in to the temptation to chew him out. Especially since I'd probably have to do it by texting, which was not nearly as satisfactory as a phone call.

The food concession area was teeming with happy tourists. The teenager behind the counter at Hamish's Hamburgers had wisely scorned his own cooking and was openly scarfing up a huge plate of fried chicken and mashed potatoes. The calypso band members were taking their bows, and the Caerphilly Country Cloggers were waiting to take their place.

"Hey, Meg. Got a minute?"

CHAPTER 5

I'd long ago learned that "got a minute" usually meant that someone was planning to take up a few hours of my time. But when I turned to see who had designs on my afternoon, I saw Randall Shiffley standing in front of one of the larger tents — the one with a neat OFFICE OF THE MAYOR sign in front.

"Good morning, Mayor Shiffley," I said.

Randall preened a little, as he usually did when we called him that. I didn't begrudge him his pride. He was the first elected mayor of Caerphilly in over a century who wasn't either a Pruitt or a Pruitt puppet.

"Want to come along with me to the courthouse?" he asked. "I'm going over to reason with Mr. Throckmorton. Implore him to come out. I could use a concerned citizen or two in my delegation."

From the way he worded it, I deduced the

presence of the reporters before I spotted them.

"Glad to help," I said.

"Meg Langslow is a blacksmith — one of the craftspeople participating in Caerphilly Days," he said to a thin, pretty, but earnest young woman standing beside him. The woman glanced at me and scribbled something in her notebook. "Meg's husband, Professor Waterston, is in the drama department over at the college."

A short, stocky man standing nearby lifted the camera that was slung around his neck, studied me through its lens for a few moments, then let it fall to his chest again, as if I wasn't worth bothering with.

"Ms. Blake is with the *Star-Tribune,*" Randall said.

"The *Washington Star-Tribune,*" Ms. Blake added, with a slight frown, as if she felt it important to avert the grave danger of my thinking she'd come from some other, lesser known *Star-Tribune.* "Call me Kate."

"Let's get this show on the road," Randall said. He strode off toward the courthouse. Kate scampered after him. The photographer and I followed at our own speeds and ended up falling in shoulder to shoulder.

"Do you think you'll finally be able to convince Mr. Throckmorton to come out?"

Kate asked, when she caught up with Randall.

"Don't get your hopes up," Randall said. "Hasn't worked the last fifty or sixty times I tried it."

"So this is just for show, then?" she asked.

"Not a bit," Randall said, without missing a beat. He didn't sound the least bit winded, even though we were climbing the tall marble stairs that stretched the full width of the courthouse façade. I thought it was rather courteous of him not to bolt up them two at a time in his usual fashion. They didn't bother me, but Kate-from-the-*Star-Trib* was panting a little, and the photographer had stopped after ten or twelve steps to wheeze and clutch his side.

"I'd be falling down on the job if I didn't do everything I could to fix this whole mess," Randall was saying. "And make sure Phinny — Mr. Throckmorton — is fully aware of all the legal complications he's bringing on himself."

"You don't agree with his actions, then?" Kate asked.

"We're after the same thing," Randall said. "I'm trying to work through the system, while Mr. Throckmorton has chosen the more difficult and controversial path of civil disobedience."

I marveled, not for the first time, at how well Randall had made the transition from the boss of a small, family-run construction company to the highly visible spokesperson for the town of Caerphilly.

Then again, he had years of experience making temperamental clients happy in spite of the delays and other perils typical of construction projects, to say nothing of keeping the peace among his large and unruly clan. Perhaps, after all that, small town politics was a breeze.

"Morning, officers," Randall called out.

He'd reached the top of the stairs, where the stairway turned into a wide marble veranda with a panoramic view of the town square on one side and a row of white marble pillars on the other. Two of the lender's security guards, looking stiff and uncomfortably warm in their blue and red uniforms, had emerged from the interior of the courthouse and were lurking at the foot of the pillars. They might have made me just a bit nervous if they hadn't been accompanied by another figure in an ordinary business suit. I reminded myself to be careful not to call them Flying Monkeys in the reporter's hearing.

"Morning, Mr. Fisher," Randall called out, nodding at the suit.

"Good morning, Mr. Shiffley." Fisher strolled forward to join us. "I gather you're about to make another attempt to remove the trespasser?"

"I certainly plan to ask Mr. Throckmorton if he thinks his act of civil disobedience has accomplished its purpose," Randall said. "Can't promise anything."

"And what entertainment does the town plan to offer us this afternoon and this evening?" Fisher asked.

"Got a clogging demo starting now, followed by the semifinals of the hog-calling competition," Randall said. "And after that a polka band all the way from Goochland County. And then Professor Waterston's students are going to do some kind of patriotic play. Tonight's another open mike comedy night."

Fisher couldn't refrain from wincing slightly at that last bit, which probably meant he'd attended one of the previous open mike comedy nights.

The two exchanged a few more sentences in polite neutral tones. Fisher was one of a handful of what Randall called "the civil ones" — executives from the Evil Lender who didn't behave badly to all of us.

"But you know they're only playing good cop/bad cop on you," I'd told him once.

"Of course," he'd said. "And if they're dumb enough to think they're fooling me, all the better. My goal is to learn just a little more about how their minds work than they learn about mine."

So I waited patiently while the two of them chatted and studied each other. They'd played out much the same scene dozens of times before. Randall tried to make a very public visit to Mr. Throckmorton every day or so, and made sure the guards saw them exchanging at least a few private words through the barricades. Not only did this annoy the lender's minions, it kept them from becoming suspicious of our knowledge of what Mr. Throckmorton was up to, or his knowledge of the outside world.

"And it also lets me keep an eye on what those clowns are doing there in the courthouse," Randall had said. "If the guards start ripping up the marble floors so they can dig down to the basement, I should spot signs."

I didn't actually think this idea was all that far-fetched. For some reason, the lender's attitude toward Mr. Throckmorton had changed in the last few weeks. For almost a year they had seemed to regard the siege as either a nuisance or a joke. The guards from the original security service had made perfunctory patrols through the courthouse and occasionally played pinochle with Mr. Throckmorton through the barricade.

And while we'd slightly resented the old guards when they were here, everyone in town now remembered them fondly. The Flying Monkeys were stiffly uniformed, uniformly humorless, and — to the dismay of our police chief — armed. I tried not to scowl at them, but I couldn't help thinking that ever since they'd arrived, things had been so much more tense in town.

I also glanced at the third guard who stood at the other end of the veranda with his left arm held stiffly out for the hawk to sit on. Both he and the hawk scanned the skies around them with similar fierce looks on their faces.

But the hawk, I reminded myself, was only doing what came naturally. It wasn't her fault her owner was trying to use her to destroy someone else's pets.

I mentally wished the hawk bad luck with her hunting.

Just then Fisher and Randall burst into laughter.

"Sorry, but I'm afraid that's out of the question," Fisher said. "But if you come up with anything we *can* help you with, just let me know."

He strolled back to the guards.

"It's okay, Lieutenant Wilt," he said. "Mayor Shiffley can go on in."

"And these other individuals?" Wilt asked, waving at the rest of us. Clearly, from his expression, he was hoping Fisher would shout "Off with their heads!"

"Reporters, come to witness my attempt at mediation," Randall said. "And a witness of my own, to make sure I don't get misquoted by the press."

"Mayor Shiffley's entire party can go on in," Fisher said. He smiled and shook his head as if inviting us to chuckle with him over the silly behavior of the guards. Randall, who didn't find the guards any more charming than I did, managed a tight smile and a nod.

"Permission to enter," Wilt said. Fisher disappeared back into the building. "Officer Reilly, escort the visitors."

"Yes sir!"

Reilly and his boss saluted each other with exaggerated military precision. The *Star-Trib* photographer snapped a few pictures of them doing it. Then Wilt walked aside. Reilly stood at attention beside us.

"Well, let's get this show on the road," Randall said.

"Yes, sir," Reilly said — still at attention,

but minus the salute. He appeared to be waiting for us to lead the way.

Randall raised an eyebrow, glanced back at the reporters, and shook his head in a gesture of amused regret.

"Is he talking to himself?" he asked, pointing to Wilt, standing twenty feet away at the far edge of the veranda.

Reilly stood stiffly at attention, pretending not to have heard. Even with his arms clapped stiffly at his sides, you could see that he had a huge and growing sweat stain under each arm, and the beginnings of a heat rash on the back of his neck. Apparently the new guard company was from someplace farther north and either didn't know how to equip their staff for the Virginia heat or didn't care about their comfort.

The reporter was staring at Officer Wilt and scribbling in her notebook.

"I think he's got a microphone in his lapel," she said.

"Yes, he's miked for sound," I said. "See the coiled wire thingy going up to his ear?"

"Just like the Secret Service wear," Kate said.

"Lordy," Randall said, shaking his head again. "Well, time's a-wastin'. Lead on, Mr. Reilly."

"That's Officer Reilly," the young man

69

said, but he did start toward the door.

Randall stuck his hands in his pockets and ambled behind our escort in a display of folksy charm that mocked the paramilitary precision of the guards. At least that's how it looked to me, and from the way the reporter was scribbling as she glanced back and forth between Randall and Officer Wilt, I suspect she was getting the same impression. A little bit ridiculous, those guards.

And maybe also a little bit scary. I hoped she got that part, too.

Randall had only taken a few steps when a series of quick reports rang out inside the building.

Were those gunshots?

CHAPTER 6

"Get down!" Randall shouted.

Reilly didn't bother glancing around to check on us civilians. He drew his gun and flattened himself against the wall on the right side of the door.

Kate and her photographer were busily snapping and scribbling away. They seemed startled when Randall shoved them down behind the pillar to the right of the door. Randall took up a position on the other side of the pillar, where he could see what was going on and still have some cover. I followed his example on the left, then pulled out my cell phone and dialed 911. I saw Randall glance at me, nod approvingly, and shove his own cell phone back in his pocket.

Officer Wilt raced over to flatten himself against the wall to the left of the door. Like Reilly, he didn't even glance at us.

"Go!" he snapped. Reilly sprang into the doorway, head and gun moving rapidly left and right as he scanned the courthouse lobby.

"Clear!" he said.

He and Wilt darted into the lobby. Kate leaped up and began inching closer to the door to peer in.

"I'd stay back if I were you," Randall said. But he looked as if he were on the verge of ignoring his own advice.

Debbie Anne, the police dispatcher, answered.

"Meg, what's going on! My lines are lighting up like a Christmas tree. If this isn't urgent —"

"Someone just fired five or six shots inside the courthouse," I said. "Two armed guards from the lender's security service have gone inside to investigate. Randall Shiffley and I are here on the veranda, along with two reporters."

"And I'm going in to investigate," Randall said. "Tell Chief Burke to get over here with everything he's got." With that, he launched himself from behind the pillar and ran through the courthouse door. Kate followed.

Rob was in the courthouse. I almost said it aloud.

"Randall and the reporter are going in," I said instead. "Randall says —"

"Yes, I heard him," Debbie Anne said. "Already happening."

"I'm going to follow, at a distance," I said.

"Stay safe," Debbie Anne replied. "Help is on the way."

In fact, help, in the form of Deputy Sammy Wendell, was already loping up the street toward the courthouse. I took a tentative step toward the door.

The photographer, who'd been peering warily through the doorway, stepped inside.

Randall had served in the Marines and Kate was a reporter, which to me meant that neither of them was a good role model for a sane person to follow in a dangerous situation. But the photographer had looked a great deal less gung-ho when the shooting started, so if he thought the courthouse lobby was safe to enter, I could at least peek through the door.

Inside, I could see half a dozen of the armed guards milling around the lobby.

"— go upstairs and protect the corporate offices," Wilt was saying. Two of the guards saluted and began running up the curved marble stairway that led to the upper levels. Another two stood by the elevators.

"But the shots came from the basement," one of the guards racing up the stairway called back over his shoulder. It spoke volumes about their discipline that he didn't let this protest slow him down.

The basement? Wasn't Rob still in the basement?

"Reilly and I will check the basement," Wilt replied.

"If I were you," Randall put in, "I'd just stay put until the police get here."

Nobody even looked his way. The elevator arrived, and two more guards leaped in, weapons drawn, as if storming an enemy position.

"We're capable of handling the situation, thank you," Wilt said. He strode over to a small doorway, flung it open, and dashed in, followed by Reilly and the reporter.

"What's going on?" Deputy Sammy stumbled into the lobby, a little winded from all the stairs.

"I don't trust those clowns," Randall said. "Follow me."

Maybe he was talking to Sammy, but I decided to assume he meant me, too. And even if he didn't mean me — my baby brother could be down there in that basement.

I glanced at Sammy and saw him suddenly topple over, clutching his leg.

"Sammy! Are you hit?" I hadn't heard a shot, but as I scrambled to his side I quickly scanned the lobby for danger.

"Leg cramp," he gasped. "Heat does it to me. I'll be fine in a second. Get outside where it's safe."

I ignored him and dashed off to follow Randall.

The narrow stairs to the basement looked as if they belonged to a castle dungeon. Both walls and treads were made of local stone, and the stairs curved around in a full circle twice. The lobby was actually on the second floor, in order to make room for all those impressive marble stairs outside, so you had to go down two flights to the basement. Two centuries of use had worn the treads slick and carved a little depression in the middle of each one.

In happier times, a visiting genealogist or history buff who wanted to consult the town records would march up the sweeping marble steps, wander around the lobby until he found the discreet sign for the archives, and then climb down the two circular flights to the basement. Savvy locals would skip the front steps to come through the back door of the courthouse and then venture through the furnace room to take the back stairs to the basement, which were only one flight, and retrofitted with a stair lift to make them handicapped accessible. The two stairways were at each end of one of the long walls of the antechamber, and the door to the archives was in the center of the opposite wall.

I suddenly remembered climbing down this same stairway on past Halloweens, when the town had used the large room at the bottom to set up a haunted house to raise money for charity. We'd creep down slowly and carefully to the tune of "Night on Bald Mountain" and other classical Halloween favorites. In the basement, we'd follow a tangled path past an assortment of ghosts and ghouls, dodging rubber bats and enormous fake spiderwebs. The door to the archive, which we passed halfway through the haunted house, was always blocked with a faux iron gate, but inside Mr. Throckmorton would arrange an over-the-top tableau of vampires or zombies — one of the high points of the evening. And at the end of the path, we'd finally reach the second spiral stone staircase at the other side of the antechamber and stumble up to the furnace room, where the elderly Shiffley cousin who served as the town engineer served out punch and cookies.

I was jolted back to the present by the sounds of someone slipping and falling below, followed by several angry oaths.

"Stay sharp!" I heard Wilt shout from the basement. "The shooter has to be nearby."

I took the steps a little more slowly so I wouldn't slip. Emerging into the basement was like leaving the Middle Ages for the Great Depression — either the courthouse hadn't been redecorated since the 1930s or someone had taken care to replicate the institutional green-painted cinder-block walls and the black-and-white checkerboard linoleum of the era. I decided I liked it a lot better as a haunted house.

I found Randall, the reporter, and Wilt standing in a semicircle just inside the doorway from the stairs. The three rank-and-file guards, with their weapons drawn, were prowling restlessly around the room as if one more search might reveal that the cinder blocks and linoleum were covering a secret hiding place.

Presumably their erratic patrol was intended to protect us if whoever fired those shots returned, but I couldn't help thinking that I was a lot more likely to get hurt by their overreaction than by anything the original shooter was apt to do.

They seemed to be paying quite a lot of attention to the ugly board-and-barbed-wire barricade on the wall opposite the stairwell, never quite turning their backs on it.

"That's right," Randall was saying into his cell phone. "The courthouse basement. And hurry."

"She's way past an ambulance," Reilly said.

"I like to let the pros make that kind of decision," Randall said.

But he wasn't trying to do anything. And I knew Randall had had EMT training. If he thought an injury was survivable . . .

I had been about to circle so I could see what they were looking at, but I paused for a moment, uncertain that I wanted to see someone who was "way past an ambulance." At that moment the photographer arrived, almost bumping into me as he exited the stairway. He saw which way everyone was looking and circled left. Within seconds I heard the rapid clicking of his camera.

"Have a little respect, man!" Randall snapped.

The clicking stopped, but the photographer had already gotten his pictures.

"Who is she?" Kate asked.

"Name's Colleen Brown," Wilt said. "She's a vice president at First Progressive Financial."

The reporter was the only person in the group who wasn't taller than my five feet ten, so I peered over her shoulder.

CHAPTER 7

Colleen Brown was a slender woman in her late thirties or maybe her early forties. I hadn't actually met her, but like most people in town, I'd seen her from afar. I remembered her as tall, though it was hard to tell from the awkward way she was sprawled on the linoleum. And I seemed to recall that she was attractive, though that was equally hard to verify right now. Her eyes were open and unseeing, and her mouth had fallen open as if to scream. We hadn't heard a scream — probably because she'd been shot in the throat. The doctor's daughter part of me was making the same assessment Randall had. I didn't think CPR would work on an airway that damaged, and there was way too much blood for anyone to try without some kind of blood barrier.

I wrenched my eyes away from the wound. There was blood all down the front of her clothes and pooled around her on the black-

and-white linoleum. Impossible to tell if her blouse had been white or pastel, but she wore a beautifully tailored red suit with a skirt that would be about knee length if it hadn't ridden up when she fell. One foot still wore an elegant red pump with a higher heel than anything I wore, even on special occasions — and probably a higher price tag than I was used to. The other shoe had fallen off and was lying on its side, half in a pool of blood, with its almost-new sole facing toward us.

I felt a brief, irrational impulse to walk over, twitch her skirt down again, wipe off the missing shoe and put it back on her foot, and then maybe throw something over her to hide her from the long, cold stares of the four guards and the reporter.

Make that five guards. Another one arrived via the back staircase, the one that led down from the ground floor furnace room. I glanced over at the barricade, hoping Rob wouldn't pick this moment to peer out.

"Shouldn't we be doing something?" the reporter asked.

"I'm afraid she's past anything I know how to do," Randall said. "Her whole windpipe's just . . ."

He let his voice trail off and shook his head. Several of the guards shifted uneasily and the reporter's pen was frozen over her notebook.

"Any sign of the shooter?" Wilt snapped. I glanced over, but he was talking to the microphone on his shoulder.

"I don't think he's armed anymore," one of the guards said. "I think I've found the weapon."

He was pointing at the barrier. We all crowded closer, and I saw, to my relief, that Mr. Throckmorton had covered the inside with sheets of plywood. So as long as that was in place, the guards weren't going to spot Rob on the wrong side of the barricade.

We all peered down into the space between the Evil Lender's outer barrier and Mr. Throckmorton's inner one. Near the floor, caught in the rather pointless tangle of razor wire the lender had recently added, was a pistol. The matte black metal of its barrel gleamed slightly, while the handgrip seemed to be made of some material that absorbed light.

We all stared for a few moments as if spellbound, then one of the junior guards reached down as if to retrieve the pistol.

"Leave that alone!" Randall and Wilt snapped out their orders almost in unison and then glared at each other.

81

"The mayor's right," Wilt said.

"Moving the gun would be disturbing a crime scene," Randall said. "We leave it there for the police to examine."

"Pretty obvious what happened," another guard said. "He shot her and then tried to throw it out."

"Out or in," Randall said. "We'll let the police decide. They're on their way, and so is the ambulance, so let's clear this crime scene."

"We'll be taking charge of the crime scene," Wilt said.

"No, you won't," Randall said. "Since —"

"This building is the property of First Progressive Financial!" Wilt was actually clutching and unclutching the butt of his gun, as if considering whether or not to shoot Randall for trespassing. Was it just my imagination or did the gun, at least what I could see of it, look exactly like the one discarded in the barricade?

Randall's eyes flicked down briefly to those fidgeting fingers and then back to Wilt's face. Either he didn't think the guy was a real risk or he was one very cool actor.

"That's as may be," Randall said. "But you and your men are private security — not law enforcement. And right now this building is a Caerphilly County crime scene. Our sheriff has jurisdiction. So unless you fancy having you and your men locked up for interfering with a crime scene and obstructing a police officer in the commission of his duty, I'd suggest you get the hell out of here."

"But since local law enforcement are not yet on the scene —" Wilt began.

"Yes, we are."

We all turned to see Sammy Wendell standing at the foot of the stairway, looking tall and stern, with one hand resting firmly on his own holstered gun.

I realized my mouth had fallen open at the sight of the normally gawky and tongue-tied Sammy suddenly turned into John Wayne. I wiped the surprised look off my face. Randall managed to keep his astonishment to a brief flicker that Wilt probably didn't even notice.

"There you are," Randall said. "And I got a bit of law enforcement experience myself when I was in the service, so I think I can assist the deputy if he needs it. How about if you assemble your troops in the big tent right next to my office? Ah, there's Deputy Morris. She can escort you."

Aida Morris was a tall, coffee-skinned woman who competed in Ironman competitions in her free time. She took up a position on one side of the door to the stairs. She put her hands on her hips, although I noticed that the right one wasn't quite touching — just hovering near her gun. Sammy took up the same position on the other side.

Wilt opened his mouth, probably to argue some more, but he took a good look at Randall and the two deputies and demonstrated more common sense than I'd have given him credit for.

"All personnel evacuate the building and report to me at assembly point Alpha Tango," he snapped at his left shoulder, where the microphone was. Then he looked up at the four guards in the room with us. They were all tall — well over six feet — with the bulked-up, twitchy look of hardened gym rats who'd done too many steroids for way too long. What kind of security company would put loaded weapons in the hands of men like these? I wished Fisher, the Evil Lender's sensible staffer, would show up. He'd been on the steps a few minutes ago — surely he couldn't have gone far.

"You, too," Wilt said, with a wave of his hand. "Alpha Tango, on the double."

One by one the guards holstered their

guns, backed away from the body, and retreated up the stairs. I was actually impressed. I'd once seen a dog trainer order three half-grown Dobermans to stop chasing a cat. They'd obeyed, visibly fighting to overcome their natural instinct to give chase. The guards gave me the same uneasy impression of barely controlled ferocity.

"You, too, ma'am," Randall said to Kate, the reporter. Her photographer had already followed the guards. "Meg, can you stay here a minute to help me with something?"

The reporter left, looking back over her shoulder until she was out of sight. Aida Morris nodded to Randall and brought up the rear. I had no doubt that the Flying Monkeys would be waiting in the tent when Chief Burke went to see them. Unless he hurried, Aida would have already taken down all their names and addresses and lined them up in alphabetical order.

Sammy, Randall, and I all looked at each other and breathed audible sighs of relief when they were gone. Sammy also slumped, and wiped his palms on his uniform trousers.

"Holy cow," he said.

"You did good," Randall said.

"Sorry I took so long," he replied. "Leg cramp."

"It's the heat," Randall said. "Happens to me, too. Keep a watch over that back stairway." Sammy nodded. He walked a few paces closer to the stairway, still limping slightly, and began staring fixedly at it. I supposed it beat looking at Colleen Brown. "Meg and I will stay here with the body until the chief gets here. If that's okay with you," he added, turning to me.

"I'm fine," I said. Actually, fine wasn't entirely accurate, but I figured I could handle being there if Sammy could. And my curiosity was kicking in.

"Who is she, anyway?" Sammy asked over his shoulder. "The bo— the deceased."

"One of the lender's people," Randall said. "Name of Colleen Brown. The only other sensible one apart from Fisher. For that matter, I thought she was even more promising than Fisher. Didn't seem to be on board with most of the crap they've been pulling. Which means if they wanted to frame poor Phinny Throckmorton, she'd be the perfect victim. Get rid of two thorns in their side in one move."

"You think they did this to frame Mr. Throckmorton?" I asked.

He pointed to the barricades and then to the body.

"Looks like she was facing the barricade

and fell back when she was shot," he said. "I'll leave it to the chief to figure out for sure, but on the surface it's certainly supposed to look as if she was shot from down in the cellar. By someone who then tried to throw the gun outside and botched it, leaving the gun between the two barriers."

"I don't believe it," I said. "Mr. Throckmorton would never have done anything like that."

"That's the point," Randall said. "It's a frame. We know that for damn sure. Proving it's going to be another thing entirely." He had moved a little closer to the body and was examining it as closely as he could without touching anything.

Just then my cell phone rang. Rob.

CHAPTER 8

"Meg, what's going on out there?" he asked. The connection was faint and fragmented.

"Out there? Are you still in the cellar?"

Randall glanced up.

"Is that Phinny?"

"No," I said. "It's my brother, Rob."

"We heard something out there," Rob said. The signal was weak and I turned on the speaker to hear better. "Sounded like fireworks or gunshots. Phinny was worried that the guards were trying to storm the barrier."

"I'm right outside the barrier," I said. "No storming going on at the moment. Hang on."

"What's up?" Randall asked.

"Maybe it's not going to be so hard to prove Mr. Throckmorton's innocence," I said. "Rob's still in there with him."

"May I?" Randall held out his hand. I gave him my phone.

"Rob, have you been with Phinny for the past half hour or so?" Randall asked.

"Yes," Rob said. "We've been playtesting my new game and —"

"Either of you out of each other's sight in that time?"

A brief pause.

"Not for more than a minute or two," he replied. "We've been playing a particularly tense part of the game."

Randall frowned, and I sighed softly. So much for giving Phinny an ironclad alibi. The shots had taken a few seconds. An alibi with a hole of even a few minutes wasn't much better than no alibi at all.

Just then Chief Burke stepped into the room. Randall handed me the phone again.

"Hello?" Rob's voice was faint, but I could tell he was anxious.

"Hang on a sec, Rob," I murmured into the phone. Then I hit the mute button.

"Welcome, Chief," Randall was saying. "Those cowboys give you any trouble upstairs?"

"None that I didn't give them back with interest," the chief said. "What happened?"

"I was coming down to parley with Phinny, with two *Star-Trib* reporters and Meg along to witness," Randall said. "We were just entering the courthouse when shots rang out. We followed the toy soldiers down here and found the body."

"Who is she?"

"Colleen Brown. Works for the Evil — for First Progressive Financial."

"The reporters get a good look?"

"And a few snapshots before we shooed them out with the toy soldiers."

The chief winced.

"And one of the guards found what may be the murder weapon," Randall added. "Gun thrown down in the no-man's-land between the two barriers."

"Wonder what made him think to look in there," the chief muttered.

Randall shrugged elaborately.

"You can see what this looks like." Randall pointed to the body and then to the barricade. The chief nodded.

"Meg," the chief said. "Is your cousin in town?"

I nodded. I had several hundred cousins, if you counted all the second, third, fourth, and once- or twice-removed ones, the way Mother did. But I knew exactly which cousin he meant — Horace Hollingsworth, who worked as a crime scene investigator in our hometown of Yorktown, and through a longstanding intercounty arrangement, here in Caerphilly when needed.

I unmuted my phone.

"Gotta go," I said to Rob. Then I hung up and dialed Horace.

"I know," Horace said instead of hello. "I'm about two minutes away."

With that he hung up.

"Two minutes," I repeated to the chief.

"Debbie Anne?" The chief was talking on his own cell phone. "See if Dr. Smoot is in town, and findable, and can get his sorry self down here with reasonable speed." He looked up at me. "This is going to be complicated," he said. "If you can find your father —"

I nodded and hit a speed-dial button. By the time I had left a message for Dad and sicced Mother on the job of finding him ASAP, the chief had finished issuing instructions to his troops. He looked grim as he tucked his phone back into his pocket.

"So, talk," he said. "Anybody."

"You want the good news first?" Randall asked.

The chief growled slightly. Randall took that for a yes.

"Phinny didn't do it."

"Randall, I know he's a friend of yours, but —"

"He may be alibied," Randall said. "Rob Langslow has been in there most of the day.

91

They've been playing one of Rob's war games for the last several hours. With any luck they were in sight of each other when she was killed."

"We can only hope," the chief said.

"Of course, even if they were, it's an alibi that would cause the devil's own kind of trouble if we had to use it," Randall said.

"Yes," I said. "I shudder to think what would happen if you had to put Rob on the stand to alibi Mr. Throckmorton. As a kid, Rob was always getting punished for stuff he didn't do because he got so rattled when anyone in authority interrogated him. A sharp DA could easily convince a jury Rob was confused or lying. Heck, they could probably even convince Rob."

"Let's hope Mr. Throckmorton doesn't need his alibi, then," Randall said. "Actually, I meant that using the alibi would give away the secret of the tunnel. Could cost the chief and me our jobs, and the town its lawsuit, and a lot of townspeople could be looking at a whole bunch of criminal charges. I'm no lawyer, but I bet there's some kind of aiding and abetting charge they could file against every one of us if they found a sympathetic DA. Like if they got Hamish Pruitt reinstated as town attorney."

The chief sighed and rubbed his forehead

slightly, as if he felt a headache coming on.

"So you believe Mr. Throckmorton didn't do it," he said. "Any idea who did?"

"Someone who had access to the basement," Randall said. "On this side of the barricade."

"FPF hasn't been allowing much access to the courthouse," the chief said. From the look on his face, I could tell he knew exactly what Randall was getting at, but he was going to make Randall come out and say it.

"No," Randall said. "Nobody much gets in here except for the guards and the creeps they work for."

The chief nodded slightly.

"I don't know whether we were a complication in their plan," Randall said. "Or whether they deliberately did it when they did so Meg and I would be witnesses. Either way, they shot her — probably crouching down low, so it would look as if it came from behind the barricade."

The chief had squatted down to get a closer look at the body. He glanced from it to the barricade as if following what Randall was saying.

"Then they could run up that back stairway while we're coming down the front one," Randall went on.

"One of the guards came down that way,"

I pointed out.

"But not right away," Randall said. "If the killer was a guard, all he had to do was run up till he was out of sight and then come down again and pretend to be in on finding the crime scene with us. If it was anyone else working for the lender, he could just trot on past the guards, get rid of his bloodstained clothes, and go back to doing whatever he was supposed to be doing when the news broke."

"Good point," the chief said. "Did anyone happen to notice which guards came down here?"

"I made a point of checking their name tags," Randall said.

"So you think the killer's either a Flying Monkey who'll be trying to barge in on my case," the chief said, "or a corporate goon who'll be complaining to you that I'm not moving fast enough and telling the media we're not competent to handle a case of this magnitude."

Randall nodded.

"And if they find out about the tunnel, the manure will really hit the fan," Randall said. "Unless, of course, we can prove one of them is the killer. Aiding and abetting a trespasser will seem like pretty small potatoes next to arranging a murder."

"So all we have to do is figure out which one of a tight-knit group of corporate crooks and their hired thugs committed a murder," the chief said. "Not just figure it out, but prove it, and all before the crooks manage to manipulate public opinion to the point that we have to call in the State Bureau of Investigation or the FBI."

"I didn't say it would be easy," Randall said. "But that's what we have to do. And if anyone can do it, we can."

Randall looked at Sammy and then at me, as if including us in the "we." Sammy, who had been looking on with big eyes, stood a little straighter and lifted his chin. I hoped I didn't look as tired and pessimistic as I felt.

"Just one thing," the chief said. "I gather you think this is a conspiracy?"

Randall frowned for a moment, then shrugged.

"Who the hell knows?" he asked. "I think some of them are capable. And if it wasn't a conspiracy to kill her, it could easily turn into a conspiracy to cover it up. Even more of them are capable of that, if you ask me."

The chief nodded, and took a deep breath.

"Sammy," he said. "You've been through that confounded tunnel a couple of times, haven't you?"

"Yes, sir," Sammy said. "To help Rob and

Mr. Throckmorton test Rob's new game."

"Tunnel bother you at all?" the chief asked.

"Well, I don't much like it, if that's what you mean, sir," Sammy said. "But I can do it if I have to."

"Good. Go in there ASAP and secure the basement. No one goes in or comes out without my orders. Keep Mr. Langslow and Mr. Throckmorton away from the barricade. Bag their hands so Horace can test them for gunshot residue. Don't let them wash or do anything until he gets there."

"Yes, sir," Sammy said. He loped off.

"Meg, if you don't mind, can you keep an eye on that back stairway till I can get another deputy in here?" the chief said. "While you're there, call your brother. You heard what I just told Sammy — brief him." I nodded and pulled out my cell phone as I took my place at the bottom of the stairs. I dialed Rob, but his phone rang on unanswered.

"Randall — you said that newspaper photographer was in here?" the chief was asking.

"Taking pictures the whole time," Randall answered, with a nod.

"Let's get his film," the chief said. "I want to see his pictures."

"These days a lot of those fellows use digital," Randall said.

"Then I need whatever he's storing the photos on," the chief said. "I could have an officer seize his camera, but maybe you could handle it more diplomatically."

"Can do," Randall said.

Rob's phone finally went to voice mail.

"Call me," I said. "ASAP."

"Make sure he understands we're not trying to take them away from him," the chief said. "He can have his camera back as soon as we get copies of his pictures, but we need to see everything he's taken so far today."

"As soon as I find him," Randall said.

"Check with Vera," the chief said. "By now he should have the folks from the *Star-Trib* rounded up along with all the guards. I told him to keep the witnesses in the big auditorium tent."

"Roger," Randall said. "Soon as you've got some help down here, I'll go over there and do what I can to make sure the media doesn't get their version of the day's events from the Flying Monkeys."

He turned to leave and had to pause in the doorway as my father burst in with his old-fashioned black doctor's bag in hand.

CHAPTER 9

"Sorry it took me so long," Dad said, as he trotted over to where Colleen Brown's body lay.

"You beat the ambulance," the chief said.

Just barely. The EMTs swept in behind Dad, laden with high-tech equipment that I could have told them was going to be useless. They could probably see it, too, but like Dad, they were wearing determined looks.

If they were going to go through the motions of trying to revive the poor woman, I didn't want to watch. I pulled out my cell phone and while I hit redial, I climbed a few steps up the stairway, to the point where I had to crane my neck to see Colleen Brown.

"She's past anything we can do," I heard Dad say, in a soft, discouraged voice.

This time Rob answered his phone.

"Where were you?" I snapped.

"At the other end of the basement," he said. "You have to be up close to the barrier to get a cell signal down here."

After relaying the chief's instructions to Rob, I climbed up a few more steps. The stone walls and steps made the stairway curiously more comforting than the cinder block and linoleum of the basement. Or maybe I just wanted a little more distance between me and the crime scene. I called Michael.

"Meg! What's going on?"

"There's been a murder," I said. "Someone who worked for the Evil Lender. Randall Shiffley and I were practically the first ones on the scene, so I might be tied up for a while being interviewed and processed and whatever."

"What can I do to help out here?"

"Keep the boys safe. Get someone to change my sign so it says next blacksmithing demonstration to be announced. Plan something for dinner that's not fried chicken, fried fish, or barbecue."

"How about pizza?"

"Pizza would be excellent."

We talked for a few more minutes, arranging all the small details of our afternoon and our evening. A welcome dose of the normal and mundane before I returned to the grim business at hand.

By the time I finished, another deputy had arrived to take my post.

"You can head over to the forensic tent," he said.

The forensic tent. This morning we'd been calling it the town hall tent. As loudly as I used to complain that nothing much changed in Caerphilly from one decade to the next, I realized that I rather missed the quiet old days.

"Dr. Smoot!" Since climbing halfway up the back stairs I'd heard only indistinct sounds from below, but the chief's bellow carried marvelously.

"I gather the medical examiner has arrived," I said.

"Acting medical examiner," the deputy said. Was he only imitating the chief, or did the entire department share the chief's disapproval of the eccentric Dr. Smoot? "And arrived? That's a matter of opinion."

"Smoot!" People in next door Clay County probably heard that. I had been planning to go up the back stairs and out through the furnace room, but my curiosity kicked in and I headed back down to the basement.

When I got to the bottom of the stairs, I saw that Colleen Brown's body was still there. Dad, Randall, several deputies, and the EMTs were anxiously staring at the chief, who stood at the bottom of the stairs with his hands on his hips and a thunderous look on his face.

"Smoot! Damn it, man, get down here!"

I was puzzled for a moment, until I remembered that our acting medical examiner suffered from crippling claustrophobia. He was probably balking at coming down the narrow, winding basement steps.

We all stared at the doorway for a few more moments.

"Maybe you shouldn't have told him to leave his cape at home," Randall said.

"We're going to look foolish enough as it is," the chief said. "We don't need the *Star-Tribune* doing a human interest story on the town whose medical examiner thinks he's a vampire."

"He doesn't think he's a vampire," Randall said. "He just likes to dress up like one. And it helps him with the claustrophobia."

"He can dress any way he likes on his own time," the chief said. "When he's on the job he should look like a blasted professional. And if he can't walk down a circular stairway or into an elevator without panicking, he should see a therapist, not an exorcist. It's not as if I can move the crime scene upstairs for him."

"We're working on it," Randall said.

"Moving the crime scene upstairs?" I asked.

"Getting your father appointed as a local medical examiner," Randall said. "In the meantime, is there anything we can do?"

"I've already pronounced her dead," Dad said. "It would be nice, of course, to have your medical examiner inspect the crime scene, but Horace and I have done so."

"Looks a blessed sight better in court if your ME can bring himself to show up at the crime scene," the chief said. "Of course, it also looks a blessed sight better if your ME's not a complete nincompoop."

Everyone looked uncomfortable. But I noticed that no one spoke up to say, "Oh, Smoot's not so bad."

"You're going down to the hospital with the body, I assume," the chief said to Dad.

Dad nodded.

"Can't you find a way to take him with you?"

"Dr. Smoot?" Dad asked. "Why?"

"Surely he's certifiable," the chief said. "If he's locked up in a psych ward somewhere I won't have to explain his absence."

"Yes, but it could call into question all of his recent findings," Dad said. "Cause the state medical examiner a lot of extra work. And these days the bar for involuntary commitment is a lot higher than you'd think."

"Heat exhaustion," I said.

They turned to me with puzzled looks on their faces.

"You could admit Dr. Smoot to the hospital for heat exhaustion," I said. "Even if he followed orders and left his cape home, you know he's probably dressed in all black. And then running up the courthouse steps in the sun? An invitation to heatstroke."

The chief and Dad looked at each other.

"I could give it a try." Dad sounded dubious.

"I'll help you." I started for the stairs. "We'll tell him he can either come down the stairs or pretend to have heat exhaustion."

Once we reached the courthouse lobby, I saw Dr. Smoot cowering against the wall opposite the stairs. He was dressed in black slacks and a black turtleneck sweater, making him probably the only person in the county dressed even less suitably than the guards for heat in the high nineties. I revised my plan of action. Ordering him to do anything was probably fruitless.

"Dr. Smoot, are you all right?" I asked.

"I'll just wait up here," he said. "You can

bring the body up here."

"I've already certified her death," Dad said. "Why don't you just come along with me, and we'll examine her together down at the hospital?"

"You're trying to trick me!" Dr. Smoot shouted. He was scrabbling against the wall behind him as if looking for a doorknob. "You're going to lead me down into that tunnel!"

"It's not you we're trying to trick." I glanced around ostentatiously, as if making sure no one could overhear, and then dropped my voice to a conspiratorial whisper. "It's the chief. He's insisting you come down. But Dad and I have a plan."

"I'm going to admit you to the hospital with possible heat exhaustion," Dad whispered.

Smoot didn't say anything, but he cocked his head to one side and stopped clawing at the wall.

"Help us out a bit with a few symptoms," I said. "That way we can keep you out of harm's way until all this crawling through tunnels is over with, and nobody will be the wiser."

"You're experiencing weakness, profuse sweating, muscle cramps, headache, and nausea," Dad prompted. "I think we can skip the actual vomiting. If you can faint plausibly, that would add a lovely note of authenticity."

"But don't do it unless you can carry it off properly," I said. "Nothing worse than an obviously fake faint."

Dr. Smoot was nodding furiously.

"Here comes the chief!" Dad hissed.

The chief popped out of the stairway door. Recognizing his cue, Dr. Smoot collapsed against the wall, clutching his head with one hand and his stomach with the other, and uttered several sepulchral groans.

"Good heavens," the chief exclaimed. "What the dickens is wrong with the man now?"

"Heat exhaustion." Dad patted Dr. Smoot on the shoulder, and Dr. Smoot sagged against him as if all his bones had suddenly turned to jelly. Dad staggered slightly under the weight. "I'm taking him down to the hospital ASAP," Dad puffed.

"Vern, help Dr. Langslow," the chief said. "Dr. Smoot, you just take all the time you need to get well."

One of the deputies hurried to support Dr. Smoot's other side, and the three of them lurched out the courthouse door.

"All the time you need," the chief repeated under his breath.

We heard cheering outside.

"What the dickens?" the chief muttered.

"Come on, Meg," Randall said. "Time we checked out how your cousin is doing with the Flying Monkeys."

"Time I did the same," the chief said. He strode briskly out of the door, and I got the impression he preferred arriving at the forensic tent first, so I paused to give him a few moments. Randall stood beside me.

"We're going to need to help the chief on this one," he said.

"The chief might not like that idea," I replied.

"I figured as much," he said. "And I don't want to pull rank on him, but I will if I have to."

More cheering from outside. Presumably greeting the chief's appearance. I was willing to bet he wasn't liking that much, either.

"So let's discuss it at tonight's Steering Committee meeting," Randall added.

I suppressed a tired sigh. Publicly, the Steering Committee was the group tasked with organizing and implementing the ongoing Caerphilly Days celebration. Its covert mission was to ensure that the celebration included a sufficient number of noisy attractions to cover the opening and closing of the trapdoor. As one of the most prolific generators of noise, I'd been re-cruited to join. The committee was impor-tant, fascinating, rewarding — and, like all committees, incredibly time consuming. I'd have resigned long ago if they hadn't taken to meeting in our library — now, tempo-rarily the fiction room of the Caerphilly public library. Having the meeting that close made it easier to attend, but also a lot harder to weasel out of.

"We had a Steering Committee meeting last night," I pointed out. "We don't have one scheduled for tonight."

"We do now," Randall said. "And what's more —"

Another cheer went up outside. Randall's head snapped toward the door.

"Let's see what that is, shall we?"

CHAPTER 10

Randall and I both hurried out the door and over to the top of the steps, where we had a panoramic view of the town square. A great many faces, tourist and local, looked back up at us from behind a barricade made of sawhorses and crime scene tape. Patrolling up and down the sidewalk just inside the barricade were several people wearing the red, white, and blue armbands we'd devised to identify the auxiliaries — citizens recruited by the Steering Committee and deputized by the chief to help with crowd control when the throngs attending Caerphilly Days grew unusually large.

Another cheer greeted our arrival, and at least a dozen digital cameras or cell phones captured it for posterity. I could see Chief Burke's stocky figure striding across the cordoned-off street. Probably still scowling. Randall responded to the cheering with smiles and waves, and it continued rather longer this time.

"Chief's going to love this," I said. "A cheering audience for his investigation."

"Soooo-EEEEEE!"

The amplified hog call rang out.

Normally our local hog callers were sticklers for competing the old-fashioned way, without microphones, but they'd agreed to sacrifice the purity of their art to the cause of making as much noise as possible. I could see people's heads whipping back and forth, torn between the certain entertainment of the hog-calling contest and the dubious pleasure of standing in the hot sun waiting to see if something interesting would happen here at the courthouse.

I hoped the hog calling would win before they brought the body out.

Randall waved one last time and began striding down the steps.

"Mr. Mayor! Mr. Mayor!"

I watched as Randall deftly fielded questions from the few journalists present — the *Caerphilly Clarion*'s one general purpose reporter, a gawky sophomore from the college rag, a stringer from the *Richmond Times-Dispatch,* and our two *Star-Trib* witnesses, who had apparently eluded the deputies on the way to the tent. Randall managed to say nothing in particular with great charm and earnestness, so that the press all focused on him and didn't even notice when the EMTs wheeled the gurney with Colleen Brown's body down the handicapped ramp that zigzagged along the right flank of the courthouse. Then Randall cut the two *Star-Trib* reporters out of the herd and guided them gently toward the forensic tent.

I had no desire to see if I was as good as Randall at dodging reporters' questions, so I gave them a wide berth and trudged on toward the waiting tent.

The tent had two entrances. I spotted Horace and the chief near the farther one and took a few steps in their direction to see what was up.

"Chief," Horace was saying, "the odds are low that these GSR tests will show anything we can use. And they're going to be hideously expensive to process."

"And we don't yet know if any of these clowns are even suspects," the chief said. "But you have to take the swabs within a few hours of the shooting, right?"

Horace nodded.

"So collect all your evidence and turn 'em loose," the chief said. "We can worry later about which samples to process. If we ever get this to trial, I don't want some defense attorney trying to make it look as if we don't know our jobs. Besides, maybe we'll all get kicked off the case and the SBI or the FBI or somebody will get stuck with processing them."

Horace nodded and ducked into the tent. The chief followed.

I was about to follow when I spotted the Caerphilly Fire Department's ambulance slowly making its way in front of the court-house. It didn't have its lights and sirens on, but people noticed. A few were point-ing. Most were standing, quietly. As I watched, one of the deputies took his hat off until the ambulance had passed.

I ducked into the tent.

Randall was standing just inside the entrance with the reporters in tow. But no one had noticed his entrance — all eyes were on the chief and Lieutenant Wilt, who were standing nose to nose arguing.

"I will not have my men singled out for special treatment!" Wilt snapped.

"Which is why we want to process them in the same way we're processing everyone else who had access to my crime scene," the chief said. "No matter how briefly. Includ-ing those reporters from the *Star-Tribune,* once we figure out where the dickens they've got to, and our own town mayor."

"Right here, Chief," Randall said.

The chief turned to where Randall and the reporters were standing and nodded. It probably looked brusque to an outsider, but given the chief's current mood I thought it was downright gracious.

Then the chief returned his gaze to Wilt. Wilt opened his mouth as if to continue his protest, then thought better of it.

Now I understood the reason for bringing along me and Randall.

"I'd be happy to go first," Randall said. "What do you need from me?"

"First Horace will swab your hands and face for any traces of gunshot residue," the chief said.

"Swab away," Randall said. Horace stepped forward, opened his kit, and began putting on his gloves and readying his tools.

"You do realize that my men are armed guards," Wilt said. "And as such they have to maintain their firearms qualification. If one of them has recently completed his required hours of target practice —"

"Then he should mention it when it's his turn to be processed," the chief said.

"I did a little tin can shooting four-five days ago," Randall said. "Getting ready for deer season. Will that mess up your tests?"

"Four or five days?" Horace said.

"Shouldn't be any GSR left. Unless you've completely forgotten to bathe or wash your hands since then. But I'll note your recent firearm use on the form so the lab can take it into account when processing your swabs."

"We'll also need to collect your uniforms for processing," the chief said.

A murmur of protest rippled down the line of guards and then died down at an instant when their leader scowled at them.

"Collect our uniforms?" Wilt echoed. "What are we supposed to do — walk around in our birthday suits?"

Guffaws erupted, and a few of the guards began unbuttoning their wool uniform jackets or pretending to pull down their pants.

"You'll be allowed to keep your under-wear," the chief said. "And one of my deputies is rounding up some temporary clothing for your men."

"Already got some, Chief." We glanced over to see Deputy Vern Shiffley standing in the doorway, holding a large cardboard box.

"Back already," the chief said. "Excellent. See if you can find something in Mayor Shiffley's size."

"Pretty much one size fits all, Chief," the deputy said. He reached into the box and held up a maroon satin choir robe.

I had to fight not to giggle, and the guards had no reason to suppress their amusement.

The chief closed his eyes briefly, but he only appeared to count to three or four before taking a deep breath and opening them again.

"I thought you were going to bring over some of those orange jumpsuits from the jail," he said, his tone carefully neutral. "Don't we have boxes and boxes of them down at the station?"

"No, sir," Vern said. He looked uncomfortable.

"We sent them over to the Clay County jail months ago." Minerva Burke, the chief's wife, bustled in carrying another box of choir robes. "Do you know how much they were charging us to rent their jail jumpsuits for our prisoners?"

"I assumed the jumpsuits were included in the steep fee they're charging us to house our prisoners," the chief said.

"Steep is the word, and it only covers the bare walls of a cell," Randall said. "Meals, sheets, uniforms, laundry — everything's extra. We could probably save money if we housed our prisoners at the Caerphilly Inn."

"So the jumpsuits aren't available," Vern said. "But the reverend over at the New Life

114

Baptist Church offered to lend us some of their choir robes."

"They're squeaky clean," Minerva said. "Which is more than I can say for our poor jumpsuits. Have you seen the condition they've been in since Clay County's been taking care of them? I wouldn't put an axe murderer in one of those filthy things, much less a respectable citizen of Caerphilly County. And what's more —"

"I think it's a great idea," Randall said. "Let's put the boxes down over there. Horace, why don't you do the reporters next, so they can get on about their business."

Minerva and Vern waited until the chief nodded his approval before scrambling to follow Randall's suggestion.

We all watched as Horace swabbed first Kate and then the photographer. Minerva escorted Kate out of the tent, while Vern took the photographer.

My turn next. I waited while Horace swabbed my hands and carefully bagged the swab. Then I followed Minerva out of the tent to a smaller one nearby that had a folding screen dividing it in two.

"Just put this on and hand your clothes out to me," she said, gesturing to the screen.

I did as she asked. The choir robe seemed voluminous when I held it up, but it only came down to my knees.

"Not a lot of people my height in the choir, I suppose," I said.

"Plenty of people take your size in a robe, especially when you factor in weight along with height," she said as she watched me tug at the hem. "But I could only borrow the smaller ones that the choir wasn't apt to use any time soon."

I could live with the bare legs, but the little tent was hot and stuffy and I only just stopped myself from reaching up to wipe the sweat off my face with one trailing sleeve. Of course, they'd probably have to wash it after I took it off anyway, but somehow deliberately using the sleeve as a towel seemed rude.

The chief strolled in.

"Oh, good," Minvera said. "I needed to ask you about something."

"Just a moment," the chief said. "Sorry to inconvenience you," he said, turning to me. "Obviously since you and Randall alibi each other, we don't really need to test your clothes."

"But it helps lull the suspicions of all those real suspects," I said. "Understood."

"Thank you," he said.

"Henry," Minerva said. "We have to do something."

"I have to do quite a few things." The chief's voice had only a small edge of testiness, probably because he knew better than to take out his mood on Minerva. "Do you have something I really need to add to my list?"

"Not your list, mine," she said. "We can't have a bunch of foul-mouthed amateur comedians performing here tonight in the town square — not with that poor woman lying dead in the courthouse basement."

"She won't be in the courthouse basement by then," the chief said. "In fact, she shouldn't be there now. She should be over at the morgue, unless the ambulance had a breakdown."

"You know what I mean," she said. "That polka music's going to be bad enough. Make it sound as if we're celebrating the murder."

The chief glanced around to make sure no one was within hearing distance and lowered his voice.

"I agree, the polka music won't be very appropriate," he said. "Anymore than the hog calling. But I've got to be able to send my officers to the basement. We need the polka music and the comics and even more the crowds they'll draw to cover the noise and bustle of all that toing and froing."

"Well, I know that!" Minerva had put her hands on her hips and fixed the chief with the exasperated look of a wife whose husband is being particularly uncooperative. I understood exactly how she felt, and yet I made a mental note to delete that particular tone and gesture from my wifely repertory. "I just wanted to tell you what we're doing to take care of the problem."

The chief raised one eyebrow, as if he wasn't really expecting to like her solution.

"The New Life Baptist Choir will be giving a memorial concert." Minerva lifted her head high in a subtle, dignified, but definitely triumphant gesture. "I talked to the reverend while I was borrowing the choir robes. It's all arranged."

"What a good idea," the chief said. "And don't tell me not to sound so surprised," he added quickly. "I'm not actually surprised, just darned pleased. The comedians wouldn't have been very good cover anyway. Just don't do too many quiet songs."

"We will be making not only a joyful noise unto the Lord but an exceedingly loud one," Minerva said, with a nod. "If that bandstand has rafters, watch out; we'll be sending them into orbit. Meg, I assume it's okay if we use your tent over by the bandstand as a changing room for the choir? We can leave someone to watch all the purses, so you can have the night off from guard duty."

"Fine with me," I said. "In fact, better than fine."

"I'll see you later then," she said. "Go on back to your tent, now. I gave Rose Noire a call, and she says you have some spare clothes over there."

I nodded, and stepped out of the stuffy tent into the almost-as-stuffy outdoors. Just as I did, the first rollicking strains of "The Beer Barrel Polka" blasted over the loud-speaker. Maybe in another mood I'd have found the music's energy infectious. Right now I just felt tired.

Ever since the heat had set in, Dad had been nagging everyone in town to drink at least a full glass of something nonalcoholic and noncarbonated every two hours. I was overdue for some liquid, so on my way back to the bandstand I took a slight detour past the food tents.

And then I paused a few steps outside the Episcopal tent. What were my chances of slipping in, getting a lemonade, and slipping back out without running into anyone who'd badger me with questions?

I had water back at the tent. I was turning to go there when —

"Meg, dear!"
Too late.

CHAPTER 11

"You look done in," Mother said. She ignored my evasive maneuvers and steered me gently but firmly into the tent. "Come sit down and have some lemonade."

I felt done in. And I must have looked pretty bad for her not to ask why I was wearing one of the distinctive New Life Baptist choir robes. Maybe, since she saw how exhausted I was, she'd postpone her interrogation. I plopped down at the table she indicated — in the far corner of the tent, behind the trash cans — and closed my eyes, happy, for the time being, to follow orders.

A few moments later I heard a slight noise and opened my eyes to see that a blond teenager was setting a glass of lemonade in front of me.

"Thank you, Shannon, dear," Mother said. "Meg, are you hungry?"

I shook my head, and Mother dismissed

her acolyte with a smile and a nod. She gazed around the tent to make sure nothing was happening that needed her attention, and then sat down across from me.

I grabbed the lemonade and reminded myself to sip, not gulp.

"Don't let me interrupt you," I said to Mother, as I sipped.

"Nonsense, dear," she said. "Everything here is under control."

Yes, if Mother had anything to do with it, everything probably was.

When Mother had volunteered to help out at the Trinity Episcopal tent whenever she was in town, the organizers had wisely refrained from assigning her a job requiring manual labor. Instead, they'd made her one of the dining tent hostesses. She greeted incoming customers as if they were long-lost relatives, made sure they found seats, had their tea or lemonade refilled until they positively sloshed on their way out, and made sure the teenagers who were bussing and cleaning the tables did their jobs with astonishing speed and efficiency.

She'd also organized the decoration of the tent. I had no idea whether the rest of the Episcopal women appreciated that or whether, like most people, they just found it easier not to argue with Mother. The long folding metal tables were now covered with bright blue-and-red-checked vinyl tablecloths and decorated with sturdy white vases full of flowers. Flower garlands looped between the inside tent poles, supporting strings of miniature red and blue Chinese lanterns. She'd even managed to get all the waitstaff to wear red- or blue-checked chef's aprons.

Before too long the Catholics and Baptists noticed that the Episcopal tent was getting more than its share of attention from the tourists and began retaliatory decorating of their own. It was, of course, an article of faith, at least in the Episcopal tent, that Mother's décor was the pinnacle of elegance, while the rival tents, though worthy efforts, were somehow lacking. I'm sure competing doctrines were held in the other two tents, but since there were more than enough tourists to keep everyone busy, everyone publicly praised everyone else's efforts and a spirit of ecumenical harmony reigned.

And I reminded myself that I should look around to see if Mother had added any more little touches that I should praise. You'd think after thirty-some years of knowing me, Mother would have made peace with the fact that I didn't share her passion for decorating, but she could still have her feelings hurt if I didn't notice some new frill or furbelow.

But I might have drifted off to sleep if I hadn't heard the ding my phone made when someone texted me. I pulled it out and saw that Michael had sent me a picture of Josh and Jamie, obviously enjoying their hay ride. I smiled at seeing their excited faces.

"We're heading back to the tent," Michael texted.

When I looked up from my phone, I found Mother staring at me.

"Is there really a murder?" she asked.

My smile vanished. I nodded.

"Oh, dear," she said. "We were all so hoping for an unfortunate accident. Was it anyone we knew?"

"Not really," I said. "Someone who worked for First Progressive Financial."

"Still distressing, though," Mother said. Was she reminding me or herself? "And at least it will keep your father happy."

I nodded and gulped more lemonade. Yes, Dad was never happier than when he could combine his two great passions, crime fiction and medicine, by taking part in a real life murder investigation.

"How was he killed?" she asked.

"She was shot," I said.

"She?" Mother looked distressed. "I didn't know the lender had any women working for him here. Unless you mean — not that nice-looking young woman with the lovely Donna Karan shoes?"

"Probably," I said. "She was about my age, more or less, probably nice-looking when she was alive, and her shoes didn't look like anything I could afford much less walk around in without tripping."

"Poor woman," Mother said, her sympathies thoroughly engaged by the knowledge that the victim was a fellow shoe aficionada. "I think I saw her wearing a pair of Stuart Weitzmans, too."

"If I hear that they're giving away her wardrobe, I'll go for the footwear," I said. "Unfortunately, her choice of employers wasn't as refined as her taste in shoes, and odds are that had something to do with her death."

The blond teenager who'd filled my glass appeared at my elbow again.

"More?" she asked.

"It's all right, Shannon, dear," Mother said. "The murder victim wasn't your young man."

An expression of relief and joy crossed Shannon's face, quickly erased by a stern frown.

"He's not my young man!" Her tone was defensive. "It's not my fault one of the Evil Lender's guards keeps stalking me."

"Of course not, dear," Mother said.

"I wouldn't talk to him at all if I wasn't trying to get useful information," Shannon said.

"And now you can continue trying to get useful information," Mother said. "Because it wasn't he who was murdered. I, for one, am very relieved that the victim isn't anyone I know personally, and I'm sure you feel the same, no matter how much you disapprove of the young man's current career choice."

Shannon looked anxious for a moment, and then a sunny smile returned to her face.

"Yes, that's just how I feel," she said. "More lemonade?"

I held up my glass. She refilled it and then bounced off.

"So she's dating one of the Flying Monkeys?" I asked.

"Heavens, no," Mother said. "She'd bite your head off if she heard you say that. But as she points out as often as possible, she has no control over where he chooses to eat his meals. And as a dedicated citizen of Caerphilly, she doesn't want to discourage him from talking to her if there's any chance he might reveal information that would be

126

useful to the cause."

"Don't encourage her to do too much information gathering," I said. "It's possible one of the guards was the killer."

"Are you sure?"

"Either one of the guards or someone they'd think nothing about letting in and out of the courthouse," I said. "So tell her not to do too much prying. Even if her boyfriend isn't the killer, it's almost certainly someone he knows. And right now the killer just might be a little suspicious of towns-people asking questions."

"I'll warn her," Mother said. From the fierce look on her face, I suspected she'd be keeping a hawklike eye on the young guard. I felt a little less worried about Shannon's safety.

"I've got to get back to the tent to change out of this robe," I said. "Thanks for the lemonade."

I strolled back to the tent to the strains of "The Pennsylvania Polka." The lemonade had restored my energy a bit. I still wasn't up to walking in time to the music, but I could at least appreciate that if you were a polka lover you were probably having a great time out here in the square.

When I got back to the tent, I found it swarming with half-dressed people. I

127

blinked, and then realized they were Michael's drama students from the college, getting ready to perform their play. I took a deep breath and put on what I called my Mrs. Professor Waterston face. I'd learned from one of the students that I had a reputation as one of the nicer faculty wives, and I didn't want to blow that.

Standing just inside the doorway holding a clipboard was Kathy Borgstrom, who served as the drama department's administrative assistant — which meant that it was her job to keep dozens of creative, temperamental, impractical, and often dangerously absentminded people from becoming completely disorganized. Today she looked even more than usual like a border collie who'd been saddled with a herd of half-grown kittens.

"Good God, they haven't added another scene at the last minute, have they?" she asked, glancing back and forth between me and her clipboard a couple of times. "Just what are you supposed to be?"

I took in the crowd. A pair of British redcoats were eating ice cream cones and talking with a World War I doughboy. A woman wearing a Caerphilly College T-shirt and a Civil War-era hoopskirt was trying to squeeze through the crowd and getting nowhere. Another woman wearing a fringed and beaded leather American Indian dress was lounging on a blanket in one corner, reading a graphic novel. A Union private and a Confederate colonel were feeding cheese crackers to Mr. Throckmorton's pigeons. A woman dressed in black pedal pushers and a black sleeveless shirt was powdering an entire row of Colonial-era wigs on wire stands. Half a dozen actors in various stages of undress from several centuries were pacing back and forth in every part of the tent, loudly doing vocal exercises.

"I'm actually here to get out of costume," I said. "What's all this?"

"The play," Kathy said. "Actually more like a series of historic scenes illustrating the high points of American history. John Smith and Pocahontas. Patrick Henry's 'Liberty or Death' speech. The Boston Tea Party. The Battle of Bull Run." She glanced around and then continued in an undertone. "It's a bit heavy on the noisy bits of history — anything with a lot of shouting or cannon fire made the cut."

I nodded. I noted, with approval, that Rose Noire had retreated to the other end of the tent, taking both dogs with her to guard the entrance to the tunnel. Eric and the twins were pressed against the fence, watching the costume parade with wide eyes.

I went to the bins where I kept useful stuff and pulled out a change of clothes — I usually kept several in the tent in case I wanted to look presentable after a bout of blacksmithing in the heat. I stepped behind a clothes rack, shed the bulky choir robe, pulled on the jeans and T-shirt, and breathed a sigh of relief. I wanted to grab some cold water from my minirefrigerator — not to drink, after all that lemonade, but to pour over myself. Alas, unlike Kathy, most of the students weren't in on the secret of the tunnel, so I refrained.

I settled for giving the boys a quick hug.

"You think the play's going to be something the boys would like?" Eric asked. "I was thinking of taking them out front to watch."

"Check with Michael," I said. "There might be a lot of battle scenes."

"They seem pretty good with loud noises," Eric said. "Even — ow!"

A deafening screech of feedback had interrupted him.

"Good grief," Eric said. "Do those guys know anything about how to run a sound system?"

"They're doing just fine," I said.

"Fine?" He was staring at me with that look teenagers get when they think adults are being particularly dense. "Fine? You mean you can't hear that feedback?"

"The feedback's part of their job," I reminded him. "If someone opens the trapdoor during the concert, the noise it makes will just sound like more feedback."

"But — but —" Clearly Eric was having a harder time than most of us accepting this now-standard feature of life during Caerphilly Days. "It's awful," he said finally. "Like fingernails on a chalkboard. Worse than fingernails on a chalkboard, in fact."

"That's an interesting comment," Rose Noire remarked. "Did you know, there's been some research done on why humans find that sound so universally unpleasant?"

"Maybe because it is?" Eric asked.

"The leading theory is that it resembles primate warning calls," Rose Noire went on. "Or possibly the hunting call of some predator that primates found particularly terrifying."

"You've been talking to my grandfather, haven't you?" I asked.

"The boys didn't even flinch at the feedback," Eric said. "So as long as there's no blood, only noise, I expect they'd love the play. But I'll check with Michael to make sure."

"Good man," I said. "See you later."

I paused by Kathy on my way out of the tent.

"Horace should be here shortly," I murmured. "See if you can find him an unobtrusive way to slip into the crawl space."

"They should all be going onstage soon," she murmured back.

"I think I'll head over to the forensic tent to return this." I was folding up the choir robe as neatly as its bulk and slipperiness would allow. "They might be running low on choir robes."

"I'm sure they have enough if you want to stay and rest before the play starts," she said.

"Not ones big enough to fit the Flying Monkeys," I said. "Besides, it will give me an excuse to snoop."

Kathy didn't argue with that logic.

I found the chief outside the tent talking to Horace.

"You want to test their shoes for GSR?" the chief was asking.

"Not GSR," Horace said. "That's hard to get from clothes. But blood isn't. And if someone had blood spatter on his clothes, that'd be a lot harder to explain away than GSR. On the shoes, it's less significant —

anyone who was at the crime scene could have stepped in the blood, but still —"

"If someone has blood on his shoes who wasn't legitimately there after we heard the shots, it'd be significant as the dickens," the chief said. "But we need to get them out of here pretty soon. The choir doesn't have special shoes to lend us. And if you think my budget will run to buying flip-flops for all of them, you're crazy."

"How about those booties workmen wear over their shoes so they won't track dirt into your house?" I suggested. "I bet Randall's construction company keeps them around."

The chief thought for a moment, then nodded.

"I'll go ask him," Horace said.

"No, I'll have someone take care of it," the chief said. "You get on over to do Mr. Throckmorton and Mr. Langslow. We've been keeping them waiting far too long already."

Was it just my imagination, or did Horace turn pale?

"Right, Chief," he said, and strode off in the direction of the bandstand.

The chief raised the tent flap and peeked in. I looked over his shoulder. At the far end of the tent, a dozen of the guards were clustered as if they felt less ridiculous in a group. Actually, I thought their numbers magnified the humorous effect. None of their gowns went down farther than mid-shin, and most displayed marvelously hairy knees atop well-thatched legs. As I watched, several of them gave surreptitious tugs at the bottom hems of their robes, in a gesture I remembered well from my own days of wearing too-short skirts.

By contrast, the flowing sleeves seemed more than adequate to cover their arms, and yet the guards repeatedly shoved or rolled them up to reveal their bulging, hairy, often tattooed biceps, and then repeated the shoving and rolling when the sleeves inevitably tumbled down.

Several of them appeared to be arguing with Deputy Vern.

"Protesting the lack of AC," the chief said. "Apparently they keep the thermostat jacked down pretty low over there in the courthouse."

"How environmentally irresponsible of them," I said. "You'd think the choir robes would be more comfortable than those uniforms."

"You'd think," the chief said. "Anyway, their employer just brought over a bus to take them back to where they're staying — mostly at that run-down motel in Clay

County, from the sound of it. Soon as we confiscate those shoes, we can get rid of them. Of course, before we do, it would be gratifying if those *Star-Tribune* reporters could find their way back here."

"I thought you already tested them," I said. "Or do you want to snag their shoes?"

"Well, that's not as critical, since you and Randall can pretty much alibi them — and each other — for the time when the shots were fired. But I expect that photographer would enjoy getting a few shots of our Flying Monkeys leaving the premises in the choir robes and booties."

"I'm sure he would," I said, trying to suppress a grin. "I will see what I can do to bring it about."

"I'd appreciate it. I suppose I should go arrange the booties."

"I'll call Randall," I said. "You're busy."

"Thanks." He nodded genially to me, then forced his face back into a more stern expression and turned back to the room.

Randall promised to have booties over to the forensic tent in ten minutes.

"And I'll convene a little press conference in front of my tent in a few minutes," he said. "It's got a good view of the entrance to the forensic tent. We've had three or four more reporters show up since the news got out. No reason the *Star-Trib* should have a monopoly on the photo op."

I was tempted to stick around and gawk, but I had things to do. I was just pulling out my notebook-that-tells-me-when-to-breathe to remind me what those things were when my cell phone rang.

CHAPTER 12

"Meg?" It was Rob. "Could you see what's keeping Horace? Phinny and I really want to go to the bathroom and Sammy says we can't until after Horace processes us."

"I'll check," I said. "I'm on my way to the tent now."

Apparently the play was about to begin. The tent was empty except for two women knitting just inside the entrance and the two dogs, sleeping in the pen. Presumably Eric had taken the twins out to watch the pageant.

"Tunnel door needs opening before your cousin can go in," one of the knitters said in an undertone. "We were going to haul it up while everyone was applauding the polka players, but there were too many students still around."

"It's okay," I said. "The play will have a lot of noisy parts."

Spike looked up hopefully when I stepped

into his pen, then sighed and went back to sleep when he saw that I wasn't bringing him one of his playmates.

In the crawl space under the bandstand, Horace was crouching by the closed trapdoor. With his back to it, actually, and his nose buried deep in the case in which he kept his crime scene tools and supplies.

"Horace?"

"I need to check my kit," he said. "It'd be pretty stupid if I got over there and didn't have some key piece of equipment, wouldn't it?"

"You could come back for it," I said. "Or send for it."

"Time's critical right now," he said. "So I'll just check my kit before I go."

Checking his kit seemed to be a rather stressful task. His hands were shaking slightly, and sweat had broken out on his forehead.

"Horace, have you been through the tunnel before?"

"No!" he snapped. "I haven't had any need to go there. If you ask me, entirely too many people are traipsing back and forth through that tunnel. Maybe it's traffic in the tunnel that's causing all the cave-ins."

"Horace, it's okay," I said. "No one's been hurt in any of the cave-ins, and we haven't

138

had any for a long, long time."

"Overdue for one, then," he said. He was hunched over slightly, clutching his kit with both hands. "And what if we have another earthquake? Remember what happened last time when —"

"Horace, we're back," Rose Noire said. She and Michael had just walked in carrying what looked like a moth-eaten bearskin rug. "Put this on and you'll feel better."

Horace blinked slightly, then put down his kit and grabbed the fur mound. He shook it out, revealing his beloved gorilla suit. There had been a time when Horace could barely have said two words to another human being when not wearing the suit, which meant that for years he'd pretended to think every single social occasion he went to was a costume party, so he could go as his big ape alter ego. Lately we'd seen a lot less of the suit — he'd worn it on Halloween and Mardi Gras, and occasionally, after a very long hard day at work, he'd put it on to watch TV at home. Ever since he'd begun his new career as a crime scene technician, Horace had blossomed.

But clearly he was more than a little spooked at the idea of having to crawl through the tunnel. So if the suit helped him deal with it, so be it.

He was putting it on now, and his body language was changing. His shoulders weren't so hunched, and the hands pulling the zipper weren't shaking.

"Excellent!" Michael said. "Now put this around your neck — under the suit."

He handed Horace what looked like a leather necklace with an incongruously modern pendant on it.

"What is it?" I asked.

"GPS tracking device," Michael said. "One of Rob's employees gave him a few of them to use for tunnel trips. In the unlikely event of a cave-in, this will let your rescuers pinpoint your location and get you out in minutes."

I was about to point out that we'd tested the GPS devices during the first few weeks we'd been using the tunnel and found they didn't work underground. And that the Shiffleys had carefully surveyed the tunnel's course, above- and belowground, and could easily pinpoint the location of a cave-in from that.

But Horace was clutching the GPS device in one furry paw and stroking it with the other, like a lucky amulet. Clearly Michael intended the GPS device for reassurance, not practical use. I took a deep breath and said nothing.

"And hold your cell phone in your hand," Rose Noire added. "That way you can keep us posted on your progress."

Only if Horace's cell phone provider had figured out a way to send a signal underground. But again, I bit my tongue.

"It's hard to hold it in my paws." Behind the impassive gorilla mask, Horace's muffled voice was anxious. "What if I drop it?"

Michael and Rose Noire looked at each other.

"I suppose you could keep it in your . . ." Rose Noire trailed off. Horace's pockets were now rendered largely inaccessible by the furry costume.

"Here, let's use this," I said. I grabbed up a roll of duct tape and pulled off a strip. "You can attach the cell phone to your hand and have it instantly accessible without any danger of losing it."

We managed to split the duct tape into narrower strips and secure the phone without covering up any of the buttons. Then, at Horace's request, we taped a pen to the other paw, since his furry gorilla fingers made it difficult to dial anything on the phone. And we topped his outfit off with a construction helmet that had a small LED light attached to the front.

"I think you're ready," Michael said.

Horace nodded. Rose Noire went out into the tent to keep watch. Michael and I waited until the battle noise from above reached a crescendo, then hauled up the trap door.

Horace waddled over to the opening, started down, and froze.

"Oh, my," he said softly.

"Horace?" I couldn't see his face, but I'd be willing to bet it had turned bone white.

"Just getting my . . . um . . ."

"Would you like one of us to lead the way?" Michael asked.

"Um . . . yeah," Horace said. He sounded eager and grateful.

Michael and I looked at each other.

"I'll go if you like," he said.

"You need to be here for your students," I said. "I'll do it."

"Take one of the helmets," Michael said.

I put the helmet on and turned on the lamp. Then I stuffed my notebook into my pocket, made sure my own cell phone was in the other, took a deep breath, and began climbing down the ladder.

It looked light, but it was actually a fairly sturdy ladder that one of Randall's carpenter cousins had made to replace the rickety original ladder. He checked it out nearly every day, and made any necessary repairs as soon as there was enough noise to cover the sound of his working. The ladder only went down twenty-five feet or so. Why did it seem so much farther? By the time I reached the bottom of the ladder, the open trapdoor seemed at least a mile away.

I heard a soft squelching sound as my shoes hit the mud at the bottom of the ladder.

"I really hate this," I muttered.

"What was that?" Michael called from the top of the ladder.

"Remind Horace to wait until I send the cart back," I said, loud enough for him to hear. "In fact, keep him up there and send him down when you see the cart again."

"Will do!"

"Hate it, hate it, hate it," I added under my breath.

There was barely enough space for me to maneuver there at the bottom of the shaft and the mouth of the tunnel. A pulley was attached to the wooden wall to the left side of the tunnel mouth, about a foot above the floor of the tunnel, with a heavy rope threaded through it. The two ends of the rope disappeared into the darkness of the tunnel.

Randall's cousin checked out the tunnel every few days, too, I reminded myself.

143

Tested all the boards and investigated the cause of any dirt sifting down. Why did that seem so reassuring when I was on the surface and so hollow down here?

I squatted down so I could grab one of the ropes and began hauling it, hand over hand, until the cart finally appeared. It was actually a small steel mesh garden cart, about two feet wide and four long. I'd removed the sides and the front handle and welded sturdy rings onto the front and back of the frame. With a rope threaded through the pulley and tied to the front and back rings, you could pull the cart back and forth from either end, or even haul yourself along by lying on the cart and pulling the rope.

I made sure my helmet was fastened on securely, lay down on my stomach on the cart, and grabbed the rope.

"Hate it," I muttered one more time. Then I began hauling myself into the tunnel.

CHAPTER 13

There was a trick to pulling yourself along without gouging your hands on the front corner of the cart. Rob had probably become expert. I'd only done this once before and hadn't planned on ever doing it again. I'd have to be careful.

Instinct told me to pull as hard and fast as I could, to get through the tunnel as quickly as possible. But if I did that, in addition to the danger to my hands, I'd risk becoming exhausted midway. I definitely did not want to have to rest and catch my breath down there in the tunnel. So I reminded myself to pull slowly and steadily.

After what seemed like half a lifetime, the cart gently bumped to a stop at the end of the rope in an area where the tunnel became slightly taller and wider before narrowing again when it took off at a forty-five-degree angle from the first stretch. I had to crawl off the cart and onto its twin for the second half of the journey.

I wondered, not for the first time, why they hadn't just dug a single tunnel. Was the jog deliberate? Or the result of a massive miscalculation? And if the builders had erred that badly on a simple compass reading —

Not something I wanted to think about while I was in the tunnel.

The second cart was, of course, at the courthouse end of the tunnel. Was I the only one who bothered to send the cart back for the next person? Once again I had to haul the rope hand over hand until the cart emerged from the tunnel into the junction area.

Waiting for the second cart to arrive was my least favorite part of the trip. For some reason, the extra foot or so of headroom at the junction only emphasized how very many tons of rock and dirt were looming over my head, waiting for just the right moment to fall down and crush me. And while the whole tunnel was damp and clammy, the junction was always the worst, with standing puddles in all but the driest weather.

Once the second steel mesh cart was ready for me, I turned around and sent the first cart back into the tunnel so it would be waiting for Horace when he climbed down. If waiting at the foot of the ladder for the cart to emerge unnerved me, I couldn't imagine what it would do to Horace. More than a few would-be tunnel rats had lost their nerve and fled before the cart loomed out of the darkness. Our chances of getting Horace onto the cart were much higher if he found it waiting for him.

Then I flopped down on the second cart and began pulling myself along the second leg of my journey. Which, according to Rob, was actually the slightly shorter leg, though you couldn't prove it by me. Several centuries appeared to drag by as I puffed and hauled, until finally I emerged in a small, stone-walled cell.

I rolled off the cart and onto my back, looking up at the stone ceiling, a spacious six feet above my head, and taking deep breaths until my heart slowed down a bit. Then I sat up and sent the cart back to wait for Horace.

That done, I lay back to savor being by myself for a few moments. No need to be encouraging for Horace or look brave in front of Michael or my brother.

And maybe before I had to go back through the tunnel, Chief Burke would decide to break up Mr. Throckmorton's long siege.

Well, I could hope.

The stone cell was about eight feet square, with the tunnel entrance in one wall, a closed metal door with a barred window in the opposite wall, and a built-in stone bunk running the length of one of the remaining walls. An oversized gray metal supply cabinet occupied the fourth wall, and a dozen or so cardboard file boxes were stacked on either side of the tunnel entrance.

I stood up and tried the doorknob. Locked. But doubtless the cellar's other occupants would open it eagerly as soon as I knocked. I reminded myself that it really had been a cell. Back in the days before the present police station and jail had been built, they'd kept prisoners in the courthouse basement.

I wondered if any of them had succeeded in escaping through the tunnel.

My heart had slowed and my breathing was back to normal by the time Horace popped out of the tunnel like a giant fur-clad missile. He propelled himself off the cart, ricocheted off the metal cabinet and then off the far wall before curling up in a fetal position, whimpering and hyperventilating.

I crawled over and patted him on the back.

"It's okay," I said. "You're safe now. And if you like, you can stay here until the chief opens the blockade."

Horace stopped whimpering.

"You think he might do that?" he whispered.

"Seems plausible," I said. "Let's get out of this tiny little room and into the main part of the basement."

"Okay." Horace bounded to his feet and looked around. I pointed to the door. He raced over and twisted the doorknob.

"It's locked," he said. I could hear a thin note of returning panic in his voice.

"You've got to give the secret signal," I said. I joined him at the door and gave the familiar "shave and a haircut — two bits" knock.

"Who's there?" Rob called.

"Open the damned door," I said.

The door flew open and Horace and I stumbled out into the basement corridor. Normally I'd have found it a little cramped and claustrophobic, but it looked as spacious as a palace after the tunnel and the cramped little cell where the tunnel came out. The ceiling was a lofty seven and a half feet. The walls might be cold stone, but they were lined with so many file cabinets and boxes of files that hardly any of the stone

149

was visible.

Sammy, Rob, and Mr. Throckmorton waited in a tense semicircle. Rob and Mr. Throckmorton were holding their hands up like prisoners, apparently to show that they were doing their best not to touch anything before Horace tested their hands. But their arms were drooping, as if they probably couldn't keep it up much longer. Sammy and Rob, who were both over six feet, loomed over Mr. Throckmorton, who was about five feet four, skinny as a rail, and had been shortchanged at birth in both the shoulder and chin departments. I knew he'd been at school with Randall, which meant he was probably in his early forties, but he could have passed for any age from twenty-five to fifty. He was dressed in gray slacks, a white shirt, red suspenders, and a neatly knotted bow tie. I had a feeling that under normal circumstances he'd have been wearing a coat or at least a sports jacket, and that the slightly retro-looking suspenders made him feel less underdressed in his shirtsleeves. He peered at us through thick bifocals and squinted as if he might be overdue for new, more powerful lenses. He radiated a sort of precise, prickly formality, which probably accounted for my strange reluctance to think of him as "Phinny" instead of Mr. Throckmorton.

"What's going on out there, anyway?" Rob asked. "Is Sammy pulling our leg or was someone really murdered out there?"

"Someone really was murdered," I said. "Shot right outside the barricade, and at first glance it certainly looks as if she could have been shot from behind the barricade."

"They're trying to frame me," Mr. Throckmorton said.

"I'm a witness that you can't possibly have done it," Rob said. He started to give Mr. Throckmorton an encouraging pat on the back, stopped just in time, and used his elbow instead, still managing to knock the breath out of him.

"Of course, they will try to claim you two were in cahoots," I said.

Mr. Throckmorton, still breathless from the force of Rob's encouragement, shook his head in despair.

"How can we possibly prove they're wrong?" he wheezed.

"That's what I'm here for." Horace drew himself up to his full height and held his forensic bag in front of him as if it were a chain saw and he were about to fell a forest of unjust accusations. "Lead me to the barricade!"

If anyone noticed that his voice was a little

151

shaky, or wondered why he had reverted to wearing his gorilla suit, no one said anything.

"Do their hands and clothes first," I suggested. "And you'll probably find it easier if you shed the suit."

"This way," Mr. Throckmorton said. He turned and led the way down the corridor. We had to walk single file to get past the file cabinets and boxes on either side. At regular intervals a gap in the file cabinets marked the doorway to another cell. A glance through each barred window showed that the cells were also filled with file cabinets and boxes.

"What is this place, anyway?" Horace asked.

"Used to be the jail," Mr. Throckmorton said over his shoulder. His voice was thin, dry, and precise. "Now we use it for the archives."

"I mean, why does it look like a castle dungeon?" Horace asked.

"Now that's an interesting question," Mr. Throckmorton said, his voice growing a smidgen more animated. "During the Revolutionary War, there was a small prisoner of war camp here in Caerphilly. Mostly German mercenaries. Apparently there were a number of stonemasons among them, and the town government put them to work building the courthouse."

"Wait — I thought the Yankees burned down the courthouse during the Civil War," Sammy said. "How could they burn down a stone courthouse?"

"The German prisoners didn't finish the whole building," Mr. Throckmorton said. "They got a little carried away with the elaborate stonework in the basement. By the time they finished that, the war was over."

"And they went home to Germany," Sammy said, nodding.

"No, most of them just disappeared into the mountains," Mr. Throckmorton said. "Throughout the colonies, about a quarter of the Hessians who survived the war never went home. They were landless men — younger sons of landowners, or the sons of laborers. Life was a lot better here than back in Germany. A few that we know of stayed here in town, intermarried with the locals — especially the Shiffleys — and took up farming or went into the masonry and carpentry trades for themselves. Most just went off into the mountains. Without the free POW labor, the town ended up finishing off the courthouse very cheaply, with wood. That's what burned. The basement survived very nicely."

He patted the stone walls in one of the few places where they weren't largely obscured by the file cabinets and boxes.

I had to admit, the Hessian stonework was impressive. If not for the utilitarian metal file cabinets, you could easily imagine yourself in the dungeon of a medieval castle. The fitted stone walls were slightly rough to the touch, but surprisingly even, considering. The vaulted stone ceiling was a little low, but looked reassuringly solid. Some of the keystones over the doorways even had little bits of carving in them. I was surprised they hadn't gone in for a few gargoyles while they were at it.

What really surprised me was the temperature. I'd heard that the Evil Lender had turned off the air-conditioning ducts to the basement at the beginning of the summer, as yet another tactic to compel Mr. Throckmorton to leave. But the stone walls felt dry and cool and the ambient air temperature was a lot lower than outdoors.

We passed through a stone doorway into a much larger area with a slightly higher ceiling. Like every other space in the basement it was packed with files and boxes, here interspersed with nests of furniture and, at regular intervals, huge stone pillars. I estimated the room was about forty feet wide by sixty feet long, but I wasn't good at estimating under the best of circumstances, and I had no idea whether the clutter made the space look larger or smaller. The short wall to our right and both of the long walls were interrupted at intervals by doors, presumably leading to other corridors and rooms full of documents. I spotted a kitchenette along one wall, and a curtained alcove that was probably Mr. Throckmorton's bedroom.

Near the short wall to our left, at the far end of the room, was the counter that, in happier times, had separated Mr. Throckmorton from the customers who came to apply for permits and licenses or access documents from the archives. He'd hung curtains across the width of the room just behind the counter, cutting off our view of the entrance door, now barricaded both inside and out. Although, come to think of it, the curtain was probably there less to shield the barricade from his view than to keep the Evil Lender's forces from peering in at his lair when he opened the plywood doors.

Most of the horizontal surfaces in the basement were piled high with stacks of paper, all weighted down with bricks, large stones, and other heavy objects to keep them from blowing away in the breeze created by half a dozen revolving electric floor and table fans. The whirring of the fans and the constant rustling of the papers made a rather restful background noise.

In the middle of the space was a battered but sturdy oak table. One half of it was piled high with dice, a hand-drawn map, and stacks of game cards and all the other paraphernalia of one of Rob's role-playing games. The other half was empty, and I suspected Sammy had cleared away a space for Horace to use.

"You're right," Horace said. "I should take off my suit."

He set down his bag and began scrambling out of it. He, it, and the clothes underneath were soaked with sweat.

"There are towels over there," Mr. Throckmorton said. He pointed with his elbow, as if that was the only way he could refrain from grabbing the towel himself and handing it to Horace. "And you'll find hangers a little to the left."

Sammy obliged by handing Horace the towel. While Horace toweled the sweat away, Sammy, under Mr. Throckmorton's close supervision, arranged the gorilla suit neatly on a heavy wooden hanger and hung it where one of the fans would blow it dry.

Horace stood in front of another fan for a few moments with a blissful look on his face. Then he straightened up, folded the towel neatly, set it on the floor, and picked up his kit.

"Okay, let's do your hands," he said.

"You should probably swab Rob's cell phone, too," I said. "He's been handling that recently. Before he got the orders not to touch anything," I added, before Rob could protest.

As I watched the now familiar process, I realized I had two options. Now that I'd safely escorted Horace here, I could go back through the tunnel to the outside world — and maybe have to come back again to coax him out when he was finished. Or I could twiddle my thumbs here until he was finished.

"While you're doing that, I'm going to call Michael and check on the boys," I said. Perhaps I could invent a child-care crisis that would require me to leave.

"The telephone is over there." Mr. Throckmorton pointed to a desk piled with one- to two-foot stacks of papers, one of which had a phone sitting atop it. "But we operate on the assumption that they're bugging it."

"That would be illegal!" Horace said.

"And you think that would bother them?" Rob asked.

"I can make the call, if you can figure out a coded way to say whatever you want to say," Mr. Throckmorton said. "But it might be easier to e-mail."

"I have my cell," I said, holding it up.

"If you get a signal, let me know and I'll switch to your carrier." His smile wasn't exactly smug, but you could tell he enjoyed knowing something I didn't. "The walls are a foot thick. Ceiling, too. No signal here."

"We got a signal outside the barricade," I said.

"Stone's not as thick up there," he said. "I can sometimes get a signal up by the barricade, but not down here. You could try going up there."

"Stay away from the area near the barricade until I'm finished with it," Horace said. "Okay — now your clothes."

"My clothes?" Mr. Throckmorton's voice sounded anxious, and he glanced over at me.

"I'll just step out for a moment," I said. "I'll come back and e-mail Michael when the coast is clear."

I made my way back to the corridor and sat down on a box to wait. As I sat, I gazed around at the books and papers surrounding me. Normally, clutter drives me crazy, but the more I looked around, the less chaotic the basement looked. Everything was definitely organized. There were very few loose papers — everything was confined to boxes, file folders, or neat string-tied parcels. And everything bore a neat tag or label. I could spot at least a dozen different styles of printing or handwriting on the labels — probably representing at least that many county clerks over the years. All of them, from spidery copperplate to neat modern block printing, were uniformly precise and tiny.

"You can come back in now, Meg," Horace called.

Mr. Throckmorton was dressed, as he had been before — gray slacks, white shirt, suspenders, and bow tie, though now the suspenders and the tie were royal blue. I suspected his wardrobe was well organized and didn't contain a lot of variety. Rob was resplendent in black-and-green polka-dotted silk briefs.

"Have either of you been near the barricade lately?" Horace asked.

"Not since just before the incident," Mr. Throckmorton said. "We heard someone knocking on the plywood door. I thought it might be Randall, but sometimes one or more of the security officers come with him."

"So he pulled the curtains closed, and I hid just inside the corridor leading to the tunnel," Rob said.

"Wasn't that overkill?" I asked. "The curtains look solid enough."

"The idea was that if they battered down the barrier, Rob could run down to the cell where the tunnel comes out and lock the door from the inside," Mr. Throckmorton said. "There's a spare key in the cabinet. And then he could retreat into the tunnel, pulling the cabinet behind him, and we might have a chance of keeping the secret of the tunnel."

"So you weren't with Mr. Throckmorton at the exact time of the murder?" Sammy asked.

Rob opened his mouth as if to say something and then shut it grimly and shook his head. Mr. Throckmorton sighed softly.

"I went over to the plywood privacy door," Mr. Throckmorton said. "And I was about to open it, but I heard raised voices. I couldn't make out what they were saying, but I could tell the tone was angry. I wasn't sure what was going on. And given how strange everything has been lately, I decided maybe I shouldn't open it until I knew precisely what was going on. I was backing away from it when I heard the shots."

"Shots?" Sammy repeated. "Plural?"

"I think so," Mr. Throckmorton said. "Two shots, very close together. Although I suppose it could have been one shot with some kind of echo. I'm afraid I don't know much about guns."

"He ran back here and told me what was happening," Rob said. "And I was going to run up there and look, but Phinny pointed out that if there was something going on up there, the area just outside the barricade would be swarming with people, and we shouldn't take the chance of anyone spotting me."

"Or shooting at him," Mr. Throckmorton added.

"So I didn't open the plywood, just stood there inside the barricade. And I couldn't figure out what was going on, so that was when I called you on my cell phone. That's the only place you can get a signal, remember?"

"I stayed well away from the barricade after that," Mr. Throckmorton added. "But I kept Rob in sight, in case he was hit by a stray bullet."

Horace nodded and picked his way along a path through the file cabinets and boxes toward the far end of the room. The counter that ran all the way across that end had a break, where you could lift up a movable segment of the countertop to exit or enter Mr. Throckmorton's part of the room. Rob and I followed. Mr. Throckmorton did, too, but at a greater distance, as if he more than half expected gunfire to break out again.

Horace drew the curtains to reveal the far end of the room. Some wide wooden steps led up six or seven feet to a raised area, eight feet deep, that ran the width of the basement. If I recalled correctly, the raised part was level with the part of the basement outside the barricade. The exit door was located in the middle of the wall on the raised area — though now the door was gone and a series of huge landscaping ties ran across the doorway. They appeared to be bolted into the stone, and on each end more huge timbers ran perpendicular to the barricade, braced at the other end by two of the immense stone pillars. Clearly, any would-be intruders who tried too hard to batter down Mr. Throckmorton's barricade risked bringing a large part of the building down on themselves.

The middle of the barricade was covered with the plywood — two sheets, on hinges, so they could swing out like double doors.

"That's to keep anyone from peeking in," Mr. Throckmorton said, when he saw Horace eyeing the plywood. "There's a latch at the top."

"First things first," Horace said. "When was the last time you opened the plywood doors?"

"Yesterday," Mr. Throckmorton said.

Horace set his satchel down on the counter, pulled out his digital camera, and climbed up the wooden stairs. Rob, Mr. Throckmorton, and I followed, although we stayed several steps down from the top, so we could watch without being in his way. He took dozens of photos of the barricade, from the front and from both sides, and of the floor in front of it.

His face was impassive. More than impassive — grim. I didn't expect him to leap up, grinning, to announce that he'd found some bit of evidence that would exonerate Mr. Throckmorton. But I was watching for some small expression of triumph or interest.

After the photography he began swabbing things, and apparently examining every speck of dirt through his magnifying glass.

And then he stood up and stared at the plywood for several minutes, frowning.

Finally I couldn't stand it any longer.

"Put us out of our misery," I said. "What have you found?"

CHAPTER 14

"Not much," Horace said. "Which isn't the worst possible outcome. I haven't found anything good, but I haven't found anything bad either. Just a big lot of nothing. No visible bloodstains on the floor — which isn't surprising; since she was shot from the direction of the barricade, the heavy blood spatter went the other way. No sign that the barricade has been removed any time lately, but also nothing to prove or disprove that anyone opened the plywood."

He went back to his satchel, removed a spray canister, and began spraying the floor just inside the barrier. Then he pulled out his digital camera and held it at the ready.

"Luminal," he said. "Shows bloodstains. Can somebody get the lights?"

Mr. Throckmorton raced down the stairs and hurried to a bank of switches along one of the side walls. He flipped all the switches and the basement suddenly became profoundly dark. We all stared in silence for a few moments. Horace clicked away with his digital camera.

"On TV, the bloodstains give off this weird blue glow," Rob said.

"In real life, too," Horace said. "You can turn the lights back on, Phinny."

"No glow," Rob said.

"This is good?" Mr. Throckmorton asked.

"It's not bad," Horace said. "If there had been blood and you'd washed it off, there'd still be enough to fluoresce when it combined with the luminal. Unless you used bleach, in which case the whole area would glow blue. No signs of any blood spatter on this side of your barricade and no signs of a recent hasty cleanup. But as I said, I wasn't really expecting any. The area just outside the barricade was clean, and so was the outside of the plywood, as far as I could tell through the barricade."

Mr. Throckmorton sighed.

Horace reached up to unfasten the latch and pulled open the plywood doors.

"That you, Horace?" Aida Morris loomed up on the other side of the barricade.

"Yes," Horace said. "I'm going to test outside of the plywood barrier for blood spatter."

"Test it how?" Aida said. "You can see

with your own eyes that there isn't any."

"Trace blood spatter," Horace added.

"Hmph." Clearly Aida didn't share Horace's enthusiasm for forensics. But she did watch with close attention as he repeated his luminal routine.

Rob and Mr. Throckmorton had been hanging back. But on hearing that there was no visible blood spatter on the door, they crowded forward. I stepped back so they could watch Horace's luminal routine at close range.

"No blood on the outside of the plywood either." His tone was glum.

"Of course not," Aida said. "It all went the other way."

She stood back and gestured at where Colleen Brown had fallen. I couldn't help looking, and realized with surprise how very much blood there was on that part of the floor and even on the wall. Perhaps Brown's scarlet-clad form had distracted me from realizing this before. And —

I heard a small thud. Mr. Throckmorton was lying in a crumpled heap on the floor to my left.

"Oh, dear," I said. "Mr. Throckmorton has fainted."

"I'll take care of it!" Rob said. "Hang in there, Phinny!"

He dashed down the steps and over to Mr. Throckmorton, threw the small, limp form over his shoulder in a fireman's carry, and threaded his way through the file cabinets and boxes back to the other end of the room. I followed to make sure both of them were all right. Rob probably would be, now that Mr. Throckmorton had given him an excuse to flee the area near the blood spatters.

He shouldered aside a curtain hanging between two high sets of shelves to reveal what must be Mr. Throckmorton's sleeping quarters. A twin-sized air mattress, neatly made up with clean white sheets, rested on some kind of platform — probably more boxes of files — while the shelves that surrounded it on three sides were filled to overflowing with books — mostly American history, at least from what I could see from my vantage point just outside the alcove.

"Here you go!" Rob exclaimed in a cheerful tone as he deposited Mr. Throckmorton on the air mattress. "Do you think I should throw some cold water over him?"

"No, I think you should fetch a glass of cold water and offer it to him when he comes to," I said. "And keep him down at this end of the basement."

"Will do!" Rob might be squeamish, but

he was also resilient.

I wound my way back to the other end. Horace had moved on to taking pictures of the gun, which was still wedged inside the barrier.

"Mr. Throckmorton okay?" Aida asked.

I nodded.

"Aida, can you reach the gun from out there?" Horace asked.

Aida squatted down and tried. Several times.

"I could if I didn't mind shredding my hand on that razor wire," she said. "But not easily."

"Whereas it's very easy to reach from here," Horace said. "The wire's not as dense on this side."

He stuck his gloved hand through a gap and snagged the gun on the first try.

"Is that important?" Aida asked.

"If you wanted to throw the gun through the barrier, and realized it had stuck there, why not pick it up and throw it again, if you could reach it?" Horace said. "That could help Phinny."

"Of course, a really sneaky person might deliberately leave it there so we'd think just that," I said. "I don't think that proves anything."

"Assuming the killer's devious enough to

169

have thought that through," Aida said. "And besides, from what I hear, he had to make tracks if he didn't want to get caught red-handed."

Horace nodded, and put the gun in an evidence bag.

"So," Horace asked, in a nonchalant voice. "Are we opening up the barricade soon?"

"Not that I know of," Aida said. "Chief told me to keep everyone the heck away from it for now. And out of this room, so no one would see you if you needed to open the plywood. You finished? We should shut it up if you are."

"Oh." Horace's face fell. "Well, I'm going to be here for a while, looking for any more evidence. You just let me know if he changes his mind."

"Chief wants to get the gun and some of that stuff off to Richmond ASAP," Aida pointed out.

"We could pass it through the barricade," Horace suggested.

"Not with all that razor wire in there," Aida said. "Unless you want to shred it to bits and yourself with it. Maybe we should get a couple of the Shiffleys in here to see if they can take the razor wire out."

"Not yet," Horace said. "It's evidence. Possibly exculpatory evidence. We need

170

every bit of that we can get."

"I'll bring the evidence over," I said. "About time I got back to take care of the twins."

"I shouldn't let you," Horace said. "Chain of custody. Sammy could take it."

"I have to stay here with Phinny and Rob until the chief says otherwise," Sammy said from farther back in the room.

Aida and I both glanced at Horace's anxious face and exchanged a look.

"Meg, I hereby deputize you and instruct you to deliver this evidence to the chief," Aida said.

"Yes, ma'am," I said. Though I refrained from saluting the way the Flying Monkeys did.

It was tricky fitting all of the evidence bags and me onto the little rolling cart, but we finally managed, and I began the slow, hand-over-hand trek back through the tunnels. Going back ought to have been less nerve-wracking, since I knew that at the other end of the tunnel I'd find fresh air and freedom, but the tunnel sloped slightly upward — enough to make pulling myself more challenging, even without baggage. And lying on top of the evidence raised me so high on the cart that my back occasionally scraped the ceiling of the tunnel, bringing down tiny avalanches of dirt and stones that set my heart beating faster. Around halfway through the second leg of the tunnel, my arms felt so heavy I wasn't sure I could go on, and all I could think of was how ironic it would be if I stopped to take a rest there in the cart and got caught in a cave-in, a few short feet from freedom. That thought triggered my second wind, and I managed the last few feet and scrambled up to the surface, leaving the evidence bags in the cart. Someone else could haul them up the ladder.

Was my claustrophobia that much better than Horace's? I thought so. Instead of popping out of the trapdoor like a jack-in-the-box I took a deep breath a few rungs from the top of the ladder and composed my face so I looked cool, calm, and collected when I stepped out into the crawl space under the bandstand.

Michael was waiting for me.

"Welcome back!" he stage whispered, giving me a hug. "How was it?"

"Interesting," I said. "I suspect Horace was hoping to find some key piece of evidence to prove Mr. Throckmorton's innocence, but so far, no dice."

"Oh, dear," he murmured.

"What's more —"

Suddenly, gunfire broke out overhead. I started, and hit my head on the low ceiling of the crawl space.

"Relax," Michael said. "It's only the First Battle of Manassas. Do you think there's any chance Horace will be coming out before World War II is over? The program gets a little quiet after that, and we'd like to close and cover up the trapdoor for a while."

"No idea," I said. "I think he'll probably find things to putter around with over there until the chief gives him a direct order to come back. He sent back all the evidence he's collected so far with me — any chance you could haul it up?"

Since I was probably not supposed to let the bags out of my custody, I peered down from the top while Michael scrambled up and down the ladder with the evidence.

"That it?" he asked.

"Rob should have some spare clothes in one of those bins," I said. "Can you take some down and send them halfway over on the cart?"

"Can do," he said.

"I'll call Rob and tell him it's coming."

But first, I called the chief to tell him that I had the evidence.

He wasn't as delighted as I thought he'd be.

"Horace really should have maintained possession of the evidence," he said. "Chain of custody."

"Aida deputized me to take it," I said.

"Well, that's better than nothing," he said. "In fact, I was a bit worried about the possibility someone would see Horace coming out from under the bandstand with a bunch of evidence bags. Any chance you could find a discreet way to bring them over to the forensic tent?"

"Sure," I said.

"Just one more thing." His voice grew stern. "You're not deputized for anything except transporting evidence. Got that?"

"Got it."

Discreet. Not usually my forte, but I could manage. I emptied out a rolling box I used to haul around heavy blacksmithing tools, put a couple of gallon milk jugs of water in it, and then Michael and I stowed the evidence bags on top of them.

"I'll just roll these over to the forensic tent," I said.

"You look beat," Michael said. "Want me to do it?"

"Chain of custody," I said.

As I dragged the wheeled box along, I found myself pondering how strange it was that the nephew I could still so easily remember as a cheerful toddler had turned into someone I instinctively trusted to take care of my own toddlers.

I found the chief and Randall talking just outside the tent that served as the mayor's office.

"Brought you some more water," I said. "Shall I stow it in here?"

"Maybe in my tent for safekeeping," Randall suggested.

Randall and the chief helped me unload the evidence bags.

"Now if I can just find someone to take them down to the crime lab in Richmond," the chief said, frowning at the sizable stack of bags. "Having to put several deputies on guard duty at the courthouse is making me shorthanded."

Maybe he was hoping I'd volunteer. Maybe if things were a little less crazy, I might have. But the arrival of Josh and Jamie in my life made me realize that I needed to do a lot less volunteering and a lot more asking for help.

Like maybe accepting Rose Noire's offer to take over talent coordination for Caerphilly Days.

Speaking of which . . .

"Got to run," I said. "By the way —"

"Can I help you, Mr. Pruitt?" Randall
asked.

CHAPTER 15

I started and turned. I didn't like anyone sneaking up behind me, particularly not a Pruitt. At least it was only Hamish, peering into the tent with a surly expression on his face.

"I need to talk to you!" Hamish said to Randall.

"Lord," Randall muttered under his breath. "Be with you in a minute, then. Chief?"

"I'll see you later." The chief rose and made his exit.

"Was there anything else you needed?" Randall asked me. I could tell from the expression on his face that he was hoping there was.

Hamish didn't wait for me to answer.

"I came to ask when you're going to take action on my request," he said.

"And which one was that, Mr. Pruitt?"

"My request that you finally do something

about that man!" Hamish snapped. "Does he have to kill off the whole town before you do anything?"

"Look, Mr. Pruitt," Randall said. "I appreciate your point of view on this. I've been going in every day to try to talk some sense into Mr. Throckmorton, without any success so far. And if you ask me, today's unfortunate events are going to make it harder rather than easier to talk him into coming out."

"He doesn't need to come out," Hamish said. "Well, of course he does, and I don't mean you should stop trying to talk him into it. What I mean is — haven't you ever tried to negotiate the surrender of the town archives?"

"Why would I try to do that?" Randall sounded genuinely puzzled.

"You have dozens of file cabinets and hundreds of boxes full of papers down there!" Hamish exclaimed. "Many of them are valuable historical documents, or official documents necessary for the governance of the town. And they're all down there in the hands of a criminal! Possibly a lunatic!"

"They're all down there in the safekeeping of our official county clerk," Randall said. He tipped his chair back on two legs and folded his arms, appearing to study

Hamish. "I grant you, it might be more convenient if Mr. Throckmorton had moved them out of the courthouse along with everything else, but we're making do."

"But we have to get them out of there," Hamish said.

I felt a sudden twinge of anxiety. Why was Hamish so stubbornly demanding that Randall do something that was clearly impossible — unless he'd found out about the tunnel and knew it wasn't impossible after all?

"We're getting along just fine," Randall said. "We really need something, we call him up, and he sends us a copy — he's got his little fax machine down there, you know. Or he scans and e-mails things to us. We've gone electronic. Joined the twenty-first century."

"But   but — that's preposterous! You can't run a town like that."

"So far we seem to be running the town and the county just fine," Randall said. "Better than it's been run in years, if you ask me. And even if I agreed with you that we ought to get the documents out, just how do you suggest we do it? Fold 'em all up small enough to fit through the chinks in the barricade? That'd take a while, and I don't think we'd want to do that to all those valuable historical papers."

"We could send them out by carrier pigeon," I suggested. "No wait — we could have, before the Evil Lender brought in that falconer to kill all the pigeons. Now I don't think that will work too well."

Randall chuckled and leaned farther back in his chair.

"You could negotiate having FPF withdraw from the basement," Hamish said. "And Mr. Throckmorton could take his barricades down long enough to move all the boxes into the anteroom, and then put them up again."

"We could," Randall said. "Except I'm not sure Mr. Throckmorton would trust FPF not to storm the basement while the barricades were down. Not for five minutes, much less as long as it would take to empty the basement. Especially after what happened today. I know I wouldn't."

"Maybe we should storm the basement," Hamish said. "It's intolerable having that man there. And besides —"

"Mr. Pruitt," I said. "Just why does this bother you so much? You're not the town attorney any longer. He's not making your job harder. I'm sure you'd be devastated if anything happened to the town archives — we all would. But they've been just fine for over a year. Why is this suddenly such a big issue?"

"It's always been a big issue," he said. "It's always bothered me. But . . . but . . . before, I just thought Throckmorton was a nut case. It's different now that we know he's a cold-blooded killer!"

"We don't know that, Mr. Pruitt," Randall said softly. "We just know someone is. Innocent until proven guilty."

Hamish opened his mouth as if to continue the argument, then changed his mind, shut it so abruptly I could swear I heard his teeth click, and stormed back out again.

"What's gotten into him?" I asked.

"Must be the heat," Randall said. "Or maybe he ate his own cooking and got Mad Cow disease or something. The archives have been just fine down there for a year, and suddenly Hamish gets a bee in his bonnet that we should get them out."

"No idea why?"

"Something he left in his office, I reckon," Randall said. "He was one of the few government employees who didn't pack up and move out when the lender took over the courthouse, you know. So when we did our inspection, about three A.M. the morning of the takeover, Vern and I ended up packing all his papers. Took forever, sorting out the personal stuff from the county stuff. From the look of it, he did more personal than county business out of that office."

"Sounds like Hamish."

"And Phinny came by just as we were finishing, and said he was taking charge of any official government documents that were in danger of being left behind. I thought he meant he'd haul them away — never dawned on me that he was dragging as much paper into his lair as he could before he put up the barricade."

Randall shook his head, but he was smiling indulgently. I wondered, not for the first time, if Randall really had been completely unaware of Mr. Throckmorton's plans. Had the diminutive county clerk really dragged those heavy timbers down into the basement and erected the barricade all by himself?

"Anyway," Randall went on. "Hamish made a big fuss the next day, but no one had much time to bother with him, and within the week, his own cousin fired him, so if you ask me, the archives are no more his business than any other citizen's, and most of the citizens are just fine with the way things are."

"Imagine the job we'd have, trying to move them out," I said. "And where on earth would we put them?"

"And how would we find anything afterward?" Randall said. "We need something, I call Phinny, and I get a copy faxed or e-mailed within the hour." I heard a faint ding, and Randall reached to pull out his cell phone. "If we move all that stuff," he went on, "I guarantee you, no one, not even Phinny, will know where all of it is for the next decade. I say we leave well enough alone. Oh, damn. Not again."

The last words appeared to be addressed to his cell phone.

"What's wrong?" I asked.

"My predecessor just sent me another snarky e-mail," Randall said. "He does that from time to time. Wonder if the news has hit the national media, or if one of his cousins who's still in town called to tell him."

"Is he still spending his ill-gotten gains in Cancún?"

"Let's see. Yes, apparently. He closes by saying he'll hoist a piña colada in my honor."

"Jerk." I was tempted to say harsher things about ex-mayor Pruitt, but the boys were on the verge of learning to talk, and I'd expunged from my active vocabulary any words that could possibly do George Pruitt justice.

"He is that. Which reminds me." He fumbled through the papers on his desk and then found the one he wanted. "I got a letter of complaint today. Someone threatening to sue Caerphilly Days for discriminating against her in our selection of entertainers."

"Discrimination?" I exclaimed. "Good grief, we let nearly anyone perform who can walk, crawl, or roll onstage, and if they're at all noisy, we ask them back. And we go out of our way to be multicultural. I can see the audiences suing us for harassment over some of the acts but the entertainers? Who is it?"

"Lady named Heterodoxia Jones," Randall said. "Name ring a bell?"

"Oh, God," I said. "The mime."

Randall winced.

"Yeah, here it is," he said. "We're guilty of holding a disparaging attitude toward the ancient and honorable profession of the mime, and also restricting her right to self-expression. And she wants a hundred thousand dollars in compensation or she'll sue us for a cool million."

"Let her sue," I said. "Last time I heard, mimes were not a protected class under the

Americans with Disabilities Act. Or would they fall under the Equal Employment Opportunity Commission?"

"Whatever," Randall said. "Wouldn't hurt to let her perform. Not that I'm eager to see another mime on our stage, mind you. Just between you and me, I don't consider shooing mimes away discrimination — more like pest control. But that's my personal taste. Speaking as mayor of Caerphilly, I'd like to think we're a mime-friendly town."

"Save the mime, apple pie, and motherhood speech for the voters," I said. "We're as mime-friendly as the next town. What Ms. Jones doesn't mention is that in addition to being a mime, she's also an ecdysiast."

Randall's brows furrowed.

"A stripper," I explained. "And while I'm more than a little curious to see what a combination of mime and striptease looks like, I thought we were trying to keep our entertainment at least PG rated."

"I agree," Randall said. "Okay, I'll figure out how to get rid of the naked mime. Keep up the good work."

CHAPTER 16

Back at the bandstand, an actor was delivering Winston Churchill's "We Shall Fight on the Beaches" speech in a remarkably good imitation of the prime minister's marvelous voice while the stage crew put on a montage of wartime scenes that included short scraps of film, strobe lights, canned sound effects, bits of martial music, small but real explosions, and occasional small parties of live actors in assorted military uniforms storming or retreating across the stage with famous battle sites rear-projected behind them. As a dramatic piece, it was short on plot and long on noise, but as cover for opening and closing the trapdoor, it was a resounding success. In fact, the whole pageant was. I resolved to speak to Michael about arranging an encore as part of the July Fourth program.

I spent the remaining sixty or seventy years of American history on the phone, making sure our entertainment lineup for the next few days was solid. We were already expecting good crowds for the Fourth of July, and I had a feeling news of the murder would attract more people than it scared away.

The Caerphilly Cloggers. The Clay County Marching Band. A chainsaw sculptor who claimed he took audience requests. Bollywood Live. A troupe of performing house cats.

"I could do that," Rose Noire said, peering over my shoulder while I was busy with the clipboard and my cell phone.

"What, training house cats?" I asked. "Yes, by now I should think we're both experts."

"Doing all that calling," she said.

"Help yourself," I said, handing her the clipboard. "I've marked the ones I've confirmed. If you can't confirm any of the others, I'm sure some of the ones who have confirmed would be thrilled to do two shows."

"And there's always the bagpiper," she said.

"There is that," I said. "And if you don't mind, I do plan to leave you in charge tomorrow."

"Taking a day off to spend with the boys?"

"I wish. Caroline Willner's bringing up

some animals from her wildlife sanctuary."

"Noisy animals?"

"As noisy as possible," I said. "And she says not to bother with her, she'll entertain herself while she's here, but you know someone's going to end up chauffeuring her around, and I could use a break from this place. If the weather's nice, maybe I'll take the boys with me to the zoo."

"It's supposed to be even hotter tomorrow," she said.

"Not a good zoo day, then," I said. "Better to keep them here where we at least have fans."

"And I can keep an eye on them and Eric while you take care of Caroline," she said.

"Just one question." I pointed to the next item on the call list. "Precisely what is Molly in Chains?"

She peered at the paper for a second.

"Oh, that. New group from the college. They do Morris dancing in red stiletto heels and skintight black-leather bodysuits decorated with a lot of chains and spikes."

"Well, that should be unique," I said. "But do we really want them doing it at two P.M.?"

"No, probably not," she said, with a sigh. "I suspect they actually requested two A.M., but that's not happening. Don't worry.

We've got that heavy metal band on at nine. I'll put the Morris dancers on just before them. Anyone who's staying for heavy metal can probably handle the Mollies."

"One quick question — they don't take the black leather off, do they?"

"I hardly think so," she said. "If the photos on their Web site are anything to go by, their costumes are probably sewed or glued on and I wouldn't be surprised if it takes them at least an hour to pry themselves out."

"Just checking."

Right outside the tent was a small roped-off area we called the outdoor green room — really just a place for anyone on duty at the tent who wanted to see one of the shows. Eric and the boys were there. He and Josh were watching the students take their bows and clapping with great enthusiasm. Jamie was fast asleep nearby in the Pack 'n Play.

"Got a future historian here," Eric said. "Josh loved the whole thing."

"He just likes noise," I said, as Josh scrambled to stand on my lap.

"So what's next?" Eric asked.

"Couple of jugglers, and then the New Life Baptist Choir," I said.

"They should love the jugglers," Eric said. "But what about the choir?" From his expression, I gathered he was hoping I'd say no.

"They'd love it," I said. "Josh would dance to the fast numbers, and Jamie would sing along with the whole concert — except there's no way they should stay up that late. In fact, we should probably take them home and put them to bed now — it'll be their bedtime by the time we get them there."

"Yeah, I figured as much." From his tone, I gathered he was beginning to feel like a child care expert. Then he looked around and dropped his voice. "You don't need to drive me unless you want to. Uncle Rob just e-mailed. He's on his way. He's helping Horace over. He wanted to know if I could pick up some food, and then he could take me and the boys back to your house."

"Going to play-test his new game?"

"After we put the boys to bed," Eric said, putting on what he probably assumed was a diligent, responsible look. And then his expression changed to sheepish. "If I can stay awake for it. Not even six and I'm yawning. Remind me to apologize to Nat. I've been giving her a hard time all summer about having such a cushy job. This is work!"

I couldn't hide my smile.

"If you like, I can pick up the food," I said.

"What did Rob say he wanted?"

"He said a church smorgasbord, whatever that is. I figured I'd ask you where to get it."

"He means a little bit of everything," I said. "Let's watch the juggling, and then I'll fetch the food after that."

Both boys adored the juggling. In fact, all three boys. I foresaw a plague of flying objects around the house for the next few days, unless something even more exciting drove juggling out of their minds.

I used my cell phone to take a picture of them tossing about twigs, acorns, and bits of gravel and e-mailed it to all three grandparents. Then I went to fetch provisions.

A quick visit to the church tents produced enough food to satisfy even Rob and Eric. And to my delight, the Episcopal tent had implemented one of Mother's suggestions, and I bought a chicken Caesar salad for myself.

On my way back to the tent, I spotted an addition to the town square: the Flying Monkeys' new headquarters. They'd erected a twelve-foot-square olive-green tent in one of the few empty spaces along the town hall side of the square — a space everyone else had left empty so the tour guides would have plenty of space to rally their parties.

The sides of the tent were rolled up to take advantage of any stray breeze, and from the number of black chests, army green foot-lockers, and other bits of gear that filled the tent, I assumed they were planning on a prolonged stay. Well, better there than in our courthouse. A uniformed Flying Monkey stood at parade rest at the front entrance, while inside we could see Lieutenant Wilt seated at a portable desk, reading papers with a self-important look on his face.

I wasn't keen on having the Flying Monkeys so close to the bandstand. Of course, in that tent they'd be a lot easier to keep track of, so perhaps it wasn't a complete disaster.

Rob and Horace returned. Horace curled up in a ball just outside the trapdoor and stayed there for some minutes, with Rose Noire patting him on the back and murmuring soothing things. I felt sorry for him, but at least it gave me a chance to ask Rob a quick question.

"Any good news?"

Rob frowned and shook his head.

"Bad news, in fact," he said. "The gun belongs to Phinny."

"Phinny? I have a hard time seeing him packing."

"He says he bought it years ago when they were having a series of burglaries in the county," Rob said. "But then it creeped him out to think that he might hurt someone if he used it, so he put it in a box in his attic and hasn't seen it in years."

A sudden doubt hit me.

"Are you sure this isn't some kind of wild rumor?" I asked.

"I heard it from the chief," Rob said. "He came and talked to Phinny through the barricade. Remember when we thought his house was vandalized last week?"

"You mean it wasn't vandalism after all?" I asked

"Burglary," Rob said. "They took his gun."

At least that was what Mr. Throckmorton said. I had to admit, my confidence was a little shaken. But Rob knew Mr. Throckmorton better than I did, and apart from his terrible taste in girlfriends, Rob was a curiously good judge of character. And he still seemed to trust Mr. Throckmorton.

I hoped he was right.

Rob took Eric and the twins back to the house. Michael and his students went back to the drama department to do a postmortem on the production and celebrate the fact that they'd been asked for an encore. Rose Noire and I peeled Horace out of his

193

gorilla suit, and after some herbal tea and deep breathing exercises, Horace pronounced himself sufficiently recovered that he could head over to the forensic tent to see what else the chief wanted him to do. Rose Noire and I seriously considered sending the suit out to be dry-cleaned, and then decided we'd better wait until there was no chance Horace would need to make another trip through the tunnel. So Rose Noire put it on a heavy clothes hanger and hung it up in the tent to dry and air out, to the great annoyance of Spike, who barked at it for fifteen minutes after she hung it up and renewed his barking whenever a stray breeze stirred it. After a while, even the normally sedate Tinkerbell joined in, though I wasn't sure whether she was barking at the suit or at Spike.

I took my folding recliner and settled down in the green room to eat my salad, drink my lemonade, and watch the preparations for the choir concert, leaving Rose Noire to keep an eye on the tent and shush the dogs. Not that the arriving choir members weren't in on the secret of the tunnel, but with so many people milling about, it would be easier than usual for someone to slip in under cover of the crowd.

I took out my phone to check on Michael

and the twins.

"They're fine," he said. "They ate a hearty supper, and right now they're having a Thomas the Tank Engine marathon with Eric. Bedtime to follow."

"Excellent," I said. "Eric used to love watching Thomas when he was their age."

"Actually, I think he still enjoys it," Michael said. "So relax and enjoy the concert. We're holding down the fort here."

I settled back to watch the action. First a trickle, then a steady stream of singers arrived at the tent, some already clad in their robes, but most carrying them in garment bags.

The audience had thinned out a little while the student tech crew cleared the stage of props and scenery, but now it began to swell again. Many of the new arrivals came bearing plates of chicken, barbecue, or fish, whose odor inspired many of those who had stayed to strike bargains with each other about who would hold their seats and who would fetch food. A small contingent of men from the church wheeled an electric organ in place.

Around 7 P.M., the choir walked onstage and launched into their first number, "What a Friend We Have in Jesus." I leaned back, closed my eyes, and prepared to enjoy the concert.

I woke up with a start when someone tapped me on the shoulder. The choir was in the middle of "Joshua Fit the Battle of Jericho."

"Sorry!" Rose Noire exclaimed. "I didn't mean to startle you."

"I hope the choir didn't notice me sleeping," I said. "I really was enjoying it, but I'm just so tired."

"Just tell them you've been a martyr to insomnia and their voices gave you the first peaceful sleep and pleasant dreams you've had in weeks."

"That wouldn't exactly be a lie," I said.

"Can you keep an eye on the tent?" she asked. "I'd like to watch the end of the concert and I'm taking the dogs with me so they'll stop barking at Horace's suit. I'll take them home in my car when the concert's over."

I nodded. I picked up my recliner and my lemonade and moved to just inside the tent door so if I fell asleep, an intruder would have to jump over me to enter.

The tent was quiet. Far from empty, though, and more chaotic than usual. The choir had brought several folding clothes racks for the clothes the singers had shed before going onstage. From the looks of it, I had a feeling most of them were wearing dressy black shoes and underwear and little else under their robes.

Knowing I was on guard duty counteracted any soothing effect the music had. And so I had plenty of time to fret about the day's events.

Had Colleen Brown been murdered because of something in her own life? Or was she just a convenient victim in an attempt to frame Mr. Throckmorton? Had Horace found anything to indicate who had killed her, or at least to exonerate Mr. Throckmorton? And what effect would all this have on the siege and the county's various legal proceedings? I thought of calling Cousin Festus to ask, but decided it could wait till morning. No sense making Festus's usual fourteen-hour days any longer. And besides —

"So this is where all the magic happens?"

I started, and looked up to see Stanley Denton standing just outside.

"No, the stage is over there," I said. "This is just where the magicians leave their wallets and purses and street clothes while they're onstage."

He chuckled.

"Mind if I come in?" he said. "I promise to keep my hands off the wallets and

197

purses."

"They're locked up anyway," I said.

The idea of letting the PI into our tent, so close to the big secret, bothered me, but he'd probably be even more suspicious if I kept him out, so I got up and moved my lounge chair aside.

"Not bad." He was standing with his hands in his pockets, gazing around with an air of casual interest that might have fooled me if I didn't know his profession. But instead of the casual smile and the relaxed body language, I focused on those rapidly darting eyes.

"Who's the pigeon fancier?" he asked, taking a few steps toward the cage.

"Mr. Throckmorton," I said. "He used to have a dozen until your employer brought in that guy with the hawk."

"Oh." His face fell, and he surveyed the cage for a few more moments. "At least he only lost one."

"Her name was Dulcibelle," I said. "And I'm told she liked to sit on his shoulder and comb his hair with her beak."

"If you're trying to induce guilt, you've succeeded," he said. "I'd have advised against that, if anyone had asked me. Shouldn't they be asleep?"

"Yes — would you mind pulling the tarp

over them?" I asked. "Rose Noire usually does it before she leaves, but it's been a little crazy."

While he obliged, I did a little tidying. I couldn't complain about the neatly arranged belongings the choir had left behind, but they did make the place feel a bit more cluttered than I could stand. I began putting away anything that didn't belong to the choir. It wouldn't make much of a dent in the clutter now, but tomorrow morning, when all the choir's belongings were gone —

"And is that the stage entrance?"

He was pointing to the flap that led to the tunnel.

"No, only storage," I said. "It's just the crawl space under the bandstand."

"That's right," he said. "I remember now — everyone had to file on from the side. Wouldn't it make things easier in the long run if you cut an entrance through there?"

"Probably not," I said. "It's not tall enough for most people to stand up straight in, and the ground's so muddy it's almost like quicksand."

"Still, if you could figure out a way to deal with the mud —"

He strode over toward the bandstand. I suppressed the urge to yell at him to stop. Maybe it was too late — maybe he'd already picked up some slight signs of anxiety in my voice or on my face when he mentioned the crawl space. I tried to keep my face calm and my step unhurried as I followed him over to the tent flap, and prayed that Rose Noire had not gone off leaving the trapdoor exposed.

"What's this?" he said, as he gazed into the crawl space.

"If you mean the refrigerator, it's mine," I said. "I hide it there because people keep raiding it."

"Shut the damned door," a voice said.

CHAPTER 17

My heart was sinking as I peered over Denton's shoulder.

"Oh, hi, Meg. Is he with you?"

It was Deacon Washington of the New Life Baptist Church, frowning back at us over a handful of playing cards. We appeared to have interrupted a poker game in progress. In addition to the deacon, two of Randall Shiffley's cousins and two men that I recognized as husbands of New Life choir members were sitting on folding chairs around a makeshift table made by placing an old wooden door over two ancient sawhorses. One end of a ratty brown wool blanket was pulled over part of the door, as if to make a slightly smoother surface for cards and poker chips, but it didn't look suspicious because you could clearly see the space under the table.

The trapdoor was hidden by the other end of the blanket, pooled with artful carelessness on the floor, and by a small nest of hats and coats draped over two more folding chairs. The only light was from a camping lantern hung from a nail in one of the joists overhead, and I suspected its position had been chosen so it would cast the maximum amount of shadow on the trapdoor area.

The five players stared back at us for a few moments with expressions of mingled sheepishness and defiance. Then Deacon Washington spoke up.

"Meg, I'd appreciate it if you didn't tell Mrs. Washington about this," he said. "Some of the church ladies can be downright intolerant on the subject of card-playing."

"Is it just the card-playing, do you think?" I asked. "Or might they also be just a little upset that you're skipping their concert for a poker game?"

"We can hear every blessed note of the choir's performance from down here," one of the husbands said.

"Hear it a damn sight too well," one of the Shiffleys muttered. "Not meaning any slight on the quality of their performance, of course," he added hastily. "It's just the volume. Last time we did this my ears were ringing for a week."

"Is this an open game?" Denton asked.

The players looked at each other.

"The man's making good money snooping around town," one of the Shiffleys finally said. "No reason to feel guilty about trying to take some of it away from him."

"In the unlikely event that I suffer any losses," Denton said, "I fully intend to include them on my next expense report. I can say I was attempting to acquire information from you."

"I like that," said the other Shiffley. "Should be a high roller, a man who's playing with someone else's money."

The players shifted to offer him an empty folding chair — on the side of the table away from the trapdoor. Denton stooped down and made his way over to the table, only bumping his head once.

"In fact," Denton said, as he took his seat, "just so I can honestly say I asked — any of you want to tell me how Phineas Throckmorton is getting his supplies?"

There was a pause.

"Don't rightly know," said Deacon Washington. "And wouldn't tell you if I did." The other men nodded and murmured in agreement. "You okay with that?"

"I'm fine with it," Denton said.

"I'll deal you in when we finish this hand,

then. One thing — house rule. As soon as the choir sails into 'Blessed Assurance,' the game's over. No ifs, ands, or buts, because that's the next to the last hymn on the program, and some of us need to skedaddle out to the audience so our wives see us whooping and hollering and clapping up a storm when the choir takes its bows. Got it?"

"Got it."

"I'll leave you to it," I said. I shook my head as if saddened by what I saw.

"Oh, Meg," Deacon Washington said. "Could you give me a call if you get wind that any of our wives are looking for us?"

I sighed.

"Give me your number," I said, pulling out my cell phone with a show of reluctance. I entered the number into my contacts list, and then called him to make sure I had it right. Which meant that he had my number, too. I assumed he wanted to call me for help in case of problems — like Denton asking too many awkward questions, or starting to ransack the crawl space. Though I had no idea what I could possibly do to help. So after the exchange of numbers, I left.

I was almost entirely sure that they'd staged the poker game as yet another diversionary tactic — one that seemed to be working well at the moment.

But what would happen at the end of the concert if Denton tried to stay behind? Offered to put away the chairs? Or what if one of the deputies was still over in the courthouse and tried to come through the trapdoor just as someone was dealing a new hand? I could e-mail Mr. Throckmorton to warn him, but what if he didn't read my message in time? Or —

Not my problem. I'd have to leave it to Deacon Washington and the Shiffleys to handle.

Of course, I wasn't good at delegating.

I went back to my post just outside the tent entrance. I wished I could kick back and enjoy the music, but I kept fretting about Denton. Should I go back and help the poker players keep the trapdoor hidden? Or would my implausible presence at the poker game only make it dangerously obvious that there was something to hide?

Then, during the final verse of "My Lord, What a Morning," I saw the tent flap pop open. Denton hurried off in the direction away from the courthouse, looking anxiously over his shoulder as if expecting someone to give chase. I waved, in case he spotted me, but he didn't seem to notice.

Was something wrong? My anxiety increased when, just as the organ played the first few notes of the next song, Deacon Washington and the other choir husbands burst out of the tent.

My heartbeat slowed a little when the choir launched into "Blessed Assurance" and I realized the men were only dashing to take their seats in the audience before the end of the concert.

Of course, that still didn't explain why Denton had made such a hasty and anxious exit.

"What's up with him?" I asked Deacon Washington, who had paused by my chair before dashing for the audience.

"Got a text message on his phone and said he had to run," the deacon said. "And he threw in four of a kind with the pot up over a hundred dollars."

He shook his head as if deeply troubled by this suspicious behavior, and then hurried after the others.

I fretted all through "Blessed Assurance" and the applause that followed it. But I refrained from dashing into the tent — the Shiffleys were still there, on guard. And what if Denton had merely faked a text message to see what we'd do when he left, and was observing from some nearby patch of shadow? On the off chance that was what was happening, I stayed put and tried to look absorbed in the concert.

An expectant silence fell over the crowd, and then a rich, mezzo-soprano voice rang out with familiar words:

"Amazing Grace, how sweet the sound,
That saved a wretch like me."

Althea, Deacon Washington's wife, and probably my favorite singer in the New Life Baptist choir. She wasn't singing full out, but deliberately holding back, making her voice sound soft and hushed. I found myself holding my breath to make sure I could hear every note, which was silly, because even when she was holding back you could hear Althea just fine from across the town square. The rest of the audience must have been holding their breath, too, because all you could hear between the notes were the frogs and crickets down in Pruitt Pond.

She sang the second verse the same way — a lot softer than we all knew she could, and with no frills or improvisations — just an achingly beautiful rendition of the familiar melody.

When she launched into "Through many dangers, toils and snares" at the beginning of the third verse, the choir began humming along — soft at first, so you almost thought you were imagining it, and then getting gradually louder and splitting off into harmonies.

By the time they got to "And Grace will Lead me home" at the end of that verse, the whole choir was singing full out in three- or four-part harmony, and the bandstand vibrated with the force of the music.

For the next two verses, the soprano section carried the tune while Althea and a soprano with almost as powerful a voice danced around and above the melody. And then for the final verse, they just sang the melody, unadorned, over a hundred voices in perfect unison.

It was so overwhelming that the entire audience was silent for a few moments, and then the applause started, all at once, like a crack of thunder. I joined in, clapping my hands together as hard as I could and shouting, "Encore! Encore!"

After the choir had taken a couple of bows, the organ struck up "When the Saints Go Marching In," and the choir left the stage in groups of eight or ten, each group coming to the front in turn, performing a few stately yet surprisingly deft line dance steps, and then taking a final bow before sashaying offstage.

"We should do this every summer."

The two Shiffleys from the poker game were standing in the doorway of the tent, clapping like the rest. They were both tall — one probably matched Michael's six foot four, and the other was at least half a head taller than that.

"I hope we don't have to every summer," I said. "Good cover with that poker game."

"We came over to do some prep work for the new trapdoor, and brought the poker fixings with us," the very tall one said. "And it's not a bad thing he showed up — not a bad thing if a rumor gets out we're having a big poker game under the bandstand. Bunch of us are probably going to be coming and going over the next day or so, and if we carry our tools in beer coolers, it'll just look like we're dropping by for the game."

"And if you look a little furtive and watchful — doesn't that kind of game skirt a little close to Virginia's gambling laws?"

They both chuckled.

"By the way," the merely tall one said. "Randall said if we saw you to make sure you remembered about the Steering Committee meeting later tonight."

I nodded. Since the meeting was taking place at our house, the only way I could possibly miss it was if I deliberately malingered here at the tent until it was over. I'd already begun racking my brain for some task that would keep me here in town for another hour, so the fact that Randall felt the need to remind me argued that he was a keen observer of human nature or possibly a mind reader.

"I'm heading home in a few minutes," I said. "As soon as I make sure the trapdoor is shut for the night. But thanks for the reminder."

The merely tall one looked around for eavesdroppers.

"We're going to be working in there for a while," he said. "Quietly," he added. "And we brought our sleeping bags, so when we finish, we're going to bed down in the crawl space. In fact, here."

He reached into his pocket and handed me a set of keys.

"Just in case anyone finds us, we'll say you caught us drinking after the poker game ended, and took away our keys, so we decided to sleep it off here."

I took the keys — wondering, not for the first time, how many of the small subterfuges townspeople had resorted to in the last year and a half were necessary and how much they merely satisfied some collective thirst for intrigue and drama.

Not a problem I could resolve tonight. I checked to make sure all my stuff was secure and that there was water for the pigeons. Then I grabbed my purse and headed for home.

CHAPTER 18

All around the town square, tour buses were loading their tired but happily chattering cargo. The sidewalks swarmed with people heading for one of the two big lots that the college had opened up for tourist parking. Luckily I was heading the other way, toward the smaller lot that Michael's faculty parking sticker let me use.

I passed Muriel picking up the daily special sign that normally graced the sidewalk in front of her diner. We greeted each other and I yawned while doing it.

"Hope you're heading for bed," she said.

"No," I said. "Steering Committee meeting."

She peered at me and frowned.

"I was about to throw out the last of the coffee," she said. "Why don't I throw it in a cup for you. Might help you get home safely."

I could see the wisdom in that, so I held

the door for her to carry in her sign and perched on a stool while she rustled up a cardboard carryout cup for the coffee.

"I see your friend's gone," she said over her shoulder.

"My friend?" I wondered for a moment if she thought I knew Colleen Brown. Was this her gruff but kindly attempt at offering condolences?

"That PI fellow." She handed me a cardboard travel cup full of coffee. "Didn't show up for his dinner. In fact, I haven't seen him since lunchtime. Just before the murder," she added, looking over her glasses at me to make sure I understood the significance.

"He hasn't disappeared," I said. "I saw him not an hour ago."

Although from Deacon Washington's description, he did exit the poker game rather abruptly.

"See? Right across the street, and didn't drop by for his pie," Muriel said. "Suspicious."

Was she suspicious of him, or insulted that he'd spurned her pie?

"It's still not what I'd call a suspicious disappearance." I took several big gulps of coffee and tried to visualize the little molecules of caffeine leaping into my bloodstream. "Maybe he found some other place where the management's less picky about who they serve. Or maybe having one of their staff murdered while he was here convinced the lender that he's not doing his job, and they fired him."

"Maybe." Clearly Muriel wasn't buying either of these explanations.

"Are you suggesting that he committed the murder and fled town?" I asked. "Or are you afraid that the killer has struck again, and Mr. Denton is also the victim of foul play?"

"Well, I hadn't thought of that last idea," Muriel said. From her expression, I gathered it was not an entirely unwelcome one. "Do you really think someone might have bumped him off?"

"Not unless they did it in the last hour," I replied. "And I have no idea why anyone would want to."

"Well, maybe if you find him, you'll figure it out," Muriel said. "Here's a lid for that. You want me to top it off?"

I held up my cup. And found myself holding my hand in midair while Muriel stared transfixed into my empty cup. I glanced in myself, half expecting to see the crystallized residue of some obscure poison, or perhaps a cryptic message spelled out in coffee grounds.

She finally shook her head and started pouring.

"I keep hoping I'll remember more of what they were talking about," she said.

"Who?"

"The PI and that dead lady," Muriel said.

"They were talking?"

She nodded.

"Here?"

"No, back in the parking lot behind the drugstore. Couple nights ago. I was walking to my car after I closed up. And for that matter, they weren't just talking. Looked to me like they were arguing."

"About what?"

She shook her head.

"I didn't catch more than a few words," she said. "They were at the other side of the parking lot, and they weren't yelling. More like snarling and hissing at each other. Only thing I caught was when the PI fellow lost it for a second and snapped out something like, 'Why the hell didn't you tell me sooner?' And then they looked around and saw me and pretended to be smiling at each other. And he said, 'Let me see you to your car,' loud enough to make sure I could hear, and they both left."

Interesting. And a little disconcerting, since I rather liked Stanley Denton. Not to the point that I wanted him to succeed on his assignment, of course. But I didn't see him as the killer, and I was strangely upset at the thought of him becoming either a victim or a suspect. And from what Randall said, Colleen Brown was civil, professional — if not a joy to work with, at least not a pain like most of her colleagues.

What had two of the very small number of apparently nice and decent people on the Evil Lender's staff been arguing about?

"You told the chief about this?" I asked.

Muriel frowned thunderously.

"I did. Fat lot of good it did," she grumbled. "He won't hypnotize me."

"He won't what?"

"Hypnotize me. I filled him in this afternoon, after I heard about the murder. He barely listened, and paid no attention when I told him maybe if he got one of those hypnotists, they could help me remember what else those two said."

"I think for a hypnotist to help you remember it you'd have to have heard it in the first place," I said. "If you were all the way across the parking lot, how could you have heard it?"

"Well, I didn't consciously hear it," she said. "But how does he know I didn't hear it subliminally? You know, like those tapes you play to help you lose weight and stop smoking. You can't hear them, no matter how hard you listen, but everybody says they work."

"You could have a point," I said.

"Chief says they don't have a hypnotist on staff, and don't have the budget to hire one," she said. "So the evidence that could break the case remains locked in my subconscious."

I wasn't quite sure what to say to that, so I just nodded and tried to look grave. It helped that when my mouth twitched with the uncontrollable urge to grin, I could hide it by sipping my coffee.

And then a mischievous thought struck me.

"Ask Dad," I said.

"Beg pardon?"

"My dad went through a fascination with hypnotism a while back," I said. "I have no idea if he learned how to do it, but even if he didn't, he might know someone who does. And you know how he is when he gets fascinated with something. Maybe if you convinced him of the importance of your subconscious, he could do something about it."

"Now that is a helpful idea." Her tone seemed to imply that she'd been fending off a barrage of unhelpful ones all day.

"Time I hit the road." I picked up my cup and slid off the stool. "What do I owe you for the coffee?"

"I was throwing it out anyway," she said. "Drive safely."

It was nearly eleven when I finally got home. I was exhausted, ravenous, guilt-wracked about dumping the boys on Michael for so long, and eager to see him and them.

Well, at least I got to see Michael.

"We missed you," he said. "But Eric was a big help, and the boys have been bathed, fed, and read to almost as well as you could do it."

"Eric's working out, then?"

"He's catching on, but he'll need a lot more stamina to keep up with the Dynamic Duo. He collapsed a little after they did."

"I'd love to follow his example," I said. "After some food. Anything that's not fried chicken, fried fish, or barbecue. I had a lovely salad for dinner, but that was five hours ago."

"Okay, so will you be pleased or dismayed that the rest of the Steering Committee are waiting for you in the library with pizza?"

Pizza. That argued that someone thought we were in for a long meeting. Unless they'd

218

just appropriated the pizza Michael had talked about ordering. I closed my eyes, controlling the urge to mutter several of the words I'd tried to expunge from my vocabulary before the twins picked them up.

"Dismayed's closer to the mark," I said. "If I'm not up in an hour or so, call and fake some kind of small problem with the boys that only I can handle."

"Will do," he said.

Encouraged at having an escape route, I headed for the library. But on my way, I stole upstairs to check on the boys. They looked so cute and angelic that I pulled out my phone and snapped a few pictures to send to the grandparents. Before the boys arrived, I'd hardly ever used the camera feature on my phone, and now I used it almost daily. And not just for my own enjoyment. I'd figured out that if I sent my mother-in-law enough baby pictures, her visits were shorter, somewhat less frequent, and a lot more peaceful.

I tucked in both boys more neatly and then, feeling slightly less guilty, I returned to the ground floor and trudged down the long hallway to our library.

CHAPTER 19

Of course, the library wasn't really our library at the moment. Call it our once and future library. When the Evil Lender had issued their eviction notices, Ms. Ellie, the librarian, and a small army of townspeople had packed up all the books, computers, furniture, periodicals, microfiche — in short, the entire movable contents of the building. The original plan was to store them in our barn until the evacuation was over. Then Randall Shiffley had made Michael and me a surprising offer: if we agreed to host not just the boxes but a living, breathing library until such time as the town regained control of its buildings, he would donate the labor to build our dream library — we only had to pay for the materials.

We had jumped at the opportunity. Some previous owner of our house with serious social aspirations and a much larger bank balance than ours had added on a two-story wing containing an enormous ballroom with a music room on one end and a sunroom on the other. We'd set up Michael's office in the music room, let Rose Noire use the sunroom to overwinter her organic herbs, and had been planning to convert the ballroom to our library when we had the money.

When Randall made his offer, our library contained half a dozen ancient Ikea shelving units, a few bits of thrift shop furniture, and forty or fifty boxes of books for which we didn't have enough shelf space. A little daunting, walking into the room and wondering when — or even if — we'd ever manage to build the library of our dreams.

Now it was built. Sturdy mission-style oak shelves ran the entire perimeter of the room, interspersed with paneled oak doors and wide-silled oak window frames. A little interior balcony ran around three walls of the room, giving access to the upper story of books and creating delightful reading nooks on the ground floor level. The fourth wall was balconyless but contained a brass ladder attached to a rail that let anyone without too great a fear of heights reach the books.

It was perfect — except that it was filled with the county's books instead of ours, and separated from us by a locked door for which Ms. Ellie, the town librarian, held the key.

Occasionally, during a bout of insomnia, I'd steal down to Michael's office, peer through the French doors into the library, and pretend it was all ours again. If I sat at just the right angle, so I couldn't see the circulation desk, I could usually manage it, provided Ms. Ellie had turned off all but the night lights, so the Dewey decimal numbers on the spines of the books weren't too obvious.

Tonight, though, the library was very much a public space. I knocked at the locked doorway that divided our part of the house from the library. And then, after Ms. Ellie let me in, I waited impatiently while she checked out books for the last few patrons and gently but firmly shooed a group of high school students out the public entrance, which led through Rose Noire's sunroom greenhouse.

"Eleven o'clock," Ms. Ellie kept repeating. "Closing time."

"But why can't we just stay a little while longer?" one of them whined. "We still need a little more time to finish our school project. Couldn't Mrs. Waterston just lock up after we finish?"

"It's July second," Ms. Ellie said. "You've

got till school starts to finish that project, and if you'd spent the last several hours working on it instead of texting people, maybe you'd have finished by now," Ms. Ellie said. "And Mrs. Waterston has too much to do to babysit you."

The teens slouched out, and I gave silent thanks once again that Ms. Ellie was so fierce about keeping our lives and library business separate. Left to my own devices, I might not have resisted the kids' guilt trip.

"I don't see why you keep the library open till eleven anyway," I said.

"We only do it on the days when we don't open till noon," she said. "I enjoy sleeping in a couple of mornings a week. I assume you're here for the Steering Committee meeting."

"I'm here for the pizza," I said. "If the rest of you can manage to have a Steering Committee meeting before I fall asleep with my face in the pepperoni, I will happily participate."

Ms. Ellie shook her head, but she cleared a space on the large central table and set down some paper plates and a stack of pizza boxes from Luigi's. I helped myself and took one of the semicircle of armchairs facing the table.

"Iced tea?" Ms. Ellie asked.

"Please."

"Did Michael tell you about the vermin we shooed away today?" she asked over her shoulder as she headed for the small refrigerator behind the checkout desk.

"Vermin? What kind of vermin?" I glanced at my feet, half-expecting to see something crawling around them.

"Relax," she said. "Two-legged vermin, and they're gone now. Two men who claimed they'd been sent to do an assessment of the house."

"Sent? By whom?"

"That's what I asked, and they tried to put me off with some vague answer about government business. Which means, of course, that the Evil Lender sent them. They didn't have any kind of paperwork — none they'd show me, anyway — so I sent them on their way with a few sharp words. As did Michael when they knocked on your front door. And to think I once described that boy as mild-mannered."

She chuckled. I managed a slight smile, but my stomach clenched.

"What do you think they were really here for?" I asked.

"Who knows?" She set a glass of iced tea carefully in a coaster on the table beside me and patted my arm. "Psychological warfare, no doubt. But wanting to buy your property doesn't give them the right to send out assessors. And if they don't know that, I'm sure your lawyer will enlighten them."

"I should tell Festus about them." I reached for my cell phone.

"I already did. He said he'll deal with it. Eat your pizza while it's hot."

Fortunately, she hurried off to do something else without noticing that I wasn't following orders. The news about the so-called assessors had unsettled my stomach. Was it just an accident that they showed up today of all days? Cousin Festus regularly assured us that he was very optimistic about foiling Evil Lender's plot to appropriate our land for their golf course and condominium project. But I wanted more than optimism — I wanted certainty. What if the Evil Lender knew something Festus didn't? What if —

No sense borrowing trouble. Festus said he'd handle it. And if he couldn't — well, we'd worry about that when it happened.

I took several deep breaths and several sips of tea and waited for my stomach to settle. I was biting into a slice of pepperoni and sausage thin crust when Dad bustled in.

"Ah! Pizza!" he exclaimed. "Of course I shouldn't."

I didn't even try to argue.

"Nice," he said. I wasn't sure if he was referring to the pizza or the library, which he was studying as if he hadn't seen it before. Well, he probably hadn't since Randall's company had installed the new lighting Mother had donated — elegant mission-style wall and table lamps whose amber shades cast a warm glow over everything. Dad was leaning back in his armchair, craning his neck to see the ceiling.

"Beautiful." Definitely the room, not the pizza. "Of course, you're going to need massive quantities of books to fill it."

Not the first time he'd said this. I suspected he was plotting huge expenditures at the Caerphilly Book Nook and all his favorite new and used bookstores once the library was ours again. In fact, I only hoped he waited until then.

"We have massive quantities, remember?" I said. "In boxes, in the attic."

"Not this massive," he said.

"I'd rather wait until we unpack them before we start planning on deliberately adding to the herd," I said. "They breed in captivity, you know — I'm sure when we open up the boxes we'll have books we don't even remember owning. And when we finally do get the library back, it could be the one moment in my lifetime and Michael's when we actually have enough shelves for all our books. We want to savor that."

Dad frowned, but didn't press the subject. Then again, he knew he could make inroads on all that empty space with his presents of books for the boys. I hoped they turned out to be readers, since Dad had already given them an extensive library, including every Caldecott or Newbery Medal-winning book ever published. Now he was hunting down all the children's books that had ever won a National Book Award, an Edgar, an Agatha, a Nebula, a World Fantasy Award, or any one of a dozen other honors.

"Evening, everyone." Randall strolled in, helped himself to pizza matter-of-factly, and leaned against the table, ready to call the meeting to order.

"Awesome!" Rob bounced in. "You got a supreme!" He transferred three overloaded slices of his favorite pizza onto a plate that would probably have given way under the weight if he hadn't set it on the table, plopped down on a nearby chair, and dug in. Ms. Ellie smiled indulgently and put the stack of napkins within reach.

"Good evening." Chief Burke entered and slumped into an armchair.

"I asked the chief to join us, under the circumstances," Randall said.

"There's pizza," Rob said.

The chief shook his head.

"Minerva would have my hide if I put even a bite of pizza in my stomach at this hour." And he winced slightly, as if the day's events had already been a little hard on his digestion. "Maybe we could get this started? It's been a long day."

"We're expecting one more — ah, there he is now."

Horace sidled into the room murmuring, "Sorry," and probably would have remained lurking by the door if he hadn't spotted the pizza.

"Help yourself," Randall said.

Horace lunged at the pizza and retired to an armchair to devour his two slices.

"So what is it you're hoping to accomplish tonight?" the chief said.

"Maybe see just how big a problem we have, and what we can do about it," Randall said. "And I don't just mean the murder. Though let's start with that — we know Phineas Throckmorton didn't do it, because he's alibied."

"Mostly alibied," the chief said. "Rob wasn't with him at the most critical few minutes."

"But what are the chances he could actually have done anything in those few minutes?" Randall asked.

"Slender," the chief said. "But not impossible."

"Damn," Randall said. "Of course, even if his alibi was ironclad, we wouldn't want to reveal it and give away the secret of the tunnel just yet. So what are you going to say if the Evil Lender asks you to haul him out and arrest him?"

"They already have," the chief said. "And I have already pointed out to them that if we arrested Mr. Throckmorton on the slender evidence we have so far he'd undoubtedly hit the county with a massive false arrest suit that we can ill afford."

"Excellent!" Randall said. "That should work, even if they start demanding his arrest."

"They can demand all they like," the chief said. "I'm not obliged to arrest anyone just because a citizen thinks I should."

"And they're not even citizens," Randall said. "Not of Caerphilly County, anyway. You could mention that if they bother you again."

"I'll let you mention it," the chief said. "Because I told them if they weren't happy with me, they should talk to you."

"Wonderful," Randall said. "Well, it comes with the job."

"I'm not worried about what to do if FPF demands Mr. Throckmorton's arrest," the chief said. "But if they whip the press up to a frenzy, or succeed in convincing state or federal authorities that we're being negligent in not arresting him, that could be a problem."

"It's also my job to keep that from happening," Randall said. I hoped he really was as confident as he looked.

"And if FPF tries to make us look inept, you might point out that if their security officers had done their jobs properly, we might have a mite more evidence to work with," the chief went on. "Not a single one of them stayed at his post when the shooting started. If they had, they might have noticed if someone was seen coming from the basement or leaving the building or taking off a bloodstained shirt. But instead, they were all running around like chickens with their heads cut off."

"So you think there's a chance the real killer could have fled the building undetected before you secured it?" Randall asked.

"The whole New Life choir could have marched out of the building singing 'Onward Christian Soldiers' without those fools noticing," the chief said. "If someone does put Mr. Throckmorton on trial — and it wouldn't be any DA who listens to me — I will make sure his defense attorney knows how bad the building security was."

"As long as they can't force you to evict Phinny any time soon, that's one less thing we have to worry about for now," Randall said.

"I'm surprised they haven't tried to file criminal trespass charges against him," Rob said. "You'd have to arrest him if they did that, right?"

I wasn't the only one who looked at Rob in surprise for a few moments. People tended to forget that before going into the computer game business Rob had managed to graduate from the University of Virginia law school and pass the Virginia Bar exam.

"You're right," the chief said finally. "So far, all they've done is serve eviction notices. If they'd ever escalated to criminal trespass, I'd have had to do something. But for some reason, they haven't."

"I suspect if they had, Cousin Festus would have filed criminal trespass charges against them," I said. "Hasn't he already notified them that he considers them trespassers?"

"Because the money that should have

gone to Caerphilly went to ex-mayor Pruitt," Rob said, nodding.

"Could be," the chief said. "Whatever the reason, I think we can count on Mr. Festus Hollingsworth to fight a delaying action if FPF tries to file criminal trespass charges. But that's far from our only problem. Frankly, if I don't solve this murder in the next couple of days, I probably won't be around to solve it at all. And some of the rest of you may have some difficult legal issues to contend with."

He stood up and handed Randall a piece of paper.

Randall looked at it and frowned.

"What the devil is this?" he asked.

"A subpoena," the chief said. "FPF is subpoenaing me to give a deposition."

"About what?" Randall looked puzzled, as if not sure what the fuss was all about. For that matter, I didn't understand myself. Subpoenas, briefs, and depositions had become a fact of life in Caerphilly ever since the legal battle with the Evil Lender had begun.

"Technically, in the matter of Caerphilly County vs. the First Progressive Financial, LLC, which if memory serves is our countersuit claiming that FPF are the trespassers, not Mr. Throckmorton. But it's obvious what they really want to do."

Not, apparently, to anyone else in the room. We all looked at him with puzzled looks. Then I suddenly realized what he meant.

"You mean it's an excuse to put you under oath and ask you what you know about Mr. Throckmorton's siege. Because they know you won't lie about it under oath."

The chief nodded.

"Can they do that?" Randall asked.

"They're allowed to try," the chief said. "And if they're smart enough to word their questions right, they'll get the answers they want. For months, I've been sidestepping their questions, or giving clever answers that weren't actual lies. I've talked it over with Reverend Wilson and he agrees that in a case like this, where there's dishonesty and injustice on the other side, what I've been doing is permissible. But I won't swear on the Bible to tell the truth and then lie. So we darn well better solve this thing in the next day or so, or I might be trying to run the investigation from a jail cell."

"How soon do they want this deposition?" Randall asked.

"They wanted it tomorrow," the chief said. "And I told them no way in Hades I was going to take time during the first forty-

233

eight hours of a murder investigation to give a deposition in a matter that's been ongoing for months. You and the county attorney may need to talk some sense into them on that front."

"Can do," Randall said. "We'll delay as much as we can."

"So, Horace," the chief said. "Tell me you've got something that will clear Mr. Throckmorton and keep me out of the slammer."

"Not much," Horace said. "When the GSR tests come back, odds are they'll show Phinny's hands are clean. And Rob's. Of course, most, if not all, of the guards will come back clean, too. No visible blood spatter on Rob or Phinny's clothes or on the inside of the barrier. But there wasn't any visible blood spatter on the outside of the barrier either."

"I guess she was killed a little too far from the barrier," Randall said.

"Or there was something between her and the barrier that caught most of the spatter," Horace said.

"You mean, something like the killer's body?" the chief asked.

Horace nodded.

"But I'm a generalist," he added. "I think we need to get a really good blood spatter specialist to come down and analyze the scene. And we need to leave the barrier in place until that happens. The exact configuration of the barrier could be critical."

"Hot dog!" Randall exclaimed. "Chief, we're not paying this man enough."

"We're not paying him at all," the chief said. "He's on loan from York County, remember?"

"Then remind me to call up my counterpart in Yorktown and recommend they give him a raise. Horace, how long do you think it would take to get that expert down here?"

"We can't even put in a request until tomorrow," Horace said.

"I will give Horace a formal, written request to take down with him tomorrow when he conveys the latest batch of evidence," the chief said. "He will make sure to deliver the evidence before the lab closes, but I think it unlikely that anyone in authority will be available to act on our request until morning."

"Thursday morning," Horace said. "They'll be off Wednesday for the Fourth of July holiday."

"Even better," the chief said. "But by Thursday I may be forced to comply with the subpoena. And after that, the game could be up."

"So we need to figure out who really did it by Fourth of July," Rob said. "That's going to be tough."

"It has to be one of those damned Flying Monkeys," Randall said. "They're the only ones with unrestrained access to the courthouse."

"Don't forget the civilian staff," I said. "The ones like Fisher, who have set up local offices for themselves in the courthouse, and the ones from headquarters who come to visit them."

"The Flying Monkeys or their corporate bosses." Randall nodded. "They're the only ones who had motive, means, and opportunity."

"Means and opportunity I grant you," the chief said. "But Ms. Brown was an employee of FPF herself. Hard to see what motive one of the guards could have had for killing someone on their own side of this whole mess."

"But what if she wasn't on their side?" I said. "What if they found out she was getting ready to spill the beans, and knocked her off before she could do it?"

"Spill what beans?" Randall asked.

"No idea," I said. "Since obviously they succeeded in knocking her off before she had a chance to spill them. Unless —"

Something occurred to me. I turned the idea over for a few moments to see if it made sense.

Chapter 20

"Unless what?" the chief prodded.

I still wasn't sure what I remembered was useful, but I'd let the chief decide.

"Suddenly I find myself remembering something Mr. Denton said," I told him.

"Mr. Denton?" Randall echoed.

"The private investigator."

"That's right — I hear you've been getting acquainted with that private eye fellow," Randall said.

"I had lunch in Muriel's today," I said. "By way of a change from fish, fried chicken, and barbecue. The PI tried to strike up a conversation with me, and unlike the rest of the town, I didn't actually run away screaming. Maybe I'm deluded, but I think I'm savvy enough to have a casual conversation with the man without giving away any of the town's deep dark secrets."

"So you really did talk to him?" Randall asked.

"We exchanged about a dozen sentences," I said. "So if that's getting acquainted, then yeah, we've been getting acquainted."

"It's more than anyone else has done," he said.

"Your cousins and some of the choir husbands were playing poker with him beneath the bandstand earlier this evening," I said. "They might know more about him than I do by now."

"Good," he said. "I keep telling people we should charm the fellow. Maybe winning him over to our side's too much to hope for — man's got to eat, after all, and we're not hiring any PIs. But maybe he knows things we'd find useful if we could winkle them out of him, and no way we can do that if everyone in town clams up the second he appears and snarls at him if he talks to them."

"And have you been setting an example?" I asked. "Chitchatting with him yourself?"

"Far as I can, but I might be the one person he knows better than to trust," Randall said. "What did he have to say?"

"Is this relevant to the case at hand?" the chief said.

"Maybe," I said. "He asked if there was anyone in town who didn't know he was the PI hired by the lender, and I told him no, we pretty much all knew. He didn't seem surprised."

Randall nodded.

"We sparred a bit. Then he said something odd." I paused to recall his exact words. "He said he was beginning to think that this time he might not be playing on the side of the angels."

Randall nodded eagerly.

"Yes," he said. "He knows something."

"Not about the tunnel, I hope," I said.

"No, about the Evil Lender," Randall said. "Something that's making him wish he hadn't taken the job."

"Maybe," I said. "Or maybe he's just figured out that we're not the raving lunatics the Evil Lender's PR department has been trying to make us seem. That we're a town of basically normal, mostly pretty nice people caught in a bad set of circumstances and trying to make the best of them. Maybe he realizes that even if what the lender is doing is legal, it's not very nice."

Chief Burke stirred slightly in his chair. He was probably exhausted and dying to go home to bed.

"And maybe none of this is relevant to the murder," I said. "But maybe it is. Just what made him think he was on the wrong side? Did he figure it out by himself? Or was it something Colleen Brown told him?"

The chief had taken off his glasses and was rubbing his forehead as if feeling a headache coming on. Or maybe doing it helped him keep from dozing off.

"It's an interesting theory," he said. "At least it would be if we knew of any connection between Mr. Denton and Ms. Brown. Apart from the fact that they both worked for the Evil Lender."

"And were seen privately arguing and behaving furtively when discovered," I said. "According to Muriel Slattery," I added, pre-empting what I knew would be the chief's next question. "Who does have a bee in her bonnet about wanting to be hypnotized in case there's more useful information lurking in her subconscious, but is in general a pretty astute observer."

"So that's what she was going on about." The chief grimaced slightly. "When she talked to me, she was so focused on the hypnosis part that she failed to mention those bits of useful information that she actually did remember."

"Hypnotized?" Dad said. "I could probably find someone who could hypnotize her if she really wants to be hypnotized. In fact —"

"I'd rather you didn't," the chief said.

241

"Juries tend to mistrust hypnotism, and a sharp attorney would have a field day with a witness who's been hypnotized. I will explain to Ms. Slattery tomorrow that for now we prefer to preserve the integrity of her potentially valuable testimony. And maybe then I can actually get her to tell me what it is."

"You should confront Denton with this," Randall said.

"I plan to," the chief said. "But Mr. Denton has already told me that his relationship with Ms. Brown, and for that matter with the several other FPF employees stationed here, has grown increasingly testy during the three weeks of his employment."

"Let me guess," Randall said. "They kept pressuring him to come up with some information they could use, and didn't believe him when he said he couldn't find any."

The chief nodded slightly.

"Speaking of pressure, Fisher's been asking me when they can get their building back," Randall said.

"It's a crime scene," the chief said.

"That's what I keep telling him. And when I do, he says that the crime scene is in the basement, and can't they have the rest of the building back."

The chief glowered.

"Are you instructing me to release the rest of the building to FPF?" he began. "Because —"

"Not what I was getting at," Randall said, holding up his hands as if in surrender. "I'm just telling you they seem to want back in pretty badly. Don't know about you, but it raises a red flag in my mind. Makes me want to keep 'em out another day or two until we can figure out what they're up to."

The chief relaxed again and smiled ever so slightly.

"I'll have it checked out. And make sure the deputies on guard there are aware that FPF may be trying to regain access. Horace, how long can you stay tomorrow?"

"Depends on the crime lab," Horace said. "I'll call first thing tomorrow to make sure they're not closing early for the holiday."

"In other words, the Fourth could add even more than a day to our wait for results," the chief said, with a sigh.

"If anyone asks why it's taking so long, send them to me," Randall said. "I'll give them my speech about the difference between TV and real-life forensics."

"As I said, I'll call and make sure someone at least stays to receive the evidence tomorrow afternoon," Horace said. "If I can make it sound interesting enough, I might get someone to come in over the holiday and work on it. No guarantees, though."

"Do as much as you can at the courthouse before you take off," the chief said.

"What about Phinny's house?" Horace asked. "Don't you want me to work on that, too?"

"Yes," the chief said. He was rubbing his forehead as if all of this wasn't helping his head. "We did a basic search after Rob reported the vandalism, of course."

"But that was before you realized the vandalism was actually a burglary," Horace said. "And that the burglar stole a gun that later became a murder weapon."

"It calls for a whole new level of effort," the chief said. "But I think we need to seal Mr. Throckmorton's house so you can focus on the courthouse. Phinny's not moving home anytime soon — at least we hope he isn't — and we need to turn the courthouse inside out before we let FPF back in. Or perhaps I can ask the SBI for some help. Anything else?"

Randall shook his head. So did Ms. Ellie and Rob.

I realized there was just one thing bothering me. I kept thinking, "Why now?"

CHAPTER 21

"What do you mean 'why now?' " Randall asked.

I started slightly. I hadn't realized that I'd said it aloud. They were all looking at me.

"Mr. Throckmorton has been in the basement for over a year," I said. "And the Evil Lender in possession of the courthouse for the whole of that time. Why wait till now to frame him for murder?"

"Somebody high up got tired of waiting?" Rob suggested.

"Maybe," I said. "But there have been a lot of other things lately. They hire a new security service. They hire a PI. They bring in a hawk to attack Mr. Throckmorton's pigeons. They maybe even burgle his house. From what I can see they've sent down quite a few more FPF personnel. Colleen Brown hadn't been here that long, had she?"

"About a month," Randall said. "And yeah, they do have more suits in town now.

You saying you know what they're up to?"

"No, just that it seems a lot's going on all of a sudden. I'm not sure we should just assume somebody got fed up. Why now? What happened?"

"Maybe it's something that's going to happen," Randall said. "There's a big court date coming up that has Festus and his legal team working long hours."

"Tell me about it," I said. "They're up on the third floor, you

know. Their lights are already on when I get up, and still on when I stagger off to bed, so I figured something big was coming up. Is it in our suit against the ex-mayor or the ongoing battle with the Evil Lender?"

Randall looked sheepish.

"I'll ask Festus," he said.

"It's a good question, actually," the chief said. He was leaning back in his chair with his fingers steepled, looking noticeably more awake than a few minutes ago. "All of you, give it some thought. What's happened recently, and what's happening soon."

We all nodded.

"And if you think of anything, don't try to act on it," he said. "Come and tell me."

"Any objection if Meg tries to use her friendly contact with that PI fellow to pick his brains?" Randall asked.

The chief winced, but he shook his head. Suddenly he looked tired again. And then he set his jaw and stood up.

"I'm so beat I can't think straight," he said. "Yes, if you run across information that might help me solve this case, I want to know it. I'd be happier if you'd all stick to running the festival and doing legal battle against FPF and leave me to solve the murder, but I'm not hoping for miracles here. Just try not to do anything illegal or anything that's going to paint a bull's-eye on your back if the killer notices you doing it."

He nodded good-bye and strode out of the room.

A few moments of silence followed his departure.

"So, Meg," Randall said. "You'll track down the PI and see what he has to say."

"Assuming Rose Noire can wrangle the festival in my absence," I said.

"I'll do some data mining to see if I can come up with any more answers to that 'why now?' question," Ms. Ellie went on.

"I'll talk to Festus," Randall said. "And I'm going to check out this new guard company a little more carefully."

"Why?" Ms. Ellie asked.

"Those clowns don't behave like any

normal guard service I've ever heard of," he said. "All this saluting and siring."

"Seems a little over the top," I agreed.

"Couple of my cousins have worked as guards, unarmed or armed," Randall said. "Talked to one of them earlier today, and he also thinks they sound pretty bogus. More like some kind of nutcase paramilitary group than a professional security outfit. He recommended I check with the Department of Criminal Justice Services — that's the state agency that regulates security companies. See if they're really operating legitimately."

"I'll see what I can find out about their management in the public records," Ms. Ellie said. "It would be interesting to know if there's any history of suspicious deaths at other properties where they've been working."

"It's all kind of futile, isn't it?" Horace said.

We all turned to look at him. Normally the prospect of a day spent microscopically examining a crime scene would have cheered Horace up, but he looked tired and discouraged.

"Futile in what way?" I asked.

"What can we really do?" he asked. "It's pretty obvious the killer's either a Flying

Monkey or someone else who works for the Evil Lender — and we don't have any inside knowledge about them. In fact, just the opposite — we've been trying to avoid all contact with them, and they with us. It's like . . . like . . . like expecting the Montagues to know what the Capulets are up to."

"Hey, it's not that bad," Rob said. "Montagues and Capulets really isn't a good metaphor. It's more like . . ."

"Like the American colonists against the occupying Redcoats," I suggested.

"Precisely," Ms. Ellie said. "We outnumber them. And we may have been trying to avoid them, but let's not pretend we haven't been keeping an eye on everything they've done since the minute they arrived here."

"And they're not from around here," Randall put in. "That puts them at a disadvantage. We know the lay of the land — they don't."

"We know the character of the locals — they don't," Ms. Ellie added.

"And most of them are doing this because it's their job," I added. "We're doing this to protect our homes."

Horace looked surprised.

"I hadn't thought of it that way," he said. "It doesn't sound as discouraging when you put it like that."

"Way cool," Rob said. "I'm getting chills. Makes me want to go and throw a truckload of tea into Caerphilly Creek."

We all chuckled, and wished each other good night. But my own good humor evaporated as I made my way up the dimly lit staircase. In spite of my brave words, I was feeling discouraged. Almost defeated. The tunnel crawling, on top of my blacksmithing, had made every bone in my body ache, and I kept seeing visions of Mr. Throckmorton and the chief led away in handcuffs, the Evil Lender triumphing in court, and the county board sadly telling me and Michael, "We're sorry. We don't want to seize your land. But we're dead broke and we owe the lender so much money and there's nothing else we can do."

As I trudged upstairs, I could see the light spilling down from the third floor, where Festus's staff was apparently still hard at it. Since our enormous old Victorian house was much larger than we needed, Michael and I had been happy to offer Festus the third floor for his support staff. Most of the time I found it comforting to know they were all up there working so hard for our benefit. But lately we hardly saw them. Most of them had taken to sleeping up there on cots and sleeping bags, and subsisted entirely on pizza, Chinese carryout, and care packages from the church food tents. Was it only the long hours that made them look so anxious? Or did they know something about the case that we didn't?

I was still in my gloomy mood when I peeked in again on the boys, both still sleeping peacefully. Jamie was clutching a stuffed boa constrictor longer than he was — a cherished Christmas present from my grandfather.

The sight filled me with a fierce determination to do anything necessary to make sure that the boys would be spending their next Christmas right here. Next Christmas and every Christmas after it, until Michael and I were little gray-haired senior citizens wrapping up stuffed boa constrictors for our own great-grandchildren.

Michael hardly stirred when I slipped into bed, or even when I slipped out again to remove the sippy cup that had gotten shoved down near the foot of the bed and brush the scattered Cheerios off the sheets.

CHAPTER 22

As usual, the boys woke us up long before I'd have gotten out of bed on my own. Michael put them in their high chairs with small helpings of whole-grain Cheerios. I gathered a selection of fruits and vegetables from the refrigerator and set them by the cutting board where Michael would be readying them for the boys, in accordance with our longstanding policy on keeping me away from sharp implements before 9 A.M.

As I was rinsing out the coffeemaker and making a resolution, for the hundredth time, to do a better job of cleaning up the kitchen at bedtime, the doorbell rang.

"At this hour?" Michael said, looking up from the cutting board.

I glanced at the clock. 7 A.M.

"Keep cutting," I said. "I'll take care of our visitor."

"Good idea." He waved the knife in the air. "I could easily be tempted to use this on someone who shows up at this hour."

I dried my hands and headed for the door. The doorbell rang again before I reached it.

"This had better be important," I muttered. There was a time when all our friends knew Michael and me better than to ring our doorbell at this hour. The arrival of children had changed things — especially since, to their parents' great dismay, both boys appeared to be more lark than night owl. But even though we were up — just barely — 7 A.M. was frightfully early for anyone to be ringing and pounding with such insistence.

I opened the door and found Kate Blake, the reporter from the *Star-Tribune,* raising her hand toward the doorbell.

"Finally," she said. "I need to get into your library."

"Around back," I said, pointing to the brick path, clearly marked with a sign, that led to the library entrance. "And it doesn't open till ten."

"But I need to get in there now!" she said.

"Sorry," I said. "I can't help you."

I started to close the door. She stuck her foot in the opening.

"Listen, lady," she said, putting her hands on her almost non-existent hips. "I'm on deadline. If you don't let me into your wretched little library this instant I'll be forced to mention you by name as one of the benighted denizens of this backwater town who have been misleading and stonewalling the press ever since we got here!"

"If you do that, then your editor will get a call from my attorney," I said, in my most pleasant tone. "Or perhaps I'll make the first call myself, and suggest to your editor that if he employed reporters who could ask civil questions, instead of whiny, entitled little brats, he might see more news and fewer defamation of character suits. Now move your foot, or you'll be sorry when I slam this door."

"Now see here —" she began.

"Look, kid," I said. "I'll give you the benefit of the doubt and assume that anyone capable of calling me a benighted denizen has some rudimentary grasp of the English language. Did you happen to notice that I didn't say 'I won't help you'? I said 'I can't help you.' I don't have a key to the library."

"But it's in your house," she said.

"And when the library moved in, we had the doors rekeyed. Ms. Ellie Draper has a set of keys, and I assume the other librarians who open do. But I don't, nor does anyone else living here. So stop taking your impatience out on me."

Her shoulders slumped.

"I'm sorry," she said. "I shouldn't have tried to browbeat you. It's just that I'm under such stress because of this deadline."

"Maybe you're in the wrong business, then," I said. "Your deadline can't be all that pressing. Today's *Star-Trib* is still being delivered. You must have at least a few hours before you have to turn in your story for tomorrow morning's issue."

"Yeah," she said. "The paper's deadline isn't until about ten P.M. *My* deadline's a lot shorter. My editor only sent me down here because he thought it would be a silly human interest story. He's sending one of his crime reporters down to cover the murder. So unless I can prove I've got some kind of inside track or hot lead, I go back to D.C. as soon as the crime reporter gets here. My editor said something about sending me to a cat show. That'll make the fourth one this year."

She glanced at her watch again.

"Ten o'clock," she said in a flat voice.

Hard to tell if her change of mood was sincere. But even if it was only another attempt to wangle information — two could play at that game.

"Ten o'clock," I repeated. "Would you like to come in and have some coffee? And you can wait inside in the air-conditioning. I can't promise any hot leads, but at least it will save you going all the way back to town and then coming out here again at ten."

"Thank you!"

From her tone, I suspected she was hoping to weasel some information out of us. Well, she was welcome to try. She stepped in briskly, waited while I closed the door, and then followed me down the hall to the kitchen. Her heels tapped on the polished oak of the hallway. I glanced down at her shoes. They were more worn than Colleen Brown's, with a lower heel, and I suspected they would inspire an indulgent smile, not envy, in Mother.

In the kitchen, Michael was sipping coffee and chopping bits of ham and cheese for an omelet. Rob was slumped over his cup of coffee and staring into it as if he could read his fortune in its depths — or more likely, in the hope that it would kick in and magically erase the ill effects of another night of minimal sleep. Both twins were in their high chairs with the breakfast Michael had prepared spread over the trays — bits of fruit, cooked vegetable, chicken, and the ubiquitous Cheerios.

"Mom-my!" Josh exclaimed, as if he hadn't seen me in days.

Jamie was so busy methodically ferrying Cheerios and bits of fruit into his mouth that he ignored my entrance.

"If Josh is finished eating, let's put him in the playpen," I said.

"How do you know he's finished?" Michael asked. "He could just be taking a break."

"Both dogs are lurking under Jamie's chair," I said. "They have an infallible instinct for these things."

"Yeah, for the dogs, babies are basically like little food vending machines," Rob said. "They tend to notice if one stops producing."

As we watched, Jamie reached for another Cheerio, knocking half a dozen off onto the floor. Spike scrambled to snatch up all of them, growling at Tinkerbell the whole time. But Tinkerbell had positioned her huge, shaggy head more strategically, and was able to snag her half of the windfall without moving her muzzle more than an inch. Spike, after chasing his half of the Cheerios to the far corners of the kitchen, returned to his place beneath Jamie's chair. He barked sharply at Tinkerbell, as if to say, "You do realize I *let* you have those Cheerios!" Then he sat down again to gaze longingly up at Jamie. Tinkerbell merely shifted her head and lifted her eyebrows to stare upward.

"Damn, that's cute," the reporter said.

"Yes, isn't it?" Rob said. He looked a lot more alert. Clearly he liked the look of Kate from the *Star-Trib.*

"I hate cute," she said. "I didn't used to, but ever since I went to work for the *Star-Tribune,* they've sent me on every human interest story that comes along. People turning in cash-stuffed wallets and refusing to take rewards. High school seniors spending their prom night passing out sandwiches to the homeless. Wolves adopting orphaned baby rabbits. Sometimes I think if I have to do another cute, heartwarming story, I'll puke!"

"Yeah, cute's a menace," Rob said. He frowned down at Spike and Tinkerbell as if suddenly disgusted by their persistent cuteness. I made a mental note not to tell her the cute, heartwarming story of how Spike, the Small Evil One, had turned into the boys' best babysitter.

"At first I thought this was another of those cute stories," Kate went on. "Town mortgages its jail, but all the citizens are bravely carrying on as usual in tents and barns. Aarrgghh! But then, just when I'm about to OD on it all — a murder!"

258

She was looking around, beaming happily — and then a look of panic suddenly spread over her face.

"Not that I'm happy the poor woman was killed, of course," she said. "I mean it's horrible. It's just that . . . I mean . . ."

"Don't worry," I said. "We understand what you mean. There's nothing cute or heartwarming about murder. My dad's the same way. He'd rather the locals didn't knock each other off, but if they must do it, he'd prefer they schedule their crimes when he's around to help with the medical side of the investigation."

"Right," she said. "I mean, I thought it was a chance for me to report on some real news! I was here. I helped find the body. And they're sending the crime reporter down to take over? Come on!"

"So you're hoping we can tell you something that will allow you to scoop your colleague, prove to the *Star-Trib* that you do belong on a serious news beat, and keep your byline on the story."

"Well — yeah," she said.

"I might be able to help you," I said. "If you help us."

She frowned and pursed her lips.

"I'm not asking you to do anything that would compromise your journalistic ethics,"

I said. "In fact, all I want you to do is what you want to do — follow the story. Using one tiny but important bit of information."

"What's that?" She had her skeptical reporter face on now.

"Phineas Throckmorton didn't do it," I said,

"I know you all think he's innocent —" she began.

"I know he's innocent," I said. "There's proof."

"What proof?"

"Proof that I'll share with you as soon as I can," I said. "With you — not any of the other reporters swarming into town even as we speak. Assuming you help us."

"Help you do what?"

"Find the real killer."

She rolled her eyes.

"It's not impossible," I said. "There's a limited pool of suspects."

"People who aren't friends of yours?" she said.

"People with access to the courthouse. Did we just stroll in yesterday?"

"You think it's one of the guards?" Her eyes had grown wide.

"Or someone the guards wouldn't think twice about letting into the courthouse."

"Like someone who works for First Progressive Financial?"

I nodded, and waited a few moments while she digested this.

"And of course you realize why you can't even share this with your management yet, right?" I asked.

I could tell this was uncomfortably reminiscent of her all-too- recent days in journalism school. She considered it, clearly suspecting a trick question, and then shook her head slightly.

"First Progressive Financial — large corporation," I said. She nodded. "*Star-Tribune* — large corporation. These days, more and more large corporations are getting snapped up by enormous multinational corporations. Or they have overlapping board members. Or one is a big advertiser with the other. Do you know for sure whether or not the *Star-Tribune* and our Evil Lender are connected in some way?"

"I have no idea," she said.

"Neither do we," I said. "So until we find out — let's not tell one large corporation that we suspect the other."

"That makes sense," she said. "But unless I can tell them I have a scoop, they're going to send me home."

"Not when you tell them how well you've insinuated yourself into the town," Michael said. "Why don't you stay here? Invited to stay with your new, well-connected local sources — that would certainly impress your paper. And we've got plenty of room, and it will be a lot more comfortable than sleeping in the back of your car."

"How did you — What makes you think I'm sleeping in my car?"

"You've got that little dent from the door handle in your left cheek," Rob said.

Her hand flew up to the cheek in question.

"He's kidding," Michael said. "Actually, one of the deputies spotted your car in the lot behind the Quick Mart. The chief scheduled increased patrols of the lot to make sure you were safe, but it must have been rather uncomfortable. Horace told me last night," he added, in response to my puzzled look.

"I couldn't get a room at the Caerphilly Inn," she said. "And that seems to be the only hotel in town. If you're serious, then yes."

"Let me help you with your luggage," Rob said. He drained his cup and leaped up with a great deal more enthusiasm than he usually showed for being up at this time of day.

"And then we can fix you some breakfast," Michael said.

"You realize that you haven't really given me any proof," Kate said.

"What do you think will happen if the killer finds out that there's one bit of evidence that can overturn the case against Mr. Throckmorton?"

"He'll go after that evidence," she said.

"And while we'd like to believe you're trustworthy, we don't really know you that well yet. So you can understand why we're keeping the evidence under wraps for the time being. Rob, get her settled in the room next to Caroline's."

Rob saluted — which I hoped indicated not just that he knew where to put the reporter but also that he knew better than to spill the beans to her just yet about his being Phineas Throckmorton's alibi. Then he bowed to the reporter and gestured to the doorway.

"Is having her stay here really a good idea?" I asked Michael, when I'd heard the front door shut behind them.

"Keep your friends close, and your enemies closer," he said.

"By which you mean that it will make it easier to keep tabs on what she's doing," I said.

"And easier for her to get to know us and

263

come over to our way of thinking," he added.

"We should warn Festus's legal team that she'll be around," I said.

"Will do." He pulled out his phone and began texting. Not his typical way of communicating with people, but I supposed he wanted to make sure he wasn't overheard if Kate came back in.

"What a lovely morning!" Caroline Willner bounced in. Clearly she, too, was a lot more of a morning person than I was. Maybe it was a generational thing. I didn't know Caroline's precise age, but she and my ninety-something grandfather were not only good friends but approximate contemporaries. And they both seemed to consider getting up at dawn a virtue on a par with kindness to animals. Or maybe they'd just gotten used to doing it because the animals did. Caroline ran a wildlife sanctuary near Caerphilly, and my grandfather, an eminent zoologist and environmentalist, now spent much of his time with his new toy, Caerphilly's small but rapidly expanding private zoo.

Caroline's small, round figure was already neatly clad in sensible slacks and a lime-green polo shirt with the Willner Wildlife Sanctuary logo on the pocket. I smiled back at her and wondered if I should add "Buy new, less ragged bathrobe" to the errand list in my notebook.

"Morning," I managed to reply.

"Meg, can you give me a ride?" she asked.

"Into town, sure," I said.

"Well, into town, yes," she said. "I need to take my animals in for the show this afternoon — but I also need to pick up Mr. Throckmorton's pigeons and take them out to your grandfather's zoo. They can stay in the aviary until the coast is clear. And we might make another little stop along the way."

I was about to beg off when I realized that this might be a useful trip. Stanley Denton was staying at the Caerphilly Inn, which was directly on the road to the zoo. I doubted Caroline would object to dropping by there on our way back. I could look for Denton in person, and even if I didn't find him, perhaps I'd learn how recently he'd been seen. And maybe some of the Inn staff would have insights on what he'd been up to and how far we should trust him.

Rob and the reporter reappeared.

"So will that be okay?" Caroline was asking.

"Will that work for you?" I asked Michael.

"Sure," he said. "I plan to stay here this

morning and splash in the pool with the boys. Unless you need me down at the tent?"

"Rose Noire can handle it," I said. "Okay, you've got a chauffeur," I added, turning to Caroline. "By the way, have you met Kate? She's the reporter who was there when we found Colleen Brown's body."

"You poor thing!" Caroline exclaimed. "Are you all right? If it had been me, I'd probably have fainted. But I suppose in your line of work you get hardened to gore and violence."

"Oh, yes," Kate said, assuming a blasé look. Since, from her own description, the most gore and violence she'd previously encountered was probably a spat between two Siamese at the cat show, I had to struggle not to laugh.

"Maybe you'd like to come with us, dear," Caroline said. "Meg and I are going to take poor Mr. Throckmorton's racing pigeons to a new foster home out at Dr. Blake's zoo. They'll be safe from that nasty hawk there. Dr. Blake is donating the space and picking up the cost of their care — it should be a nice, heartwarming human interest story."

Kate visibly suppressed a shudder.

"Thanks," she said. "But I'm afraid I'm

going to be awfully busy covering the murder."

"Well, if you change your mind, let me know," Caroline said. "Come on, Meg. Time's a-wasting."

Of course, before we could take off we had to load all of Caroline's baggage onto the ancient van I normally used to haul my blacksmithing equipment. Under normal circumstances, I might have wondered why she was traveling with an African Grey parrot, a brace of small monkeys, an adolescent hyena, a three-legged wolf, and an eight-foot boa constrictor. But I assumed they were props for her appearance on the bandstand this afternoon. She'd be giving a talk on the important work the Willner Wildlife Sanctuary did by rescuing wild and exotic animals. I only hoped she made her presentation noisy, and that none of the exhibits ate any tourists.

Once the animals and all their accoutrements were on board, we took off for town. To avoid overworking the air-conditioning, I kept the van's windows open, so all the way to town, passersby could hear the laughter of the hyena, the hooting of the monkeys, and the parrot's occasional cries of "Danger, Will Robinson."

CHAPTER 23

I always liked arriving at the town square before the crowds. I pulled up as close to the tent as possible, unloaded Caroline and her charges, and headed on to the college parking lot a few blocks away. I took my time strolling back to the town square, and as I had hoped, by the time I got there, Caroline and the cages had vanished. No doubt she had charmed someone into hauling them to the tent.

I spotted Rose Noire watering one of the growing number of planters scattered around the town square. Whenever we had to haul dirt out of the tunnel, after one of the few cave-ins or as part of the routine maintenance, the Caerphilly garden club would drop off a few more faux stone planters, which we'd fill with tunnel dirt topped off by an inch or two of topsoil. Then Rose Noire would plant geraniums and the Shiffley Movers would haul the planters to some part of the town square that didn't already have planters. At first, they'd added a cheerful note of color, but the Shiffleys were having a hard time finding spots for the latest ones — at least spots where they wouldn't block traffic. And Rose Noire now spent the first hour of her day hauling water to them all.

Two Shiffleys came ambling up. The two who'd slept in the crawl space.

"Mission accomplished," one of them said to Rose Noire. "And we'll keep an eye out in case he does it again."

With that, they saluted and strolled off.

"Mission?" I asked.

"They've been rearranging the planters for me. Last night, someone moved all the ones over in the food tent area so they made a path leading directly to the Hamishburger stand. You couldn't even get to any of the church tents without either climbing over geraniums or going a block out of your way."

"What a jerk," I said, shaking my head.

"Of course, we can't prove Hamish did it," Rose Noire said.

"Do we need proof?" I asked. "It's obvious who did it."

"We need proof if we're going to kick him out of the town square," Rose Noire said. "There's a lot of sentiment in favor of it, but we can't kick him out just because no one likes him and we suspect he's been up to something sneaky. If we catch him in the act . . ."

"Brilliant," I said. "Although I still say we should get rid of those damned things, too." I paused beside her little cart, loaded with the gallon plastic milk jugs in which she carried the water, and waved at a line of planters.

"Don't be negative," she said, her hands fluttering over the geraniums as if she wanted to block my harsh words from their ears and couldn't quite figure out how. "Plants are living creatures! How would you feel if someone walked up and told me we should get rid of you?"

"They're annuals," I said. "I'm sure they're philosophical about their tiny roles in the great pageant of life. And actually I didn't mean getting rid of the flowers. They're very nice. What if you hauled them all someplace, dumped the dirt, returned the planters to the garden club, and planted the geraniums in a nice sunny place where someone could easily sprinkle them with a hose every day or two? They could live out the rest of their short lives in peace and quiet. I'd even volunteer our yard, and I'm sure Mother would say the same thing."

"It's a thought," Rose Noire said. "But we don't exactly have time to do that today, do we? Caroline's waiting for you at the tent."

Yes, Caroline would be waiting for me, and who knew when I'd have another moment to call my own. So I found a quiet, shady spot by the food tents, pulled out my cell phone, and fished Stanley Denton's card out of my wallet.

When I called his cell phone, I got voice mail after four rings.

"Hi," I said. "This is Meg Langslow. I wanted to ask you something." I added my cell phone number and hung up.

Not the most informative message in the world, but I didn't think any of the questions I wanted to ask him were ones he wanted to answer, so I thought vagueness would be my best tactic.

Then I left the same message on his office voice mail.

At least I got a live person at the Caerphilly Inn, although asking them to put me through to Denton produced, after seven rings, yet another voice mail. I called back and left my message at the desk instead. Now if I went looking for Denton at the Inn, I could honestly say I'd been trying very hard to reach him.

By the time I finished that, I saw Caroline

271

trotting toward me. Behind her were the two Shiffleys again, now carrying the large pigeon cage.

"There you are!" she said. "I'm ready to go to the zoo now. If you go and fetch your car, these nice young men will load the pigeons on it."

"If I'd known you'd be back so fast, I wouldn't have gone all the way to the parking lot," I grumbled. "I really should check on what's going on at the tent."

"Rose Noire's there," one of the Shiffleys said. "Watching the wildlife."

And the trapdoor, I assumed. I turned and trudged back toward the parking lot. On my way, I spotted Horace, trotting briskly up the courthouse steps with his evidence kit in his hand. He waved at me. No, he didn't just wave. He gave me a Churchillian V for Victory salute with his free hand. I responded in kind, and felt strangely light-hearted.

The pigeons proved to be far less entertaining companions than Caroline's wild animals. They cooed and fluttered occasionally. Caroline seemed lost in her thoughts. I had resigned myself to a quiet drive when Caroline finally spoke up.

"Don't turn around and gawk or anything, but there's a black van following us."

CHAPTER 24

I glanced in the rearview mirror, being careful not to move my head.

"I see him," I said. "What makes you think he's following us?"

"He's been behind us ever since we left town."

"Once you get past the town limits there are only a couple of places to turn," I pointed out. "If you're not living along the road or staying at the Inn, you'd have no reason to turn off. And this is the only road to take if you're going to Clay County, and not a bad way to go if you want to get to Route Seventeen."

"Don't you think we should at least take rudimentary precautions?" Caroline asked.

"Good idea," I said. "Shall I fire a few warning shots across his bow with the aft phasers, or just activate the Romulan Cloaking Device?"

"I'm serious," she said. "After all, there's

a killer loose. We should do something."

I thought about it for a moment. Then I pulled out my cell phone, punched a few numbers, and handed it to Caroline.

"Talk to Grandfather," I said. "Have him get a welcoming party ready in case this guy is following us. And then if you're really worried, call 911 and ask Debbie Anne if they have any patrol cars in the area."

"Hmph," she said. "I expect your grandfather can handle it."

I grew a little more concerned when we turned onto the zoo access road with the van still following. It was a little hard to think of an innocent reason for that, since the zoo wouldn't open for another hour or so.

When we pulled up in front of the zoo gates, Grandfather and the zoo's night watchman were standing in front of it. Zeke, the watchman, might have looked like a harmless old geezer if he hadn't been holding a shotgun, barrel pointed to the sky but clearly ready to swing down and into action if needed. Grandfather was holding leashes attached to two young wolves.

I pulled up a little past them, so they'd have a clear view of the road.

"So what's with this menacing van?" he asked.

"We don't know that it's menacing," I said. "But it is a little odd that someone would follow us all the way out here."

We all looked over at the black van, which had slowed to a stop at the same time we'd stopped at the gate.

"Hmph!" Grandfather said. "Not so brave now, is he?"

The wolves whined and snarled a little, and Zeke hefted his shotgun as if testing the balance.

The van started moving again and pulled up a few car lengths behind my truck. Then the driver turned off his engine.

We all waited for a few moments.

"This is ridiculous," I said. I strode up to the driver's side of the van, keeping a safe distance. The window rolled down and a face looked out. I'd seen him before, but I couldn't quite place him.

"The zoo's closed," I said. "Why are you following us?"

"I wanted to see what you were doing with the pigeons."

I remembered him now. The falconer. I'd have recognized him sooner if he'd been in uniform instead of jeans and a black T-shirt. Close up I could see that the shirt had THE ART OF FALCONRY in white letters over a

275

picture of a large hawk chasing a hapless rabbit.

"Why do you care what happens to the pigeons?" I bristled slightly, and took a step closer to the door of the van. "Is your hawk having a craving? Can't you find something for her to eat that isn't someone's pet?"

He flinched as if I'd struck him.

"I'm sorry," he said. "You have no idea how sorry. I didn't know those pigeons were pets. If I had, I'd never have flown Sheba at them."

"Then what were you trying to do?" Grandfather stepped forward and fixed the falconer with his most savage frown.

"Doctor Blake!" People's faces didn't usually light up like that when Grandfather frowned at them. "I am such a fan of your work — you have no idea how exciting it is to meet you!"

He scrambled out of the van, grabbed Grandfather's hand with both of his, and pumped it with enthusiasm. I hoped Grandfather was too surprised to retaliate with his customary bone-crushing grip.

Then again, we still weren't 100 percent sure that the falconer was on the side of the angels.

"The work you've done with breeding endangered raptors in captivity is incredible," the falconer was saying.

Grandfather began to preen slightly.

"Getting back to those pigeons," I said. "You claim you didn't know they were pets?"

The falconer's face fell again.

"Absolutely not," he said. "FPF told me they had a major pigeon infestation at their property here in Caerphilly. And they claimed they wanted to do the environmentally responsible thing — to control the infestation with natural predators. That's where I came in."

He dashed back to his van, reached in, and pulled out something. I saw Zeke shift the shotgun a little, but the object the falconer was pulling out was one of those magnetic signs people use when they want to advertise their business without doing a permanent paint job on a vehicle. In black letters on a red background, it read SOME LIKE IT HAWK: NATURAL PEST CONTROL. CHARLES DOANE, PROPRIETOR.

"Interesting," Grandfather said. "So you have a lot of hawks?"

"Just the one," Doane said. He opened the driver-side rear door to show us a large cage containing a hooded hawk. "Sheba."

"Red-tailed hawk," Grandfather said — to me or possibly Zeke, since presumably

Doane knew what kind of bird he had, and Caroline had been fostering assorted injured raptors for decades. "Not a bad specimen."

Doane beamed proudly as Grandfather peered in at the hawk.

"No offense," I said, "but exactly how is one hawk supposed to tackle a major pigeon infestation? Unless it eats a lot more than the average bird, it could probably only chow down on a pigeon or two a day. That wouldn't even slow down the growth of a real infestation. Unless Sheba's the advance scout for a whole army of hawks you plan on bringing along now that you've scouted things out."

"No, one or two hawks should be fine for most bird abatement jobs," he said. "Pigeons aren't dumb. They figure out most of the things we do to chase them away — all those ultrasonic noisemakers and hawk profiles and such. They get used to them. But a natural predator — that they don't get used to. Once they learn a hawk is flying the territory, they leave."

"And the pigeon problem is gone, as long as you and your hawk are around," I said.

"Once you convince the pigeons that an area's not safe, they pretty much avoid it," he said. "I'd only have to come out once or twice a week to keep the area clear."

"Any reason they were having you disguised as a guard?" I asked.

"It wasn't supposed to be a disguise," he said. "Mr. Fisher — he's the one who hired me — he asked if I would mind wearing the company uniform. I have T-shirts with my company name on it, but he didn't think that would go over well with his management — he said some of them can be real sticklers for decorum. Plus, he thought if I just blended in with the security staff, I'd be less of a target if any of the locals were softhearted. And he even agreed they'd pay me a beginning security officer's salary on top of my company's fee, and it included the uniforms and laundry service so . . ."

He shrugged.

"They probably thought you'd be a more menacing figure in the uniform," I said.

"Menacing? Me?" His voice squeaked slightly.

"So you had no idea what was going on when they hired you," I said. "But you've figured it out now?"

"Not really," he said. "All I know is that they're pretty frantic to get that guy out of the cellar. They think there's a secret passage he's using to get in and out, and there's a standing reward of ten thousand dollars if anyone finds it. A few of the security officers spend all their free time tapping on walls."

I didn't like the sound of that. What if they branched out from tapping on walls on the inside of the courthouse to probing for tunnels on the lawn outside?

"If they find any, the Caerphilly County Historical Society would love to hear about it," I said aloud. "I'm afraid they find the courthouse embarrassingly lacking in local color. No ghosts, no secret passages."

"Well, they've got a murder now," Caroline said. "That should keep them happy."

"No." I shook my head. "If it happened a century ago, maybe, but a grisly modern murder — that's not local color, it's scandal."

"You're probably right," Caroline said. "Well, time's a-wasting. Let's take care of these pigeons."

Doane frowned. He threw the magnetic sign back on the passenger-side seat of his van and straightened up.

"Just what do you plan to do with those pigeons?" he asked.

"Put 'em in a cage where they'll be safe until Phinny Throckmorton can claim them again," Caroline said.

"He probably thought we were going to feed them to our raptors," Grandfather said.

"Kid, you've been hanging around the wrong people," Caroline said. "Why don't you quit that horrible job?"

"I would if I could get another one that would let me pay the rent and feed Sheba."

"Hmmm." Grandfather peered at him, head cocked to the side as if Doane were a new and interesting animal he wanted to identify. "If you're looking for work in the wildlife management area, you're talking to the right people. What qualifications do you have?"

Doane wilted slightly.

"I was working on my bachelor's at Virginia Tech. But I had to put it on hold. No money."

"What were you majoring in?" Caroline asked. "And what do you want to do when you finish?"

Doane looked uncomfortable.

"It's not that I don't want to talk about this — but could we take Sheba into a cool place first? Even with the door open, the van's going to be an oven before long."

"Follow me," Grandfather said.

"Bring the birds," Caroline said over her shoulder.

They strode off toward the aviary section of the zoo. Doane grabbed his hawk, Zeke and I hoisted the pigeon cage, and we

281

scrambled to follow.

We turned the pigeons loose in a big empty cage. They fluttered around nervously for a while, possibly because Sheba was keeping them under close observation. So we took her with us to Grandfather's air-conditioned office and he poured cold waters for everyone, Sheba included.

"Rather large for a red-tail," Grandfather said. "So — you planning to specialize in ornithology? Focus on raptors, maybe?"

"Actually, hawks aren't really my main interest," he said. "Not that I'm not very fond of Sheba. She's a great little hunter. But I've got something more interesting I'm working on."

He looked as if he were waiting for us to ask what — for that matter, dying to be asked. We all exchanged glances, and then Grandfather cocked one eyebrow. It was enough.

"Cadaver birds!" Doane exclaimed.

I glanced over at Grandfather. His face bore a look of puzzlement that I'm sure was echoed on mine.

"Vultures," Doane added, as if that explained everything.

"You're planning on specializing in vultures?" Grandfather asked finally.

"Not just that," Doane said. "I'm training

them. You've heard of cadaver dogs."

"Also known as human remains detection dogs," I said. "Yes. My cousin Horace has worked on some cases where they've used dogs to find buried remains, or clues at a crime scene."

"And they do a great job," Doane said. "Don't get me wrong. But you know what's the greatest problem with your typical cadaver dog?"

"Attention span, maybe," I suggested. "They're right in the middle of a hunt and — squirrel!"

"No, actually it's mobility," he said. "Especially in your rough terrain, like woods and mountains, it could take a cadaver dog hours to cover a few square miles of territory. But one of my vultures can soar above the treetops and pinpoint its target in a fraction of the time."

"Along with every bit of roadkill in the immediate vicinity, I should think," Grandfather said.

"It's a training issue," Doane said. "It's slow, but we're making very real progress in teaching them to hunt for human remains."

"And what happens when they find remains?" I asked. "Do they fly back and fetch you?"

"We mount a GPS device on their legs,"

Doane said. "And we track them, with a monitoring system, and when the vulture becomes stationary, we head for that location."

"And damn well hope your vulture isn't far away," Grandfather said with a snort. "Or are you also training them to wait until you give them permission to eat?"

Doane sighed.

"We do have some obstacles to overcome, I admit," he said. "But just look at the potential benefits."

"You could fit them with little muzzles, like dogs," I suggested.

"Now that's an idea," Grandfather said. "Much the way fishermen put bands around the throats of trained cormorants to keep them from swallowing the fish they catch."

"We're actually doing some work along that line," Doane replied.

"Maybe I'm picky," I said, "but I'm not sure they'll ever replace search and rescue dogs. If I get lost in the wilderness and a vulture shows up, I'm not going to be reassured."

"If you're merely lost, they won't show up," Doane said. "Not until you're dead."

"So how are you teaching them to prefer human remains?" Grandfather asked.

I decided this was not an explanation I

needed to hear.

"I should probably get back to town," I said.

"Much as I'd love to hear about the vultures, I'll go with you," Caroline said. "Remember, I've got another little errand you could help me with."

Precisely the words I'd been dreading.

"We'll leave you gentlemen to your discussions," I said.

Caroline and I returned to the truck, and headed for the main road.

"So what's your little errand?" I asked.

"We're going by the Caerphilly Inn on our way back to town, aren't we?" she asked.

I nodded.

"Great," she said. "We're going to burgle it."

CHAPTER 25

"Please tell me you didn't really say what I just thought I heard," I said.

"Relax," she said. "I have a plan."

"Exactly what does your plan think we're going to find at the Caerphilly Inn?"

"No idea," she said. "But since the Evil Lender's executives are staying there, stands to reason if we poke around enough we'll find something interesting. Did you have a better plan for finding out what's going on in what your dad's calling Redcoat head-quarters?"

"I was thinking maybe Grandfather could learn something from his new raptor and carrion bird specialist," I said. "Or were you going to hire him?"

"We'll sort that out once your grandfather has assessed his credentials and charmed him," she said. "And the best plan would be to let him keep working for the Evil Lender for the time being. Sort of a mole in place.

Moles are useful."

I couldn't argue with that. And maybe Caroline was just being dramatic when she used the word "burgle." Unless she'd recently acquired the skills needed to circumvent a four-star hotel's pricey security system, odds were we wouldn't manage anything more than eavesdropping and skulking.

"We're getting close to the Inn," I said. "Where should I park the van?"

"The parking lot would be my suggestion," Caroline said.

I looked at her in surprise. Knowing Caroline's love of drama, I'd fully expected that she'd want us to park a mile or two away, cover the car with branches, hoof it over the pastures and the back nine of the golf course, and then scout the hotel with binoculars from the shrubbery for an hour or so before finally creeping toward our goal. Was she going normal on me?

Then again, if she was having a brief flirtation with normal, perhaps I shouldn't complain.

"Do we really want to put the van in plain sight?" I asked. "Because we're going to sneak around once we get there, right?"

"No, we're not sneaking," she said. "Once we get the key from Ekaterina, we're going

287

to do a little discreet investigation."

"Ekaterina?"

"My mole inside the Inn," she said. "She's a supervisor in housekeeping. She's lending us her master key. We need to be discreet, so we don't get her in trouble. But there's no need to sneak. And for that matter, there's nothing more conspicuous in a four-star hotel than someone acting furtive. We march right in like people who have a perfectly good reason for being here."

"And just in case anyone asks, what is our perfectly good reason?"

She pondered for a few moments. I hoped she came up with her good reason soon, because we were turning into the Inn's driveway. Which meant we were still a mile or so from the front door, but I was nervously expecting to be stopped at any moment.

"I'm planning a fund-raiser," she said finally. "I want to see if the Inn's a suitable venue."

"Wouldn't they assume you already knew whether it was a suitable venue?" I asked. "You've only been here a couple of dozen times, visiting Grandfather."

"But never when I was planning a fund-raiser," she said. "You look at a place differently when you're thinking about whether you can squeeze in four or five hundred well-heeled guests and how much trouble it will give your caterer. Don't worry — if you don't think you can carry it off, just leave it to me. You know nothing, you're just being kind enough to give me a ride. Ah, here we are. Try for a shady spot near the door."

Normally we'd be lucky to find even a sunbaked spot a quarter mile from the hotel, but to my surprise the lot was half empty. I actually could find a spot relatively close to the wisteria-framed door and shaded by the huge, raspberry-colored flowers of the crepe myrtles that dotted the parking lot. Not that the shade would help much — the car would still be an oven when we returned. The parking lot was paved with gleaming white gravel and the whole thing shimmered with heat in the July sun. I hadn't even stepped out of the van and I was already eager to get inside where it was air-conditioned.

I parked, and Caroline helped me arrange the sun shields in both sides of the front windshield before we headed for the entrance. We were halfway across the parking lot when a voice rang out.

"Stop!"

Caroline and I both started guiltily, froze, and whirled to see a young man in the

289

muted green uniform of the Inn's landscaping staff running after us, waving his arms.

"Come back!" he shouted. "You can't park there."

"Get rid of him," Caroline hissed. She strode on toward the front door, leaving me to deal with the groundskeeper who was so intent on spoiling our unobtrusive arrival.

"You can't —" the groundskeeper began.

"Shh!" I said. And then I grabbed my head as if suffering from a hideous headache. "No yelling, please," I whispered. "Do you know what it's like when you have a migraine and someone keeps yelling?"

I was very proud of myself. I hadn't actually lied and said I had a migraine.

"Sorry," he whispered. "It's just that you can't park there right now. We're about to regravel."

Of course. The Caerphilly Inn prided itself on the perfection of its housekeeping and landscaping, and the pristine white gravel of the parking lot was marred here and there with spots of oil — no doubt from plebian vehicles like mine.

"Oh, right," I whispered back. "I always wondered whether they regraveled or power washed the stones."

"Power washing!" He snorted, and forgot to whisper. "Yeah, management thought that would be such a great idea, because labor's so cheap. You know what happens when you power wash a gravel parking lot?"

I shook my head — gently, with one hand to my temple, to maintain the appearance of someone who shouldn't be interrogated while bravely coping with a migraine.

"Neither did management," he said, dropping back into a stage whisper. "You turn a power hose on this sucker and it's going to send all that gravel flying. Could have graveled the parking lot a dozen times with what they paid out in paint jobs and new windows for all the Mercedes and Jaguars they didn't move far enough away. And they fired the poor guys they ordered to do the power washing. Like it was their fault. No, we're back to re-graveling. And we make sure all the vehicles are well clear of the part we're working on. Even the ones that look like that."

I winced, and then realized he wasn't pointing at my van but at an old and somewhat battered Chevy sedan at the far end of the lot.

"You don't happen to know where he is, do you?" he asked.

"He?"

"Belongs to that PI fellow," the grounds-

291

keeper said. "Didn't I hear that you know him?"

My, how rumors got around in Caerphilly. I shook my head.

"Not well," I said. "Though as it happens, I've been looking for him myself. I take it you've checked his room?"

"Called three times this morning, and knocked once. But apparently he never came back to his room last night." From his tone, I gathered that this was unacceptable behavior for a guest. Or was it Denton's profession that put him beyond the pale? "His car hasn't been moved since last night. And we sent out notices yesterday afternoon and again this morning about moving all vehicles to the south lot. So if you find him, you might tell him to come and move it. The tow truck's on its way. If he hurries up and moves it in the next half hour or so, he can save himself the cost of the tow."

"If I see him I'll tell him. You do realize that he works for some of your more distinguished guests."

"Yeah, but they don't know where he is either," he said. "And from the sound of it, they're not too pleased with him at the moment. You could tell him that, too."

I nodded and returned to my van. Now that I was looking for it, I spotted the small tasteful sign, printed in the sort of frilly, elegant cursive typeface normally reserved for wedding invitations. Once you got close enough to decipher it, you could see that it read

Please park in the south parking lot today due to construction. Management apologizes for the inconvenience.

Probably more of an inconvenience for the valet parking staff than anyone else. Odds were at least half the guests couldn't care less where their cars were parked as long as someone fetched them quickly enough when they wanted them. I found a space at the far end of the south parking lot, and trudged back to the Inn.

I cringed inwardly when I reached the front door and the uniformed attendant scrambled to hold it open for me, bowing deeply.

"Good afternoon, Ms. Langslow," he said. So much for anonymity.

Caroline was waiting inside, tapping her foot impatiently.

"Don't skulk," she said to me. "You have just as much a right to be here as any of them."

She waved her arm as if the lobby were

filled with haughty plutocrats sneering at us. Actually, it was empty, except for two bored-looking businessmen seated by the fireplace reading copies of *The Wall Street Journal* and looking at their watches every few seconds.

"They're paying to be here," I murmured.

"So has your grandfather, plenty of times over the years," Caroline said.

"Are you sure we can't help you, madame?"

We both started slightly at finding the bell captain at our elbows.

"No, no," Caroline said. "For now, I just need to visualize."

She held up both hands to create a frame in a gesture I'd seen painters and photographers make to assess the pictureworthiness of some bit of scenery. Then she nodded approvingly.

"Very nice," she muttered. "Meg — follow me!"

She began striding briskly through the lobby. I had been trying to study the two businessmen out of the corner of my eye, wondering if they worked for the Evil Lender, and she caught me by surprise. I had to hurry to catch up with her.

"So whose room are we burgling first?" I asked, sotto voce.

"Inspecting," she said. "And I think we'll do the PI first."

"Not that way, then," I said, grabbing her arm. "That leads to the cottages. I doubt if they put the PI in the cottages."

"Oh, right," Caroline said. "Force of habit."

I understood. I'd almost taken the same route myself.

Nowadays, Grandfather had his own suite at the farm that Mother and Dad used as their summer cottage. But back when he had first begun coming to Caerphilly, he'd frequently stayed in one of the Inn's three cottages. The Washington Cottage was a miniature replica of Mount Vernon, the Jefferson Cottage resembled Monticello, and the Madison Cottage was loosely inspired by Montpelier. All three were decorated with acres of chintz and a mixture of real antiques and pricey reproductions. And given their inflated price tags, even the Evil Lender hadn't rented the cottages for their minions — although they had been known to house visiting senior vice presidents there.

A pity we didn't have any senior vice presidents to burgle. All three cottages had multiple French doors opening out onto the terraces with their panoramic view of the golf course. They'd have been relatively easy to break into, even without Ekaterina's help.

Caroline had been fumbling in her purse and emerged, triumphant, with a slip of paper.

"Here it is," she said. "The Annex, room 212."

"That makes sense. This way." I turned away from the elevator and led the way to a long and much more modest corridor tucked away nearby.

"What is this Annex place, anyway?" Caroline asked. "Is it new?"

"No, it's fairly old, although they've renovated it nicely," I said. "It's the servants' quarters. If someone brings along their personal maid, or their nanny, or their private secretary, the Annex is where the Inn puts them."

"Rather insulting for poor Mr. Denton," Caroline said, with a sniff.

"I expect he's seen worse." I stopped by a smaller elevator. "This leads to the Annex. Shouldn't we get the key before we go up? Where is Ekaterina meeting us?"

"She doesn't want to be seen with us," Caroline said, as she punched the elevator button. "She's hidden the key in a dead drop near Mr. Denton's room."

"A dead drop?"

"Her idea," Caroline said. "Her father

used to spy for the CIA in Moscow back in the Cold War days. Or so she says. Don't worry — she gave me instructions."

When we stepped out onto the second floor of the Annex, I decided that the maids and nannies weren't too badly treated. We were walking on lush wall-to-wall carpet instead of an oriental rug, and there was far less marble and gilding than in the other wings, but I felt a lot more at home.

Caroline was slowly walking up and down the hallway, studying each of the paintings. I'd never known her to be particularly obsessive about art, so I deduced she was looking for the key.

When she reached the far end of the hall she stopped and turned around with a puzzled look on her face.

"That's odd," she said. "I don't see it."

"Don't see what?"

"The dead drop. Ekaterina was going to tuck her master key — actually it's one of those electronic key cards — behind a bit of loose baseboard beneath the painting of a policeman."

I walked back down the hall. None of the paintings contained a policeman. They were all landscapes. Landscapes or seascapes. Some of them had tiny figures, but they appeared to be peasants waving scythes, or sailors pulling oars. Some of the paintings looked vaguely familiar, so I suspected they were expensive reproductions of works by well-known landscape painters.

"Very odd," Caroline said. "Look more closely to see if any of the landscapes have policemen in them."

Looking closely took a while. I'd peered at every tiny little human figure in half a dozen paintings before enlightenment dawned. I straightened up.

"This," I announced. "Is a Turner. I remember it from art appreciation class. I didn't quite sleep through the whole lecture on eighteenth-century English painters."

"Does it have a policeman in it?" Caroline asked. She scurried over and began peering at the Turner.

"No, it's a landscape," I said. "Turner was noted for his landscapes."

"If he doesn't paint policemen, I don't care what he's noted for," she said. "Find me a policeman."

"Noted for his landscapes," I repeated. "So was Constable. John Constable, Turner's fellow landscape artist."

Caroline straightened up and frowned at me.

"Come to think of it, Ekaterina probably did say constable," she said. "She learned her English from the BBC before she moved here. Uses a lot of Anglicisms. I just thought this was another of them. So which one is the Constable?"

"Damned if I know," I said. "All those eighteenth-century British landscapes look alike to me. And none of them seemed to have signed their work. Ekaterina must be an unusually literate maid."

"She's working her way through grad school," Caroline said. "I suppose we'll have to check under all the paintings."

"You take the left side," I said. "I'll take the right."

It took another ten minutes and another rush to hide, this time in the ice/vending room.

"In the unlikely event that we ever burgle the Inn again," I said, as I fumbled at yet another spot on the baseboard, "let's ask Ekaterina for a better dead drop."

"This was a better dead drop than her first idea," Caroline said. "She wanted to leave the key card inside a rat."

"A rat? Like a dead rat?"

"Freeze-dried, actually," Caroline said, with a grimace. Rats, apparently, were one of the few inhabitants of the animal kingdom that hadn't won her heart. "Standard CIA issue, according to her. Her father and his handler used to exchange messages that way all the time."

"What do you do with it once you've put the message in it?" I asked.

"Leave it on a street corner, I suppose." Caroline shrugged. "The idea is that no one but the intended recipient would pick up a dead rat."

"Wouldn't that make the spies rather conspicuous, then?" I suggested. "Going around picking up dead rats all the time. 'Oh, look, Boris! That man over there is picking up the dead rat! Must be another CIA operative!' "

"It's no stranger than the exploding cigar story," Caroline said. "And it doesn't matter if it's true or not. Ekaterina believes it. The only way I could talk her out of the idea was to point out that neither of us happened to have a dead rat available for freeze-drying, and as an animal lover I could never condone killing one on purpose. Aha! This must be it!"

She waved the key card in triumph.

We returned to room 212. There was a DO NOT DISTURB sign on the door. I grabbed Caroline's arm as she was about to use the key card.

"What if he's here?" I pointed at the sign.

"I asked Ekaterina to do that." She gently

shook off my hand and reached to insert the card in the reader. "I thought it would be better if we could see the room just as he left it."

I had a sudden, vivid image of Denton's body sprawled on the floor of the room in the same awkward pose in which we'd found Colleen Brown.

"Let me go first," I said.

Maybe Caroline had the same vision, because she made no protest as I took the key card out of her hand.

I stepped up to the door and knocked.

"Mr. Denton?" I kept both voice and knock low, designed to be heard inside the room, not up and down the hall by any fellow guests who happened to be in their rooms. I knocked a second time, then, after listening at the door for a few more moments, I dipped the key card in the slot, opened the door, and stepped inside the room.

CHAPTER 26

The room was empty. Empty, at least, of humans, living or dead. Apparently I wasn't developing psychic powers after all, just an overactive imagination.

It wasn't my imagination that Caroline also breathed a sigh of relief.

"Well," she said, as she looked around. "It's certainly not the Washington Cottage."

Actually, Denton's room in the Annex wasn't bad at all. The ceilings were normal height; the furniture was nice but didn't look as if it belonged in a museum; and best of all, there wasn't a scrap of chintz in sight. Lots of tweed. The huge reproductions of landscapes had given way to reproductions of antique botanical prints. I had the feeling if I were one of the maids or nannies I'd probably breathe a sigh of relief when the end of the day arrived and I could flee the expensive, impeccable, and overwhelming halls of the main wings for the more plebian yet cozier comfort of the Annex. I shut the door behind us, and Caroline and I both relaxed slightly at having put a barrier between us and any onlookers. Well, I did. Caroline was looking around in her sharp, birdlike way.

"Not too bad," she said. "Now what are we looking for?"

"You're the one who arranged the key," I said. "What did you plan on looking for?"

"I have no idea," she said. "That's why I also arranged you. Use that brain Monty keeps bragging you inherited from him and figure out what we need to find."

"Like pornography, I will know it when I see it," I said.

I was looking out the window. Carefully, at first, since the curtains were open, and I had no idea if there was anyone outside to see me.

Clearly Denton had not found favor with the management. His room looked down on the loading dock and its concrete apron lined with Dumpsters. Though if you kept your eyes elevated, you could gaze out at a small copse of trees that shielded the loading dock from the view of any golfers on the course. You could even catch a glimpse of one of the greens.

A lesser hotel might have advertised this

as a room with a balcony, since the window was actually a sliding glass door — clearly added during a modern remodel — with a foot-wide ledge outside. The ledge was fitted with a nice, sturdy waist-high railing to keep the guests from plunging down to the concrete if they had any momentary lapses of memory and thought they were in a room classy enough to have a full-sized balcony. The ledge extended beyond the window on either side, and each end was decorated with a large clay pot containing bright purple petunias.

I glanced up and down the side of the annex. I saw no other curtains open and no one leaning on their railings to take the air — not that the air would be all that delightful this close to the Dumpsters baking in the July heat. And even if the distant golfers took a break from their game to look our way, the distance and the glare would keep them from seeing what we were up to, so I left the curtains open.

"Leave the lights off," I said. "And let's start with a general search, paying particular attention to any interesting papers we find."

"Good thinking," she said. "Here."

She handed me a three-inch by four-inch plastic zip bag marked EXAM GLOVES: 2 LATEX-FREE, LARGE, POWDER-FREE VINYL

EXAM GLOVES. Dad kept dozens of these in his doctor's bag. I wonder if Caroline had raided her own first aid kit or if Dad had helped provision our expedition.

I pulled the gloves on, pocketed the little bag, and began my search.

Luckily Denton appeared to be a light packer, which would make our search a little easier. His empty suitcase was in the closet, along with a sports jacket, several pairs of pants, and a couple of shirts. They filled the closet — an incredibly tiny closet for a hotel room. Presumably maids and nannies weren't expected to bring extensive wardrobes. Denton's shaving kit sat on the bathroom counter, and the few toiletries not inside it were arranged neatly on the counter.

"Tidy, for a man," Caroline said.

"Unless the maids have tidied up after him," I said.

"No." Caroline shook her head. "I thought we'd want to see it just as he left it, so I had Ekaterina put it at the end of her schedule. So it's him who's neat."

"Or he hasn't been home since they cleaned yesterday. The bed's still made."

"Some people do make their beds, you know," she said.

"In a hotel? Not many. He travels light,

305

doesn't he?"

Caroline gave a last look around and abandoned the bathroom. I poked around for a few more minutes, but I had to admit that if there was something to be found, it would take a more expert hunter than me.

"This armoire is locked!" Caroline called out.

I stepped out of the bathroom to find her rattling the armoire's doors vigorously, as if she hoped to shake them open.

"Don't get too excited," I said. "The key's sitting right there on the dresser."

I found only the usual Bible and stationery in the bedside drawer, so I went over to see what Caroline had found in the armoire. A modest TV with two drawers underneath filled the right side while the left offered more hanging space to make up for the small size of the closet. Denton hadn't needed the overflow. He'd stashed his socks and underwear in the top drawer. The second one contained a laptop and a small collection of papers.

"Bingo!" Caroline said. "You boot up the laptop; I'll start photographing these."

She set the papers on top of the desk and pulled out a small digital camera. I brought the laptop over and set it beside the papers.

"Here," I said, as I hit the laptop's power

switch. "You watch this while it boots. I can take the photos for a while. I'm tall enough to get a better angle anyway." I also knew, from seeing the fuzzy, crooked pictures she took of the animals at the Willner Wildlife Sanctuary that Caroline was a singularly inept digital photographer, and while my shots of the boys might not be award winners, they were at least in focus more often than not.

"Thank you, dearie," Caroline said.

I concentrated on getting good, sharp shots of Denton's papers, but I scanned them as I worked, and I wasn't spotting any earth-shattering new information. I found three weekly progress reports, addressed to Mr. Leonard Fisher of First Progressive Financial, the last one dated three days ago. Not exactly page turners — mostly they were long lists of the people he'd interviewed and the tiny scraps of information he gained from them.

"Not making much progress, is he?" Caroline said, when I'd finished photographing the last of the reports.

"Don't gloat," I said. "Neither are we."

"At least he does appear to be doing what he said he was doing," she said. "Trying to find out how Mr. Throckmorton has been getting his supplies."

"I don't like how much energy he spends asking about secret passages," I said. "And looking for them."

"Looking inside the courthouse," Caroline said. "He won't find anything like that inside the parts of the courthouse he can reach. Speaking of not finding things — your PI fellow has a password on his laptop. We're not going to find out much information from it unless you can guess what it is."

"Then we won't find out much from it," I said. "Because I haven't a clue what he'd use as a password. Get Rob to find you a hacker with a password cracking program."

"Okay," she said. "If you won't even bother to try, I'll turn it off and see if I can fit it in my purse. Then —"

"We are not taking that laptop with us," I said. "You snuck in once with me, you can sneak in again with Rob's hacker, once he finds you one."

I could tell she was about to argue with me, but just then someone knocked on the door.

"Denton!" a male voice said. "Are you in there?"

Caroline and I froze. Then she scrambled toward the armoire.

"Lock me in," she whispered. "And then

you can get out through the window."

"They probably won't come in," I whispered back. "And if they do, then they're burgling the place, just like us, and the armoire is the first place they'll look. We'll both just have to go out the window."

"What about the laptop? And the papers? We —"

"Leave them!" I whispered. "Let's move!"

"Denton?" The man outside knocked again. And he was using the same discreetly low voice and firm but soft knock I'd used.

"There's no one there," another voice said. "Shut up and hurry up."

"Quick!" the first voice said. "Someone's coming."

The door didn't pop open immediately, which probably meant that this new set of burglars was hiding from someone passing by, just as Caroline and I had.

Thank goodness for passersby. Meanwhile, we'd reached the window. I looked down. We were only on the second floor, but the ground sloped down behind the hotel, and it was at least a two-story jump to the concrete loading dock below.

I pulled the sliding glass door open and grabbed the left curtain to pull it closed.

"Grab the other side," I whispered. I was moving the potted petunias so they were in front of the window, leaving the less visible ends of the ledge for us. "Pull it closed. And then take the other end of the ledge."

"We shouldn't jump?" Caroline whispered.

"They'd hear the sound of our bodies going splat on the loading dock," I whispered back. "This is the best we can do."

I backed out onto the ledge and then stepped sideways over the petunias. It wasn't easy to wedge myself into the narrow space between the railing and the side of the hotel. I suddenly wondered if Caroline could do it.

Caroline grabbed the other side of the curtain, pulled it closed, and then began trying to squeeze into her end of the balcony. After a few fruitless attempts to wedge herself in, she used the petunia pot to give her a leg up and sat on the railing with her rump hanging over the outside. I suspected her perch felt as precarious as it looked and wondered, for a moment, if the ledge and the railing were really designed to hold this much weight.

I thought of closing the sliding glass door, but before I could do it, we heard the door opening.

The carpet underfoot muffled the intruders' footsteps — that and the wool curtain between us and them — but we heard the door close again.

"Not much here," one of the voices said after a moment.

"He's not stupid enough to leave anything important lying out in the open," said another voice. A familiar voice — one of our rival burglars was Leonard Fisher.

"No, sir."

"Do a thorough search," Fisher ordered. "And bring me any papers you find so I can check them out."

"Yes, sir." Two voices, in almost perfect unison.

"Stuffy in here, sir," one voice said after a moment. "Shall we open the curtains?"

Caroline shifted slightly. I hoped she was preparing to come out fighting, not to go over the railing.

"Just turn up the AC," Fisher said. "I don't want to take any chance of being spotted."

"Yes, sir."

A few seconds later, I heard the hum and rattle of the HVAC unit kicking in. I breathed a small sigh of relief. Not that we'd benefit from the cold air, since we were outside in the broiling sun with the curtain between us and the AC, but at least the noise of the compressor would camouflage any small sounds Caroline and I made.

If only we could camouflage ourselves from possible onlookers outside. Luckily, the Annex was the only part of the hotel with windows overlooking the loading dock area, and the occupants of those rooms would have to step onto their ledges to see us. But the golfers would have a great view, if any of them happened to look this way. Or anyone who made a delivery to the hotel. Even a staff member coming out on the loading dock to smoke, as a discreetly placed ash tray suggested some did. To anyone who bothered to look up instead of straight ahead, we were about as unobtrusive as a black cat on a snow-covered roof.

But since there was nothing I could do to make us any less visible, I focused my attention back to what was going on in the room.

"If anyone spots us, pretend to be washing the windows," Caroline hissed.

I realized that if I leaned as far as I could to the left, I could get one eye next to the place where the two sides of the curtains came together. I could only see a small fraction of the room, but since that fraction included the desk, on which we'd left the papers and the laptop lying, it was potentially an interesting fraction.

Leonard Fisher was sitting at the desk, leafing slowly through the papers I'd photographed. I caught an occasional glimpse of an arm or a leg clad in dark blue with red trim. From those glimpses, and from the sounds we were hearing, I deduced that uniformed Flying Monkeys were doing a rapid and thorough search of the room — and probably being a lot less careful than Caroline and I had been to avoid leaving any signs of our presence. Meanwhile, Fisher had booted the laptop and discovered the password screen. He made a few unsuccessful attempts to log in before frowning, muttering something under his breath, and turning the machine off again.

Caroline and I had a bad moment when one of the guards came over and searched the folds of the curtains. I jerked my head back from the opening. Caroline actually tucked her head down and under one arm, in a fair imitation of a sleeping bird, as if she could prevent him from seeing her if she didn't see him.

Luckily, the guard was so focused on the curtains that he never looked out. And also luckily, he left the curtains very much as he had found them, so there was still a tiny gap for me to peek through when he moved off again.

A few minutes later the guards had fin-ished their search.

"Nothing, sir." One of them came to stand at Fisher's elbow, rather like a dog coming to heel.

"Take that." Fisher pointed to the laptop. I saw Caroline stir slightly. For a moment, I was worried that she'd leap out from behind the curtains to wrestle the guard for the laptop. I reached over and patted her shoul-der a couple of times. She became still again, but I could tell from the tension in her shoulder that she didn't like it.

"Wait for me down at the car," Fisher said.

"Yes, sir," the two voices said in unison.

The room door opened and closed again. Fisher glanced over, as if to make sure the guards were on the other side of it. Then he pulled out his cell phone and punched some buttons.

"It's me," he said. "No luck."

Evidently whoever was on the other side of the call had a lot to say in response, and was saying it rather loudly. Fisher moved the phone ever so slightly farther away from his ear and waited, staring at the botanical print above the desk.

"I realize that," he finally said. "But I can't find it if it's not here to be found. And if you want my guess, I don't think he has it."

More listening.

"Absolutely," Fisher said. "It's the only reason I can see for that whole crazy stunt."

I found myself wishing Fisher would find some reason to put his phone on speaker. I had a feeling I could learn a lot if I heard both sides of this conversation.

"No." Fisher was starting to sound annoyed. "It's the only copy. . . . Well, it is now. . . . No, like I keep telling you, a photocopy's useless. Same thing for a scan. Too easy to forge. If both sides show up with a photocopy, it's a he said/she said thing, and we can win that. They show up with the original and we're sunk."

Caroline poked me, and pointed at the crack in the curtain. Did she think I wasn't already listening to every word?

"That's what I'm trying to do," Fisher said. "I'll fill you in later."

He punched a button or two and then stuck the phone in his pocket as if glad to be rid of it.

He looked around, frowning, as if dissatisfied with his surroundings. Was he doubting the thoroughness of the guards' search? Had he only just noticed that they'd not only searched but trashed the room? I'd assumed either that they didn't care who knew the room was searched or that they were hop-

315

ing to leave a message for Denton.

Suddenly he strode over to the window. Caroline and I drew back and quailed in our separate corners of the ledge.

"No wonder this place is such an oven," he muttered. I heard him slide the glass door closed and then latch it.

"Great," I muttered. "Now we're really stuck."

CHAPTER 27

"Sssh!" Caroline hissed.

"If we keep it quiet, he can't hear us with the window closed," I whispered. I was peering into the room again. "And it's okay. He's gone now."

"It's not okay," Caroline said. "I'm stuck here on this wretched little balcony with my bum hanging over the railing, clinging for dear life to a geranium plant."

"They're petunias," I said.

"Whatever. I'm not a botanist. How are you going to get me down from here?"

"I have my cell phone," I said. "Do you have Ekaterina's number?"

Of course, it took rather a lot of careful wriggling to extricate my cell phone from my pocket without knocking myself off the balcony. And after all that, Ekaterina's phone rang on unanswered.

"She probably turns it off when she's working," I said.

"She could put the damned thing on vibrate!"

"Maybe she has and will call us back as soon as she can," I said, in my most soothing tone.

"As soon as she can may be too late," Caroline said. "I'm not sure how much longer I can hang on."

I took a closer look and realized that she wasn't exaggerating. I'd managed to wedge myself between the rail and the side of the hotel, but even so my perch felt precarious. Caroline was perched on the rail and wobbled alarmingly. To keep from falling, she had to hold on to the rail and the petunia pot, which meant she was supporting a lot of her weight with her arms — and she didn't have the same upper body strength that my blacksmithing gave me.

I had to do something.

If I'd had any kind of metal tool, I might have tried breaking the window, but the closest thing I had to a hard object was my phone, and I didn't think it would survive an abrupt encounter with triple-paned glass. I glanced down. If I could crawl over the railing and dangle from it as far down as possible before letting go, I would probably survive the fall. I might not even break anything if I relaxed.

At least that was what Rob would tell me. He was a total klutz but claimed he'd never broken a bone in any of his mishaps. According to him, the key was to retrain yourself so when you realized you were falling, your reaction was not "Oh no! I'm falling! I'll break every bone in my body!" but "Hey, cool, I seem to be falling again."

But so far, my attempts to retrain myself had not been successful, and I suspected that the most important factor in falling safely was having a laid-back temperament. I'd never qualify.

Think positively, I told myself.

"Where do you have the key card?" I asked Caroline.

"In my right pocket," she said. "But I don't dare let go to fish it out."

At least it was in the pocket on my side. I managed to lean over and fish out the room key card. I also snagged her cell phone and put it on the dirt in the geranium pot, where she might have a chance of reaching it if she needed it. Then I began carefully climbing over the rail.

"What are you doing?" Caroline asked.

"I'm going to use my ninja training to jump down and land lightly on the loading dock," I said. "And then I go around to the front of the hotel, walk in like someone who knows she has a perfect right to be here, and hurry back up to the room so I can unlock the sliding glass door from the inside."

"Use your ninja super-speed while you're at it, dearie," Caroline said.

"I'll try." By this time, I was dangling from the bottom of the railing, arms stretched as far as they would go. The gap between my feet and the concrete seemed to be at least the length of a football field, Maybe two football fields. "If by some chance I kill myself, is there any chance you could manage to call 911? Just tell them to come and pick up the dead ninja on the loading dock."

"I'll tell them two dead ninjas," Caroline said. "Because if you go splat, I don't think I can hold on until they get here."

I closed my eyes, took a deep breath, and let go.

CHAPTER 28

"Meg? Are you all right? Speak to me!"

Easier said than done. I'd dropped and rolled with beautiful form — my old martial arts teacher would have been proud of me. Unfortunately, while rolling, I'd managed to hit my solar plexus on something — probably my own knee — and I didn't have enough breath to answer her. And her back was to me, and she couldn't turn around without falling off the ledge.

"I'm fine," I croaked.

Apparently she didn't hear me.

"Help! Help!" she began shouting.

"Ssshhh," I hissed, as loudly as I could. The hissing sound carried only slightly better than my feeble croaks.

"Meg?"

I was near a garbage can. I tapped out "shave and a haircut — two bits" on it with one foot.

"Lost your breath?"

I kicked the can twice. Then I staggered to my feet.

"Fetching help!" I wheezed. I checked the loading dock doors, but unfortunately they were all locked, so I stumbled off to circumnavigate the hotel.

By the time I reached the front door, I'd gotten my wind back, and my stomach had mostly stopped hurting. I nodded graciously to the doorman as he let me in. If he was puzzled that he'd now let me into the hotel twice without letting me out in between, his calm face didn't show it.

The two businessmen were still by the fireplace — or two others remarkably like them had taken their place. Leonard Fisher was sitting at a table in the lobby bar with a glass and a Perrier bottle on his table, reading some papers. I wasn't sure my imitation of someone with a good reason to be at the Inn would hold up nearly as well if I had to talk to him, so I was relieved when I made it through the lobby without attracting his notice. I picked up the pace once I got into the corridor to the Annex, ran up the stairs instead of waiting for the elevator, and sprinted down the hall to 212.

"What took you so damn long?" Caroline said when I opened the sliding glass door.

"Nice to see you, too," I said.

It took a while to get her inside the room. I finally leaned out and grabbed the back of her blouse and the waist of her pants so I could haul her in.

"Just stop gripping the railing," I ordered. "I've got you now."

"I'm not sure I can," she said. "I think my hands are paralyzed."

"Hurry up, or I'm going to lose my grip on you."

That worked. She let go so suddenly that we both landed in a heap on the floor inside the door. I managed to roll out from under her and lay back on the floor panting.

"Okay, they're not paralyzed, but they have gone numb from holding on so tightly," she said, grimacing as she slowly flexed her fingers. "And I'm dehydrated as hell. I'll be lucky if I don't have heatstroke."

"You want me to call Dad?" I said. "I could take you over to have him look at you."

"Maybe later," she said. "Follow me."

I was expecting her to lead the way to our next burglary target, but she charted an unerring course to the lobby bar. Leonard Fisher was still there, nursing his Perrier. We nodded at each other. Caroline and I took a table as far from him as possible, and a waiter scurried up.

"How may I help you, ladies?" he asked.

"A pitcher of water," I said.

"I'll have a martini," Caroline gasped.

"If you really are worried about dehydration, you should have some water," I said.

"Make it a double," Caroline said. "And a pitcher of water for me, too."

"Good," I said. "And you should drink the water first."

"Drink it?" Caroline snorted. "I plan to pour it over my head."

The waiter bowed and disappeared.

"I don't think I can go on," Caroline said.

"Of course you can." I wanted to ask "Go on with what?" Surely our adventure hadn't soured her on life.

"No, I can't. We'll have to finish this another day."

I was relieved. Apparently she was only giving up on today's plans. I glanced at my watch. Almost noon. Amazing how time-consuming a life of crime could be.

"That's okay," I said. "I think we got the most important burgling done. I doubt if the Evil Lender's execs keep many sensitive documents in their rooms."

The waiter returned. He set Caroline's martini in front of her, and put a pitcher of ice water and a tumbler of ice on my side of the table. Then he set a second pitcher, this one without ice, at Caroline's elbow, along with a thick white bath towel, a matching washcloth, and a large porcelain bowl. Then he bowed and slipped away. Much as I railed against the Inn's inflated prices, I couldn't fault their notion of service.

"Ahhh." Caroline took a large sip of her martini — actually more like a gulp — and sat back in her chair.

"I think he overheard you," I said. "And took you seriously about dunking yourself."

"I may yet," she said. "You're probably right — burgling anyone else would be useless as well. Denton was our best chance of learning something, and that was a complete bust."

"What do you mean a bust?" I asked. "We may not have found any interesting papers, but we did learn something. Or were you too busy hanging on to eavesdrop on Fisher?"

"I might have been a little distracted," she said. "Remind me."

I glanced over at Fisher. It seemed doubly odd to be sitting across the bar from him, discussing a conversation we'd overheard because his burglary coincided with ours. I repeated what he'd said.

"So they were looking for something they thought Denton might have," she said.

"Same as we were."

"Only ours was a random fishing expedition," I pointed out. "And they seemed to have something very specific in mind. They're looking for the original of some document that would cause them problems if we showed up in court with it."

"Doesn't help us much, does it," she said. She poured a little of the water from her pitcher onto the washcloth and began patting her face and the back of her neck with it. "Should we tell the chief?"

"It might be a little hard to explain how we happened to hear it," I said. "Besides, all we know is that they're looking for the original of a document. We have no idea what document."

"We could call your cousin," Caroline said. "Festus," she added, before I pointed out that I had enough cousins to populate a small city. "Isn't he still handling all of Caerphilly's battles with the Evil Lender?"

"Yes," I said. "Do you want to ask him to represent us when we're arrested for burglary?"

"We could ask him what kind of document would totally upset their applecart if we produced it in court."

I nodded, already pulling out my cell phone.

I got Festus's voice mail. At least a dozen times, Festus had reminded me and everyone else who would listen to him never to say anything in a voice mail or an e-mail that we wouldn't want to see on the front page of *The Washington Post.* So I left a cryptic message suggesting that we had some new thoughts on the case, and could he call me as soon as he got a chance.

"We should be going," I said, as I pocketed my phone again.

"Fine," she said, taking another strong pull on the martini. Another swallow and she'd have it finished. "I'll settle the bill if you bring the van around. I'm not sure I can walk with all this heat."

"Sounds like a plan," I said.

Outside I saw that the truck from Shiffley Towing had arrived, and Osgood Shiffley was hooking it up to Denton's old Chevy. I waved at him as I plodded toward the south parking lot.

As I expected, my van was an oven. I started it, rolled down all the windows, turned the fan on full blast, and then set the parking brake so I could step out and wait for the fan to blow out the worst of the hot air. I pulled out my cell phone to call Michael, then decided to wait a little while. If I called now, the shakiness in my voice might worry him.

A car drove up to the front door of the Inn and one of the bellhops stepped out. Leonard Fisher strode out of the hotel's front door, pressed a tip into the bellhop's hand, and drove off.

I watched him go with narrowed eyes. Just because he was the friendliest of the lender's minions didn't actually mean he was a good guy. Maybe he was just the designated good cop to the Flying Monkeys' bad cops.

Over at the far end of the lot, Osgood had finished hooking Denton's Chevy up to the tow truck and had stopped to take a long pull on a plastic water bottle.

Water. I'd finished most of my pitcher in the hotel, but I already felt parched again. I could get a bottle at the hotel gift shop. Or poach some from Caroline's pitcher. I stepped into the van and drove up to replace Fisher at the front door.

Fisher drove out at a faster pace than I'd have taken, spraying little bits of super-heated white gravel behind him. Osgood Shiffley was lumbering across the parking lot at a more stately pace, so Fisher beat him to the exit and gunned his car on the asphalt driveway.

Caroline met me at the curb.

"Damn," she said. "They're towing Denton's car. I was hoping we could search it before we left."

"I doubt if he left anything interesting in it," I said. "And if he did, what are the odds the Flying Monkeys didn't already get it?"

"Not good," she admitted.

"I'm going to run in to get some water," I said. "I'll leave the car running so you'll have the air-conditioning."

"I don't suppose you want to run over and ask Osgood to stop and let us have a look at the car?" she asked.

"No, I don't," I said. Osgood had reached the asphalt of the driveway now. "I plan to call Randall to see if we can ransack it once it gets to the impound lot."

"Good thinking," Caroline said. "Do you suppose —"

Just then Osgood accelerated and Denton's car exploded.

CHAPTER 29

"Call 911!" I shouted to Caroline as I dashed across the lot. "And stay back!"

"You stay back, too!" she shouted.

"Someone needs to check on Osgood."

We'd both been frozen for the first few moments, as bits of glass and metal rained down on the parking lot. Denton's car — what was left of it — was burning now, and since it was between me and the tow truck, I couldn't see what had happened to Osgood.

The explosion had set off the alarms in four or five of the cars in the south parking lot, but so far Caroline and I were the only people visible on the scene.

I made a wide circle around the burning car. To my relief, the tow truck wasn't totaled. The towing end of it was pretty badly damaged, but the cab was intact, and Osgood was sitting in it, blinking, looking stunned.

"Are you okay?" I had to shout to be heard over the car alarms and the roaring noise of the fire.

"What?"

Oh, great. I suspected he was temporarily deafened by the explosion. At least I hoped it would be temporary. But I figured it would be a good idea for both of us to get away from the car and the truck, in case the truck was about to explode, too. I opened the driver's side door and jerked my thumb over my shoulder in what I hoped was a pretty obvious "move it!" gesture. Osgood got it. He scrambled down from the cab and began half-walking, half-staggering away from the tow truck. He kept stopping to look back at the wreckage, and every time he did it, I'd tug at his arm again.

By the time we reached the hotel entrance, several guests and hotel staffers were standing on the sidewalk, gawking at the fire.

"Police, fire, and ambulance are on their way," Caroline said. "Osgood, are you okay?"

"My truck," Osgood said. "My truck." Knowing how he felt about his tow truck, I wasn't sure this was a non sequitur.

"Is the driveway completely blocked?" Caroline asked.

"I have no idea," I said. "Were you about

to suggest that we try to sneak away before the chief gets here?"

She sighed.

"Well, if we're not going to make a get-away, shouldn't we try to search some more rooms?" she asked quietly.

"In a few minutes the whole place will be crawling with cops," I said. "I think we should postpone doing anything illegal or even suspicious-looking until they're gone."

"But they're all our cops," she protested. "Chief Burke and his men."

"Not anymore," I said. "They already borrowed a bunch of officers from Clay County yesterday, and the chief said last night he was going to ask for help from his friend, the sheriff of Goochland County. And for all we know, the State Bureau of Investigation may have shown up by now. Maybe even the FBI."

She nodded.

"I'll be in the bar," she said. "I need another martini."

I turned to follow her inside.

"Ma'am? You can't leave that van here!"

I contemplated the long walk back from the south parking lot and turned to the bell-man.

"Unfortunately, my van is now part of the crime scene," I said. "Chief Burke would be very displeased if I moved it before he got here. Come on, Osgood."

I grabbed Osgood's arm and steered him inside. No use adding heatstroke on top of shell shock.

We joined Caroline in the bar. The notion of a martini sounded tempting, but I decided to stay optimistic and assume I'd be driving us home soon. So I ordered an iced tea for myself and one for Osgood.

Caroline looked as if she had something on her mind. When the waiter left with our orders, she looked at Osgood and frowned.

"Do you have the dingus?" she asked me.

"The dingus?" I repeated.

"The borrowed dingus," she elaborated.

"Oh, that dingus," I said. "Yes, it's in my pocket."

"Its owner called," she said. "She wants it back, ASAP. Can you put it back where we got it?"

"I'm not sure I remember exactly where we got it," I said. "And I think that's a place both she and we should be staying away from right now. But I have an idea. Tell the owner to go down to the loading dock in fifteen minutes. I will leave the dingus in a dead drop there. Don't worry — she'll recognize it immediately."

Caroline frowned, and clearly wanted to

ask more questions, but Osgood's presence inhibited her.

I went to the hotel gift shop, which I knew from previous experience contained an uncannily large selection of plush toys, at least a dozen of which had made their way into Josh and Jamie's cribs, courtesy of my doting grandfather.

I picked out a plush mouse with a long pink tail. I stopped off in the ladies room, where I used a pair of nail scissors to un-pick a few stitches and make a hole large enough to contain the key card.

I sat the mouse down at one edge of the loading dock with a fallen petunia blossom between his paws and made it back to the lobby in well under fifteen minutes.

Back in the bar, Osgood had begun to recover from the worst of his shock.

"It was a Vulcan," he was saying. "Brand-new this May."

"Was your insurance current?" Caroline asked.

"Of course," Osgood said. "But what a terrible thing to do to such a beautiful piece of machinery. A Vulcan."

He took a gulp of his iced tea and then stared at it with displeasure.

"I could use something a lot stronger than that," he said.

"So you could," Caroline said. "But not until after you talk to the chief. When you're finished with that, the first round's on me. And what luck! There he is now."

The chief was standing in the lobby, looking around. When he spotted us, he frowned.

"Uh-oh," I said.

"Do we come clean about what we were doing here?" Caroline asked.

"I think we have to," I said. "But I'm not looking forward to it."

But the chief left us to cool our heels while he interrogated first the groundskeeper who'd called the Shiffley Towing Company, and then Osgood.

Finally it was my turn. A deputy led me to the conference room the chief was using as his temporary office. Not, I noted, a Caerphilly deputy — I knew them all, at least by sight.

The chief was sitting near one end of a mahogany conference table only slightly smaller than my first apartment. He indicated a seat diagonally across from him, probably because if I sat directly across the table he'd need binoculars to see my expression. When I was seated, he fixed me with a look of stern disappointment, but he didn't say anything until the borrowed deputy left the room.

"And I'm sure there's a good reason why you and Caroline were here today," he said at last.

"No," I said. "Not a good reason — at least I don't expect you'd find it good. Caroline and I were . . . searching Mr. Denton's room."

The chief nodded. I reminded myself that just because he wasn't chewing me out for breaking and entering and, worse, interfering with his investigation, didn't mean we were off the hook. He could be saving up to do it later when he had time to do a really good job of it.

"I presume you'd finished by the time the car exploded," he said. "Did you find anything interesting?"

"Yes," I said. "Burglars. Other burglars," I clarified.

I could see his jaw clench, but he didn't immediately start chewing me out. Not necessarily a good sign.

"Are you sure these other people were not there with Mr. Denton's permission?" he asked.

"They ransacked the room," I said. "And took his laptop. They were wearing Flying Monkey uniforms. Leonard Fisher was with them, and he told them to leave the curtains closed so they wouldn't be spotted."

The chief nodded.

"And after the guards left, we overheard Mr. Fisher's side of a very interesting cell phone conversation."

I gave him a detailed account of our afternoon, including Leonard Fisher's hasty departure just ahead of the tow truck. When I'd finished, he sat, frowning for a few moments.

"Before you arrest me," I said, "or at least chew me out, may I ask a question?"

He raised one eyebrow in what I recognized as grudging permission.

"Do we know for sure that Stanley Denton wasn't in the car when it blew up?"

"No sign of human remains in the wreckage," he said.

I breathed a sigh of relief.

"We don't know he's all right," the chief said.

"But at least we know he's not blown to bits."

"Not here, anyway," he said. "If you hear from him before my officers find him, encourage him to drop by the police barn for a chat."

"Will do."

"And try a little harder to stay out of trouble."

He looked down at his notebook and I realized I was being dismissed.

I thought of half a dozen other questions I wanted to ask, and I was opening my mouth to start asking them, and then thought better of it. I seem to have survived the interview without ticking him off. Maybe I should keep it that way.

I tripped over my own feet in my haste to leave while I was ahead.

CHAPTER 30

Of course, once I had made my own escape,
I had to wait while the chief interviewed
Caroline. But within half an hour, we were
ready to depart. The wreckage was still
blocking the driveway, but one of the bell-
men directed us to a service road — after
apologizing profusely for the inconvenience,
giving the impression that he considered
the explosion an unforgivable departure
from the hotel's normally impeccable customer service.

I dropped Caroline as close as possible to
the tent, and then as soon as she was out of
earshot, called Rose Noire to warn her that
Caroline had had a tough day and could
use some cosseting.

"I'll fix her some herbal tea," Rose Noire
said.

"Good luck getting her to drink it," I said,
as I pulled my van into Michael's space.
"Unless you chill it and serve it to her in a

martini glass."

I hadn't meant it literally, but when I got back to the tent, I found Caroline sitting in my recliner with two fans blowing over her, a compress on her forehead, and another on her feet. She was staring dubiously at a highball glass containing a liquid that probably bore little resemblance to any concoction in the bartender's manual.

The fact that she hadn't already poured it out and demanded something better made me realize that Caroline was far from her usual energetic self. So when I had a chance I slipped back outside again, pulled out my cell phone, and called Dad.

"Could you drop by the tent when you get a chance and check on Caroline?" I asked him.

"Caroline? What's wrong?"

I hesitated. If I told him about our morning's adventures, would he be disappointed that I hadn't included him in on the burglary? Even if his morning had been filled with an unusually large number of interesting cases, I felt sure Dad would much rather have witnessed the car bomb.

Then again, he'd hear about it soon enough on the news anyway. In fact, I was surprised he hadn't already.

"Nothing in particular," I said. "Except

being chased by a sinister black van, clinging to the side of a building to avoid being
caught as a burglar, and seeing a car get
blown up. A day like that might be a little
hard on a senior citizen."

"Oh, my!" he exclaimed. "You have had a
morning! I wish I could have been there."

I braced myself for recriminations.

"Is she complaining of anything?"

"Only that Rose Noire won't bring her a
martini," I said. "But she looks a little wan.
Can you stop by?"

"I would if I were in town, but I'm down
in Richmond. For the autopsy on Colleen
Brown. I've got Dr. Smoot filling in for me
at the first aid tent. I could have him stop
by."

I had a momentary vision of Dr. Smoot
slipping furtively into the tent wearing his
black cape, looking like a refugee from a
cheesy fifties vampire flick.

"Dr. Smoot doesn't even have a good
bedside manner with dead people," I said.
"He'll either scare her to death or tick her
off."

"Good point," Dad said. "I'll send Clarence."

"I'm sure Caroline will love having a vet
examine her."

"He doesn't have to tell her he's examining her. He can pretend to be just fussing over her. And he's got enough medical knowledge to tell if she should be packed off to the ER, and she likes him well enough to go if he tells her to. And I'll check on her when I'm back this evening."

Back in the tent, Caroline appeared to be napping, her untouched herbal cocktail at her side. Rose Noire was poring over the clipboard.

"Clarence will be dropping by to make sure Caroline is all right," I said.

"Why not your dad?" Rose Noire asked.

"Dad's in Richmond," I said. "Ostensibly for the autopsy, although he might also be doing a little campaigning to get himself appointed as a local medical examiner."

"Oh, that would be so nice," she said. "He'd love that."

But would the chief love it? Maybe he would, if he knew Dr. Smoot was the alternative.

"Here comes another rug rat," Caroline called out. Not really asleep, then, but playing possum.

"Oh, dear." Rose Noire rushed toward the tent door. Lad, Seth Early's border collie, was herding in a toddler in a pink sundress. While Lad guarded the door in case his charge made a break for it, Rose Noire squatted down beside the girl — who, I was relieved to see, looked more cross than scared.

"What's your name, honey?" she asked.

"Bad doggie," the girl said. I suspected this wasn't an accurate answer to the question.

"He's not a bad doggie," Rose Noire said. "When little girls and boys get lost, he brings them here to wait until their parents can come to pick them up. Now what's your name, so we can tell your parents to come get you?"

"Emma," the girl said.

"Would you like to play with the other children until your parents come?"

"Other children?" I echoed. I glanced over at the pens. Three other children of assorted sizes and genders were playing in the front pen with the twins' toys or cuddling with Tinkerbell. Spike, I was relieved to see, had been exiled to the back pen.

"Here you go." Rose Noire lifted Emma into the pen, where after a moment, she toddled over to whack Tinkerbell affectionately on the head. "Juice, anyone?"

As soon as Emma was safely inside the pen, Lad gave a brisk, businesslike bark, then turned and trotted off.

"He's been herding in lost children all

343

day," she said. "We've had fifteen come and go already."

"Seems like an unusually high number," I said. "Are you sure they were all lost?"

"Well, they are now," she said. "As soon as we find Seth, we're going to see if he can train Lad to herd them over to the police tent instead."

"Better yet, get him to take Lad home," I suggested.

Just then Rose Noire glanced at her watch. I checked mine. Almost one.

"Light-years ago, before the murder, we had scheduled me to do a demonstration at one P.M. today," I said. "Please tell me you found a substitute."

"The bagpiper was available," she said.

"The good one?" I asked. "Or —"

Just then the bagpiper struck up his first few droning notes and answered my question.

"Don't worry!" Rose Noire shouted over the din. "Most people can't tell a well-played bagpipe from a badly played one!"

Just my luck to be in the unhappy minority. We'd had this particular bagpiper any number of times over the summer — though usually only as a last-minute substitute. I could already feel another bagpipe headache starting.

So while the bagpiper murdered his first number — probably, though not definitely, "Scotland the Brave" — I racked my brains for something that needed doing elsewhere. As far from the bandstand as possible.

Lunch.

I was ravenous, and in no mood to forage far afield. So I trotted over to the food tent area to test a theory.

And I was right. The salad wars had begun. The Episcopalians were doing such a booming business with the chicken Caesar salads that the Baptists had added a Cobb salad to their menu. Normally I waited in line with the tourists, but not today. I slipped behind the counter and caught Minerva's eye.

"Could I have a Cobb salad to go?" I said.

"Coming up," she said. "You see Henry out at the Inn?"

I nodded.

"How'd he look?"

I thought about it.

"Not too frazzled, under the circumstances."

She shook her head grimly, handed me two Cobb salads and a pair of iced teas, and pushed my hand away when I tried to pay.

"Thanks," I said. "But I only need the one."

"You keep the other one there in the tent, and if Henry shows up, make him eat it."

"Roger."

I was planning to go straight back to the tent, but I spotted my grandfather striding down the sidewalk, so I gave chase.

It took me till the far end of the town square to catch him. He was mopping his face with his handkerchief.

"What are you doing here?" I asked Grandfather. I realized a few seconds too late that the words sounded a bit rude. "Shouldn't you be inside out of this horrible heat?" I added.

"I won't be out here for long," he said. "Just going to sit here in the shade. I could even cool off by sipping some iced tea if I could find anyone thoughtful enough to bring me some."

"If I gave you one of these, do you suppose I could persuade you to sip it inside where it's cooler?" I asked. I held one out without waiting for his answer.

"Inside won't work," he said. "I'm going to inspect that vulture trainer's work. Ah, there he is now."

Mr. Doane was approaching us. Instead of carrying a bird on his arm, he was pulling a small wheeled cage. Grandfather rose and stood with crossed arms, frowning slightly.

"Here she is!" Doane's voice reminded me strangely of the proud tones with which Michael introduced the twins. I'd also seen the cool analytical gaze with which Grandfather was inspecting the occupant of the cage. I'd seen him turn it on the boys often enough, and I could never tell if he was feeling family pride or comparing their behavior to the young of other primates. He sipped his iced tea several times during his leisurely inspection.

"Cathartes aura," he said eventually. "Turkey vulture," he translated for those of us not up on our scientific Latin. "One of the few vultures that finds carcasses by smell."

"Exactly!" Doane exclaimed. "Most New World vultures and all of the Old World ones are sight hunters, and that would be useless for my project. I call her Nekhbet," he added. "After the Egyptian vulture goddess."

"Good name," Grandfather said. "And she's a fine specimen."

I wasn't sure what was so fine about her. Nekhbet was about two and a half feet tall, with brownish black feathers. Her legs and feet were chalky white and her head was

347

bright red, featherless, and oddly small compared with the rest of her. I could easily imagine that head perched atop a rather large lizard.

"You do realize it's illegal to keep them in captivity?" Grandfather asked.

"I am a certified wildlife rehabilitator!" Doane drew himself up to his full height. And then his face fell. "That's part of the problem, really. Up until recently, the only birds I've had to work with are the ones I'm rehabilitating. And around the time I began to see some real progress with them, I'd have to release them back into the wild. But now that I've finally got permission for my work, I hope to make more progress."

"You going to show me now?" Grandfather asked.

"If you want to, sure," Doane said. "Beats hanging around waiting in case your police chief releases the courthouse and we can all go back on duty."

"Although as long as you're getting paid for it, waiting around's not such bad work," I said.

"Wouldn't be if we were getting paid, but they put us all on furlough," Doane said. "The jerks."

"Well, I'll put you on my payroll," Grandfather said. "And your first assignment is to hang around with the other furloughed guards and keep your ears open for any information that would help solve this murder case."

"Yes, sir!" Doane said.

"No, wait," Grandfather said. "That's your second assignment. Your first is to show me what your vulture can do."

"Awesome," Doane said. "I'll have to run back to my car to get my baiting material. I use small airtight capsules that can be broken open to release cadaverine and pu-trescine."

"Too bad we don't have a real corpse to work with," Grandfather said. "I don't sup-pose there was anyone in that car you blew up out at the Inn, was there?" he asked, turning to me.

"I didn't blow it up, and the chief said there were no signs of human remains," I said.

"But is he sure?" Doane asked. "The Inn's only a few miles from here. Let's turn her loose and see if she heads there."

"And if there wasn't a body in the car, maybe she can find that private eye fellow," Grandfather said. "He's missing, right?"

"Missing, yes," I said. "But we have no reason to presume him dead."

"And no proof he's alive, either," Grandfather said. "Let's send Nekhbet out and see what she can find."

Doane began fumbling at the door of Nekhbet's cage.

"Why don't you two find a more private place to set her loose?" I suggested. "We've already had a murder here — if people see a vulture flapping around, they'll think the worst."

"Let's do it from the parking lot," Doane said, "since I need to go back to the truck anyway, for the bait. And the GPS anklet."

I watched as the two of them strode off, dragging the caged vulture behind them.

"Please don't find anything," I murmured.

CHAPTER 31

After watching my grandfather and Mr. Doane disappear with the vulture in tow, I shook my head and headed for the tent to eat my salad.

I had only strolled a few paces when my cell phone rang. I set down the salads and my tea on the edge of a nearby planter and answered it.

"Meg? Randall. Can you drop by my tent for a couple of minutes? Quick meeting of the Steering Committee."

"If it's about the bagpipes —"

"No, it's about the car bomb."

I picked up the salads and the tea and headed for the other side of the town square.

I found Deputy Sammy standing outside the tent, glaring at anyone who came within ten paces. Inside, Randall, Caroline, Ms. Ellie, and the chief were sitting on the green plastic stacking lawn chairs that served as the mayor's guest seating.

"Here." I handed one Cobb salad to the chief. "With Minerva's compliments, and I'm under orders to see that you eat every bite."

He blinked, then took the salad.

"Thank you," he said. "It has been a busy day."

While the chief and I poured little packages of dressing over our salads, Randall cut to the chase.

"Caroline tells me you overheard something that might explain why the Evil Lender is suddenly so fired up to get Phinny out of the courthouse basement," he said.

"Not exactly," I said, through a mouthful of lettuce. "They're not really trying to get Mr. Throckmorton out."

"Could have fooled me."

"I mean they are, but it's only incidental," I said. "They want to get him out of the basement because they think that's the only way they can get in."

"Okay, I'll bite," Randall said. "Why do they want to get into the basement?"

"To find something," I said. "A document, I assume, since that's about all there is in the basement. And also because they were talking about whether it was the only copy."

"And Leonard Fisher said it was," Caroline added.

"No, actually what he said was, 'it is now,'" I said. "Which sounded to me as if they'd snagged or destroyed the other copies."

"Whatever it is, we have to keep them from getting it," Caroline said.

"That's easy to say," Randall replied. "But how are we supposed to do that if we don't know what it is? Unless you're about to suggest we haul all of the documents out of the courthouse — and trust me, that's not an option. It'd take weeks — maybe months."

"I told you we should have started moving the files out last year," Ms. Ellie said. "If we'd started moving the files out as soon as the siege began —"

"Then maybe we would have moved whatever they want to someplace where they could already have found it," Randall said. "Never mind what we maybe should have done a year ago. What should we do now? And dammit, emptying the courthouse basement is not an option!"

"Sorry," Ms. Ellie said, drawing back from Randall's frown.

"No, I'm sorry," Randall said. "I didn't mean to snap at you. It's just that I had this same damned discussion with someone else already today."

"With Hamish Pruitt," I said. "I remember."

"Actually, Hamish was yesterday, but he makes two someone elses within the last twenty-four hours," Randall said. "He's been after me for weeks about it, but now your cousin Festus is taking an interest in the archives."

"He was disappointed to find we didn't have them in the library," Ms. Ellie said. "I suppose he's looking for documents that might help him in that big court date that's coming up."

"Or bite him in the rear if the other side has them and he doesn't know about them," Randall said. "That's the impression I got, and when I asked him what kind of documents, he said he'd know them when he saw them."

"The lender should have provided him with a copy of any documents they plan to use at trial," the chief said. "That's what the lawyers mean by discovery."

"Maybe he thinks they cheated," Randall said. "Or maybe it's a document we have and they don't."

"That would make more sense," the chief said. "Because if it's a document he planned to use in the trial, he'd need to get them a copy ASAP, or he couldn't use it."

"I think we already gave them all the documents we had," I said. "Wasn't Mr. Throckmorton quite busy scanning and faxing and stuffing papers through the barricade all winter?"

"True," Randall said. "So maybe it's something he only just figured out was relevant. I don't rightly know why, but Festus was asking about the archives."

"He could go over to the courthouse," I said.

Randall nodded.

"I get the idea he's not keen on it," he said. "I did offer to lend him some overalls so he wouldn't sully that fancy white suit of his on the trip over."

Cousin Festus invariably dressed in retro-styled three-piece suits. At this time of year they would, of course, be white linen. He always beamed with delight when people said that he reminded them of Gregory Peck playing Atticus Finch in *To Kill a Mockingbird.* I tried to imagine him in a pair of Randall's overalls and failed miserably.

The chief, who, like me, had been working away steadily on the Cobb salad, wiped his mouth and spoke up.

"I presume that since Festus is contemplating making the trip through the tunnel, he thinks it's tenable for us to keep Mr.

Throckmorton in place for the time being," he said. "Although keeping him under guard is putting a severe strain on our resources."

"Can't be helped," Randall said. "By the way — we're a little worried about getting the trapdoor done during the Fourth of July orchestra concert. Apparently this *1812 Overture* isn't all that long."

"Fifteen or sixteen minutes, I should think," Caroline said.

"Which should be enough time for the really noisy bits, but you know how construction is. So the boys and I are going to make a start during tonight's rock concert."

"Good idea," I said. "It certainly should be noisy enough."

"Oh, it will be," he said. "My cousin Vern's son Orvis is the drummer. Vern won't even let them practice in his barn anymore."

"So they're loud and underrehearsed," I said. "Great."

"They get plenty of practice over in Granddaddy's barn," Randall said. "Being deaf as a post tends to enhance your appreciation of Orvis's musical abilities. But they'll be good cover. And if we finish off tonight, we can kick back and enjoy the fireworks tomorrow. One more thing —"

"Chief?" Sammy stuck his head in the tent door. "There's some kind of commotion over in the food tent area. Deputy Morris says maybe you might want to see what's going on."

The chief set down his empty salad container and took off at a fast trot. Randall, Caroline, and I followed in his wake.

I came around the corner of the ice cream stand and almost bumped into the chief. Randall did bump into me.

"Good Lord," the chief said. "What's that fool thing doing there?"

We all turned to see what he was pointing at and saw a vulture perched on the roof of Hamish Pruitt's hamburger stand.

"You mean, apart from sending a very negative message to all our tourists?" Randall said. "Beats me."

"I hereby take back any doubts I had about turkey vultures' ability to find carrion," I said. "Nearly twenty food concessions, not to mention several dozen sun-ripened trash cans throughout the square, and he heads unerringly to Hamish's booth. The only question is whether it's Nekhbet, or a freelance vulture."

"Nekhbet?" the chief echoed.

"What a lovely name!" Rose Noire exclaimed. And then seeing my unspoken question, she added, "Michael's on duty at the tent."

I explained, as well as I could, the demonstration Mr. Doane was giving to Grandfather.

"I see," the chief said. "You think you could call your grandfather or Mr. Doane and ask them to come and collect their vulture?"

"He doesn't have a cell phone," I said. "He hates them, so he just borrows them from whoever he's with and gripes about them. And I don't know Mr. Doane's number. But if this is their vulture, they should be showing up shortly to see what she's found. They were going to put a GPS anklet on her."

As we watched, the vulture scuttled sideways slightly until she was on the very edge of the roof. Then she stooped and leaned down, trying to see what was inside the booth.

"Wish we didn't have that ordinance against shooting off firearms within the town limits," Randall remarked.

"Even if we didn't, I can't believe you'd shoot a harmless turkey vulture," Rose Noire said. "They're such an important part of the ecosystem."

"And besides," I said, "it probably is Mr. Doane's tame vulture. I think I see the GPS device on her leg."

"I wouldn't shoot her," Randall said. "But I'd love to fire a few warning shots to scare her off. Chief, couldn't one of your men oblige? Fire a shot or two in the air?"

"Don't you think the shots might spook the tourists even more than the vulture?" the chief asked.

"Don't think of the tourists," Rose Noire said. "Think of that poor vulture. What if she eats something from Hamish's booth? He's very careless about refrigerating his supplies. I'm pretty sure he's responsible for those cases of food poisoning that keep turning up."

"She's a vulture," I said. "She's looking for carrion."

"I'm sure even vultures can't eat everything," she replied.

"I'll put Deputy Shiffley in charge of ensuring that the vulture relocates to a safer environment," the chief said. "With or without Dr. Blake's assistance." He had pulled out his phone and was peering over his glasses at it. "And I'm going to sic the county health inspector on Hamish."

"Good plan," Randall said.

Just then I spotted Mr. Doane and Grandfather pushing their way through the crowd. I pointed them out to the chief.

"I'm going back to the tent," I said. "Call

me if there really is a body in Hamish's
booth."

CHAPTER 32

Back at the bandstand, the bagpiper appeared to be performing a medley of "Flight of the Bumblebee" and *The William Tell Overture.* Backstage in the tent, everyone was counting the minutes until his time was up and he'd have to cede the stage to Henrico Taiko, a Richmond-based troupe of Japanese drummers.

Michael, clipboard in hand, was supervising. Rob was napping in one of the folding recliners, which astonished me until I noticed the bits of cotton sticking out of his ears. Caroline was sitting in one of the lawn chairs. She was also festooned with cotton tufts and smiling blissfully.

The boys were in the pen, happily mauling Spike and Tinkerbell. Eric was sitting nearby with an anxious expression on his face, as if he still didn't quite trust Spike's doting canine uncle act.

Michael strolled over to greet me.

"I thought they'd enjoy the drumming," Michael said. "I hope this stuff doesn't give them bad dreams."

The bagpiper finished at last, and left the stage to more applause than I'd have expected. Of course, perhaps the audience were applauding not his performance but his departure.

Michael turned to Caroline and mimed pulling something out of his ears. Caroline removed her cotton and joined us.

"Your grandfather and I are on after the drummers," she said. "Assuming he can tear himself away from chasing vultures long enough to show up."

"He'll be here," I said. "You know how he loves an audience."

"What's after us?"

Michael handed her the clipboard and she studied the afternoon and evening's schedule. She looked up after a few moments.

"What the dickens is Rancid Dread?" she asked.

Michael shrugged and looked at me.

"It's a heavy metal band," I said. "That's kind of like —"

"Heavy metal? Puh-lease!"

I looked around to see the diminutive, black-leather-clad figure of Rancid Dread's drummer, sixteen-year-old Orvis Shiffley.

He was rolling his eyes and wearing the long-suffering expression teenagers so often adopted when adults said or did something particularly lame. I'd seen a milder version of that expression earlier, on Eric, but Orvis was treating me to a full-strength blast of withering adolescent scorn.

"Well, then what do you play?" I asked.

"Like we started out playing *some* heavy metal," Orvis said. "But we pretty much moved into retro thrash metal right away, and then into sort of a combination of metalcore and melodic death. Now we're kind of working our way into dark medieval ambient. And some other stuff that really hasn't got a name yet. You'll all probably hate it."

He strolled off, head high, looking remarkably triumphant at the prospect of our collective hatred.

"You were expecting maybe easy listening?" Michael asked.

"I think I'll plan on an early night," Caroline said.

Rob snickered. Apparently he'd awakened and removed his earplugs in time for Orvis's tirade.

"Eric would like to see Rancid Dread," Michael said. "And Rob's going to keep an eye on him and bring him home after the concert. So once Josh and Jamie start to fade, I'll take them home. Come on, boys. Let's watch the drummers."

He and Eric grabbed the boys and took them outside. I picked up the clipboard and returned to wrangling the talent.

Caroline and Grandfather were a hit with their wild animal presentation. So was the old-fashioned barbershop quartet that followed, although they were a little too quiet to be of much use if we'd had to open the trapdoor. Shortly after the Irish step dancers took the stage, producing an impressive amount of staccato noise, assorted Shiffleys began showing up making deliveries of musical instruments and enormous wooden crates with RANCID DREAD stenciled on them. Some of the Shiffleys disappeared into the crawl space, with or without crates, so I assumed they were taking advantage of the Irish decibels.

"What are all these crates?" I asked the Shiffley who delivered the eleventh and twelfth ones.

"Sound equipment," he said.

I looked around to see if Caroline was still there, so I could ask her where she'd found the cotton earplugs.

The afternoon wore on. Irish step dancing gave way to yodeling. Then the polka band from Goochland County went onstage for an encore performance. They'd been rather miffed at the small number of listeners the day before, but now, without competition from a real live murder investigation, they had a much larger audience and received a warm welcome.

While they were performing, the members of Rancid Dread began slithering into the tent, and now all five were hanging about backstage, sweating heavily in their black leather and black denim stage garb. Since Orvis was not only the oldest, at sixteen, but also the tallest, at five foot six, their collective presence was not quite as menacing as they probably intended. In fact, they looked rather like a party of kids going for one last trick-or-treat before they became too old, and more than a little sheepish about the whole thing. I hoped, for their sake, that they got through the evening without hearing those words, so dreaded by tiny Darth Vaders and miniature Freddie Krugers: "Aren't they cute?"

It didn't help that they were all eating Popsicles that stained their mouths bright blue and added another layer of sticky grime to outfits that had already been worn too often without cleaning.

"A penny for them," Michael said, seeing

me frowning at the band members.

"Is it too late to take away those toy drums and ukuleles we gave the boys?" I asked.

"I'll whisk the boys away before the polka players finish," he said. "And tomorrow we can look into some toy accordions."

I said good night to Michael and the boys.

"Your parents are coming over to see the boys, and bringing dinner," Michael said.

"They must have a surplus of something in the Episcopal tent," I said. "Don't let Dad talk about the autopsy with the boys around."

"Why don't you try to get off and join us?" he suggested.

I tried, but the only trustworthy substitute I could find was Rose Noire, and my attempts to enlist her to fill in for me fell flat.

"Oh, no," she said. "I don't think I could possibly stay here for a heavy metal concert."

"Dark medieval ambient," I corrected her.

"It's the same thing," she said. "So much raw, dark, hostile energy! It's all about death and violence and primitive emotions. I'm going to go home and beam some positive vibes to dispel some of the toxic energy they generate."

"It's only Orvis Shiffley and some of his friends going through an adolescent phase,"

I said. "I don't think it's about death and violence as much as hormones and trying to be cool. But do what you need to do."

"I think I'll do a cleansing on the bandstand tomorrow morning," she said. "I'll gather the herbs tonight, and do it at dawn."

"Lovely," I said. I'd long ago learned better than to argue with Rose Noire about subjects like toxic energy. And except for the occasional foul-tasting herbal concoction, all her cleansings and energy beamings seemed, at worst, harmless, and more often than not curiously comforting.

Molly in Chains, the Morris dancers in black leather, turned out to be twelve very shapely and athletic young women, and while their act was just as strange as I expected, it was definitely entertaining. The Rancid Dread musicians spent the entire performance outside gawking. The show almost didn't go on after the dancers finished their final number, bowed to the applause, and hurried offstage. Most of them pulled off their towering stilettos and iced down their aching feet. The prospect that they might follow this up by removing their sprayed-on leather garb so distracted the Rancid Dreads that they almost forgot they were due onstage. Luckily, they weren't trying to double as their own roadies. Half a dozen adult Shiffley men began hauling instruments, microphones, and many of the enormous speakers out onto the bandstand. By the time they finished their setup, I'd managed to pry the band's eyes off the dancers and shoo them out into the tiny offstage area.

We still had at least half of the equipment in the tent, but apparently the adult Shiffleys had decided they had enough amplification onstage. Probably a wise decision, since the only way they could fit any more of the speakers onstage would be to dispense with a musician or two. The volunteer roadies ambled off the stage and the crowd, realizing that the last and presumably biggest act of the day was about to begin, shushed each other until silence reigned.

Rancid Dread exploded onto the stage, all pumping both fists in the air as if to acknowledge the frenzied cheers of their fans. Unfortunately their audience was a mix of indulgently smiling locals, who had known the musicians since they were in diapers, and the tourists, who were perfectly happy to applaud politely for almost any act that walked onstage.

The fist-pumping petered out as the five Dreads took their places. Orvis scurried over to his drums and crouched behind them, peeking out from time to time as if surprised that no one was throwing anything at him. The vocalist clung to the microphone stand as if in need of support, while the guitar, bass, and keyboard players stumbled around onstage, peering at all the available instruments as if unsure which they'd been assigned. Finally the vocalist turned around and stage whispered, "One! Two! Three! Four!" All three instrumentalists quickly grabbed an instrument and began to play.

My initial thought was that they'd also failed to reach agreement on what their first number would be. The guitar player and the keyboardist were playing something that resembled a reggae version of Steppenwolf's "Born to Be Wild," while the bass player and Orvis launched into the rhythm of "Louie Louie." I cringed, expecting that after a few bars they'd stop and regroup, or perhaps one side or the other would give in gracefully and switch. But either they were all incredibly stubborn or the mishmash they were playing was exactly what they had in mind.

After a few bars more, the vocalist joined in with an earsplitting wail, sort of a cross between chalk on a blackboard and the feedback our sound crew had become so adept at producing. The band responded by turning up the volume — a feat I wouldn't have dreamed possible — and the first few ashen-faced tourists began stumbling toward safety.

I decided to put the tent between me and Rancid Dread, so I ducked inside.

Randall and a posse of Shiffleys had arrived and were springing into action. The reason for the surplus sound equipment became evident — the extra speakers were not actually speakers but cleverly camouflaged cases holding tools, lumber, and other construction supplies.

"We're going to do some prep work for the trapdoor," Randall shouted to me. "We're hauling a bunch of tools and equipment over to the courthouse basement, and then we're going to work inside the tunnel shaft for a while. So once we get in there, I'd appreciate it if you could close the trapdoor and keep watch."

"Do you really think anyone will come near the bandstand while this is going on?" I bellowed back.

"Never hurts to be cautious," he replied. "Specially since one of the band members is a Pruitt. Bass player. He's the mayor's second cousin once removed. According to Orvis, he hates his whole family, and maybe that's true, but . . ."

"Better safe than sorry, then," I said. "So he's not in on the secret of the trapdoor and we want to keep him that way."

Randall nodded.

We hauled the trapdoor open during one of the vocalist's glass-shattering screeches. I watched the Shiffleys lug tools and equipment down into the tunnel. I helped them arrange the big faux speakers in a rough circle around the trapdoor, as if we were using the crawl space as an overflow sound equipment area. They even strung a few cables from the fake speakers up into the tangle of real wires overhead. I had to admit — it was impressive camouflage.

"We should keep this stuff around indefinitely," I said. "No one would ever guess the tunnel was there. You can probably keep the trapdoor open if you like."

Just then the band reached the frenzied crescendo of a song. The cacophony made us both wince and clutch our ears.

Then the sound ended. A few seconds of stunned silence followed, and then the patter of applause so faint that I suspected everyone not related to the band had fled during the last number.

"Keep the trapdoor open? And listen to that?" Randall asked. "No thanks."

He reached up for the trapdoor, but the

band spoiled his snappy exit line by waiting until the last feeble claps died away before starting their new number. When the first chords of the second song rang out, Randall winced and slammed the trapdoor shut.

This time it was the guitarist's turn in the spotlight. He launched into a solo riff that seemed to have no redeeming characteristics, apart from the virtuoso speed with which he executed it. And "executed" was definitely the right word. Like the emperor in *Amadeus,* I found myself muttering, "Too many notes."

About a century later, the guitar solo ended and the vocalist leaped back into the fray. I braced myself against the noise and stepped outside again. And remembering Rose Noire's tirade about death, violence, and primitive emotions, I tried to focus on the words, to see if they were as bad as she claimed.

The guitar player's frenzy prevented me from even hearing the vocalist during the second number. But the third song started out with a much slower tempo. More of a rock ballad. Now that was more like it. And instead of leaping about like a frog on a hot-plate, the vocalist had draped himself over the microphone like a weary praying mantis. I could not only see him, I could see his mouth move. Surely I could decipher the words of this song.

The singer rather mumbled the verses, as if he'd half-forgotten them, and I caught only a few phrases — "nasal chains," and "a drywall knight." But he belted out the chorus.

In a cowbell
Honesty has arrived
Oh bwana
Dental align!

"I give up," I said aloud — not that anyone could possibly have heard me. "It could be death and violence and primitive emotions. Or his mother's to-do list. The kid needs a speech therapist."

I brooded through the rest of the song. Was I turning into my parents? Completely unable to understand the music of the new generation? Actually, I reminded myself more of my childhood friend Eileen's father, who during our teen years regularly outraged us with what I now realize were probably rather amusing parodies of our favorite rock songs.

"Psst! Meg!"

I wouldn't have heard the whisper if it hadn't come in the several seconds between the end of "In a cowbell" and the moment when the stunned audience began dutifully applauding. I turned around to see who was calling me.

Stanley Denton was peering out from behind a large trash can.

CHAPTER 33

"Meg?" Denton called. "Is the coast clear?"

I strolled over toward the trash can and pretended to deposit something in it.

"I don't think there's anyone in the tent, if that's what you mean," I said, as I smiled and clapped along with the rest of the audience. "But let me go inside first and check."

I strolled casually back inside the tent. No one there. No one visible in the crawl space, either. I pulled out my cell phone and sent a text message to Mr. Throckmorton: "Tell Randall to keep his crew in the tunnel. Possible hostile in the tent."

I tapped the send button, then walked back to the tent flap and gave a thumbs-up sign to the waiting night. I stepped back inside, and a few seconds later, Denton burst into the tent. He pulled the flap closed, looked around, and then sat down behind one of the big wooden instrument cases that hadn't gone into the crawl space.

"No one here," I said. "What in the world is going on?"

"Don't let anyone know I'm here."

"I won't," I said. "But tell me why not? And where have you been all day, anyway?"

"Long story," he said. "You don't happen to have anything to eat, do you? I've been hiding out all day. Haven't eaten since lunch yesterday."

"Lots of leftovers in the mini-fridge," I said. "And a microwave to heat them up with. Help yourself."

I was a little nervous at letting Denton into the crawl space again, but he barely glanced at the huge speakers and other clutter. He ransacked the mini-fridge and inhaled several slices of country ham and about a pint of cole slaw while I microwaved a plate of leftover pulled pork and mashed potatoes and found some bread to transform the pork into a sandwich. And then I led him out of the crawl space again by putting the sandwich on a plate and taking it with me. He sprawled on my folding recliner and dug in.

He still wasn't giving the food the attention it deserved, but at least he was eating the sandwich slowly enough that I stopped worrying quite so much that he'd choke.

"Thif if great," he said. Under the circumstances, even Mother wouldn't have rebuked him for talking with his mouth full.

"So why are you hiding out?" I asked him, when he'd slowed down a little.

"Someone took a potshot at me last night when I was getting out of my car," he said.

"At the Caerphilly Inn?"

He nodded, still chewing.

"I didn't hear about it," I said. "Wait — I bet you didn't report it to the police, did you?"

He shook his head.

"You told your employer?"

He shook his head again.

"You didn't tell anyone?"

He swallowed the food he was chewing.

"I'm telling you now," he said. "And I'm not opposed to telling your chief of police if you can let him know I'm here without giving away the show to anyone who has a police radio. But I'd really rather not let my employer know where I am. Make that former employer. I have a strict policy against working for anyone who tries to kill me."

"Not that I want to argue with you, but is there a particular reason you don't trust the Evil Lender?" I asked.

"Because I'm more than half convinced that it was someone in their employ who shot at me."

I nodded.

"I'm betting they're also the ones who blew up your car this afternoon," I said.

He choked on a bite of pulled pork sandwich at that and had to be pounded on the back.

"They blew up my car?" he asked when he could speak again. "How? When? Was anyone hurt?"

"No one was hurt," I said. "It blew up when the Shiffley Towing Service was hauling it off the parking lot of the Inn at a little past noon today. While I was waiting for the chief to interview me, I overheard one of the State Troopers speculating that it was an acceleration detonation device, but we won't know until the State Bureau of Investigation finishes analyzing the debris."

"Debris," he said. "Not wreck or hulk — debris?"

I nodded.

"Maybe the rumor mill exaggerated the damage?"

I shook my head.

"I saw the explosion," I said. "It was raining car parts. Tow truck's not in such good shape, either. Debris. Charred debris."

"Damn," he said. "I was fond of that car. Two hundred and twenty thousand miles and still chugging along. More to the point, I'm damned lucky. I was considering sneaking back to get it at around three A.M., but I decided they might have staked it out."

"It's possible they didn't rig it to blow up until after that."

"Also possible if I'd tried it they'd be picking pieces of me out of that debris. And identifying me with DNA."

I didn't argue with him. He took another bite of his pulled pork sandwich and chewed thoughtfully.

"You saw the explosion?" he asked, when he'd finished that bite. "How'd you happen to be over at the Inn just then?"

"I went over to burgle your room," I said.

He paused in the middle of a bite.

"Find anything interesting?" he asked.

"Only Leonard Fisher doing his own burgling."

"He caught you?"

"No, I hid on the balcony." I figured there was no need to implicate Caroline as well.

"Wrong room, then," he said. "My room doesn't have a balcony."

"Actually, it's more like a window ledge with a view of the loading dock," I said. He nodded. "I could tell you what brand of toothpaste and dental floss you use if you want me to prove I was there, or you can take my word for it. I saw Fisher take all the papers you left behind — not that there were many of them, just copies of your weekly reports to him. And I hope you didn't have anything interesting on your laptop. I couldn't check myself because of the password protection, but I'm sure the Evil Lender can find someone to get past that. Why do you think someone from FPF shot at you?"

"Presumably because they think I'm a liability to them," he said. "Or maybe even a threat. Wish to hell I knew why. Nothing I've run across in the past few weeks seems all that useful or interesting to me."

"Actually, I didn't mean what their motive was for doing it, but why you were so very sure it was them," I said.

"I've got no evidence it wasn't, say, some gun-toting local who resents my being here," he said. "But every instinct I have says it's FPF."

"And you trust your instinct even with no evidence?"

He leaned back in the recliner and looked thoughtful.

"In my experience," he said, "instinct is your subconscious adding up the evidence before you even know you have it. I trust my instinct, absolutely. I'd be long dead by now if I didn't."

I was tempted, briefly, to repeat the words I overheard Fisher say. Maybe he could make more sense of them than we could.

And maybe I should wait until we were a little more sure what side he was on. After all, we only had his word for it that anyone had taken a shot at him at all.

"Any objection if I stay here in your tent tonight?" he asked. "I don't much fancy going home — or anyplace else where FPF knows where to find me."

"Bad idea," I said. "The whole town square is swarming with tourists, townspeople, police, and Flying Monkeys. You couldn't take two steps out of the tent without being spotted."

"Then I'll stay here in the tent."

"Apart from the lack of a bathroom, what are you going to do when all the performers and craftspeople start showing up in the morning? I can't swear that they'll all keep your secret."

"Hide under the bandstand?"

"Where half the women stow their purses, and the tech crew from the college spends half its time crawling around trying to fix the antiquated sound system? No, actually, you won't have to worry about the people showing up in the morning. This place will get pretty busy when that wretched band finally knocks off, and you can't hide under the bandstand because they had so much crap I made them shove half of it in there. You might as well hide up there onstage."

"I'm open to suggestions," he said.

I thought for a few moments.

"Michael and I have plenty of room," I said finally. "You can come home with me and hide in one of our spare rooms."

"And just how am I going to get out of the tent now without being spotted?"

Good question. The rolling box I'd used for the evidence bags was a little small. Maybe in one of Rancid Dread's humongous speaker boxes?

Then inspiration struck.

"I have just the thing." I ducked into the crawl space and plucked Horace's gorilla suit down from where Rose Noire had hung it up to air.

Denton studied it dubiously.

"I just put this on and walk out?"

I nodded.

"No offense, but that doesn't exactly sound like the most unobtrusive way to get around."

"Trust me," I said. "If you walk out of here beside me wearing that, no one will give it a second thought. A few people might say 'Hi, Horace!' "

"Your cousin wears this?" Denton took the suit and held it out at arm's length.

"Not all the time, just when he needs to relax."

"Been wearing it quite a bit today, apparently." He wrinkled his nose.

"Not since yesterday." I reached out to touch the fur. No longer still sopping wet, but still a little damp. Not surprising. The suit took forever to dry under optimal conditions, and a humid Virginia heat wave was about as far from optimal as you could find. "Look, it's scruffy and smelly and more than a little weird, but it's the best way I can think of to get you out of this tent without anyone being the wiser. You want to stay here until someone with no reason to keep your secret shows up?"

Denton opened the suit's zipper and began to step in.

"Just one thing," he said. "What if we run into your cousin while I'm wearing this?"

"Last I heard, he was down in Richmond delivering some evidence to the crime lab," I said. "And he's only on loan to Caerphilly — his real job is in Yorktown, and he'll be on duty there tomorrow, doing crowd control at their Fourth of July celebration. And if anyone who knows his schedule spots you, both places are only about an hour away — he could easily have popped back for some reason."

"Okay," he said. "Just stick close so I don't have to pretend to be Horace if anyone comes up to us."

"Slouch a bit, and I'll explain that you've had a very long day," I said. "Horace often goes nonverbal when he's wearing the suit. But I vote we don't stay for the end of the concert. Let's take off as soon as you're ready."

I called Rob and asked him to take over for me at the tent. Then Denton and I slipped out and hiked to my van. The rest of the town was curiously deserted, as if everyone not actually attending the concert had either fled to the surrounding countryside or retreated to the most soundproof portion of their houses and hunkered down to ride it out.

I waited until we were on the road to interrogate him.

"So what were you and Colleen Brown arguing about the night before she was killed?" I asked.

He sighed.

"Nothing's very private in a small town, is it?"

I waited. I was about to prod him again

when he finally answered my question.

"It wasn't really an argument," he said.

"You were heard shouting 'Why the hell didn't you tell me sooner?' " I said. "Told you what sooner?"

He frowned slightly.

"I don't remember," he said. "She'd probably just told me about Leonard Fisher bringing in the falconer to harass Mr. Throckmorton. Something about Fisher, anyway. That was what our whole conversation was about. We both thought he was up to something."

"What?"

"We had no idea. She kind of thought maybe he was trying to set her up to take the blame for the fact that they still hadn't gotten the hermit out of the basement."

"Seems a little far-fetched," I said. "Since she only came here a month or two ago, and he's been here since the day they seized the building."

"That's what I thought," Denton said. "But according to her, half a dozen FPF execs have seen their careers wreck on the shoals of Caerphilly. Apparently, assigning you to come down here and work on the problem is FPF's way of saying, 'Hey! Get your resume ready!' So maybe it's not so paranoid."

"And what did you think he was up to?"

"No idea," he said. "That's not what we disagreed about. She wanted to confront him about what he was up to. Have it out. Clear the air."

"You thought that was a bad idea?"

"The guy's a seasoned corporate weasel," he said. "You don't have it out with someone like that. You get the goods on him if you can, and otherwise you steer clear. I told her it was a stupid thing to do. Stupid and dangerous."

The last word hung in the air for what seemed like a long while. Then he spoke again.

"Of course, I only thought it was dangerous to her career," he said. "I didn't think her life was in jeopardy."

"You think Fisher killed her, then?"

Another long pause.

"No idea," he said. "I'd have pegged him as sneaky, not violent. A knife in the back, maybe. Or setting it up so it looked as if she committed suicide. Something well planned and executed. And unless the picture has changed a lot since last night, the murder doesn't sound very well planned. More like a crime of impulse or opportunity, and one the killer didn't think through very well — at least not if he was trying to frame Mr.

Throckmorton."

"True," I said. "Of course, maybe it was planned to look like a crime of impulse. Is Fisher that devious?"

He shrugged.

"Yeah," he said. "I just can't figure out how he'd benefit from this. But one thing I can tell you — if the theory is that the murderer changed his clothes between the time of the murder and the time they evacuated the building, Fisher could do that, easy. He always wanted to look snappy if some corporate dignitary showed up or if one of the local TV stations wanted to interview him. He'd always have a change of clothing in his office, and in weather like this, probably several changes. The guards, on the other hand — can't see any reason for them to keep a change of uniform lying around."

I nodded.

When we got home, I ushered Denton into a room on the third floor — one of the few not already occupied by Festus's paralegals.

"You've got your own bath," I said. "The door beside the bureau. I hope you won't be insulted, but I'm going to lock you in and keep the key myself."

"How can I possibly be insulted?" he asked with a yawn. "I'm not actually conscious. Thanks, and good night."

As I walked downstairs again, I pulled out my phone, intending to tell the chief that I'd found Denton. But when I hit the second floor, I ran into Kate Blake trudging up the stairs from the front hall.

"There you are!" she exclaimed.

CHAPTER 34

"Evening," I said. "What can I do for you?" With luck, she wouldn't have seen the moment of panic on my face as I realized how close Denton and I had come to running into her on our way in. And I couldn't remember whether I'd let Denton take his gorilla head off before he got to his room.

"I was going to leave you a note," she said. "I have to go back to Washington."

"Now?"

"They're pulling the plug," she said. "I have to be at Mount Vernon at nine to cover another story."

"Not the cat show, surely."

She shook her head.

"Someone pretending to be General Washington is inspecting a bunch of reenactors dressed up as Revolutionary War soldiers." Her voice was flat and joyless. "And then I'm supposed to interview a whole bunch of people becoming citizens. I'm sure they've selected a picturesquely diverse bunch with heartwarming stories. Back to the human interest beat."

"Just because it's human interest doesn't mean it has to be cute, you know," I said. "And General Washington and his citizen army still seem pretty fascinating to me. Don't just assume it's fluff. Find the meat. Run with it."

She blinked for a moment, then smiled.

"I'll try," she said. "Sorry I can't stay around to help. Not that I've been much help. I really only found out one new bit of information, and that's probably pretty useless."

"You never know," I said. "What is it?"

"The paper's been trying to get a comment on the murder from your ex-mayor," she said. "And so far we haven't been able to track him down."

"He's in Cancún," I said.

"Actually, he's not," she replied. "We have a couple of stringers in Mexico. One of them was actually in Cancún on another story, so my editor sicced her on him. He was there earlier, but the Thursday before Memorial Day he packed up and left."

"Does she know where he went?"

"Yes, she bribed a ticket agent to find out. He caught the seven-fifteen A.M. American

Airlines flight to Dallas with a connecting flight from there to DCA."

My mouth fell open.

"He could be here!" I exclaimed.

"Do you think he's the killer?" she asked.

I reminded myself that however helpful she was being, she was still a reporter.

"No idea," I said. "But I'm sure a lot of people will be very interested in finding out where he was yesterday. Thanks."

"Anyway," she said. "I'm going to grab my stuff and head out. You'll let me know if that story breaks?"

I nodded and took the business card she offered. She continued down the hall to the room we'd given her.

I peeked into the nursery. Both boys were sleeping peacefully. In our room, Michael had fallen asleep with a red pencil in one hand and a draft copy of a student's dissertation in the other. I eased both out of his hands and turned out the light.

Then I went downstairs and puttered about until Kate came down, purse and tote in hand, and said good-bye. After locking the front door behind her, I slipped into the kitchen, poured myself a glass of milk, and called the chief.

"Good news," I said. "Stanley Denton is safe, and sound, and locked in one of our third floor bedrooms. And while it's always possible he's the killer you're looking for, I have an interesting new suspect for you."

I filled him in on Denton's arrival at the tent, and what I'd learned from Denton and from the reporter.

When I'd finished, he remained silent for a few moments.

"Any marching orders?" I asked.

"How early will you be up?" he asked.

"We have toddlers," I said. "If I'm not up at dawn, Michael or Eric will be. I'll put the key to Denton's room in my bedside drawer. Michael can give it to you."

"I'll see you tomorrow, then," he said. "And thanks."

I glanced at the clock. Nearly one. The boys were always up by seven, and sometimes six, and try as I might I had a hard time going back to sleep once I knew they were up. Five, maybe six hours if I dozed off immediately, and while I was physically exhausted, my mind was restless and I was afraid I'd toss and turn until daybreak.

I crept upstairs as quietly as I could, slipped into bed, and lay there for a while, breathing as slowly and deeply as I could, and consciously letting go of the day's events.

Which were already yesterday's events.

For some reason I found that fact curiously soothing.

CHAPTER 35

The fireworks woke me shortly after dawn.

"I'm sure they didn't sign the Declaration of Independence until the afternoon of the fourth," I muttered, when Michael tiptoed in to fetch the key to Denton's room.

"Actually, the majority of them didn't sign it on the fourth at all," he said. "Most of the signers weren't in Philadelphia at the time, so they sent the document around to them over the course of the next month."

"It's too early in the morning for cold, hard facts," I said, as I pulled both pillows over my head. "Let me go back to sleep with my historical illusions intact."

But even through the pillows I could hear the intermittent pops and bangs from the yard below. The backyard, which meant it wasn't just neighbors or passersby doing it but someone from our household. I also heard barking and shrieks of laughter. I finally gave up, dragged myself out of bed, and stumbled to a window where I could see what was going on.

Down in the backyard, Rob, holding a lit sparkler in each hand, was running around in circles while the dogs chased him, barking furiously, and Eric and the boys looked on, laughing and clapping their hands.

I wasn't thrilled that Rob was setting such a bad example — had he completely missed Dad's annual lectures about the perils of fireworks? — but at least he appeared to be keeping the sparklers well away from the boys.

Downstairs, I noticed that the door to the dining room was closed. I continued past it into the kitchen.

"I see the chief's using our dining room," I said.

"I thought you were going to sleep in." Michael was working busily. Clearing up the remains of a toddler meal and, I was pleased to see, working on some grown-up coffee, bacon, and eggs.

"I was," I said. "But Rob had other ideas."

"Sorry," Michael said. "He started setting off something noisy while I was letting the chief in. I chewed him out and told him to stick to sparklers until noon. Rob, that is."

I nodded and began gulping down the coffee he set in front of me.

"Good morning, Meg." I looked up to see the chief walking in, followed by Denton. The PI was already in the gorilla suit, although he was carrying the head under his arm rather than wearing it.

"Morning, Chief," I said. "I trust you were as relieved as I was to see Mr. Denton still among the living."

"Indeed," he said. "I'm assuming you would have no problem if Mr. Denton continued to wear Horace's gorilla suit for the time being?"

"As a disguise, it's a pretty useless one except in Yorktown and here in Caerphilly," I said to Denton. "Does this mean you're staying in town?"

"If someone from FPF took a shot at me, they know where to find me in Staunton," he said. "And besides, I want to search the courthouse."

"I thought it already had been searched," I said, glancing at the chief.

"Very thoroughly," the chief said.

"Yes — but by police officers looking for evidence in the murder," Denton went on. "This would be different — I want to look for evidence that will help sort out precisely what's going on within First Progressive Financial. Evidence of corporate skullduggery. Which may or may not have anything to do with the murder, but will definitely have a bearing on Caerphilly's various legal battles."

"Mr. Denton suggests, not unreasonably, that his knowledge of the inner workings of FPF might enable him to spot useful evidence," the chief said. "I'm inclined to consider his suggestion."

"And if he goes into the courthouse wearing the gorilla suit," I said, "no one will pay any attention, because they'll all assume it's Horace."

"Precisely," the chief said. "So I see no reason not to continue the rather ingenious masquerade you used to spirit him safely out of town. However," he added, fixing Denton with a stern look, "I am not comfortable with having him wandering around town by himself in it or sending him solo into the courthouse. So if you don't mind lending us the suit for a little while longer, I'll take Mr. Denton with me into town. He, and the suit, will be in the mayor's office. When I can free up a deputy to accompany him, I'll let him do his search of the courthouse, and after that we can return the suit."

"It's Horace's suit, and I'm sure he'd consider this a good cause," I said.

"And should the occasion arise," the chief added, "you might mention to a few people that Horace is back, just for a few hours, and working so frantically on a few forensic items that it would be a kindness not to disturb him."

I nodded.

"Of course, if you deputized Meg to go along and babysit me," Denton said, "you wouldn't have to pull any of your deputies off their regular duties."

"I've already told you I'd rather try to free up a deputy," the chief said. "Meg has her hands full already."

"You mean you'd actually consider deputizing me again?" I asked.

The chief winced.

"For the sole and specific purpose of supervising Mr. Denton's inspection of the courthouse," he said. And then, in a more conversational tone, he added, "But it shouldn't be necessary. Right now, the roads around the town square are bumper to bumper. If I had to pull another deputy off traffic control this morning, we might just achieve total gridlock. But things should get better this afternoon."

"By this afternoon you'll be neck deep in lost children, heat prostrations, teenagers mishandling fireworks, belligerent drunks, and people who think 'no parking' signs don't apply to them," Denton said. "And another day will go by without our finding critical evidence. Not to mention that every day increases the chance that any evidence will be lost or compromised."

"If it hasn't been compromised yet, a few more hours won't hurt," the chief said. "And if the day goes to hell in a handbasket the way you're expecting, I'll reconsider deputizing Meg. If she's willing."

I glanced at Michael.

"Your call," he said softly. And I knew that, like me, he was probably thinking about what could happen if the Evil Lender got its way. The threat to our house, Dad's farm, and our working farmer neighbors — all of us whose land FPF was hoping to seize and hand over to a developer. I imagined condos covering the pastures where Rose Noire grew her herbs and a sleek but soulless clubhouse swallowing up the house we'd worked so hard to get in shape and the yard where even now our sons were playing so happily. And no doubt strip malls, parking lots, and fast-food joints after that.

"I'm in," I said. "Chief, consider me deputized, and if you decide you want to use me, just call me. Until then, I'll be in the tent."

Before the chief left with Denton, I pulled

out the spare forensic kit Horace kept at our house and carefully transferred its contents into a box.

"Horace would never go out on a case without this," I said.

"Any objection if I put my clothes in there?" he asked. "I'm just wearing my shorts under this outfit."

"Good idea," I said. "No need to risk a fur-induced heatstroke. And remember," I added, probably for the tenth time, "if anyone tries to talk to you, just nod or shrug or shake your head. Horace often gets pretty preoccupied when he's on a case, and he hates talking in the suit. Spoils the effect."

Denton nodded, took a deep breath, and slid the headpiece on. Then he followed the chief out to his car.

"So you're going to be helping the chief with his investigations?" Michael asked.

"I wouldn't bet on it," I said. "He only said that to placate Denton."

"We'll see," he said. "Help me load the llamas into the trailer, will you? I promised Caroline I'd bring them in for her petting zoo."

"Petting zoo? She brought hyenas and wolves. Who's going to want to pet them?"

"I think she's borrowing some sheep and goats for the petting zoo," Michael replied.

"Plus the usual assortment of cute animals from the shelter."

"That's more like it," I said. "Just make sure they know to keep the fans going so none of the animals get overheated." Caerphilly Days had been a boon for the county's new animal shelter, thanks to an innovation Caroline had introduced. In addition to displaying the adoptable animals from the shelter on one weekend a month, we also had several large, clearly marked donation boxes for guilt offerings from people who saw the cute animals but couldn't take one home. For the moment, the county shelter was almost self-sustaining.

It took both Michael's truck and my van to haul the llamas, Eric and the boys, Rob, and Caroline. Eric and Rob were telling Josh and Jamie all about the upcoming fireworks. I wasn't sure how much the boys understood, and I knew it wasn't wise, working them up to a fever pitch of excitement about something that wasn't going to happen for hours. But keeping them happy till things went boom would be Eric's problem. Well, mostly Eric's problem.

I unloaded everyone else at the petting zoo and parked the truck. I could see what the chief meant — traffic was already bad.

But that was good for the festival. All three

of the churches were selling coffee as fast as they could brew it and they'd all come up with a breakfast menu. Tourists were lining up for Baptist ham biscuits, Episcopal coffee cake and fruit smoothies, and Catholic doughnuts still warm from the fryer.

Apparently Rose Noire had anticipated the traffic and arrived even earlier than usual. I found her standing in front of the tent, broom in hand, staring up at the sky.

"Good morning," I said. "Planning to take a ride before things get busy?"

"Look!" She pointed up at the sky. "There's a huge bird circling overhead. Is it the hawk or the vulture?"

I studied the bird's silhouette for a few moments.

"The vulture, I think."

"How horrible!"

"Actually, I think it's rather reassuring." I shaded my eyes as I watched the buzzard's slow, stately flight. "She's not circling tightly over a particular area. She just seems to be looking."

"And she'll find something sooner or later."

"Yes, but so far today she hasn't. No dead bodies, animal or human, anywhere nearby. I like that thought."

Once the first act, a country music group,

took the stage, Shiffleys arrived with discreet shipments of parts and tools for the trapdoor construction. Since Rose Noire had everything under control, I spent a happy hour at the petting zoo with Eric and the boys. I arrived back in time for my 11 A.M. blacksmithing demonstration. While I hammered madly, the Shiffleys started the final stage of demolition work on the old trapdoor and continued it while a fife and drum corps marched and played overhead. The cousin who was selling my ironwork and Rose Noire's herbs texted me to say that she was running low on everything, so I recruited a couple of burly cousins to go with Rose Noire to load the truck and resupply her.

For the first few hours Lad showed up occasionally with a lost child, but eventually Seth's retraining program took effect, and we'd see Lad trotting by, driving his charges before him, en route to the police tent.

Since the banks were closed, every hour or two Caroline would send someone over with money from the petting zoo's donation box. I set a sturdy box in the pen where Tink and Spike could guard it and we poured the cash and coins into that. We'd probably need another box before the end of the day.

At lunchtime, I called Mother's cell phone and asked her if she could gather some provisions for me to pick up.

"Of course, dear," she said. "And while you're here, there's someone you should talk to."

CHAPTER 36

The someone turned out to be Shannon, the pretty blond teenager who either was or wasn't dating one of the Flying Monkeys. Mother whisked us into a back corner of the kitchen area.

"Now just tell Meg and see what she thinks," she said.

Shannon turned to me with an anxious look on her face.

"I don't know whether I should tell the chief something I saw."

"When in doubt, tell," I said. "That's my policy."

Of course, whether this was a good day to tell him was another question. I knew I'd hesitate to bother him today unless I was pretty darn sure my information was important.

"Shannon and her young man were over in Clay County last night," Mother said. "I am allowed to call him that now that he's

405

quit his job — right?"

"Yeah." Shannon's sunny smiled returned. "Andy got hired at the hunting goods store over in Clay County. He doesn't want to do that forever, but he's going to go back to school in the fall if he can transfer his credits to Caerphilly."

"Excellent," I said. "So what did you and the former Flying Monkey see?"

"I took Andy over for his second interview yesterday, and after they said he was hired, we went across the street to the diner for a little lunch, to celebrate. And as we were coming in, you know who was coming out?"

I shook my head.

"Ex-Mayor Pruitt!"

"You're sure?" I asked.

"I know everyone thinks he's in Cancún, but he's not," she said. "And Andy said 'Afternoon, Mr. Mayor,' and Mr. Pruitt just grunted, and I asked Andy why he called him that, and how he even knew him. Andy thought he was still mayor. He's seen him hanging around over at the courthouse a lot lately, talking to Mr. Fisher."

I glanced at Mother, who wore the same pleased expression our family cat used to wear when bringing us a particularly large and succulent mouse.

"Definitely tell the chief," I said. "He will

be very pleased with you for reporting this."

Shannon looked anxious again.

"Or if you'd rather, I'll tell him," I offered. Her smile returned, and she nodded vigorously. "Is Andy around today?" I added.

"Helping your father in the first aid tent," Mother said. "Dr. Smoot wasn't working out — too unsettling for the tourists. But Andy volunteered, and he's had EMT training. Such a nice young man!"

Clearly Andy had been forgiven for his brief sojourn on the dark side and was being welcomed into the Caerphillian fold. Mother would probably soon be asking if Michael could put in a good word for him at the college admissions office.

"Good work," I said to Shannon. "I'll take it from here."

If Andy was available for interrogation, the chief might not even need to talk to Shannon.

When I got back to the tent with my food, I called the chief. He sounded harried.

"I'm only calling because if you found out later I knew this and didn't tell you, you'd be mad," I said. Once I'd relayed what I'd learned from Shannon — well, he didn't sound any less harried, but he did sound a little more cheerful.

I did more blacksmithing at two. When I

showed up at the tent at three, Randall looked jubilant.

"We're making great progress," he said. "We're going to take a break during all this quiet stuff, and then pick up again during the high school band concert. We might even finish while the history pageant is on."

I glanced at the program to remind myself what the "quiet stuff" was.

"Oh, right — the politicians." Randall had extended an open invitation to all our state and national representatives to speak during today's festivities, and to my surprise, most of them had accepted. So the next two hours would be devoted to what Randall called "the speechifying."

"Probably the only time on record I've complained about politicians being too quiet," he said. "Plenty of hot air, but not nearly enough noise. And after that there's the ballet."

"Don't discount the ballet," I said. "They're doing *Appalachian Spring, An American in Paris,* and *Stars and Stripes.* None of them are that quiet, and the last one's to music by Sousa."

"Really?" he said. "Then I'll tell the crew to be back for that."

When the politicians went onstage, Michael decided to flee.

"I'm taking the boys and the llamas home," he said. "I'll bring them back in plenty of time for the fireworks, but they won't enjoy it unless they get a nap."

"I doubt if the llamas would enjoy the fireworks under any circumstance," I said. "You don't think it will be too scary for the boys?"

"They've been hearing small fireworks go off all day and loving it," Michael said. "Eric and Rob have already trained them to shout 'boom!' whenever a firework goes off. Or, for that matter, whenever they would like a firework to go off, which is pretty much all the time. Could take a while to settle them down."

I kissed the boys and waved bye-bye to them, hoping that either they'd forget about "boom!" during their nap or that it would grow old while they were still in Eric's charge.

I was relishing the ensuing peace and quiet — okay, I was napping myself in the folding recliner — when my cell phone rang. It was the chief.

"You still willing to babysit that PI on his trip to the courthouse?"

CHAPTER 37

"I thought I dodged that bullet," I muttered. But I made sure Rose Noire knew I was going.

"It could be worse," she said. "You could be going back through that horrible tunnel!"

When I got to the mayor's tent, the chief looked harried and maybe a little cranky. Apparently my experience of the day as a relatively quiet and peaceful one was not shared by the Caerphilly police. And he was laying down the law to Denton.

"And if you find anything, I want to hear about it immediately," he said. "Not a few days from now when you've had a chance to play with it yourself."

"Absolutely," Denton said. "Here she is now."

"You're in charge," the chief said, turning to me.

"Yes, sir."

He stormed out.

"What's gone wrong?" I asked Denton.

"What hasn't?" He was gathering things and stuffing them into Horace's bag. "Let's see — skinny dippers in the college fountain. Seventeen lost kids — only three of them still unclaimed. Semi full of eggs overturned on Stone Street. Third vanload of drunk and disorderly just left for the Clay County jail. Five ambulance runs — three heat prostration, one suspected heart attack, and a woman from Winchester whose baby your father delivered in the ER a few minutes after they got to the hospital. Oh, and your grandfather's missing a snake. Keep your eyes open — something called an emerald tree boa."

"That should be easy to spot," I said. "It really is emerald green, and dry as it's been all summer, there's not a lot of green grass for it to hide in. If you're ready, put your head on."

Denton pulled on the gorilla head, grabbed Horace's forensic bag, and led the way out of the tent.

I glanced over at the Flying Monkeys' tent. Only Lieutenant Wilt and one other guard were there. I wondered, briefly, where the others were.

Aida Morris was at the top of the courthouse steps, pacing restlessly.

"Whole town's gone crazy, and I'm guarding an empty building," she said. "Hey, Horace, Meg."

Denton grunted and trotted inside.

Was she not in on the secret, or was she being careful in case of eavesdroppers?

"At least you'll have a good view of the fireworks if you're still on duty then," I said.

"What's up with him?" she asked.

"Long story," I said, shrugging. "Looking for a stray piece of evidence. I'm supposed to be the spare pair of hands if he needs me."

"Good hunting then."

I walked inside and she returned to her pacing.

Denton was waiting in the middle of the huge, two-story entrance hall.

"Can I take my head off now?"

"Okay by me," I said. I was reassured when I realized that his voice was so muffled by the gorilla head that even people who knew Horace might not realize it wasn't him inside, so odds were his presence had gone undetected by anyone who wished him ill.

We finished exploring the first floor relatively quickly. Denton seemed focused on finding papers, and there weren't any to be found in the entrance hall, the courtrooms, or the emptily echoing judges' chambers. Then we ascended to the second floor and the real search began.

And for the first two hours, it was uneventful to the point of boredom. We methodically ransacked the few offices used by the FPF onsite staff. We learned that Colleen Brown had collected McCoy and Roseville pottery. Lieutenant Wilt of the security staff had decorated his borrowed office with taxidermied heads, presumably of things he'd shot himself, since his walls also contained a number of framed photos of him holding up newly slaughtered animals. Leonard Fisher appeared fond of motivational slogans and posters, and owned a copy of nearly every business-related self-help book published in the last decade.

But most of the offices were empty. If we'd been Horace and his colleagues, we'd still have gone over them carefully — for a murderer looking to change from blood-stained clothes to clean ones, what better than a vacant office? But for our purposes, vacant was useless.

From time to time, when we were on the town square side of the building, we could hear snatches of the entertainment on the bandstand. The ballet gave way to a swing band, and eventually I could hear the opening strains of the patriotic music from Michael's students' pageant. About the time the Revolution began, we left the second floor for a quick scan of the third, which I gathered was unoccupied. I assumed my tour of duty in the courthouse was nearly done. I was almost sorry. The air-conditioning wasn't down at the arctic level where the lender had been maintaining it, but the building was still cooler than the outside. And it was restful. No tourists asking questions. No fretting over whether all the acts would show up — and finish — on time. No pangs of anxiety every time an outsider went near the entrance to the crawl space. Just trailing after Denton, who seemed to find no need for small talk as we rummaged through the drawers, shelves, closets, and in-baskets of the enemy.

Then, peering into the first room we came to on the third floor, I spotted something suspicious.

CHAPTER 38

"This is odd," I said, stepping in and gazing around. "This was the mayor's office. Our old mayor — by the time Randall was elected, we'd vacated the courthouse. Actually, this is where Mayor Pruitt's administrative assistant sat. The mayor himself sat in there."

I pointed to the door leading to the inner office. Denton went over and tried the handle.

"Locked. So what's odd?"

"Why would someone be using this office, instead of one down near everyone else?"

"Are you sure anyone is?" He was looking around with quick, darting eye movements.

"Computer's on. The screen's gone dark," I added, following his gaze. "But the power button's lit and the fan is whirring."

He cocked his head, listened, then nodded.

"You're right," he said. "Could be nothing. A lot of people just leave their computers on all the time. I think the idea is that shutting it down and turning it on again causes more wear and tear than just letting it run. No idea if that's true. Maybe someone just left it running and never came back."

"Not turning it off at the end of the day, okay," I said. "But someone's been using it since the mayor and his secretary left. It's been over a year. We had power outages this winter. Look, there's trash in the trash can."

"Could be they use it whenever distinguished visitors from headquarters need a temporary space."

"Could be, although they'd probably put the distinguished visitors in the main office, not here at the secretary's desk." I sat down, pulled on my gloves, and touched the space bar. The screen sprang into life. "You check the trash can. I'll poke around in the computer."

"You're not afraid you'll mess up any evidence it contains?"

"I won't save or delete or close anything," I replied. "Considering it's been running here unguarded for who knows how long, I don't think my doing a little careful snooping is going to compromise anything that hasn't already been compromised."

"Snoop away, then, and on your head be it." He walked over and began peering into the trash can while pulling his gloves from his pocket.

I started by looking to see what programs were open. Firefox, Microsoft Word, and Adobe Photoshop.

Firefox was showing the Caerphilly County Web site's page about the week's activities in the town square.

Interesting, but I had no idea what it meant. Except that it was more evidence that the computer had been used recently. The page it was showing hadn't existed a few weeks ago.

"Now this is interesting," Denton said.

I glanced over and saw that he had a handful of what looked like standard sheets of eight-and-a-half-by-eleven-inch paper that had been torn in half. He moved over to a clear space on the office floor and began arranging them.

"What are you doing?" I asked.

"Matching the tops to the bottoms," he said. "Although I'm starting to think that's not so useful. They're all copies of the same document."

"What document?" I asked.

"Looks like the signature page of a con-tract."

I knocked over a chair in my haste to take a look at his find.

"Appears to be a copy of the loan document between Caerphilly and First Progressive Financial," he said.

"Yes, but why haven't all the county board members signed it?" I pointed out.

We put aside the identical top halves for the moment and compared the bottom halves. All of them had been signed by Mason Shiffley, Randall's uncle, who had been and still was county board chairman. And all of them had been signed by Quintus Washington, the vice chair. But while Mason's signature was unchanged from document to document, Quintus's signature varied wildly. On one copy it was way too large. On another, too small. On several it slanted left or right, or fell a little below or above the signing line. But even in all these tries, it was the placement of the signature that varied. The loops and lines themselves remained curiously static. They all even had the same little broken bit on the capital W where the ink flow had stuttered slightly.

"Someone's working on forging these signatures," I said. "Or is it counterfeiting?"

"No idea," Denton said. "But yeah, he's digitized their signatures, and he's working on adding them to a copy of the contract."

"He's got Mason's signature the way he wants it," I said. "And he was interrupted while working on Quintus's."

Denton nodded.

I raced back to the computer and began doing one of the few computer tasks in which I was expert.

"What are you doing?" Denton asked.

"Running a search," I said. "If you forget where you filed a document, but can re-member something about it, you can find it again. The mayor was supposed to have vacated his office about a week after the recall election. I'm searching for any docu-ments created since then. And look — I'm finding some."

The search screen was gradually filling up with the names of documents. Most of them were either Microsoft Word files or graphic files. When the search feature finished, I ar-ranged its findings in date order.

"So this computer has been used on — call it six occasions in the last year," Den-ton said. "Two of them were single day uses, and the others stretched from two to four days. The most recent being a three-day ses-sion that started on June thirtieth and ended on July second, the day of the murder." He had pulled out a notebook and was scrib-bling. I pulled out my trusty notebook-that-tells-me-when-to-breathe and followed his example.

"And look what he was doing on July second," I said, pointing to a group of files with that date. "He or she; I'm sure forgery is an equal-opportunity crime."

Denton studied the file names I was pointing to for a few moments, then shook his head.

"Apart from the fact that they're all graphics files, I'm not sure I get it."

"Look at the file names. Atkinson.jpg. Hallett.jpg. MShiffley.jpg. Vshiffley.jpg. Washington.jpg. It's the members of the county board."

"Didn't they already sign that contract years ago?"

"They signed *a* contract," I said. "And there are plenty of copies of it floating around, so I can't imagine anyone would need to forge signatures on that. But what if someone came up with a bogus version of the contract? With terms far less favorable to Caerphilly?"

"There would still be the originals," he said. "There's a pretty obvious difference between a signed original and — well, one of these." He held up one of the sheets from the wastebasket.

"But what if the originals were missing?" I

said. "And all you had were our photocopies and that — once the forger finished adding all the signatures?"

"Are they missing?"

"No idea," I said. "I don't even know how many of them were signed. But I know that there would be at least one copy with FPF and one with us. And I'm betting FPF's copy will inexplicably turn out to be missing or replaced."

"Where would the county's copy be?"

"In the county archives," I said.

"You mean in the basement?" he asked. "With Mr. Throckmorton?"

I nodded.

"Holy — okay, I think you solved the question of why my former client was suddenly so eager to get into the basement. But wait — why would they be doing this forgery here? They've got plenty of computers back at FPF's headquarters, and probably graphic artists who could do this kind of graphic manipulation very easily. Why risk doing it here?"

I thought for a moment.

"Because the crook is here," I said. "Not that there couldn't be any number of crooks back at FPF headquarters, but I get the impression they operate on a grand scale, in clever ways that usually pass muster with the IRS and the court system. This is someone stationed here in Caerphilly."

"That makes sense," he said. "Someone desperate who is getting increasing pressure from his management to resolve an increasingly embarrassing situation playing out on his watch."

"You're thinking Leonard Fisher?" I asked.

Denton nodded.

"Could be," I said. "Would it change your mind if you heard that our former mayor is in town?"

"Is he? I thought he was in Cancún."

"He was, but he flew back to the states just before Memorial Day. And was spotted in Clay County yesterday. We don't know that he's in town, but . . ."

Denton pondered.

"My money's still on Fisher," he said. "But I wouldn't laugh if you suggested they might be in on it together."

"Let's call the chief," I said. "And Festus. They need to see this."

CHAPTER 39

Considering how interesting Denton and I thought our find was, we were a little frustrated at how long it took the chief to arrive. But we whiled away the time by photographing various bits of evidence and e-mailing them to Festus.

When the chief arrived, accompanied by Randall, it was obvious that the delay was frustrating to him, too.

"Sorry," he said. "I'd have been here sooner if I hadn't been so busy chasing down and arresting intoxicated Flying Monkeys."

"They'll catch hell from Wilt when he finds out," Denton said.

"That would be highly unfair," the chief said. "Considering it's his fault they're blotto. Gave them all the rest of the day off to celebrate Independence Day — which would have been a nice gesture if he hadn't already put most of them on leave without pay — and provided several cases of beer to fuel the celebration. If I were a paranoid man, I could easily imagine he'd done it just to complicate my life."

"I'm not paranoid and it sounds perfectly in character," Denton said.

"So what is this new evidence you've found?" the chief asked.

Denton and I displayed the forgeries-in-progress. While we were waiting for the chief's arrival, we'd heard back from Festus, who called to say that no, these were definitely not the real contracts, and he'd be back in Caerphilly at eight in the morning. I suspected his parents, with whom he was supposed to be celebrating the Fourth in Yorktown, were not altogether happy with the interruption. I made a note to warn Mother to expect a complaint about my behavior.

We also continued snooping in the contents of the computer, so we could give the chief a more coherent picture of what appeared to have happened.

"Started on June thirtieth," I said. "Someone took a digital copy of the real contract and began using a graphics program on this computer to capture just the county board members' signatures."

"He wasn't very good at it," Denton said.

"So he made a lot of mistakes and had to start over a lot. But he was patient and motivated, and eventually he got digital copies of all the signatures."

"And then he started working on adding those signatures to another version of the contract," I added. "Ours is twenty-three pages long, and in this one, the signature page is page twenty-five."

"But he was still working on the second of the five signatures when something interrupted him," Denton broke in.

"And the date and time stamp on the last file he saved was about forty-five minutes before Colleen Brown was shot."

"So you think whoever was using this computer was interrupted by our evacuation of the building?" the chief asked.

"Maybe," I said. "Or maybe he was interrupted by Colleen Brown."

"What if she found the killer doing this and demanded an explanation?" Denton said. "And then the killer says, 'It'd be easier just to show you — follow me.' "

"And he leads her down to the barricade," I said. "And says, 'Stand there a minute while I knock on the barricade.' "

"And blam!"

The chief looked from me to Denton a few times, blinking slightly.

"Your theory's not inconsistent with the evidence," he said finally.

"Yes!" Denton exclaimed, pumping his fist in the air. He probably hadn't seen the Rancid Dreads doing the same thing.

"I don't suppose you came up with any clues to who the killer is?" the chief asked.

"Whoever was using this computer," I said. "They probably weren't expecting anyone to find out they were here, so they probably didn't wear gloves while using it."

"And we didn't touch it without our gloves," Denton said. "So you might get fingerprints."

"Or there might be some other evidence in the computer," I said.

"We'll work on that," the chief said. "But right now, we need to get that document."

CHAPTER 40

"I'm sure if we tell him what it is, Mr. Throckmorton can find it almost immediately," I said.

"I'm sure he can," the chief said, "but we need to get it out of the courthouse basement and into someplace safe. Someplace where it will be guarded a lot more carefully than I can do here."

"Mr. Throckmorton has kept it safe for over a year," I replied.

"A year during which no one knew the document was there," the chief said. "Now we know, and even if we manage to keep it a secret, I think it's pretty obvious from what's been going on that the lender knows, too. Or do you want them murdering any more people trying to get it?"

I shook my head. I understood his point, but Mr. Throckmorton struck me as a person with very definite notions about things. Especially things like where official

Caerphilly documents should be kept.

"We go public," Randall said. "Let them know we have the document safe in our archives, and —"

"I'd rather not go public until we have that document safe somewhere else," the chief said. "I'm thinking a bank vault."

"I can talk to Phinny." Randall pulled out his cell phone. But he looked dubious, as if he shared my reservations about how Mr. Throckmorton would react.

"I wouldn't," Denton said. "I can't prove it, but I think they've tapped his phone line. I wouldn't say anything over the phone that you don't want them to know."

We all looked at each other. Randall put away his cell phone.

"Not a big surprise," I said. "We've been acting all along under the assumption that they might do that. We could go talk to him through the barrier."

"He nailed it shut this afternoon," the chief said. "I think having a murder so nearby shook him up a lot more than we realized."

"Someone needs to go in there and get it," Randall said.

"Go in there?" Denton echoed. "You really do have a way in?"

"You should do it," the chief said to

Randall. "You're friends."

"We go way back," Randall said. "To grade school. But we're not exactly buddies. And I think it might be my fault he's in there. I was the one who went down to tell him about the evacuation. Apparently I came across a little too bossy and told him he had to pack up and get out now. Phinny always had trouble with authority figures."

"Then I don't suppose he'd take it well if I went over," the chief said.

"No, I'm afraid you're even worse at gentle persuasion than me," Randall said. "But I have an idea."

I realized he was looking at me. He was going to ask me to go over in that damned tunnel again.

"You could deputize Meg," Randall was saying. "And send her over."

"If you're worried about her safety," Denton said, "I'd be happy to go along and help."

"You just want to find out how to get there," I said.

"There is that," he admitted. "But it's for my own curiosity, not to help my former employer."

We all looked at the chief.

Just then his cell phone rang. He pulled it out and glanced at it.

"Damn," he said as he flipped it open. "What now? . . . No, I'm inside — I can't see the courthouse steps from here."

I strolled over to the window where I could see them.

"Demonstration? What kind of . . . Good lord. I'll be right out. Okay, what else? . . . Blast!" He snapped his phone shut.

"Meg," he said. "If you're willing to talk to Mr. Throckmorton, go."

My stomach churned slightly, but I kept my face calm and nodded.

"And can I go along to help?" Denton asked.

The chief studied him for a moment, then nodded.

"You've earned it," he said. "I admit, I didn't think your fishing expedition here in the courthouse would turn up anything. I was wrong. Now get moving, both of you. Apparently there's an army of naked mimes doing the cha-cha on the courthouse steps."

"Only nine of them, actually," I reported, from my post at the window. "And I think they're doing more of a line dance."

"And worse," the chief went on, "one of those wretched Flying Monkeys is on the roof of my old police station, waving a gun. They don't know if he's firing rounds or just setting off firecrackers."

The police station. It was a good ten blocks from the town square, where Michael and the boys were. But still.

"Good lord," Randall said.

The chief hurried out.

"Call me when you're back and I'll take charge of the document," Randall said. "Maybe I can get my cousin Melvin to put it in the vault at the First Farmer's Bank."

He scrambled to follow the chief.

Denton joined me at the window.

"How come the people who insist on taking their clothes off in public are never the ones you want to see in the altogether?" he asked.

I decided to assume this was a rhetorical question that I could ignore. Although I agreed with him.

"So how do we get to the basement?" Denton turned away from the window with a final shudder.

"I'll show you."

When we got out into the hall, I suddenly realized I needed to go to the bathroom. Was it because we'd been so absorbed in the documents before that I only noticed it now? Or were my nerves affecting my bladder? And should I call to check on the boys?

"Hang on," I said. "Pit stop."

I peed as quickly as I could and washed

431

up in a hurry. Normally I'd have stopped to clean up the water I'd splashed around, but I tossed my paper towel in the trash can and pulled out my cell phone.

Michael answered on the second ring.

"The boys are fine," he said. "We've heard there was some trouble over at the police station, but everything's quiet here."

"Are you sure? You could always take the boys home."

"They'd pitch a fit," he said. "They've been saying nothing but 'fah-wah!' and 'boom!' for the last hour. Every time someone waves around a sparkler or lights a small cracker, it sets them off again."

"The Flying Monkeys are drunk, and they've all got guns," I said.

He was silent for a few moments.

"Okay, I tell you what. Muriel offered to let us watch from the roof of her restaurant if we wanted to. Really good view, and she only lets a few friends and relatives up there. I'll tell her I'd like to take her up on it after all."

"I like that idea," I said.

"Are you still in the courthouse?"

"Yes," I said. "And will be for a little while longer. Long story; I'll fill you in later. But I'll try to get there in time to watch the fireworks with you."

As we finished our conversation, I jerked the bathroom door open and strode out. Denton was standing where I'd left him, adjusting the gorilla head. I couldn't see his expression, of course, but his body language screamed impatience. He pushed the elevator button.

"Gotta run," I told Michael. "Love you. Follow me," I added, to Denton. "And keep your head on and don't talk to anyone."

As we rode down in the elevator, I called Rose Noire.

"Is the coast clear?" I asked. "Or can you make it clear?"

"Students coming and going, but if you need a moment, I'm sure we can find one," she said. "It's pretty much all hands onstage whenever there's a battle scene."

We hurried across the entrance hall, waving at Aida, and loped down the courthouse steps. We had to dodge mimes, the deputies who were hauling them down to the fleet of patrol cars, and the scattered groups of people sitting on the steps, getting good places for both the current show and the fireworks to come, no doubt.

I half walked, half ran, with Denton trailing behind me. He was winded by the time we got to the tent.

"Damn," I said. "It's one of the quiet parts."

"They're signing the Declaration of Independence," Rose Noire said. "But don't worry — the Shiffleys finished their work during the Sousa ballet."

"Awesome!" I said. "Come on," I added, motioning to Denton, who was still leaning over, hands on his knees, wheezing. "You're about to find out what you've been seeking for so long."

Denton muttered something unintelligible, straightened up, and stumbled behind us as Rose Noire led the way to the crawl space.

The old trapdoor had stuck up several inches out of the ground. The new one was a lot more unobtrusive. All you could see was what looked like a large storm-drain grate flush with the ground. Rose Noire lifted that up, revealing the trapdoor.

Then she leaned down and grabbed the trapdoor handle. I winced instinctively as she pulled, but the door came up with only a faint swishing noise from the brand-new, well-oiled hinges.

Denton looked down and made a sort of strangled noise.

"Don't worry," I said. "It's perfectly safe. As long as you're not claustrophobic, you'll be fine. And if you are claustrophobic — well, just stay here and help Rose Noire guard the trapdoor."

I heard Denton swallow, and then he straightened his spine.

"Right," he muttered.

"I'll go down first," I said. If he was claustrophobic, like Horace, maybe he'd buck up after seeing me do it. And if he froze in the tunnel, I could let Rose Noire talk him back out of it while I accomplished my mission.

"Okay," I said to Denton. "Ever seen the World War II movie *The Great Escape*?" He nodded. "Remember the little carts they had so they could ride through the tunnels instead of crawling?" Another nod. "Down the ladder. Take the first cart. Pull yourself hand over hand to the end of the line. Transfer to the second cart. Same thing until you get to the courthouse basement. Wait up here till you see the cart reappear."

With that I scrambled down the ladder.

CHAPTER 41

You didn't have to be claustrophobic to hate the tunnel, I decided. You just had to have a reasonably good imagination. As soon as I entered the tunnel, I could think of all kinds of things that could go wrong. What if a water main broke and flooded the tunnel? What if another earthquake broke all the wooden supports again? Or what if termites had been slowly and insidiously working on them? What if the recent work had severed a power line that I could run over with the metal-wheeled cart? What if some joker dropped a bottle rocket down the tunnel?

When I got back to the world, I was going to ask if the Shiffleys in charge of tunnel maintenance ever just sat in it thinking of all the various things that could go wrong and then doing everything they could to prevent them.

Back to the world. As if this wasn't the real world. It didn't feel that way when I crawled out of the tunnel into the tiny little cell.

I wanted to lie there and recover, but the sooner I finished my errand, the sooner I could go back and rejoin Michael and the boys. So I got up and knocked on the door.

"I didn't know anyone was coming over." Mr. Throckmorton appeared flustered, but not displeased. "Come in," he said. "If you can pardon the mess."

"There's someone else coming over," I said. "The private investigator who used to work for the Evil Lender. He's helping us now."

"I'll leave the cell door open, then." As he walked down the path to the main room, he was tidying things — moving a paper from one stack to another, pushing a file cabinet drawer shut, picking up a fallen paper clip. More than ever I had a sense that beneath the outer chaos there was an inner order that mattered deeply to Mr. Throckmorton. Every horizontal space might be piled with papers, but they were tidy piles, their edges neatly aligned. He placed the paper clip he'd picked up in a small glass jar on his desk, and I could see that he had three identical glass jars — one each for large, small, and colored plastic paper clips.

And when he learned my mission, would

he consider me an unwelcome subverter of all that lovely order?

"Have a seat." Mr. Throckmorton lifted a stack of papers from a chair, tapped them gently on the table to align them, and anchored them with a large binder clip — I could see now that there were also shallow boxes for small, medium, and large binder clips. Then he did the same with the rather larger stack occupying the table space immediately in front of me, although he used a large rubber band instead of a binder clip, and invited me to sit with a surprisingly gracious gesture.

"Would you like some tea?" he asked.

As Mr. Throckmorton fussed over making the tea, I suddenly realized that for all our focus on him over the last year, I'd barely given much thought to him as a person. My presence seemed to agitate him, but not unpleasantly.

Mr. Denton appeared, still completely encased in the gorilla suit, but I could tell from his body language that he hadn't enjoyed the trip over. Only his eyes showed through the eye holes, and they were definitely a little wild.

"Horace?" Mr. Throckmorton asked. "I thought you'd gone down to Richmond."

"He has," I said. "This is Mr. Stanley

Denton. The PI."

Denton raised one paw in a weak salute, and then buried his face in his paws, taking deep breaths as if to calm himself.

Curious. I'd been embarrassed about the anxiety I felt about going through the tunnel, and did my best to disguise it. But now that I thought about it, I realized that to my knowledge fewer than fifty people had ever completed a trip through the tunnel, and fewer than half of those had repeated the experience. And since the earthquake, the number of people willing to brave the tunnel had shrunk down to Rob and a handful of Shiffleys. If the chief or Randall had ever done it, it wasn't on my watch. Maybe they weren't entirely disappointed that urgent town business had kept them from making this trip. Should I share this with Mr. Denton? Lie to him and say that going back was much easier? Congratulate him on being one of the proud, the few, the tunnel rats?

I didn't actually think he'd appreciate any of those things. So I just said, "It's strenuous, hauling yourself along in that cart. Just rest until you get your wind back."

"Tea, Mr. Denton? It's Earl Grey today."

Denton shook his head without even lifting it from his paws, and uttered a muffled, "No, thanks."

"And what will you take in yours?" Mr. Throckmorton said, turning back to me.

"Plain is fine."

"Very sensible." Mr. Throckmorton was nodding his approval. "Silly to spoil the taste of a fine tea. Now what can I do for you . . . I'm sorry — should I call you Ms. Langslow, or Mrs. Waterston?"

"I answer to either, or you can just call me Meg," I said.

"Then you must call me Phineas!" He beamed as if we had just accorded each other rare and important honors. "Now what can I do for you? Because I know very few people make the difficult journey here without a good reason."

"Yes, not enough people make the effort." Why was I suddenly envisioning Mr. Throckmorton — or Phineas, as I resolved to learn to call him — as the noble sentry at a lonely and dangerous outpost? "I'll try to do better in future. But for now, I'm afraid I've come to make a difficult request."

He composed his face into a serious expression.

"I need to check out a document," I said.

"Why, that's not difficult at all," he replied. "I'd be happy to show you any document you like."

"I mean check it out in the sense that one

checks books out from the library," I said. His face stiffened a little at that.

"I know it's not common," I said. "But surely there must be an official procedure for conveying a document from the archives to someone who is authorized to use it."

"Yes . . . but it's all . . ."

"Unusual," I said. "Perhaps even unique."

"Not quite unique," he said. "Unusual. But what's the reason for the transfer? What's the document?"

"The original copy of the loan document between Caerphilly and the Evil Lender."

Phinny stood frozen for a few very long moments. Denton lifted his head as if suddenly interested, now that we'd cut to the chase.

"But why?" he asked. "What's so important about the original? I would offer to make you a copy, although I can't see the point. There must be dozens of copies floating around."

"Yes," I said. "But they're not all the same. Someone connected with the Evil Lender has been trying to forge a new version of the contract. We haven't seen the full text of the forgery yet, but I bet when we do, the terms are going to be a lot less favorable to Caerphilly than they are in the real contract."

"But what good are the forgeries unless
—"

He stopped, and turned suddenly pale.

"Exactly," I said. "We believe the copy
here in the archives is the last surviving
signed original of the real contract. We were
incredibly lucky that it was down here while
we didn't know about the danger."

"In that case, why not leave it down here?"
he said.

"Because now the lender also knows it's
here," I replied. "In fact, they probably
knew well before we did. And they've been
taking steps to get at it. We have no idea if
Ms. Brown was killed merely to frame you,
or if she, perhaps, was aware of the scheme
and tried to stop it. We need to get that
document to a secure location unknown to
the Evil Lender — where our lawyer can
produce it to prove any new versions of the
contract are false."

"You don't think I can protect it!" He
drew himself up, and I found myself suddenly reminded of Spike facing down a
neighbor's German shepherd.

"I think you've done a great job of protecting it so far," I said. "But these people are
unscrupulous. They've already killed once
to get it. As long as it's here, not only will it
be in danger, so will you. And anyone who

comes near the courthouse."

I could see the talk of danger was only stiffening his spine.

"In fact," I went on, "the entire archives could be in dire peril. These people will stop at nothing! Who knows what they'll do."

Dire peril. Had I gone a little too far with the melodrama?

No. Phinny studied my face for a few moments, then nodded.

"To protect the archives," he said. "Yes. You'll convey it to the county's attorney personally?"

"If you like," I said. "Actually, he should be here in the morning to take it, and Randall is arranging a highly secure place for it tonight. I'll personally see it stowed there."

"All right then," he said. "Done."

"Well, there is the small matter of finding it," I said.

"No problem," he replied. "As a matter of fact, I may have a little surprise for you."

He sipped the last of his tea, stood up, walked briskly to his desk, and pulled out a large brown mailing envelope, which he handed to me. Then he opened a nearby file drawer and pulled out a folder.

"The original contract," he said. "Take the whole folder; it's tidier that way."

While I tucked the folder into the envelope, he had pulled out a piece of cardboard
and was writing on it.

"There we are," he said. "Name of the file.
Today's date. Purpose: use by attorney. And
your name. I put the full name, so there are
no questions. Sign here, please."

I signed the cardboard, which was halfway
filled already with the names of other files
checked out by other people. Evidently letting files leave the nest wasn't completely
unfamiliar to Phinny.

Denton had risen and stood watching. He
was still wheezing slightly. He hadn't looked
that out of shape. Maybe it was stress —
probably induced by claustrophobia. I made
a mental note to have Dad check him out
when we got back on the other side.

"But that's not all!" Phinny said. With the
air of a magician unveiling a dazzling new
illusion, he led us through the room to one
of the cells.

"The former town attorney's files," Phinny
said, pointing to several stacks containing
perhaps a dozen neatly labeled cardboard
banker's boxes. "When everyone else evacuated the courthouse, he left all his papers
behind, and I offered to take them in, for
safekeeping. And shortly after that he was
fired, and then the mayor was recalled, and

— well, they've been here ever since."

"Do you know if Hamish had a copy of the contract, too?"

"I believe I recall seeing one," he said. I suspected that meant he knew precisely where it was. And I was right. He ran his fingers down the box labels until he found the one he wanted, and pulled out the folder within five minutes.

"Here you are." He handed me the file folder and pulled out another cardboard placeholder.

This folder was a lot thicker. I flipped it open and began leafing through the contents.

"Now this is interesting," I said. "He does have another signed copy of the real contract. He also has two other contracts. One signed, one not."

Phinny took the folder from my hands and leafed through it.

"Ah, yes," he said. "This second document is the original loan contract Mayor Pruitt presented to the county board. They felt several clauses were dealbreakers, and told him they'd only sign it if he brought them a version without those clauses. Which he did. That's the version they signed."

"And what's the third one?" I asked.

Phinny studied the third contract both

through and over his glasses. Then he set it beside the second contract and began flipping the pages of each.

"It appears to be a signed version of the unfavorable contract," he said.

"Signed by the county board."

"Well, no," Phinny said, looking over his glasses at me. "In my job, I tend to see a lot of documents with the board members' signatures. These aren't even good forgeries."

"But if you sent these to someone who wasn't familiar with the board members' signatures, they'd have no idea it was a forgery." I said. "He faked it. The mayor."

"Ex-mayor," Phinny corrected.

"Right. They wouldn't sign, so he faked their signatures — he probably had plenty of examples in his files."

"Incredible," Phinny said. "And so obviously a forgery."

"It's not really such a bad forgery," I said. "Most people don't know the board members' handwriting as well as you do. But I bet a handwriting analysis will back you up. We don't just have proof of the real terms of the contract — we've got evidence of a crime. We definitely need to get all these to a safe place."

"They've been in a safe place all along,"

Phinny said softly. "A secure, climate-controlled environment in which the only people aside from myself who have had access have been persons well known to me and under my close supervision."

"I stand corrected," I said, throwing up my hands as if in surrender.

"But you're right," he said. "We need to get these out where Chief Burke and Mr. Hollingsworth can use them."

"I don't think so."

We turned to see that Denton was pointing a gun at us. The seams of Horace's gorilla suit had been ripped open at the wrists, and his hands were sticking out. The right one was holding the gun. The left one was fumbling at the gorilla head.

Then he pulled the headpiece off and I could see it wasn't Denton.

It was Hamish Pruitt.

CHAPTER 42

"Oh, dear," Phinny gasped. He looked as if he might faint.

"Into that small room over there," Hamish said, pointing slightly with the gun. "Now."

He was indicating one of the cells — one that wasn't quite as chock-full of file cabinets as the others and had a key stuck in the lock.

Phinny stumbled obediently into the room. I followed more slowly. In fact, I lingered outside the door until Hamish snapped at me again.

"Inside!" he said. "This place is pretty well soundproofed, you know. Would you rather be locked up while I escape, or dead?"

I couldn't see a way out of it, so I stepped into the room and sat down on a box of files. Phinny was already sitting on a nearby box, curled up as if trying to take up as little space as possible. Hamish slammed the door and I heard him turn the key in the lock.

"Now hand me your cell phone," he said.

I blinked at him as if I didn't understand.

He raised the gun, and I gave in. I handed the cell phone out through the barred window in the door.

He threw it on the desk beside Phinny's computer and disappeared from view. I heard sounds of rummaging elsewhere in the basement.

"What's he doing?" Phinny asked.

"No idea," I said.

Phinny got up and came to peer with me through the cell door window.

Hamish reappeared. He had taken off the gorilla suit, revealing that he was wearing a navy blue track suit. He was carrying a can of kerosene. He unscrewed the cap, tossed it aside, and began pouring a trail of the liquid around the base of some of the nearer filing cabinets.

"Oh, my," Phinny murmured.

"Do you keep a lot of kerosene here?" I whispered.

"Several cans," he said. "I run a space heater on really cold days."

Hamish finished and came to stand where we could see him through the cell window. He was holding the files we'd found in one hand, and a pocket lighter in the other.

"Shall I?"

Phinny closed his eyes and stifled a whimper.

"I wouldn't," I said. "At least not until I was sure I didn't need them."

Hamish looked puzzled, and then a look of cunning spread over his face.

"You're right," he said. "Properly used, these could be worth a lot of money. Thank you. In gratitude, I'll give you a choice: smoke inhalation, or a bullet."

He cocked his head as if waiting for an answer.

"Still thinking about it? Well, you have a little bit of time."

He chuckled mirthlessly and disappeared again, this time in the direction of the barricade.

"If he's thinking of going out that way, he's in for a disappointment," Phinny said.

We heard a creak. Then another creak.

"He's opening the plywood privacy doors," Phinny said.

And then a clink.

"And throwing the cell door key outside," I said. "Pretty pointless."

"I think it's intended as a gesture," he said. "To unnerve us."

Hamish was whistling, rather off-key, as

450

he passed by the cell door on his way to some other part of the basement.

The idea of waiting until Hamish finished his preparations and set the basement on fire didn't appeal. I studied the old lock.

"Do you have a screwdriver?" I asked.

"A screwdriver?"

"Or anything like a screwdriver. Something I can use to pick the lock."

His face looked blank for a second.

"I don't have a screwdriver unless — well, I do have this."

He reached into his pocket and pulled out a Swiss army knife. One of the really large, complicated ones with at least a dozen various implements on it.

"Fantastic." I knelt in front of the door and began testing all the knife's attachments.

"Are you a skilled lock picker?" he asked.

"I've had lessons," I said.

I didn't look up to see if he found that explanation reassuring. I suspected he didn't. If I hadn't been trying to concentrate so hard on the lock, I'd have told him about the long-ago summer when Dad had become obsessed with lock picking, and I'd been the only one of his three children who really put my heart into what Mother called "your father's little burgling project."

451

I'd been the star pupil — better than Dad, even. But while my skill had proven useful a few times since, when I'd lost my keys, my successes had been on the cheap locks of rental apartments in my salad days. Who knew if the ancient cell door lock was harder or easier?

Hamish reappeared with an axe. He glared at us, and I was suddenly very glad we had a locked door between us.

He whirled and smashed Phinny's computer with a few savage whacks. Phinny flinched with each blow.

He picked up the telephone, and I was expecting him to throw it on the floor and give it the same treatment, but instead he dialed a number.

"It's me," he said. "Don't give me that. You're the one who really knows all this explosive stuff."

Explosive stuff? I looked at all the kerosene glistening on the papers. I'd been starting to worry about the effect a match could have on the paper-packed basement. If someone was planning to set off explosives . . .

"Besides," Hamish went on, "I've been doing something even better — I've got the paper and Denton. Yeah, it was him running around in the gorilla suit all day, not the policeman. I was hiding in my uncle's office and overheard that they were going to take him over to the basement to hunt for the paper, and I found a chance to jump him and steal the suit."

He'd probably done it when I'd made my quick trip to the bathroom. Too bad we hadn't thought to search that locked inner office.

"And you'll never guess where I'm calling from," Hamish went on. "Bingo . . . And I've doused the whole place with kerosene. It'll burn like a grill with too much lighter fluid on it when we blow up the rest of the courthouse."

Maybe it was that phrase "blow up the rest of the courthouse" that gave me new energy. Suddenly, I felt the tumblers inside the lock moving, and —

Click!

"You did it!" Phinny whispered.

I tried to look blasé about my accomplishment, as if I organized jailbreaks on a regular basis.

Of course, now all we had to do was overpower a man with a gun.

"I've taken down the plywood," Hamish was saying. "So those bombs you put just outside the barricade will do as much damage as possible. Yes, I saw them just now, and laid a trail of kerosene from there back into the room. So I'm taking off in a few minutes, and I can just lay the paper on top of . . . well, yeah, if you like. And we can burn it together."

He removed the contents of the thicker of the two folders — the one that contained not only the real contract but also the forged one. He folded up the papers and stuck them inside the jacket of his track suit, and then stuck the other copy of the real contract in his pants pocket.

"See if you can call him over," I whispered into Phinny's ear. "And we'll knock him down with the door."

He nodded.

"Listen," Hamish was saying, "Denton's in the janitor's closet on the third floor. I whacked him on the head and tied him up. Might be a good idea to leave him somewhere near one of your bombs, so there's no chance he survives to tell tales."

I felt a surge of relief that Denton was alive. At least for the moment.

"How long till *The 1812 Overture? . . .* Well, what's playing now? . . . Hold up the phone, then . . . That's the *New World Symphony.* We've got the rest of that and then the "Battle Hymn of the Republic," and then boom! No, I'm coming out now.

Meet me in the tent by the bandstand — the tunnel's in the crawl space under the bandstand, and you get there through the tent."

The tent. Surely someone would notice him when he came out. Unless, of course —

"I'll be the one in the gorilla suit," he said. "And remember — nothing goes boom till I'm safely out of here. Or you'll never be sure I didn't leave this incriminating little piece of paper behind in the fireproof safe. . . . How do you know there isn't? . . . About fifteen minutes. Right."

He hung up. He whacked the phone to bits and disappeared from our field of vision.

"Maybe we should just run out," Phinny said.

But Hamish reappared almost immediately, carrying the gorilla suit.

I gestured to Phinny to wait.

A few moments later, Hamish had to put the gun down to wriggle into the suit.

"Go!" I said.

We slammed open the cell door and both launched ourselves at Hamish. My flying tackle was better, but Phinny's wasn't bad. We went down in a tangle of fur and loose papers. Hamish was facedown, half in and half out of the gorilla suit. I managed to pull both of his arms behind him.

"Get the gun," I said. "And then find something we can use to tie him up with."

Phinny scrambled to follow orders. Once we had Hamish's arms and legs trussed up with heavy-duty packing tape — with a strip over his mouth to block out the foul insults he was hurling our way — Phinny and I stood up and took a deep breath.

"Of course we can't just leave him here," I said. "I'll go out the tunnel first. Then you can put him on the cart and I'll haul him —"

"I'll take care of him, and myself," Phinny said. "Just take these and go. Warn them. Save the courthouse."

He reached into Hamish's pockets, pulled out the various papers, and thrust them toward me.

I hesitated for a few moments, then nodded. It made sense. I shoved the papers into my pockets, grabbed Hamish by one foot, and began dragging him toward the tunnel.

"I said leave him," he said.

"I will," I said. "But I can at least leave him close to the exit. Up to you if you want to bring him out —"

"Or send him out," Phinny said. "I keep a lot of fire extinguishers here. I'm going to gather them all, close the plywood doors, and maybe I can prevent any fire. Or contain it."

I thought it was a crazy idea, but I didn't think I should take the time to argue with him. I kept seeing all those people sitting on the steps of the courthouse. The deputies guarding it. Denton.

And if the courthouse really blew, how far would the destruction go? As far as the audience gathered around the bandstand?

As far as the roof of Muriel's restaurant, where Michael and the boys would be waiting for the fireworks?

"Your decision," I said. I had dragged Hamish with me into the cell that contained the tunnel entrance. I shoved him into a corner where he would be convenient for dragging farther, but not in my way.

"Wish me luck."

"Most fervently," he said. Then he dashed back into the main part of the basement.

Hamish wiggled a little, and tried to say something through the packing tape. I took a deep breath and got down on my hands and knees, ready to enter the tunnel.

"Let's hope your friend really does wait for you to arrive before he sets off his explosion," I said to Hamish. He squirmed slightly.

I climbed into the cart and set out.

"Slow and steady," I told myself. Easier said than done. My arms ached by the time I arrived at the junction. I was about to send the cart back, so it would be there if Phinny changed his mind, when I heard the faint squeaking of the pulley wheels.

Someone was coming through the other tunnel toward me.

CHAPTER 43

I told myself that the person riding toward me on the cart didn't have to be Hamish's fellow thug. It was probably someone else. One of the Shiffleys, checking on some small detail of the construction. The chief, coming in person to find the documents. Rob, intent on talking Phinny into sneaking out to watch the fireworks.

But if it was a bad guy, the junction wasn't the place to meet him. Especially since I'd left the gun with Phinny. I hopped back on the cart and pulled myself as fast as I could back to the cell.

Maybe not such a smart idea. If I could hear the wheels, he could, too. I stood by the opening of the tunnel, waiting either to greet a friend or to ambush a foe.

No squeaking.

"Hamish?" Someone was calling from inside the tunnel. The sound was slightly muffled, and I couldn't identify the voice.

Hamish made some noises through the duct tape. I made a gun with my forefinger and mimed shooting him. He shut up.

Phinny came back in.

"Meg, what —"

"Shhh!"

He stopped immediately. I mimed the gun again, this time pointing my finger in the air. Phinny handed the real gun to me, looking anxiously between me and Hamish.

"Hamish?" The voice from the tunnel again. "We're running out of time."

Phinny and I waited in silence.

Then I heard the faint squeaking. But the pulleys on our end weren't moving.

"He's going away," Phinny whispered.

"To blow up the courthouse," I said.

I launched myself into the tunnel — just me, not riding the cart, so whoever it was wouldn't hear the squeaking. Trying to crawl quickly and quietly through the tunnel made me really appreciate the cart. The rails dug into my body as I crawled, and the ground under them was alternately muddy or pocked with small sharp stones. I tried to keep my breathing regular instead of panting noisily.

About ten feet into the crawl, I heard a small explosion ahead, followed by the muffled sound of dirt falling.

"He blew the tunnel," I muttered.

I kept crawling until I reached a place where my way was blocked with dirt. I turned my headlight on. Blocked solid.

Curious how calm I felt now that what I'd been dreading so long had actually happened. Oh, I could feel the impulse to panic, scream, claw the walls, and curl up into a little ball. But it was surprisingly easy to push those thoughts to the back of my mind and focus on the practical. I'd break down later when I got out. When — not if.

I dug with my hands until I encountered a splintered bit of wood. One of the side supports. Not good. Should I keep digging? Or go back and see if Phinny and I could remove the barriers?

I remembered those huge landscaping logs, bolted to the wall.

I grabbed the splintered board and dug with that.

At first it felt like bailing a bathtub with a thimble. Then I realized that I could see something other than dirt ahead.

A stretch of intact board ceiling on the other side.

I dug with new frenzy, and while I was far from clearing the tunnel, I was opening up a space near the ceiling. After what seemed like forever, I finally got the hole large enough to crawl through.

"I'm not doing this again," I muttered. "Phinny will have to come out and visit me."

I resumed my crawl. I had no idea how long I'd been digging. Five minutes? Five hours?

Not five hours. I could hear music ahead. The concert was still going on.

Not *The 1812 Overture,* though. Which must mean they were still playing Dvorak's *New World Symphony.* Not a piece of music I knew well enough that I could tell how far along they were. But the music was fast, loud, and dramatic. Damn. Probably meant they were working up to the grand finale.

I stopped long enough to pull the gun out of my pocket and hold it in one hand for the final ten feet of the crawl.

But the junction was empty.

And the pulley at the mouth of the other leg of the tunnel was still softly squeaking.

I studied the rope system. We'd mounted it on the wall rather than the ground, on the theory that it wouldn't be as easily covered up by any dirt that fell. Which meant if I was careful, I might be able to crawl through the tunnel without pressing on the rope.

At least I hoped so. Because whoever was creaking along in the cart — rather slower than I'd have been going — would probably be alert for any signs that he'd failed to block the tunnel.

I crawled. Beside me the ropes slid slowly along.

Then they stopped. I kept crawling, but more slowly, so I could listen.

I heard someone squelching through the mud at the bottom of the ladder. And then a shoe scraping on one of the treads.

Could he hear me as well as I could hear him? If he could, he might be planning to ambush me when I reached the top of the ladder. I paused long enough to wipe the sweat off my right hand and get a better grip on the gun.

I reached the bottom of the ladder only to see a foot disappearing at the top.

I ducked back into the tunnel and was peering up to see what happened next when I heard a report that sounded like a gunshot, a low bass growl, a human howl, and then frenzied barking from Spike.

"What is he doing to Spike?" I muttered, and scrambled up the ladder. I managed to drop Hamish's gun in the process. It went splat in the mud at the bottom of the shaft. Was it still usable? I didn't climb back down to find out, but leapt out of the open trap-door.

Spike was fine. Lieutenant Wilt was not. He was sprawled on his stomach with Tinkerbell standing on his back, growling in a deep rumble whenever he twitched a muscle. Spike was dancing around the pair of them, barking in triumph.

"Good dog!" I said. "Stay! Guard him!"

I considered stopping to tie Wilt up. But that would take time. And I had no idea how much or little time I had. He was safe with the dogs for now. If Spike took a few chunks out of him, I didn't think anyone would complain.

I patted down Wilt's pockets. I couldn't find anything that looked like a detonator device. Only his wallet and his cell phone. Of course, I had no idea what a detonator device looked like. Maybe he could do it with his cell phone. I put the wallet back and pocketed the phone.

Or maybe he had it on a timer.

"How are you detonating the courthouse?" I asked.

His answer was singularly uninformative, and if he'd uttered it on network television it would have come out as one long bleep.

I whirled to see if there was anyone else in the tent to help. No, apparently they'd gone off to watch the fireworks, leaving the dogs to mind the trapdoor. They hadn't even tidied up — the whole tent was littered with stuff from the history pageant. A British redcoat's uniform. Several oversized quill pens. Assorted reproduction guns.

Guns. I should go and retrieve Hamish's gun. Maybe that would make Wilt more co-operative. But I wasn't sure I wanted to brave the tunnel again.

An idea struck me. I grabbed one of the stage guns — a sleek musket with a bayonet attached to the muzzle. I ran to stand where Wilt could see me.

"Let's try again. How were you planning to detonate the device?" I asked. I shoved the bayonet right next to his eyes, so he could see it, but I hoped a little too close for him to see that it wasn't sharpened.

He looked up at me and grinned.

"Wouldn't you like to know?"

Given time, I could probably have ex-tracted the information from him, with Tinkerbell's and Spike's help. But time might be the one thing we didn't have. There could be a timer. Or some third confederate with a detonator.

I raced out of the tent.

Rose Noire was standing about ten feet away.

"Call the chief!" I shouted to her. "They're planning to blow up the courthouse!"

"Who?" She looked at me strangely, and I realized I was still holding the musket.

"Just tell him!" I said. "It could go up any minute!"

She pulled out her cell phone and began punching buttons.

I ran toward the courthouse. The wide marble steps were packed with people. People were standing on the plaza at the top of the steps, and the street below was also crowded with people.

"Everybody out!" I shouted. "Evacuate! Evacuate!" I repeated it a couple of times, and I wasn't even sure anyone heard me.

I spotted Aida at the top of the steps. I raced up to her, earning quite a few harsh words from the people I bumped into or stepped on.

"The Evil Lender has wired the courthouse to blow," I shouted in her ear. "We need to get these people off the steps. And Stanley Denton's inside."

Aida sent another deputy inside to look for Denton and began trying to help me. But we didn't make much headway until Seth Early figured out what we were trying to do and deployed Lad, his Border collie. Lad's efforts tipped the scales in our favor. Within minutes, he had several hundred tourists on their feet and moving. And when

Aida took out her service revolver and fired several warning shots into the air, the tourists really took off.

Then two police cars pulled up, sirens shrieking and lights flashing, and Sammy and Vern Shiffley leaped out and helped guide the flocks of tourists into a more orderly evacuation. We had the steps clear and were working on the road when suddenly the music reached a huge crescendo and an enormous "boom!" shook the air.

I dropped to the ground and covered my head, hoping a huge chunk of courthouse wasn't going to fall on me.

Then I felt someone shake my arm.

"It's okay, Meg." Aida. "It's only the cannons and the fireworks."

I lifted my head and looked around. Dozens of people, like me, had dropped to the pavement to shelter in place.

I rolled over onto my back and watched the firework show. I can't say I enjoyed it as much as I normally would have. But when it was all over and the courthouse was still in one piece, I got up, still a little shaky on my feet, and nodded my agreement when I overheard several townspeople say that this had been the most exciting Fourth in years.

CHAPTER 44

"At least you did get to see the fireworks," Michael said, for about the seventeenth time. I didn't mind. I'd figured out right away that what he would have said, if little ears were not around to hear, was "Thank God you weren't shot, buried alive, or blown up."

And it was nice, sitting quietly with Michael and the twins in a corner of our tent — now temporarily the chief's crime scene headquarters. The former forensic tent was serving as a field hospital where Dad and several doctors from Caerphilly Hospital could patch up all the minor injuries people had incurred while being stampeded off the courthouse steps. And a squad of FBI agents had commandeered Randall's office tent. I was looking forward to hearing how they happened to be so close by that they could show up less than half an hour after the end of the concert. And odds were I would hear — the tent was buzzing with people dashing out to tie up the evening's loose ends and then dashing back in to report on them.

"Fah-wah!" Jamie was wiggling excitedly on my lap.

"Yes, you saw the fireworks," I said.

"More!" Josh demanded, from his perch on Michael's shoulder.

"More fah-wah!" Jamie agreed.

I was afraid we'd have a small rebellion on our hands when we told the boys that no, we were going home without any more fireworks. But just then Rob showed up with frozen juice cones to distract them, and within a few minutes both boys were asleep in the pen, using Tinkerbell as a cushion while Spike ate the remains of the cones and licked their sticky faces.

"More ice, Mr. Denton?" Mother asked. I wasn't sure if she was offering to freshen his tea or replenish the ice pack he was holding on the bump on his head.

"I'm fine, thanks," he said.

He still looked a little shaky to me, but he'd assured us he didn't need to lie down.

"I want to hear everything that happened after that jerk sidelined me," he said whenever we tried to send him over to the hospital tent.

469

And he was looking better than when they'd first brought him out of the court-house. Dad kept popping in to check on him, and was still insisting that Denton stay with him and Mother overnight. "So I can watch for any signs of concussion," he'd said. But knowing Dad, I assumed he was less worried about Denton's health than interested in hearing war stories from a real private eye.

The chief strode in and slumped into a plastic lawn chair. Randall followed on his heels.

"Good Lord, what a night," the chief said. "The bomb squad from Richmond is finally here, and they say it'll take them all night and maybe into tomorrow. Apparently Wilt snuck in while we were evicting the mimes and wired that building six ways to Sunday."

"How come Meg and I didn't see any sign of it when we searched the courthouse?" Denton asked.

"They didn't do anything on the second or third floors," the chief said. "They mainly hit the furnace room and the part of the basement they could reach, and apparently they did that at the last minute, while you two were upstairs. They may have put some stuff outside, near the foundations. We'll find out soon enough. Incidentally, he was going to set it off with his cell phone. Thank God Meg was sharp enough to take it away from him."

He'd have been thankful in any case, but two of his grandchildren had been in the crowd that Lad, Aida, and I had shooed off the courthouse steps.

"Where is that damned snoop?" Muriel Slatterly strode into the room. She looked around, frowning as if searching for someone who'd stiffed her on his check. Her eyes fell on Denton, and her frown intensified. She stalked over and stood over him, glowering.

"Here," she said finally, tossing something into his lap.

A small cardboard take-out box. Denton opened it, his fingers fumbling with eagerness. Inside were three slices of pie — apple, blueberry, and pecan.

"On the house, this time," she said. "On account of your helping save the town. And you can have the space if you want it, but board's not included."

With that, she strode out.

"Space?" I asked.

"The vacant office space over the diner," Denton said. He had picked up the fork Muriel included in the box and was hovering indecisively between the three slices of pie. "I've got no family ties in Staunton, and I hate the winters. Been thinking of relocating to someplace closer to D.C. and Richmond. Someplace that gets a lot less snow. I expect Caerphilly will work just fine."

He finally stabbed his fork decisively into the blueberry pie and leaned back to chew with his eyes closed and a blissful expression on his face. Convenience and climate my foot. Clearly Muriel's cooking was the real attraction.

I glanced around the tent to see that several other people were concealing grins. And the chief wasn't doing a very good job of hiding an enormous yawn.

"Why don't you get some sleep, Chief?" Randall said. "Nothing to do tonight but watch the bomb crew and the FBI work. I can call and wake you if they ask any questions I can't answer."

The chief frowned for a moment, and then his face cleared.

"You're right," he said. "I'll head out in a few minutes, as soon as I clear up a few more things. Thank you kindly, Randall."

"Just why were the FBI in town?" I asked. "Because we know they couldn't possibly have shown up so fast unless they were here already."

"In hot pursuit of our ex-mayor, I expect," Randall said. "They're from the financial crimes unit. Apparently they were thrilled to find out he was back in their jurisdiction."

"And do we know why he came back?" I asked. "And where —"

"This is incredible!"

Festus Hollingsworth had arrived. As soon as I'd realized that the fireworks were over with and the town was still in one piece, I'd borrowed Aida's cell phone to make two calls — one to Michael, and then one to Festus, to tell him what we'd found.

His parents would definitely never forgive me.

And then, before I handed the phone back, I'd made a quick call to Kate Blake, offering her — and her only — an exclusive interview.

"But not until tomorrow," I'd added.

"I'll be there at seven," she'd said.

"And I'll let you in at nine."

And even nine would come much too early. Assuming she waited till morning. I just hoped she wouldn't show up tonight. But I'd wanted to stay until Festus arrived.

"And I'm very interested in hearing the answer to Meg's question," Festus said. "But first, do you have all the crooks safely in custody?"

"I can't swear we've got all of them," the chief said. "But we've already sent Mr. Wilt and Mr. Hamish Pruitt down to be locked up in Richmond. I don't want to entrust them to Clay County. Everyone there must have known the ex-mayor was hiding out there for weeks, and not a one of them had the decency to tell us."

"Maybe we should find a new home for all our prisoners," Randall said. "The Goochland County sheriff's a friend, right? We could check with him."

"We could," the chief said. "After all, we'll also need someplace to put Mr. Fisher and Mr. George Pruitt — we just picked them both up for questioning."

"Were they all in on it?" I asked.

"We might be a while sorting that out," the chief said. "Right now it looks as if Hamish and Mr. Fisher cooked up the phony contract, either on orders from our ex-mayor or with his full knowledge. We could have a mite of trouble proving that, of course."

"I doubt it," Festus said. "I'd be astonished if we don't find e-mails back and forth, especially after George fled to Mexico."

"Let's hope so," the chief said. "Hamish

was definitely the killer. Ms. Brown caught him working on his forgery, and he was terrified she'd blow the whistle on him. He claims he doesn't remember what happened next, but I think we can guess. He lured Ms. Brown to the basement on some pretext and tried to solve both his problems with one bullet."

"But how did he get out afterward without being seen?" I asked.

"He didn't," the chief said. "He ran up the back stairs and hid in the furnace room until the guard had raced past him into the basement. Then he popped out into the lobby and managed to look so helpless and terrified that one of the guards took pity on him and hustled him out the back door. They all knew him, apparently because he would sneak in regularly to confer with Mr. Fisher."

"And to work on his forgery," I said. "Strange that the guard didn't think to mention it when you questioned him."

"He thought we already knew," the chief said. "He said he'd told his superior officer — that would be Mr. Wilt — and assumed Mr. Wilt informed us. A bit short on common sense and long on blind obedience, these guards."

"And instead of telling you, Wilt dashed

off to become an accessory after the fact?" I asked.

"It looks that way," the chief said. "Supposedly, Hamish skulked down the handicapped ramp while all eyes were focused on the main steps, and hid his bloodstained clothes in the Hamish-burger booth, from which we have now retrieved them. And while Hamish may have suggested blowing up the courthouse, it was Mr. Wilt who had the expertise in demolition, according to his military record. Festus is right — with any luck, an examination of their phone, text, and e-mail records will prove enlightening."

"What baffles me is Mayor George's return," Randall said. "He could have holed up in Mexico forever — why would he come back on his own?"

"Because he was worried that the whole phony contract business would blow up in his face," the chief said. "Evidently, it was making him nervous, watching from afar Hamish's bumbling efforts to fix things, so he came home to keep a closer eye on the situation."

"And perhaps to confer with his buddies at FPF," Festus said. "Some of whom may be indicted themselves on Federal corruption charges."

"Ah," the chief said. "I expect that's why

the FBI were so keen on having a chance to interview Mr. George Pruitt."

"So do you think all of this will be useful?" I asked Festus. "In getting our courthouse back without selling anything to the developer?"

"Useful?" Festus exclaimed. "FPF will be lucky if we don't end up owning *them!* Talk about a smoking gun! I confess, for a while I was worried the FBI would offer him a deal to rat on his cronies at FPF. But the closer we can tie him to the murder, the less chance of that. You'll have your courthouse back, no strings attached, and sooner than expected."

And with the courthouse safely back in Caerphilly's hands, our passionately antidevelopment county board would have no reason to cooperate with anyone's plans to seize our land for a golf course.

"Speaking of FPF," Randall said. "Did I tell you I got a call back from my contact at the Department of Criminal Justice Services? Apparently the Flying Monkeys were not operating legally in the state of Virginia. It may be minor compared with what the FBI has in store for them, but FPF's going to have a lot of explaining to do on that front, too."

"And more legal charges, most likely," the

chief said. "And furthermore — are we keeping you up, Ms. Langslow?"

I hadn't been able to stifle a particularly broad yawn.

"It's been a long day," I said. "I'm delighted to hear that none of our local future felons are still running around loose, and I've got a million more questions, but they'll keep. Michael, let's grab the boys and go home."

ABOUT THE AUTHOR

Donna Andrews is a winner of the Agatha, Anthony and Barry Awards, a Romantic Times Award for best first novel and two Lefty and two Toby Bromberg awards for funniest mystery. She is a member of MWA, Sisters in Crime and the Private Investigators and Security Association. Andrews lives in Reston, Virginia.